Also by Laura Anne Gilman from Gallery Books

Flesh and Fire

WEIGHT OF STONE

WEIGHT OF STONE

BOOK TWO OF
THE VINEART WAR

LAURA ANNE GILMAN

GALLERY BOOKS
New York   London   Toronto   Sydney

Gallery Books
A Division of Simon & Schuster, Inc.
1230 Avenue of the Americas
New York, NY 10020

First Gallery Books hardcover edition October 2010

GALLERY BOOKS and colophon are registered trademarks of Simon & Schuster, Inc.

For information about special discounts for bulk purchases, please contact
Simon & Schuster Special Sales at 1-866-506-1949 or business@simonandschuster.com.

The Simon & Schuster Speakers Bureau can bring authors to your live event.
For more information or to book an event contact the Simon & Schuster
Speakers Bureau at 1-866-248-3049 or visit our website at www.simonspeakers.com.

Designed by Renata Di Biase

Manufactured in the United States of America

10 9 8 7 6 5 4 3 2 1

Library of Congress Cataloging-in-Publication Data
Gilman, Laura Anne.
    Weight of stone / Laura Anne Gilman. — 1st Gallery Books hardcover ed.
        p.   cm.—(The Vineart war ; bk. 2)
    1. Vineyards—Fictions. 2. Magic—Fiction. I. Title.
PS3557.I4545W45 2010
813'.54—dc22

                                                                    2010021180

ISBN 978-1-4391-0145-2
ISBN 978-1-4391-2688-2 (ebook)

For my editor, Jennifer Heddle,
for reasons dating back to 1997 and still counting

ACKNOWLEDGMENTS

The list of people who contributed their knowledge, their wisdom, and their occasionally strained sanity to this project is long. Specific to this book, I need to single out Bill Ricker, Walter Zilonis, Patricia "Pooks" Burroughs, and the entire madhouse crew of the Word Wars chat room, who kept me company at all sorts of odd hours. And, as always, my folks, Janet and Aaron Gilman, who were with me, draft after draft after draft. . . .

WEIGHT OF STONE

*T*he *Washers tell us, over and over again, that Sin Washer came to save us from destruction.* They speak of the distant Emperor in far-off Ettion, and how he cared not for his subjects, only the wealth and power they might accrue to him. Too, the Washers say that the prince-mages who ruled the Lands Vin in the Emperor's name in those distant days were cruel and unjust, hoarding the power which the magic of the Vine gave them, and that the people cried out for someone to save them from overwork and despair. I, sitting in my library, surrounded by the documents of a dozen generations of land-lords, might argue otherwise: that the people were protected by the prince-mages, that the magic of the Vine was what kept their lands fertile, their borders safe, their health secured.

The veracity of these stories can never be judged. Truth is overrated; what matters is what people believe.

In the Washers' stories, the people cried out and the gods, who then were active in the affairs of man, heard those cries, and came down and delivered unto them Zatim, the son of Baphos Harvest King, and Charif, patron of the farmer. And this Zatim, in his anger and pride, took the First Growth, the Vine that bore the fruit of magic, and cast it down, shattering it to the root. The prince-mages could no longer cultivate the magic, and their power waned and faded in a single season.

The Brotherhood of Sin Washer say this was salvation, and praise the name of Zatim Sin Washer.

Those of us who bear the burden of power, who see the long view, know differently.

Far from saving the people, the Breaking of the Vine cast the Lands Vin into such chaos as had never been seen. Without the spellwines to protect them, the people died of cold, of hunger, of diseases that swept across the lands where no such illness had been seen before. The Emperor died, and his successor had no care for lands without the riches of the Vine to harvest. Without that wealth, the far-flung Empire crumbled, and the once-mighty princes could not maintain control, leaving lesser princelings and land-lords warring over who might control this village, that town, while the once-mighty vineyards were abandoned. Culture and prosperity faded, knowledge was lost, and we were left little more than savages.

This was the "salvation" Zatim Sin Washer brought us.

All was not lost, however. Slowly, gradually, those slaves who had maintained the vineyards during that chaos learned the ways of the lesser magics, even as the princelings and land-lords settled their differences with blood and fire, claiming their lands and defending them, slowly rebuilding what was lost. They came to an accommodation, these lords and vine-mages, to save what was left of our wisdom and knowledge; that the Lands Vin might yet survive.

And yet, all that time the Washers roamed among us as though *they* had saved the people, proclaiming the Commands of Zatim Sin Washer and demanding that all adhere; that the men of power refrain from magic, and the slaves of magic refrain from power, that Sin Washer have no cause to come down and smite us once again.

FIFTEEN HUNDRED YEARS have passed since the Breaking of the Vine, since the Lands Vin were cast down and shattered as well. Fifteen hundred years of reclaiming what was lost, of relearning what was forgotten during the darkest years of chaos. Fifteen hundred years of searching for the wisdom and glory that was denied us. Ever harried by the words of the Brotherhood of Sin Washer, watched and scolded as though we were children, Lords and Vinearts nonetheless made good that which was laid to waste, protected what was given to us to serve.

The land-lords, we lesser inheritors of the prince-mages of old, have come to terms with the restrictions laid upon us. If the magic is less powerful now, and we must buy or barter for it like tradesmen, still it comes to our hands and responds to our decantations. The land itself thrives, our people live and prosper, and the Vin Lands are still known and respected throughout the greater world. It should have been enough.

And yet, among many of the lords, those with access to the histories as I have, and who were not bound as were the Vinearts to a life of soil and seasons, there has always been the hunger, the desire to be more than we are, to reclaim the glory Sin Washer took from us. . . .

I was one such man. I was a fool.

Prologue

THE GROUNDING

Autumn

*W*e are running out of time."

The other occupant of the room seemed not to hear—or heed—this gloomy prediction, continuing to sip from his cup and read over the journal open on the table in front of him, every so often moving the leather strip to mark another page.

The speaker turned his back on his companion and leaned against the stone windowsill, looking down on the scene in the plaza spread out below him. The view from the window was unpleasant, but he watched without flinching. It was his responsibility to witness and be seen witnessing the sacrifice, even if he, by tradition, was not allowed down among them.

The families of the chosen watched as well, clutching wreaths of crimson-leafed vines, their sleeves fluttering with dark green ribbands pinned there for the occasion. The crisp air was scented with the smell of woodsmoke and the distant, more acrid stench of a blacksmith working in the outer ring of the Holding, away from the Praepositus's House, and the center of the city.

The *praedicator* finished his chant, and the voices of those gathered rose in response to the call to serve, and then fell silent again.

It was almost done, now. The watcher no longer held his breath as the names were called; he watched, dry-eyed and calm-hearted, sorrowing only as much as was required and no more. Six for the autumn harvesting. Six to feed the soil and appease the gods of this harsh land. Six, to protect so many more.

The *praedicator* raised his hands in a benediction, his voice rising clearly up from the plaza. "The faith of our children sustains us. The love of our parents protects us. The strength of our strength defends us."

The sacrifice was swift, the Harvester's blade moving without hesitation, and none struggled or fought—a good sign. His people understood the need for what was done, and few argued against the lottery's results.

Prisoners or the mortally ill might have been a less wasteful choice, but the results, they had learned over long years, were not as effective. The vines responded to vitality.

The Praepositus turned from the window even as the lifeblood was being collected from the channels carved in the stone, his gaze unfocused as though looking at some inner landscape and not the austerely appointed chamber he stood in.

Six for the Harvest. Six at the Pruning. Another six to feed the Planting. Eighteen lives, each year, to protect the greater population. It was not so high a price, in truth. . . . There had been so much knowledge lost since the Grounding, in the decades of struggle that followed . . .

were there any way to pay but the blood and sorrow of his people, he would have grabbed it with both hands, but there was not. Without the sacrifices, the vine-mages told them, the magic would have failed, and the Grounding destroyed long ago.

But it would not be forever. If his plan succeeded—and it would, he would not doubt—then he would bring this exile to an end, finally.

He could practically taste that promise, sweet and juicy, to wash away the taste of ashes he had carried since he had learned the truth of why they had come to this place generations before; come, and been abandoned. His people might believe that the Grounding had been an accident, a twist of fate that crashed three ships onto these unwelcoming shores. He knew otherwise.

He knew, and could never forget, or forgive.

"We are running out of time," he said again, this time looking at his companion as though to demand a response. "The Harvest is upon us, and if we are not ready this time . . ."

The other man in the chamber laughed, a rusty sound, as though he did not often speak, and even more rarely showed humor. "Ximen, old friend. All is on schedule. In the old lands, their vine-mages turn on each other, the safe-ports close against strangers and allies alike . . . rumors spread and fear grows. We are ready. There is no need for concern."

The vine-mage was thrice Ximen's age, half his weight, and had a core of hatred that burned in him brighter and hotter than the summer sun. And he was no man's friend, old or otherwise. You challenged him at great risk, and almost certain failure. The Praepositus did not fear the vine-mage, precisely, but normally kept a cautious tongue around him. Today, the weight of reports burdening his desk, the growing sense of time passing and risk increasing, made Ximen incautious.

"And yet, I have concern. We are pouring so much into your scheme, *old friend*, that there is less to use here." A real worry: the land beyond the limits of the Grounding were harsh, the beasts vicious, and only spellwines kept them safe—and only this one man before him could craft those wines. He would not risk his people, not even to save them. "You are certain it is working?"

Ximen did not know the details of the vine-mage's scheme, only the broad strokes. That was not optimal, yet he had no choice but to trust the other, and that knowledge was a knife's point to the back of his neck, every waking thought and most of his sleeping ones as well.

"Patience a little while longer, Praepositus of Grounding," the vine-mage said, smiling a little, without real humor.

The Praepositus frowned, not pleased with the answer, and the vine-mage noted that displeasure. Ximen was short but well muscled, with a wrestler's build and the clean-shaven head of a fighter, and were he to suddenly become enraged, it was not certain magic alone would stop him, not if he acted swiftly. If he would not willingly anger the vine-mage, the vine-mage was also wary of him. It was a delicate dance between them, to push thus, and no more.

"I wish you would tell me exactly why you hesitate, now, when all has been set in motion," Ximen said, pulling his robe more closely around his frame as though he were cold, although a fire burned warmly in a nearby hearth, and the air was comfortable, even with the open window. "Merely to ease my foolish concerns."

The vine-mage put down the manuscript he was reading, keeping his place with one finger, and gave Ximen his full attention. "The vines are deep and the roots spread far."

Every child heard that saying from the teat, mostly to remind them that, no matter how far away they might feel, they were still connected to their distant homeland, far away and silent. From this man's mouth, it sounded more ominous.

"Yes, so you keep telling me. If they spread so far, why have we not yet—"

"Roots take time to grow," the mage said, cutting off a discussion they had repeated many times before. "I wish to make sure the moment is right, before I allow them to flower. Patience, Praepositus."

The now-patronizing tone irritated Ximen, but he tried not to show it. Others might think that the vine-mage was subject to him, but Ximen knew better. Magic made men odd, and this one had drunk deeper than most.

"Still. I do not like this delay, so late in the game. A single discovery, and—"

"There will be no discovery, not until I wish them to know who they face." The vine-mage's arrogance was no less frustrating for being well earned. "Did I not deal with the single Vineart who managed to track me back? Have I not dealt thus with every Vineart who might be a threat?"

Ximen nodded once. He had. From an impossible distance, the mage had reached out and plucked the spying eye from that Vineart's head, then crushed the body into dust, leaving no trace behind to be found. Others, too, unaware and unprepared; it was no great matter for his vine-mage to reach his heavy hand and take them. Silently, swiftly, slaying them where they slept, or tearing them apart as they tried to resist.

But a Vineart who was not unprepared, who was not unaware . . . would he be as simple to destroy?

Ximen held those doubts deep within his darkest thoughts. Five years. Five years since he had approached the vine-mage, a daring plan in mind, and found him already halfway there. No guard or personal vigilance could stop the vine-mage if he felt that Ximen were suddenly an obstacle rather than an ally. And yet Ximen needed reassurances, even if this need pushed too far and angered the other man.

For the moment, the vine-mage seemed to be amused, rather than annoyed. "We have had confidence in you for these many years, worthy Praepositus. Now, have confidence in us. Magic beast and sudden storm are all very well, but the strongest storm cannot batter a well-built house. We weaken the foundations, sow chaos in their soil, and the house falls with a single blow. Soon we shall sweep in and take our revenge."

Ximen nodded again, less reluctantly. This, too, they had discussed before. For generations, the people of the Grounding had survived, accepted the abandonment, made the best of the harsh land they had been given. But that ended with his rule. Never again would his family be cast into shadow, his people forgotten like an unpleasant chore. Not even if the gods themselves demanded it. He would not crawl before Sin Washer himself, if it came to that. He would not be denied the power that was rightfully his, for the failure of others seven generations before.

The fact that the vine-mage most likely had another agenda in mind did not bother Ximen, so long as it marched in step with his own. This land taught the necessity of compromise, the virtue of the long view.

The vine-mage pushed a wooden cup across the table toward his prince. "To justice, my old friend. Though it took generations, it will be ours."

The Praepositus reached out and took the goblet, letting the warm scent of the *vina* reach his nose. It smelled of ripe berries, and warm spices, and the bitter branch of vengeance too long denied. His people, his *family*, abandoned for the political aims of a single man, the foolish trust of those who should have known better, who followed the promise to this harsh, unloving land . . . and were there betrayed to their death.

But they did not die. And they would return and take payment for that betrayal, not just on the blood of the one who had sent them but on all who thrived while they were gone.

He raised his cup in turn. "To justice."

PART I

Fugitive

Chapter 1

THE WESTERN SEA

Spring

erzy of the House of Malech, Vineart-student and currently accused apostate under the mark of death, heaved his guts over the side of the ship and wished, not for the first time, that a wave would simply sweep him over the side and be done with it.

"Beautiful day, isn't it?"

Ao had come up behind him while Jerzy was losing what was left of his previous evening's dinner, and was standing by the railing, glancing out over the calm blue waters. The trader was barefoot and shirtless, his straight black hair slicked away from his round face, emphasizing the narrow, heavy-lidded eyes that, even when things were going badly, held some inner amusement—often, as this morning, at Jerzy's expense.

Above him, the wind snapped the canvas sails and rattled the main. The air was sweet and salty; large white birds sailed overhead, calling out in harsh, high voices as they searched for breakfast in the waters below; and the sun was only just rising, turning the briny blue-green depths into a brighter aquamarine.

Jerzy would have traded it all for a miserably rainy day in the dankest room anywhere on solid land.

"I hate you," he said, leaning against the wooden railing and wishing that his limbs would stop shaking already.

Ao laughed, but there was real sympathy in his voice. "No, you don't," he said. "Here." The trader handed him a towel to wipe his mouth. The cloth was scratchy linen, air-dried and smelling of mildew and sea spray, but Jerzy barely noticed at this point. They had been at sea for ten days now, and he had been sick every single morning.

Jerzy pushed a sweat-damp lock of hair off his forehead and mopped his skin with the towel, then looked up at the dun-colored sail snapping in the breeze above them. The creaking, slapping noise still sounded dangerous to him, but he freely admitted that he knew nothing about boats or sailing, leaving that to Ao and the third member of their party who was currently at the helm, steering them through the waters.

The thought of her made him look over his shoulder to where Mahault stood tall and proud at the wheel, her attention on the far horizon, where water seemed to merge into sky without a single obstacle to mar the view.

Her blond hair was no longer caught up in the formal, complicated knot she had worn as the daughter of the lord-maiar of Aleppan, but was instead braided into a thick plait, hanging halfway down her back. The time under the open skies had bleached it from deep gold to the color of straw, and darkened her smooth skin to a pale brown, almost exactly the color of tai, the bark brew popular back home. Her lady-mother would have been outraged to see her daughter looking so much like a common sailor.

The fact that Mahault seemed happier now, free and browned, than she had been the entire time he had known her in Aleppan, took away some of the regret Jerzy felt at his involvement in her exile.

The thought made him grimace. Mahault would have glared at him if she knew he was taking any responsibility at all for her actions—she had made the decision to leave on her own; in fact, she had used their rescue of him to make her own escape. An exile, yes, but a chosen one, against worse options.

And at that, she was faring better than he—not only was he a poor sailor, but his skin pinked under the sun, burning at the bend of his arms and back of his neck unless he kept them covered. Ao assured him that the skin would darken over time, adapting to the different weather, but Jerzy didn't want to spend enough time here to discover the truth of that. He wanted to go home.

Unfortunately, that was the one place he could not go.

Eleven days ago they had fled the city of Aleppan, barely one step ahead of Washers who named Jerzy apostate, oath-breaker, saying that he had broken Sin Washer's Commandment forbidding one Vineart from interfering with the vines of another.

It was a crime punishable by death.

Jerzy was not guilty of that crime, but he was not innocent, either.

Master Vineart Malech, Jerzy's master and teacher, had sent him to Aleppan under the guise of studying with Vineart Giordan—itself an unheard-of breach in tradition—to listen, in that city of trade and gossip, for further news of recent, disturbing events: magic-crafted serpents attacking shoreline villages, strange disappearances of Vinearts, out-of-season vine infestations, and more they had not yet heard about.

Instead, Jerzy had discovered that the strange happenings went deeper than Master Malech could have dreamed, attacking not only Vinearts and villagers, but men of power as well. While trying to investigate, he had been caught up in lines of deceit and magic entangling the lord-maiar, Mahault's father, and turning Aleppan into a deadly trap for both Jerzy and Vineart Giordan.

Ao and Mahault had risked everything to help Jerzy escape, fleeing the city on horseback with only what Mahault had had time to throw into packs, and no idea where they would go or what they could do.

Unable to contact his master, with not only his own survival but his companions' to consider as well, Jerzy had decided to go to the one place where he could not be easily tracked: open water. As a member of the Eastern Wind trading clan, however junior, Ao had been able to barter their two horses and Mahault's jewelry for this ship. It was seaworthy but small, and not meant to be taken out of sight of the shoreline.

Given a choice, Jerzy would never have willingly set foot on another boat, after his terrible sickness on the way from his home in The Berengia to Aleppan. The risk of illness was welcome, compared to the options: if they stayed on the shore, they would have been retaken, he would have been killed, and Ao and Mahault . . . he did not know what would happen to them, but it would not have been good.

The three of them had agreed that until they determined how far the search for them had spread, it was safer here on the empty waters, where they could see any pursuit coming. Their supplies were limited, though, and they needed to replenish their fresh water or they would die of thirst, surrounded by seemingly endless blue waves.

Jerzy felt the responsibility for their situation keenly; it was his fault, his failure that had brought them to this. He had promised to give his companions a chance to recoup the losses incurred when they linked their fates to his . . . but he had no idea how to do that. More, he could not allow that promise to become his foremost priority. He was Jerzy of the House Malech; his first and only obligation was to warn his master of what he had learned in Aleppan.

But Jerzy had no way to contact Master Malech; the enspelled mirror he was meant to use had been broken when he was arrested, and he had neither messenger birds for the sending nor knowledge of a decantation that would cast his voice into his master's ear, even if he had access to the proper spellwine.

He had no spellwine at all.

"Mahl says we should be able to see the shores of the next island by midday," Ao said. "The map shows a village there, large enough for us to find what we need, without standing out so obviously as strangers. We can bargain for supplies there, restock, and listen for news."

Ao barely seemed to notice the sun's intensity, the copper highlights of his skin merely darkening to bronze. More annoying to Jerzy, the trader's natural enthusiasm, high already, increased dramatically at the thought of new people to bargain with.

Jerzy changed his mind. He didn't want to go overboard; he wanted to throw *Ao* overboard.

Unaware of his friend's emotions, or simply ignoring them, Ao clapped him on the shoulder. "And once we discover what is what, my friend, we will be able to solve our little dilemma, and return us all home, covered in glory."

Home. The thought gave Jerzy an unexpected pain in his chest, like a hollow ache. Home to The Berengia. Sloping hills and low stone walls, the welcoming smell of warm earth and fruit ripening on the vine.

Home, now forbidden him, thanks to the tangled plots of Washer Darian and Sar Anton, who claimed to have caught him in the act of stealing Vineart Giordan's vines, and the betrayal of Giordan himself.

Jerzy could not find it in himself to blame Giordan, who had thrown Jerzy to judgment in order to save himself. Holding anger at what served no purpose; that Harvest was done, and Giordan had suffered for it, was likely dead now, for his efforts. Jerzy had Ao and Mahault to concern himself with now, and the mission that his master had set him upon.

Even now, Jerzy did not know if Sar Anton, the man who had accused both Jerzy and Giordan of breaking Sin Washer's Command, was part of the greater taint, or merely using the unsettled situation there to advance his own political purposes.

Jerzy's mission was to bring what he knew to Master Malech. Simple enough—except that the moment he went home, the Washers would take him and possibly his master as well. If that were to happen, all hope of defending themselves against the true threat would be lost.

"As simple as that?" he asked Ao, returning to the matter at hand. "Sail in, ask a few questions, discover the answer?" Jerzy had tried that in Aleppan, and even with Ao's help, it had not turned out well, leaving them with more questions and no answers. "Even if we did discover who set all this in motion, I can't see the Washers admitting that they were wrong, can you?" Jerzy had learned some of politics, in Aleppan.

The trader didn't hesitate, shaking his head ruefully. "No. Not without proof they could not ignore, and maybe not even then." The brotherhood was secure in their mission: they were Sin Washer's heirs and keepers of the Commands, the living barrier standing between power and abuse.

Once, Jerzy would have agreed with their role without thinking. Now . . . he found himself thinking, and mostly it gave him a headache. Thinking left them here, hiding on open water, unable to return, unsure of where to go.

It was, Jerzy had quickly discovered, easier to announce he would come up with a plan than it was actually to come up with one.

"Ha, Jerzy, Ao!" Mahault turned just then and waved, beckoning them to join her. Walking was easier now than during his first few days, the slide of the boat on the waves and wind barely noticeable, although he kept a constant hand on the rope lines Ao had strung along the length of the boat for him to use. Mahl and Ao might dash from one side to the other like birds flitting among their birth branches, but he trusted this boat, and the sea itself, not at all. Not even when one of the sleek gray spinners that followed in their wake in the evening leaped into the air and then slid back into the waters as clearly as a hoe cut soil, or when the sun passed out of sight in the evening, leaving sparkles of red and gold in the sky and reflecting off the water. It was beautiful, but it was not *his*.

Jerzy wanted his feet flat in the warm earth again. But for now, it was safer here, on the featureless surface of the sea, where, even if he could not reach his master, neither could spells and searchers find them.

Time. It was both their ally and their enemy, but in either case, it was running out.

"So, where is this island you promised us?" he asked Mahault, squinting at the horizon but not seeing anything save more seemingly endless waves and large-bodied birds soaring overhead.

Unlike Ao, Mahault had patience with him. "There, do you see?"

Jerzy looked again, but all he saw was a hazy smudge in the distance. "There?"

Mahl nodded, her hands working the wheel that controlled the ship without hesitation. Her father ruled an inland city, but she claimed that she had learned to handle a ship during one of her father's state visits to the smaller towns along the Corguruth coast. Before he turned inward, seeing threat and plot behind every member of the Aleppan Court, and his own family. Before the magic-tainted aide had whispered in his ear and poisoned his thoughts, and shut his ears to reason.

Mahault had her own reasons to hate the source behind all this, and wish it destroyed.

"By dusk we'll be there," Mahault reassured him, seeing only the worried crease between his brows. "If the maps are correct, there's a small village where we can take on more fresh water."

"And check for news," Ao said.

She nodded, her gaze returning to the horizon. Ao was a known harvest: he was there for the adventure, the chance to discover something new to reclaim his status within his clan. But Jerzy could not grasp Mahault's reasoning; she was a maiar's daughter, born to wealth, who had dreamed of joining the solitaires, the women soldiers, until her father forbade it. She had helped Jerzy for her own reasons, but in exile, she had neither name nor wealth to recommend her to the solitaires. He wondered what she thought when she woke each morning, and remembered. If she hated him for it, or resented their journey, she gave no sign. He did not know how long her loyalty would last, or how far she might go. He could not rely on her . . . and yet he had no choice.

"You're steering too hard starboard," Ao said suddenly.

Mahl frowned and glared at him. "No, I'm not."

"Yes, you are, I can feel it."

Jerzy took a step back, away from the argument. Ao claimed to have spent half his life on one sort of ship or another, and the two of them had been squabbling over who should be captain since first setting foot on the ship, neither admitting the other had any skill whatsoever.

The two had been like this since their first meeting, as often hissing and spitting like cats and then laughing as though there had never been a quarrel at all. Like politics and sailing, Jerzy did not understand it. This world beyond the walls of the vintnery, outside the reach of his master's hand, was often too confusing, and he could feel the headache press within his skull once again.

Leaving them to their exchange of insults, Jerzy went forward to the very front of the ship, as far away from their voices as he could get, wrapping his fingers firmly around the knotted rope there. It was, Jerzy admitted as the sunlight caught on the polished wooden planks and the copper fittings, a pretty little ship. Originally made in Seicea for the *meme-couriers*, meant to carry a member of the Messenger Guild to his destination as swiftly as possible with a minimum of fuss, it could be managed—if barely—by a small crew. Acquiring this one thirdhand had been a stroke of luck on Ao's part, although he would doubtless insist it merely good trading.

The problem was they couldn't stay here forever, dodging from one tiny island to another, avoiding all other people for fear of being discovered and taken back to Aleppan, and the charges facing Jerzy.

The charges—and the danger.

His throat dry, Jerzy reached for the palm-sized waterskin hanging at his belt and swallowed a scarce mouthful of tepid water, aware of how little they had left; the flat, stale taste triggered a memory he would gladly have forgotten.

Soil. Stone. Pulp and juice . . . but something more. Something darker, more dire. Heavy and weightless, smooth and slick, and the very touch of it even in this no-space made Jerzy's flesh crawl and his heart sorrow.

The taint he had discovered in Aleppan, in the halls and minds of men of power, corrupting their hearts with fear and distrust. The same taint he and Master Malech had discovered in the flesh of the sea serpents that harrowed the shores of The Berengia, and left a wasting melancholia in their wake.

They had no proof it had been in Aleppan, though, save Jerzy's own magic-sense—and the accusation of apostasy ensured that no one would believe him save Master Malech. His master would know how to proceed, but if Jerzy returned home without proof to clear his name, the Washers would take them both.

And Jerzy's muddled thoughts were back where he had started, trapped on this gods-forsaken sea.

It tangled him up inside, trying to determine what to do. Little over a year ago he had been a slave, doing as he was ordered, knowing nothing beyond the confines of the yard. All that had changed when Master Malech took him as student, and Jerzy could no longer imagine a life other than this, but recent events were beyond his ability to manage. He was lost, more confused than he had ever been, more troubled than he could remember. Even as a new-taken slave, he had known what was expected of him, how he was to behave, how to survive.

The waters that protected him from discovery likewise kept him from advice. Vineart Malech was not here to tell him what was best, what was wise. The Guardian, the stone dragon who protected the House of Malech, and had prompted him before, no longer whispered in his ear.

Jerzy alone had to decide—and where he decided, Ao and Mahault would follow. The weight of that was an additional burden Jerzy did not want.

Still. Nether Ao nor Mahault were slaves. They had seen the wrongness in Aleppan for themselves, believed enough to follow not for friendship, but survival, to root out the cause and bring it to light. That made the pressure of their company easier for Jerzy to bear. A slave did not have friends. A Vineart did not have companions. He did not know what to do with either. Easier, clearer, to look at them as having their own goals to achieve, that had nothing to do with him.

But they expected him to have a plan.

With that thought in mind, Jerzy stared up into the sky, at the wings of a seabird soaring far above them, and tried to reach the Guardian's stone-heavy presence with his thoughts, once again.

And, as every time he had tried before, silence—failure—was his reward. The Guardian might be able to reach him, but it did not seem to work in reverse, and either the stone dragon was not looking for him, or whatever magic animated it could not stretch this far, over so much spell-diluting water.

Finally, Jerzy gave up, and heard, over the ever-present sound of the waves sliding against the sleek hull, and the creak of the sails, the sound of Ao and Mahault still arguing.

No, not arguing. Quieter, more determined.

"It's my shift. Go."

"But—"

"Go." Ao's voice sounded amused, not annoyed. "You lost the toss, you get to tell him."

Jerzy figured they were going to change the watch schedule around again. He wasn't insulted; if they could spare him from having anything to do with the ship's handling, they would, and he would have been grateful. But someone had to keep a hand on the wheel, and they were already stretched too thin, with only the three of them.

He could hear Mahault's gentle steps coming up behind him, for all that she moved like a cat on grass. Back when they had first met, the maiar's daughter had been clothed in simple but elegant dresses, her hair coiled neatly, her expression and voice quietly composed, as befitted her position in the world. Now he looked sideways and saw a tall, lean figure dressed in a man's rough brown tunic, the sleeves cut away so her arms could move freely, and an equally drab brown skirt that failed to decently cover her bare ankles. She, like Jerzy, was barefoot, and her toes flexed and curled against the wooden planks as she walked.

They were an odd crew, the three of them—noblewoman, trader, and Vineart-student. Apostate, and fugitives by choice. Jerzy still did not understand the comfort he found in their presence, but he was thankful for it.

Mahault stood next to him, watching the prow cut through the waves. He waited for her to collect her thoughts, for this one moment at peace.

"Ao and I, we think . . . ," she said finally, in the tone of voice he was learning to recognize, the one that said she didn't like what she was saying but had to say it anyway, because if she didn't nobody else would. "We think that you should stay on the ship when we go in for supplies. If someone sees you . . ."

It made sense. He was hardly memorable—taller than Ao, shorter than Mahault, with a sturdy build more suited to a horseman than a farmer—but the shaggy red hair and pale skin would make him easy to identify among the darker-skinned folk Ao said were common in the southern islands. Mahl's golden hair would stand out, but the Washers should not be looking for a woman, and Ao was of a trader clan, and so had reason to be in strange lands.

No, if word had made it here from Aleppan, they would be looking for a male his age, with dark red hair and brows not even a hat could hide. It was doubtful word had spread this way—that was why they had come south, not gone directly north toward The Berengia—but it was a risk they could not take.

"It's all right. I'm fine. I'll guard the ship."

Mahl's posture eased a little with his acceptance. "Truth, having a Vineart onboard should be a useful deterrent. No would-be shipwraith would be foolish enough to attack, once you announced yourself."

Jerzy let her think that. The truth was that, although he had been able to start fire to warm them on their flight, and keep their ship lights lit, he was too young, too green to have much more magic than that. He had no spellwines to decant, and the quiet-magic in his veins was barely a whisper, fading faster the longer he was away from the touch of the vines.

He was near-useless.

As though hearing his thoughts, Mahault reached out to touch his arm. "How are you doing, in truth? I mean, I've never heard of a Vineart going to sea, and you're always sick. . . ."

Jerzy bent forward, away from her touch, resting his hands against the railing, and wished, again, for the waves to take him overboard. "Ao would have believed me when I said I was fine."

Mahault made an indelicate noise that would have horrified her lady-mother. "Ao wants to believe you're fine. He also doesn't know a thing about Vinearts, or magic. I lived with Giordan in my father's house long enough . . . and I pay attention."

True enough. The trader folk didn't use spellwines, and they drank the dark ale or the hot spirits of Caul rather than *vin ordinaire* to ease a long day. When Jerzy had created fire for them on the trail, when he eased their sore muscles, or illuminated their night shifts . . . Ao in his ignorance took it for granted that a Vineart could do these things, even without a spellwine at hand.

But it wasn't that simple. Anyone could work a spellwine, if it was properly incanted. That was the basis of magic: the Vineart incanted the spell onto the *vin magica,* allowing anyone who knew the decantation to release the magic on command.

All that Jerzy had done since they fled the maiar's palazzo, he had done without access to spellwine. It came from inside him, what his master called the quiet-magic. And the quiet-magic was the one thing that was never spoken of, outside master and student.

Sin Washer had broken the First Vine, and made Vinearts to be crafters, not masters . . . but in the process of crafting magic, of working so intently with it, the residue remained within them. Enough, over years, so that they themselves carried magic itself inside their blood and bones.

A Vineart, trained and experienced, could work a spell merely by calling on the quiet-magic within him. But it took time, and exposure, and Jerzy had only recently been an ignorant slave, only the past year accepted by the mustus; his quiet-magic was still weak.

Quiet-magic was never spoken of. And yet Mahault had seen him work magic without spellwines, and she used her mind, thought quickly and wisely. She must suspect something.

"I'll be all right." He hesitated. "But if you happen to find any spellwines, when you're bargaining for water . . . ?"

He knew that they didn't have money for spellwines, not even a rough sort that a small village might have—and that without him, they could easily be sold a *vin ordinare* instead, and never know. Forged spellwines were not common—the penalty for any selling such, when caught, was death—but it happened. But if there was even a chance of a *vin magica* . . .

"If they have any, we'll bring it back," Mahl said, and her hand covered his on the railing, as though to seal the promise. Touching still made him uneasy, too many memories of nights when he was smaller, too appealing to the slavers, and then to the older slaves who had craved some kind of physical release—another thing he did not understand, was not comfortable with.

Jerzy could sense the movement of magic within the roots and fruit, but other people, their desires and fears, mystified him. He wanted to move away again, but at the same time was afraid of insulting Mahault, if his reluctance was obvious. So he let her hand rest there and didn't say anything.

Near the end of Ao's shift, the trader called the sighting of shore. The other two, roused from their rope-tied hammocks, joined him to watch as the mass of gray on the horizon slowly turned into the clear silhouette of land: sloping beaches, thick trees, and craggy rocks reaching high into the air. If there were any settlements larger than a village, they were not visible from this edge.

"Sardegna," Mahault confirmed, after glancing at the map and checking the position of the sun overhead. "Good. There should be a small cove to shelter, over there."

While Jerzy stayed out of the way—past experience having taught them that he was more a hazard than a help—Ao and Mahault did a flurry of things required to lower the sails and slow their progress enough to drift carefully into a sheltered bay between a midsized rock outcropping and the island itself. The cove was barely large and deep enough for their own craft, but the outcrop would keep them hidden from any ships passing in the open water while still far enough from the shore to be safe from intrusions from that direction.

They dropped the weigh-anchor to keep the boat from drifting off, and Jerzy felt the boat bob and weave more distressingly than it had when they were moving, but managed to keep his stomach from rebelling. He took a long drink of warm water—almost the last of that barrel—and used the kerchief holding his hair back to wipe his forehead. Once again he was reminded that the sun was far more intense here than he had ever experienced in The Berengia, especially now that the breeze off the water had been stilled.

"You should be safe here," Ao said, stripping down to his bare skin without the slightest hint of embarrassment, and stuffing his clothing and the small items he thought might be useful for trading into an oiled sack. Off to the side, Mahault, wearing a short shift for modesty, waited, her sack already filled and sealed tight with wax. Jerzy took Ao's sack from him and wrapped the coil of wax around the closed mouth of the sack, then pressed his fingers around it, calling on the smallest flicker of quiet-magic, creating a seal stronger than ordinary flame could, to protect the contents from becoming water-soaked.

"Just . . . keep your voice down and your head low," Ao said, accepting the sack back with a nod of thanks. "We'll be back before nightfall."

First Mahault, then Ao slipped over the side of the ship and into the water, swimming the distance to the cove's shore. Jerzy watched them go, his forehead creasing in worry until he saw them reach the sandy beach, unmolested by any beast under the blue-green waves.

He had told them about the sea serpents, how they had ravaged the coastline of The Berengia, but not how close up to shore the beasts came—or how they looked as they swallowed men whole. That nightmare, he kept for himself.

Once they were gone from sight, Jerzy turned back to survey the ship. The three of them had not made much noise that it should feel so much quieter now, and yet within minutes Jerzy was acutely aware of the creaking of the wood, the slight sawing of the now-slack sail, and the watery sounds of the waves sliding against the hull of the boat, those noises far louder now than they had been before.

It struck him suddenly that this was the first time in his entire life he had ever been alone.

Jerzy had no true memories from before the slavers came. As a slave, he had slept with dozens of others in the sleep house; had worked in the fields every day, one of many nameless bodies. Once Master Malech found him, he had moved to the House, but even there, Malech and the House-keeper, Detta, and the kitchen children had surrounded him every day. In Aleppan, although he had a bedchamber to himself, he had shared the wing with Giordan, and the palazzo itself had housed hundreds of people going about their routines, from servants to courtiers to the visitors like Ao and his clan members. The fact of their presence always surrounded him, the hum of bees in their nests, constant and comforting.

Even when they fled Aleppan, the three of them had stayed close together—he had shared a horse with Mahl, hearing her heartbeat as closely as his own at times, and there was no way to avoid one another in these close quarters.

Now . . .

Now there was no sound save the ship's creaking, the relentless waves, the occasional cry of a bird overhead, and his own breathing, too loud. His heart raced, and he could feel blood surging under his skin, the warm sweat of the sunshine battling with a cold sweat of fear.

The last time he had been so wracked, he had been waiting for the overseer to kill him, for failing in his responsibilities, allowing the precious mustus to spill to the ground. Then, Master Malech had saved him with a single word.

Master Malech was not here. The overseer was no longer a threat to him. There was no danger here in this cove, to make his piss loose or his skin prickle.

"Enough. This is . . . enough. I am a Vineart. I am not afraid of being alone!"

The echoing silence that greeted his announcement was like a scornful laugh, and Jerzy felt himself flush. The sun was directly overhead; he was hot and sweaty, and his head was beginning to ache again, despite the kerchief over his head and the seawater he kept splashing on his face. He needed to do something to cool off, but the thought of going belowdeck, to the close, dark sleeping area, did not appeal; the sway of the boat was even more noticeable there. He went down there only to sleep, after Ao insisted it was too dangerous to doze above deck.

Up here at least, there was fresh air, although with the weighted line keeping them moored, that terrible side-to-side movement made him feel even more ill than before.

Jerzy pulled off the kerchief again and walked over to the open barrel of seawater they had been using to clean themselves. The water left them feeling sticky and smelling of salt, but it was better than the sweat and stink that would have accumulated otherwise. Plus, the act of washing often made the dizziness fade away.

He paused as the cloth dipped into the water, reminded of the clean strokes of his companions as they swam to shore.

Jerzy could not swim—or rather, he could, but only enough to keep from drowning. He never had cause to learn more than that; the river Ivy that bordered Master Malech's lands was wide but not deep, and if his childhood before the slavers involved bodies of water, those memories were lost forever. The first time he had ever seen the ocean was only a few months past, when Malech sent him with a spellwine to cure a bout of melancholia that had struck a town, in the aftermath of a sea serpent's attack. He remembered again the sight of that monster, and yet . . . there had been no more serpents reported since that second one, and he had no reason to believe that any were to be found this far south.

All of his thoughts of being washed overboard had ended there; he had not allowed himself to consider what might happen after, be it from drowning, or being eaten, or anything else that could happen to a fool Vineart caught in the deep waters so far from his home. Now, left alone with only his thoughts and the hot sun for company, surrounded by water, he had time to think of it, and his fears were soon overpowered by how much better the fresh water might feel against his skin than water from a barrel, stagnant and stale.

Before he could stop himself, or think again of the sea serpent's massive form rising up from the deep waters, villagers caught in its gaping maw—this water was too still, too shallow, he would have seen sign of it, and there was no reason to believe another was here anyway—Jerzy dropped his trou and pulled his tunic over his head, leaving them in a pile on the deck. Taking one of the coiled ropes in his hand, he tied it to the railing with a secure knot, jerking at it twice to make sure, and then he climbed over, carefully letting himself down the side of the ship and into the water.

The moment his toe touched the surprisingly cold water, Jerzy flinched and paused, the memory of his initiation from slave to student forever vivid in his memory.

Drown. Drown yourself. Breathe in and breathe out and let the liquid enter your lungs. And then the feel of the mustus around him, supporting him—filling him, until there was no difference between his flesh and the soft, ripe liquid . . .

His master had thrown him, unprepared, into the deep barrel of mustus, only his own instincts to guide him. After the initial panic, he had followed that instinct and let the liquid into his body, but not drowned.

This was salt water, not wine, but he would not drown here, either, with the rope to keep him safe. He would not be afraid.

Taking a deep breath of the salty air, Jerzy played out a little more of the rope, closed his eyes, and let his entire body drop the remaining distance into the water.

The comparison to mustus was fulfilled in another way: the moment he was immersed, his skin came alive, every bruise and scrape on his body reacting sharply to the water, tingling and aching as though brand new. At the same time, he felt invigorated through the pain, the exhaustion that had been on him since this entire mad race began suddenly falling away as though the sea had washed him clean.

His eyes opened once he was fully submerged, and the seawater stung them, but he stared, fascinated at how very different things looked through the glaze of water. A large pale blue fish swam by, incurious about this strange interloper, and a long wriggly creature passed below him, equally unconcerned.

His lungs started to burn, warning him of the need for air. The rope still wrapped around his left fist, Jerzy kicked experimentally with his legs, pushing himself toward the water's surface. He popped out of the water much like a cork on a spoiled bottle of *vina*, gasping for breath even as the water streamed off him. He had moved farther out from the ship than he'd planned, but the rope was still his tether. He tugged at it gently, and then drew himself back, hand over hand along the length, until the side of the boat was within reach once again.

The fish below might have ignored him, but he wanted easy access to the relative safety of the deck, in case something larger and more hungry came along. The thought made his toes curl, and the water seemed colder suddenly.

Taking a deep breath, determined not to let fear win, Jerzy used his free hand to push against the ship, forcing himself back underwater again. His hair floated in his face, and he luxuriated in the strange feeling of being suspended, without any support. It was surprisingly soothing.

Then something touched the bottom of his foot, a gentle but unmistakable pressure, and he shot out of the sea, rising clear out of the water and into the air. Jerzy hung there, almost even with the ship's railings, for a long shocked second, his mind too busy trying not to think about whatever had touched him to realize what he had done.

The moment he realized it, his body started to fall back down into the water. Only reflexes kept him from splashing back down into the gaping maw of whatever had nibbled at him, grabbing the rope up with both hands and swinging his body toward the boat. The hard slam against the hull was almost a relief, compared to falling back into the water, and he scrambled up the rope and threw himself onto the deck, panting with the effort.

Logic told him that it had probably been one of the small fish he had seen, or even one of the larger ones they had caught for dinner, or even maybe a curious spinner coming to play with this strange, two-legged swimming creature, as Ao claimed they were known to do. But he couldn't banish the image of a great-toothed maw rising up from the depth, the milky-white eyes and tremendous muscled neck of a sea serpent coming up after him. . . .

He braced himself, but nothing knocked against the boat, nothing rose from the water to attack and devour him, and slowly his heart stopped racing, and the roaring in his ears subsided.

Only then did he realize what he had done.

He had used quiet-magic to escape. More quiet-magic than he should have been able to summon, even as panicked as he was, in a way he had never before encountered. He had . . .

"I lifted into the air," Jerzy told the sky, blinking at the sunlight. "And I didn't mean to. I didn't prepare, or try to decant a spell . . . I just did it." That shouldn't have been possible: magic required conscious thought, the drawing of moisture from within to mimic spellwine, the uttering of a decantation to force the magic into action.

Still. He had done it, and therefore in his panic he must have blanked out, the salt water masking the spittle in his mouth, the words uttered and forgotten in his fear. It was the only answer that made sense . . . and it terrified him even more than the idea of a sea monster below him.

Not the fact that he had forgotten, but that he had been able to do it at all. Where had it come from?

Once his breathing calmed down a bit, Jerzy was able to look over his actions with the dispassionate evaluation a Vineart needed. With any taste washed away by seawater, he could only evaluate the spell by its results. A windspell. It had to have been a windspell, to lift him that way.

His body shuddered involuntarily as the realization hit him. A windspell should not have been part of his quiet-magic. The House of Malech did not grow weathervines; he had none of that legacy within him. Vineart Giordan grew those vines, but the time Jerzy spent in Aleppan could not have been enough, should not have been enough. . . .

The shudder turned to a cold dread in his stomach. There was more quiet-magic within him than he recognized—a legacy he had not felt within his veins. Now, though, it had woken; he could taste it in his throat, feel the thrum of it in his blood. That pocket of magic, if he had taken that much from working with those vines, that wine . . . then the Washers were right, and he had broken Sin Washer's Command, all unknowing.

He was, in truth, apostate.

KAÏNAM, ONCE NAMED-HEIR of the island Principality of Atakus, now a homeless, nameless sailor with only his honor to recommend him, stared at the maps spread out in front of him and felt a burning in his stomach that had nothing to do with the meal he had just finished. According to his charting, he should be nearing the coast of Tursin. The thought left him dizzy. A normal voyage would have taken three times as long, but a normal voyager would not have had access to the magics he could command.

It was those magics that left him feeling queasy, discomforted, and not sure if it were he rocking back and forth, or his ship. He, who had been born on a swiftship, who had spent his entire life as much in the water as on land . . . there could be no other cause of this illness. Kaïnam smoothed out a tiny wrinkle in the topmost map and brought the spell-lit lamp closer in, refusing to give in to the toss of his stomach, no matter how it complained.

Kaïnam plotted his position on the chart and frowned, then replotted it, getting the same result. He drew in a deep breath and then let it out. Incredible, and yet it was exactly as he had hoped.

It should have taken him months to cross this distance with a larger ship and a full crew of men. Alone, it would have been impossible.

Knowing that had driven him to desperate measures. The night before his departure he had taken aside Master Edon's student, asking him what spellwines of Master Edon's were best suited to speeding a vessel along. The student had unthinkingly, unhesitatingly pointed them out. Why should he not? Kaïnam was the son of Erebuh, the Principal of Atakus, and as such had every right to ask about the magics that kept his island home safe and wealthy.

Later that night, Kaïnam entered the cellar where those spellwines were stored and took what he thought he might need, then another two flagons more. In their place he left his marker, a silver coin with the icon of his rank engraved upon it. When they came to question him . . . he would already be gone.

It was not the action of a Named-Heir, but the disgrace that would follow his theft and disappearance was outweighed by what he needed to accomplish with this mad journey. In the past sixmonth, his sister had been murdered within the safety of their own lands, and ships under their Vineart's protection had been destroyed. Those acts had driven his father—aided by the Vineart Edon—to a mad plan masking their island home with spells, hiding the once-welcoming harbor from all outsiders. Edon and his father thought it would protect them against further assault by enemies who brought magic and men against the island.

Kaïnam had warned them against such an act—warned, and been ignored. As he had feared, that protection had turned into a spear at their heart when Caulic ships attempted to find the now-invisible harbor. It would have been bad enough, had the Caulic ships gone away unscathed—but they were instead set upon by firespouts in the night and destroyed, down to the last.

Firespouts: a work of magic only a Master Vineart might accomplish. A Master like Vineart Edon, who had advised Kaïnam's father, Erebuh, to close off Atakus from the rest of the world, and given him the means to do so.

Kaïnam did not suspect Edon; the man had been devoted to Atakus more years than Kaïnam had been alive, and if he said that he did not cast that spell, *could not* cast that spell, then Kaïnam believed him. But it had been done, and none would believe Atakus's innocence, now.

His sister had been known as the Wise Lady for the quality of her advice. Kaïnam had learned much, listening to her—enough that when she had been killed, his father had named him, out of all his sons, the Heir on the strength of her regard. It had been the whisper of her voice in his ear that had told him not all was well, that the events were not coincidence, were not attacks, but rather prods designed to herd them like fish into a net, to cast them not as victims, but dangers. To destroy Atakus's reputation as a safe haven, and make them a target instead of suspicion and fear.

His sister's murder had been the bait, and Edon and his father had taken it. Circles closing in on circles, locking them inside, apart from the rest of the world, while Sin Washer alone knew what might happen next.

He could not convince his father to relent, and he could not remain and stay silent. Instead, Kaïnam took the spellwines and the sleek little *Green Wave*, and set out to find the villain who had set the trap, ordered ships under Atakus's protection attacked, his sister foully murdered. Only by exposing him could Atakus's honor be regained.

His sister's whispers, and his own knowledge and training, told him what he must do.

The obvious place to begin was the far-distant island of Caul, origin of the ships that had had come searching. Normally, his little *Green Wave* would never be able to manage it, built more for races between islands than for any long journey. But Master Edon's spellwine had conjured a wind that encased them and lifted them, carrying both ship and sailor distances impossible on their own.

All it had cost him was several days of utter exhaustion and gutsickness, a sense that he had somehow overslept, or not slept enough, watching the white-capped waters as the *Green Wave* slipped through them on her way to their final destination. When the spellwine wore off, he would need to put a hand to the rudder again, but for now, he needed only sit and wait.

And think.

Kaïnam lifted one of the wine sacks and stared at it. The sigil of Master Edon was clear on the side: the stylized olive tree of Atakus against the outline of a wine leaf. Rare, for a Vineart and a land's ruler to coexist so well, rarer even for them to cooperate the way those two had, for so many years.

Before all this, they had been equals but not partners, not a single combined force. Every child in the Lands Vin knew that, in the mists of time and legend, Sin Washer had broken the First Vine to prevent exactly that; had Commanded that never again should a leader of men work magic, and men of magic never lead men.

And yet, that was exactly what Edon and his father were doing; two men, yes, but combining their powers to a single goal. That they did it to protect Atakus was noble, but it would not save them when the Washers came to demand an answer for their actions. Spells, even a master like Edon's spellwork, even with the aid of his students and lesser Vinearts who owed their loyalty to him, would not be enough to protect Atakus from Sin Washer's judgment, then. And the Washers would come; Kaïnam had no doubt of that. The Brotherhood would not let such a thing pass unmarked.

Their only hope was to discover who had set them up in such a manner. And Kaïnam was the only one who was searching.

He considered the wine sack in front of him again. Master Edon crafted windspells, primarily. But he also had a small vineyard on the leeward edge of Atakus, where he grew grapes that were never shipped off island. Those grapes produced only small amounts of wine every year, and most of it became not spellwine but *vin ordinaire*, served at his father's table when special guests came to visit. In rare Harvests, however, when the conditions were ideal, a spellwine was made from these delicate fruits. The decantation of that spell carried messages through the air, whispering from one ear to the next. Aetherspells: rare and valuable.

He had never seen such a spell used, did not know if they would carry the distance needed. He did not know, either, if this was a wise thing he was doing. But he needed to try.

Uncorking the skin, he took a careful sip, letting the wine rest on his tongue in proper decanting fashion. He had never learned to enjoy the taste of spellwines, finding them acrid and hard to swallow, but he did not need to understand how spellwines worked, only what he needed to do to make it happen.

Once he felt that the wine had soaked into the flesh of his tongue and mouth, the words of the decantation came to him, a long-ago, never utilized lesson:

"Thought to words. Words to ears. Go."

The air itself seemed to pause around him, waiting. Not daring to breathe, Kaïnam let his lips form his most heartfelt message. "Wise Lady. Thaïs. Can you hear me? Can you help me?"

He felt the words leave his mouth more than he heard them, and then an invisible gust of air flashed past his mouth, snatching the query up and disappearing with it.

He stoppered the wine sack and set it back into the especially con-structed cabinet with the other skins normally stored there. His mouth felt puckered and tight inside, as though he had not drunk water in days. Did that mean the spell had worked?

His sister was dead. No spell could reach her now. And yet, after her death, he had been woken by her whispered warning, had felt her coun-sel one last time, setting him on this path. If she could reach him, might he not reach her as well? Or had he, in his grief, imagined her touch, her wisdom? Was this all a fool's quest, and he the fool?

He had no sooner thought that than a hard wave slapped the side of the *Green Wave*, rocking it violently, even as she flew forward through the water. Kaïnam steadied himself with a hand on the table, keeping the maps from sliding to the floor despite the weights on them. He swallowed hard; no son of Atakus would disgrace himself by being ill, not when the sea was calm and the winds fair. . . .

Another slam against the side of the ship, and this time Kaïnam realized it was no wave hitting so violently. He left the cabin, bare feet touching the polished wooden steps so lightly he might almost be flying in his speed. As he reached the deck, he, without thought, lifted a long spear off the hooks where it rested. It had enough range to fend off even the most determined toothfish or shark without endangering the thrower, and could be used to knock aside closer opponents as well. Kaïnam had been using fish spears since he was a youth, and the feel of the shaft in his hands renewed his confidence and settled his stomach.

The hatch to the lower deck was shielded by an alcove made of the same watertight wood as the stairs, meant to protect anyone using the steps from wind or rain. That meant that he did not see the creature until he was already on the deck itself, and within range.

The first and only warning he had was the sense of a shadow falling over the back of his neck. He turned, bringing the spear up instinctively. It crashed against something heavy and unyielding, even as the wind brought him the heavy scent of brine and dead flesh and the faint hint of overripe fruit.

He looked up, following the path of the spear, and staggered back in shock at the huge, scaled muzzle that was turned away from him, a jagged rip in the side above its gaping maw of a mouth from where he had struck it. The black flesh underneath did not bleed, the flesh showing no signs of injury beyond that surface tear. Above it, a handspan higher, a great white eye the size of his head glared down at him, and then the muzzle swung back, knocking the spear out of his hands. Kaïnam went down on the deck in a controlled collapse, even as the mouth opened and countless sharp teeth snapped at him, like a deep-sea snake grown impossibly huge. His hands reached out and he found the spear, rolling onto his back even as he grasped it, and as the great head darted down off an impossibly long neck, he jammed the spear point up, into the creature's mouth. The point slammed home, and the shock went through Kaïnam's entire body, the butt end of the spear pinning him to the deck with the force of the blow.

The beast screamed, rearing back, taking the spear with it as it went, and then slid back down into the water, length by length of that sinewy neck, until the head itself followed. The bright, wave-lapped waters closed over it; the *Green Wave* sailed on through magic-powered winds; and Kaïnam lay on the deck, on his back, his shoulder and spine aching and his hands cramped from the memory of that grip, and tried to remember how to breathe again.

"Sin Washer and Deep Proeden, what *was* that?"

Not even the calling of seabirds answered him, much less the silent god of the tides, the *Wave* moving too quickly still for the usual winged scavengers to be wheeling overhead. His memory, unbidden, showed him flashes of what he had seen: the great scaled head, the long narrow muzzle with the double rows of small, sharp teeth; the great white eye with its thin lid overhanging . . .

A serpent, risen from the depths of story and legend. Every child knew that Master Vineart Bradhai had destroyed the last of them generations ago, clearing the seas of their lethal presence. Since then, every few years a merchant ship would claim to have seen something that might perhaps have been a serpent's head, or the slip of its tail in the distance, but there were no attacks, no bodies, no confirmed sightings. The great serpents were gone from the seas, turned into things you might frighten a child with, or tease an old sea hand about.

Had they been out here all this time, lurking? The one that attacked him . . . as his heart slowed slightly and his breath calmed, Kaïnam realized that it had been relatively small—not quite the length of his ship, only four or five fathoms long. A young one? Or had they gotten smaller since the days of legend?

Or, a practical part of his mind asked, had the reports of those larger beasts been exaggerated, in the days when superstition and fear traveled with sailors once they passed out of sight of land, and every encounter was greater the longer it took to reach safe harbor?

Either way, small as it had been, the beast could easily have knocked the *Wave* over, or swamped her with a determined wave, or snatched him right up off the deck, spear or no spear. Whatever it had been, it had come not out of hunger or fear, but . . . curiosity? Could you accuse such a beast of emotions? Of the intellect to have such an emotion? And if so, what had brought it . . . ?

"The spell," Kaïnam said, realizing, his gut clenching at the thought of how he might have put himself directly into such danger. "The aetherspell."

Somehow his request had summoned that beast, roused it from the depths. How, he did not know—could a beast such as that intercept magic, or scent it on the air, the way a dog might a hare or lamb? Or was he overreacting? Had it merely sensed the ship slipping through the waters overhead, and risen to the surface to investigate?

Either way, it was gone, and he was still alive, if with one less weapon to his name. From what he had read of encounters with great serpents, he had done well indeed.

Still on his back, he placed his hands together over his belly and cupped them together, forming the ritual cup. "Sin Washer, we thank you for your mercy and loving forgiveness. We praise your wisdom and wash our lives in the blood of your bones, that we, too, may be clean of malice and fear."

Malice, he had none. Fear . . . it still shivered on his skin and caused his stomach to tighten. Just the thought of the beast returning, or bringing more—or larger—of its kind was enough to make Kaïnam blanch.

"Enough." He sat up, flexing his fingers to make sure they had not been injured when the serpent wrested the spear from his hands. "You

are no bay swimmer, to fear the unknown. There are dangers behind
and ahead; why did you think there might not be dangers alongside, as
well?"

The speech sounded silly, spoken into the quiet air around him, but
they settled his nerves and allowed him to step forward into the helm,
checking the compass-piece set into the mast.

Stop.

You must stop.

He did not question the familiar voice in his ear, but moved toward
the wheel set at the crest of the mast house and placed both hands on
the wheel, curling his fingers around the brass fixtures and feeling their
cool smoothness under his flesh. For a dry second the words to end the
windspell would not come back to him, and then they returned in a
flood. "Wind, calm. Ship, slow. Go."

He felt it through the soles of his feet first, the change in the rhythm
of the ship. Still moving forward, but not as swiftly, not as surely; more
subject now to the rocking of the natural waves, the push of the sun-
warmed winds. His ears picked up the distant scream of a seabird, then
the whisking of the wind against his sails, and the hundred tiny sounds
that made up the normal music of shipboard life.

The haze around him cleared, and he could see rocky outcroppings
to the starboard, large enough to be called an island, although he did
not think anything lived there save seabirds and seals resting during
their journeys. No sign of any creature of menace, slipping below the
waves; he must have left it behind. Not far behind the first outcropping
there was a larger island, this one with trees, and farther behind that the
outline of a larger mass, fading into the distance. Kaïnam reached below
the wheel and pulled an oilskin case from the cabinet, withdrawing a
smaller, waterproofed version of the maps he had been studying belowdeck. The map was old, but the land had not changed since the day
it was inked. He looked up to confirm his impressions, then back down
at the map, letting one finger trace the path his *Wave* was taking. Yes, he
had estimated correctly. Starboard was the distant mass of Corguruth,

where he had no interest. To port side, the dry cliffs of Tursin. He had relatives there, a distant family connection. If he were to pull into port there, they would welcome him. . . .

And he would be no further along on his quest. Tursin was not where his answers lay.

Ahead.

The whisper was a soft curl of air around his ear, subtle and warm. The fact that he could not possibly be hearing the voice of a woman now dead for months did not stop him from following it. She had warned him of danger before, had saved him, had set him on this journey . . . if this was madness or the answer to his whispered spell he did not care; he would follow her counsel until the end.

Ahead, she told him again. *Your answers wait directly ahead.*

Not Caul, then. He checked the compass rose, then looked at the sea. Iaja? The wind shifted slightly, sending the *Wave* off to the starboard as though in answer. No, not the Vin Land of Iaja. Sardegna.

Chapter 2

HOUSE OF MALECH, THE BERENGIA

Spring

The great wooden doors shuddered as someone thumped on them with a heavy fist, demanding entrance, even though the doors themselves stood open, as always.

"Master Malech! Master Vineart Malech!"

Malech had known they were coming the moment their horses' hooves had crossed the border into The Berengia. There was no magic to it, merely the common means of tongue and ear, and the willingness of the villagers around him to bring such news to his attention. In other lands, they might fear their Vineart, or ignore him unless they had a specific need, but Malech would forever be the healer who had kept the rose plague from devastating the villages and farms, and the folk here did not forget, not even a generation after. When Washers came riding, asking after him, word spread.

The timing could have been worse—they might have appeared during the Harvest—but Malech was annoyed nonetheless. It was spring, the second busiest time at the vintnery. There were things that needed doing, without delay, and without Jerzy's assistance it all fell upon his shoulders.

He had managed to take care of the most pressing work, mainly by driving his slaves and Household staff into exhaustion, and their unwanted visitors were now quite literally at his front door. And rather irritated, from the sound of it.

In his study on the first floor of his House, the Vineart turned in his chair and looked up at the stone dragon the size of a large dog, perched atop the doorframe.

"And so it begins." Malech's lips pressed together in a grim smile, and he touched his fingertips together. "But no"—he shook his head, the smile fading—"no, it began long before, long before I sent the boy out, long before I woke to the dangers in our land. This is but the next cycle, old friend. The next cycle, inevitable as flowering and Harvest, and we must be ready to reap what has been sown—and make of it a vintage of our own."

The dragon looked at him, its blind, unblinking eyes nonetheless finding exactly where the Vineart sat. Its exquisitely carved face showed no change in expression at its master's speech, no blink or frown, but a sense of heavy disapproval radiated from it.

You are too confident.

"You worried that the boy was lacking in confidence, and now warn that I am too confident? Would you blend us together, Guardian?"

Yes.

When his House-keeper, Detta, escorted the Washers in, Malech was still chuckling.

There were three of them in the impatient delegation, wearing the dark red robes of the Washers, the heirs of Sin Washer's Legacy. Two of them had the double belt around their waists, similar to his own, only where he carried the tools of his trade—the tasting spoon, the wax knife, and the waterskin, they carried only a shallow wooden cup. The third had only a single belt and a smaller cup, indicating that he was yet a novice. Behind them, at a respectful distance, there were two others, dressed in leather trou and sleeveless tunics bearing the cup-and-root emblem of the Brotherhood. Not Washers, but hired men. The sort who protected valuable cargo—or high-ranking members of the Brotherhood. They carried no weapons—Detta would not allow that, inside her House—but their arms were corded with enough muscle to break an old man's back without trouble.

Malech did not believe it would come to that.

"Come in, please," he said, standing and gesturing to the chairs placed in front of his desk. He had forgone the usual dressings that might impress visitors—no grand display of his bottled wealth, no ornate tapestries on the walls, no embroidered robes adorning his person. Instead, they saw him as he was: an old man in brown trou and white collared shirt, the lacings worn and his left sleeve stained from an incident with a wine cask months before. The study was likewise plain, if comfortable, the only impressive thing within the great wooden table he worked at, glossy brown and sturdy enough to support a horse. The sole tapestry on the wall, a map of the *Lands Vin*, was so worn with age that only a master weaver might discern that it was in fact priceless.

The Washer who came in first, tall and balding, with a curly brown beard, scowled at Malech. "Something amuses you?" Malech recognized the voice: he had been the man calling out, at the front door.

"Brion." The second Washer, an older, shorter man, laid a hand on his companion's arm the way one might calm a skittish horse. "We are uninvited visitors. Our mission does not negate the requirement of manners in another man's House."

He stepped forward and made Washer's blessing, his palms cupped in front of his chest in the shape of a bowl, then pouring it outward toward Malech. "Solace to you, Master Vineart Malech of the House of Malech."

Malech nodded, standing to accept the gesture. There was, indeed, no need to be impolite. This would end badly enough without starting in ill will.

"You have the advantage of me, gentle Washers."

"Our apologies." The clean-shaven man smiled, but the expression was nothing more than a polite mask. "I am Neth, and these are my brothers Brion and Oren." The guards remained nameless.

Washers gave up their *nomen familia*, their birthlines, when they joined the Collegium, and by the time they were sent back into the land, it was doubtful they identified themselves as anything other than Washers. In that, they were much akin to the Vinearts, who came from the ranks of slaves in the field, taking on the name of their Master's House. Only the brothers' intentions—and their training—were rarely as single-minded. Malech did not trust them: unlike Vinearts they were not enjoined from political power, and unlike land-lords fell under no restrictions on how they might use magic to further their goals. The populace trusted Washers to be the benign inheritors of Sin Washer's Legacy. Malech had been taught how easily Sin Washer broke the First Vine, of the demigod's anger at the mage-princes' perceived insolence, and made no such assumptions as to his human interpreters' beneficence.

The Vineart showed none of his distrust in voice or manner, however, merely a blandly curious façade. "And you have come to my lands . . . why?"

He knew why, of course. Just as word of their coming had outpaced them, he had already learned of the disaster in Aleppan, of the mockery of a trial that had resulted in the death of a promising Vineart, and his own student, equally promising, accused of apostasy, of rejecting Sin Washer's Commands and taking power he was not entitled to, and of meddling with the rights given to secular lords. Malech believed none of it. But he was curious how these men might phrase it, how they saw the situation, and what they expected to achieve here.

He believed in being prepared, before he took his own direction.

"You are the master of the young man known as Jerzy." It was not a question, but rather a statement, so Malech merely reseated himself and steeped his hands under his chin, feeling the hairs of his neatly trimmed beard against his fingers. The Washers remained standing despite the chairs waiting for them, while the two bullyboys waited in the hallway. Detta, as per his earlier instructions, had already returned to the main part of the House, taking with her all the kitchen-children.

"Is he here?" Neth asked.

"He is not." In point of fact, Malech had no idea where the boy was, and that worried him. The mirror he had sent with Jerzy, enspelled so that they could communicate if there was need, had been broken, the spell rebounding back to his primary mirror and making it shiver hard enough that he worried for its safety as well. Violence. Violence, and then silence.

"You expect him back." Another nonquestion.

"Gentle Washers, please, sit. You make me tired, craning my neck to look at you. Please."

They had a choice: be seated, and lose some of their physical authority, or remain standing, and risk antagonizing their host.

They sat.

"I do indeed expect the boy back. Word has come to me of the tragedy in Aleppan, of Vineart Giordan's sad end. The boy is doubtless confused and frightened, and in need of guidance. He will return."

Eventually. But if he had not returned already, then he was staying away intentionally. That was Malech's hope, anyway; that he was hiding, and not harmed, or, the silent gods forefend, dead.

No. If the boy were dead, he would know. Certainly, the Guardian, linked to all members of the Household, would know, no matter where the boy was hidden.

Malech risked glancing up at the Guardian, still as the stone it was carved from. No, there was only a calm waiting in the dragon. Jerzy was alive.

"When he returns, Master Vineart, we will be taking him back with us, to the Collegium." Neth was polite but firm, as though expecting Malech to give way before his authority.

Malech had no intention of giving so much as a slave to these men. But he was wise enough to keep that fact to himself. For now.

"Indeed, Washer Neth. I understand your concerns that the boy might have taken some injury by his association with Giordan, and for that I assume responsibility; I sent the boy to him in ignorance of any taint about the other man."

True, and true, mainly because there had been no taint to be found. Giordan had been flawed, yes; arrogant and too willing to break tradition, but not apostate. The charges were false, or trumped in such a fashion to make harmless actions reviled. He had sent Jerzy to Aleppan to discover if that city-state was infected with the rot that was spreading across the Vin Lands, the danger that had caused Vinearts to disappear, crops to fail, innocent villages to be attacked. . . .

Apparently, it was indeed infected, if he read these events correctly. But how, and by whom . . . and to what purpose? Those questions were yet unanswered.

Jerzy might have the answers. But were he to arrive with them now he would be taken by the Washers and, in their vital ignorance, silenced forever. Malech could not allow that. These men must be gone by the time Jerzy returned.

"You would take my student into your hold . . . for the mere association with Giordan, a few weeks' time?"

"The boy was accused first of apostasy," the second man, Brion, said. Anger simmered under his words, most un-Washer-like. They were trained to take pain and sorrow from people, not to inflict it. Neth must have seen Malech's surprised reaction to Brion's tone, because he sighed and leaned back in the chair, giving the impression of one old friend about to confide in another.

"Master Malech. The boy was charged and the charges supported by a man of good standing, who had no cause to wish the boy harm. In fact, Sar Anton protected the boy when another servant would have attacked and killed him."

That was new information to Malech. The violence he had sensed through the mirror, when the smaller spell-cast mirror broke? Perhaps.

"Then Sar Anton has my deepest thanks," Malech said, not letting his concern show: a Vineart did not form attachments, and the Washers would note if he seemed unduly worried. "But I do not believe his claims about Jerzy. The boy is talented—very talented—but young and easily influenced. I am sure that it is all a terrible misunderstanding."

The impression of old friends disappeared as though it had never been. "He has been accused and tried, Master Malech. Your thoughts in this matter are no longer relevant. Be thankful that the Collegium has not turned its attention to you, as his master."

The threat was clear, even though it was issued in mild tones. Interfere, and he, too, would be named apostate, his lands seized, his spellwines destroyed, and his name blackened to history. It had not been done since the memories of the prince-mages finally faded and Vinearts accepted their role more than a thousand years before, but the Washers, by Sin Washer's grace, still had the power to do so.

Malech was a man of patience. You could not become a Master Vineart without patience in your very bones: years as a slave, to teach the importance of waiting and listening; years working the vineyards, to teach calm readiness; years tasting and crafting, to teach the art of sensing the proper moment—and how to resist moving too soon.

"You should not threaten me," he said now, his tone as cool as the earth in morning, his face still and composed. His dark blue eyes, usually heavy-lidded, were open and staring directly at Neth the way a cat would watch another predator; cautious, but unafraid. "Not here, and not now."

The novice stirred, picking up on the undercurrents rising fast to the surface, and Neth straightened in his chair. "Indeed? We are—"

"You are Washers," Malech said. "You are the caretakers of the people, the watchdogs of the Vin Lands, the inheritors of Sin Washer's Legacy, sworn to comfort and protect us, as Sin Washer did." His voice grew harder, all pretense of agreeableness shedding from him now. "And yet you have allowed evil to grow in the land, at your very doorstep. You have allowed a wicked magic to rise, to threaten what Sin Washer created. Or have you not heard of the attacks along the coastlines, the missing souls torn from their homes, their ships? The whispers of illness out of season, and infestations that should not have happened . . . have you heard none of this, O gentle Heirs of Sin Washer?"

He heard his voice grow too harsh and modulated it, but did not allow the anger to fade, waiting for their response.

"We have heard of these things," Neth said, refusing to be cowed. "And we have investigated. It was thus that we heard of your actions in sending the boy, and were there to investigate when—"

"When what? What happened, exactly? This you have not told me, this none of my sources can tell me. The boy was seen . . . working in a vineyard? Working some magic the observer knew not of? And your response is to accuse an innocent boy—a boy!—of a terrible crime, on the basis of . . . What? One man's word? Is he himself free of taint? Has he no cause, no agenda, no priority he would forward at the expense of another?"

Malech shook his head, his anger controlled but visible, the strands of hair normally tied back at the base of his neck falling free, loosened by the vigor of his movement. "No, gentle Washers, no. There is more here that you are not telling me. If you come into my home, my study, and raise threats, then you must support them, as a vine must be supported to reach the sun."

Neth stared at Malech, dark brown eyes meeting darker blue ones, and neither of the men blinked, or looked away.

"Oren." The novice looked up, startled and expectant and, if Malech read the boy aright, torn between wanting to stay hidden in the storm and feeling proud of being called on. "Take the guards and, with your permission, Master Malech, settle the horses and set up our encampment for the evening."

He addressed the next directly to Malech. "I presume the yard behind your House will be acceptable for our use?"

The Vineart accepted the fact that he would not be rid of them just yet with scant grace. "Indeed. The patch just beyond the icehouse is level ground suitable for your tents, and there is a stream that flows beyond the far side of the building where you may draw fresh water for your needs." Fortunately, the early spring weather was mild enough for comfort, and the ground was not unduly muddy. He would not have them within his House, not even for a night.

The boy—older than Jerzy, but barely—stood and bowed to the three men, then escaped the study with almost unseemly haste.

"And so," Malech said, once the door closed behind the novice, "what is it you wish to tell me, that your student should not hear?"

"You have heard of the disappearance of the island-nation of Atakus?"

Malech kept himself still, not giving any sign of surprise—or knowledge. "Rumors, yes."

"More than rumors," Brion said, leaning forward, pulling at his robe with the displeasure of a man still more used to the trousers and surcoat of a fighting man. Not all Washers came to the cup as children, and suddenly the bullyboys accompanying the Washers made more sense. The Collegium had expected Malech—or Jerzy—to give them trouble. Giordan must have . . . resisted.

"Recently," Brion continued, "ships sailing in that area tried to make port, to exchange news and take on new stores, as usual. The island could not be found. Attempting to reach the island blind resulted in ships being pushed off course, finding themselves leagues from where they should be."

"You think it caused by magic," Malech said, but his tone made it a question.

"Nothing else could accomplish such an event," Neth said. "Not unless you would believe that the silent gods have once again taken an interest in the doings of men."

The gods had not intervened since Baphos and Charif sent their son, Zatim who became Sin Washer, to remonstrate with the prince-mages, and in his anger the First Vine had been broken. Almost two thousand years of silence . . . no, Malech did not think that would suddenly change, now. The gods had washed their hands of mortals when Zatim died.

"I know of no spellwine that could hide an entire island so," he said. "That does not mean it cannot be done, merely that it is beyond my ken."

"Or you could be lying to us," Brion said.

"I could. But I am not. I have no need to lie." He simply would avoid telling them the truth, if it did not suit his purposes. But in this, he could be honest. "On my vines, I did not work that magic, nor could I. Master Edon"—the Vineart of Atakus, a Master Vineart already when he, Malech, was still a slave—"he might, perhaps. It would be a thing of weather and wind, not fire and healing, as are my vines." Vineart Giordan, who had worked those vines, might have known—he did not think he would point that out to these men.

Neth nodded, and even Brion seemed satisfied by Malech's denial.

"It is not the fact of the magic which disturbs us," Neth said, "so much as it is the way it was used. Atakus was a major port and kept itself neutral to maintain its status, making no alliances save those of trade and parley. Now it has not only drawn a cloak over itself, but attacked those who venture too near where it once was."

"Attacked?" That, Malech had not heard, and the not-hearing disturbed him greatly. "How, if the island itself is not to be seen?" Months ago, they had received an order of bloodstaunch, a very particular spellwine of his crafting, from Atakus. He had dismissed it at the time as being none of his concern, but now he wondered at the timing. Had their cloaking in fact been a prelude to something more fierce? Was the menace he sent Jerzy to find coming from Atakus? He would not have thought it of Edon, but he had admitted that he did not know the man personally.

No. A man of Edon's years would not suddenly break Commandment so brutally, not without some pressure brought to bear on him. Who was the princeling there? Naïos? No, his son Erebuh. What was Erebuh up to?

"A fleet of Caulic ships approached, during a storm," Neth said, picking up the thread of the story.

"Approached?" Malech felt one eyebrow rise at that.

"Attacked," Brion admitted, less reluctant to use the word than his elder companion. "The Cauls have always been on the hunt for any crack in Atakus's neutrality. They take offense at anyone telling them how they must behave while on the seas, even beyond their own island."

Caul boasted of the greatest fleet, their rocky, cold island growing not spellwines, but sailors. Unlike the Iajans, they were not known as explorers, but as warriors and merchants.

"And they feel that Atakus's disappearance . . . is an act of aggression?"

Neth sighed. "Master Malech, do not play the fool; it does you no service and merely wastes our time. For magic to be used in such a matter . . . Principal Erebuh and Master Vineart Edon have long held too close a relationship for the comfort of many. And they are not alone. Your Vineart Giordan and lord-maiar Niccolo of Aleppan, Vineart Conna and his town council, they overstep the Command to keep the vines separate from men of power. We have overlooked these transgressions in the past, thinking them distant enough, bonds of temporary convenience. But in recent years there are signs that they have become stronger, more significant—and then this, on Atakus.

"Master Malech, your oath clears you, but it does not address the fact that you yourself suspect that Edon might be capable of such an act. And so I ask you, on your oath: If a spellwine of such power did exist, could any soul who knew the decantation be able to control it? Or would the magic overwhelm them?"

Malech narrowed his eyes but did not immediately speak. On the surface it was a simple matter: Should the Washers look to a Vineart, specifically, or might anyone have used such a spell? However, the question brushed against knowledge Vinearts held as close—closer, even— as the intricacies of vinecraft itself.

Any spellwine properly incanted, no matter how powerful, could be decanted if the speaker knew the proper words. But a spell that could adapt and expand to such a task as this? That spellwine had not been incanted, had remained a *vin magica*, which meant that it required quiet-magic to command it.

Quiet-magic, the physical expression of the ability that turned a slave into a Vineart. More than the small aid he had described to Jerzy; quiet-magic, blood-magic, meant that no Vineart was ever tied to a specific decantation so long as the magic recognized his authority.

If Sin Washer had sought to neuter magic-users entirely, he had failed. And that was what no Washer could ever know. No Washer could ever know of the quiet-magic. No one could ever know that Vinearts were more than they appeared. The moment that truth escaped, fear of the prince-mages would return, and all hands would turn against the Vinearts.

"If such a spell were to exist . . . ," he said, holding Neth's gaze steadily, aware of both Brion looking intent and the presence of the Guardian overhead. If he gave the word, the Guardian would kill both men, its stone talons crushing their spines without hesitation. It would be a simple matter, after that, to dispose of the bodies. . . .

The thought came and went. Killing two Washers meant only that more would come, bringing with them worse trouble for the House of Malech.

But carefully, carefully. Truth won more than the best-spun lie.

"If such a spellwine were to exist, it would require a Vineart to properly decant it, I suspect. The potency would overwhelm a man not well accustomed to handling spellwines on a daily basis. However, I do not know of a vine that could create it and have never met a man who could place such an incantation."

Sin Washer's Commands were clear: those of magic shall hold no power over men, and those princes of power shall hold no magic, nor covet or manage that given to another. No matter how the original language was translated, what he had done—sending the boy to Giordan, poking his fingers into events outside his yards—was not traditional, but it was not explicitly against Command, either. Edon, if he had done this thing, even if he had merely been the one to decant the spell, had broken Command—no, he had *shattered* it.

These Washers wanted to blame Edon; he would throw Edon to them willfully.

"The fleet that . . . attacked Atakus has disappeared. The Caulic king is most wroth and demands repayment for his losses." Neth's tone was dry, indicating what he thought of Caul's chances for reparation. "The petty squabbles between one nation and another are none of our concern; they will resolve them in the usual fashion. However, the Collegium has determined that it is no longer able to turn a blind eye to the events leading up to this . . . unfortunate incident. It is time for us to take a stand in the matter. No more indulgence, no more allowance."

Malech stroked his pointed beard thoughtfully, feeling his way along the man's words, alert for traps while setting his own. "That would be dangerous," he said finally. "Perhaps even more dangerous than leaving it be. In fact, you may already have made things worse, with your intervention in Aleppan."

Neth looked startled, clearly expecting Malech to be cowed, not countering him. Brion, on the other hand, leaned forward with bright-eyed interest. "How so?"

Malech kept his voice even but did not soften his words. "You said it yourself: the Collegium has remained true to its roots as the common folk's advocate, all these ages. Where princeling warred over territory and pride and Vineart stood apart, you were walking the roads, sleeping in the cots of the common folk, listening to their woes."

"That is our calling, yes," Neth said, but this time it was Brion who gestured for him to remain silent. Malech, however, had spoken his piece.

"You think that our actions in this matter could be seen by the princelings as a rebellion against them, an affront to their given authorities?" Brion sat back, taking his words into his own thoughts, juggling them into a new shape.

"Impossible," Neth snorted, the voice of a man secure in the strength and righteousness of his position.

Malech was suddenly weary beyond even his age. For a year, he had been watching events unfold, keeping his own counsel and hoping that he was wrong, that they were merely isolated events that he could ignore as was proper, and look only to his vines, his yards. But now, Jerzy missing, Washers on the offense . . . it could undermine everything Vinearts had accomplished in the past two thousand years, picking up the shards of the First Vine and protecting their own. "You are, I trust, trying to prevent full-scale bloodshed rather than instigate it, but recent events have placed both princelings and Vinearts on such edge, those actions could have exactly the opposite effect, yes." He could not imagine it . . . but he could sense it, waiting to happen.

Neth snorted again, but suddenly it was Brion, and not Neth, who led their little delegation. "Master Vineart Malech. Tell us what you know." When Malech hesitated, trying to find his way through the verbal thicket of truth and near-truth, the Washer played his final card. "If you would save your student—and yourself—tell us."

Chapter 3

*A*o *and Mahault* would not return until closer to sunset, but after the shock of his experience in the water, Jerzy decided to stay within the safer confines of the ship itself. Boredom, just then, seemed a better option.

Stretching out in a shaded spot toward the stern of the ship, he tried to relax, but his thoughts kept him tense, and the headache returned, not helped by the oppressive heat. When sitting quietly did not help, he decided to use the time instead to clear out the area belowdeck where they had been sleeping. At least it would be darker, and cooler, there.

The space below was open, but the ceiling was low, and there was no way for the breeze to circulate, so the air had gotten stiff and stale. Jerzy stood in the middle of the space and tried not to gag. They slept in this? How had he not realized how bad it had gotten?

With the right spellwine, he could clean this space in a matter of minutes. Jerzy made an exasperated noise at the thought. A full assortment of the Vineart's tools, and he could have made the entire journey one of pleasant experiences, not hardships. Wind, to freshen the air. Fire, to light the shadows and make it seem more hospitable. Aether, to relieve some of the echoes of previous sleepers, their bad dreams and fears still hanging in wood and metal. All those spells he knew, if only from study.

He had none of those, not even a basic waterspell to rinse the floors, but Jerzy had been a slave for years before he ever tasted a spellwine, and he was not afraid of hard work. Especially if it kept him busy enough that he no longer thought—or remembered.

The space echoed; the three of them had no belongings save what Mahl had thought to load onto the horses when they escaped: a few changes of clothing each; a small bag of coins, including several silver pieces with her father's image on them, similar to the copper token with his master's sigil imprinted on it that Jerzy carried on a leather thong around his neck as safe passage and promise of payment throughout The Berengia. There was also a single blade, the length of his arm, sheathed in a dull-looking leather cover. Other than that, and the few items that had come with the ship, the sleeping quarters were barren.

What would Detta do? The answer came to him as though the House-keeper of the House of Malech were standing beside him, hands fisted on her ample hips, her gray curls bouncing as she scolded him. Air the bedding out, and wash clean the floor.

Jerzy unhooked the cloth hammock pads and lugged them up the steps, hanging them carefully over the railing and tying them again to the frame so they would not fall into the water if the ship rocked the wrong way. That done, he dipped a bucket over the side of the ship and brought the seawater back down the steps, using it and a stiff brush he found to scrub some of the dirt and grime off the wooden planks of the floor.

The work was slow, but when he had scrubbed his way from one end of the space to the other, Jerzy sat back on his haunches, wincing a little at the ache between his shoulders and in his knees, and could see a difference.

It wasn't up to Detta's standards, but it was better.

He stood, hearing his knees crack a little, and, dropping the brush into the bucket, brought it back up to the deck. The sun had passed into the far corner of the sky while he worked, and the rays were softer now on his skin. He left the bucket in the corner where he'd found it and checked the bedding. The ticking was warm, and the stuffing smelled of salt air and green spray rather than dank wood and mildew. Pleased, Jerzy wrestled them off the railing and back down into the sleeping area, tying them back down in place. When he went back above deck to get the blankets, he heard a distant sound that made him freeze in place, suddenly alert and tense. Splashing on the water.

Then his eyes spotted the source of the noise: two figures heading in from the shore on a raft barely worthy of the name. No creature from the depths, only Ao and Mahault, returning from their expedition.

By the time they reached the ship, their raft—a makeshift wooden thing held together with coarse rope—was already starting to come apart.

"Some help here?" Ao asked, even as Jerzy was leaning over the side, reaching down to take casks and bags off before they sank.

They had secured two small water casks and a bag of dried meat strips, plus fresh fruit, including the green, egg-shaped fruit called pieot Master Malech had given him to try during the early months of his training.

"I'm sorry," Mahl said, seeing the way his gaze flitted over their acquisitions. "The village was so small—there were no spellwines to be had, not at any price."

Jerzy hadn't really expected that there would be; while those at Mahault's social level might consider them daily essentials, the price kept even the most basic healwines out of the reach of most farmers or guildsmen, and the more powerful or well known a Vineart, the more coin a spellwine with his sigil would earn. A land-lord or guild master might distribute spellwines among his people, at need, but a small island village without direct patron or generous lord? They would likely never see magic used in their lifetime.

"No matter," he said to Mahl, feeling the lack in his gut and on his tongue, the accomplishments of the morning floating away like dust.

A Vineart without a vineyard. A Vineart without spellwines. A Vineart without enough experience to have a deep quiet-magic, and what he had done that morning likely used up the little he had left. No Vineart at all, without even his belt and knife to identify him. He was useless except as physical labor, nothing more than the slave he had once been, the absence of soil under his feet and fingers like a physical ache once again.

"You aired out belowdeck?" Ao spotted the last of the bedding and drew the proper conclusion. "Good man! I think I'd have rather drowned than spend another night in that stink hole. Why they couldn't design these ships with sleeping quarters above the water-line . . . oh yes, I know the whys, but it still frustrates. I once spent an entire month belowdeck, on my first trading voyage. I was barely ten, along only to listen and haul freight, and had to sleep under the bunk of my sponsor, for there was no room anywhere else . . ."

Ao's usual chatter was good cover, but Jerzy didn't think that his mood had escaped either of his companions. Ao was a trader, trained practically from birth to read people, and Mahault was the daughter and granddaughter of maiars, and had grown up surrounded by politics and negotiations as her birthright. A simple slave had no protections against them.

Mahault, not even pretending to listen to Ao, finished handing their acquisitions up from the raft to the ship itself, and then climbed over the railing, the skirt of her dress trailing damply against the deck. As usual, she did not waste time with niceties. "I hope that you had brilliant thoughts about what we should do next, because as much as I enjoy being at sea, we can't be aimless much longer. Ao used the last of his baubles and tricks on this trip—we've nothing left to barter save ourselves, and I doubt any of us are good enough fishers to feed us that way."

Jerzy looked at Mahault, both flattered by and quietly resenting her assumption that he would have their next move decided, as though he were the oldest and wisest of the three, rather than the youngest and least experienced. Hadn't he already proven that he didn't know what he was doing?

He was spared having to answer for a moment, when she looked over the railing and said something in a language he did not recognize, but sounded rude. The sodden ropes had loosed, and the driftwood planks were floating away. Ao threw the paddles they had been using overboard as well, watching as they sank below the surface. "Barely worth the riddle I traded for them," he said. "Not that it was a very good riddle anyway."

"You traded words for a raft?"

Ao grinned at him, for a moment the worry and exhaustion sliding off, his attitude that of the cocksure know-everything Jerzy had first met. "In a small village like this? A song or riddle or new story can make the poorest, most homely of men into a lord among the ladies," he said, clearly pleased with himself. "You've never won a fair maid's attention with a well-turned tale of life among the vines?"

Jerzy had never tried for a maid's attention, fair or foul. While a female might occasionally work in the vineyards—usually an older woman without family to house her—slaves were all male, and he had never wished for those attentions, or invited them to himself, although a few had taken without his asking when he was younger and unable to say no.

There were female servants in the House, of course. Detta, and Lil, and Roan. Lil and he . . . flirted, he supposed. But neither of them had ever gone beyond that. He liked Lil, but it was the same way he liked Mahl, or Ao, for that matter.

Giordan had commented on that when he had first met Mahault, warning Jerzy that he should act on such feelings before the vines took them. The vines, Jerzy suspected, had already taken everything. He understood the way men and women went together; he simply had no urge to do so himself.

It puzzled him a moment, how he felt about that, then Jerzy shrugged it off. He was as he was, and now was not the time to worry about things that did not matter.

"You got what we needed?" he asked instead.

"That and more—Ao is almost as good as he thinks himself to be—and although we found no spellwines, we did hear news," Mahault said, taking several odd-shaped pieces of fruit out of the rough sack and placing them into the storage chest, a box lined with a thin layer of hammered tin in order to keep out rats and seabirds.

"Yes," Ao said, changing topics easily. "Only the news is that there is no news. The village was large enough to have a relay tower, so they know what happens across the island and even on the mainland coast, and the tower-keeper said that it had been quiet of everything save the marriage of the local lordling's eldest daughter to a liege of Seicea. That is going to do wonders for their trade." Ao was diverted for a moment by that thought. "If the marriage is successful, they'll have a direct line into the newest ships Seicea turns out, at a better price than most. That could decrease their travel time, and—"

Jerzy waggled his fingers in front of his friend's face, attracting his attention. "Ao? The matter at hand?"

"Right." The trader looked abashed, glancing down and then up again, a sparkle in his eye. "Sorry. I really can't seem to stop."

"Traders," Mahl said in tone of dramatic disgust, and Jerzy had the sense that they were both playing the fool intentionally, to entertain him out of his dour mood. "Do you know what it is like to go anywhere with him? Always finding the price of this, the cost of that, trying to talk people into selling things he didn't want, and trying to buy things we can't afford!"

"Negotiations," Ao protested. "Keeping my hand in. You never know what someone might say that might be useful later."

"We have no need to know the price of this year's crop of . . . whatever it was that you were discussing."

"Telkberry. A good telkberry crop means the dyers will be able to get their hands on red and purple dyes easily, and that means . . ." He finally took notice of Mahl's expression. "Nothing that matters right now. I know."

Jerzy cut into their wrangling, wanting to hear what they had discovered. "So there's no alert for us, no reward for my return?" That had been one of their concerns: if the Washers had spread their accusation throughout the Vin Lands, his only freedom would be in one of the Outer Lands, where vines did not grow, and Sin Washer's Command— and therefore the Washers themselves—held no sway. For a Vineart, a land without vines was a walking death. Jerzy had known that, intellectually. It was only after a week with only water underfoot, and a sense of severed longing in his flesh, that he understood that such a fate was not death, but a more terrifying madness.

"None," Mahl said. "No rumors of anything involving Vinearts— they were full of a Caul fleet that went missing, which I suppose worries them more. Oh, and fishing's down. The tides changed, they think, or something's scaring off their usual catch."

Jerzy suppressed a shudder, thinking again of that touch on the bottom of his foot. He would be so pleased to be off this ship, never crossing any body of water deeper or wider than the Ivy, ever again.

Finished with her report, Mahault took an armful of the bedding off the rail and carried it belowdeck. She returned a moment later, an expression of rare pleasure on her normally solemn features. "Oh, that looks so much better. Smells much better, too. Now, if I could only take a bath . . ."

Ao made a face, and Jerzy chuckled. The bathing rooms in Aleppan had been built on the old Ettonian style, sunken tubs that were filled via pipes that ran from a great furnace, giving everyone in the palazzo equal access to steaming hot water. Jerzy shared the maiar's daughter's longing for a long soak in water that didn't smell of fish and salt, even if Ao thought it a foolish indulgence when there was so much bracing seawater around them, free for the taking.

The heated baths were long behind them, now. Jerzy turned away from the others, looking over the railing at the quiet shoreline, wishing again that he could be there, on solid land, not here on this boat, on the endless water.

He realized then, suddenly, that his near-constant nausea had faded, and his legs did not wobble even as the ship bobbed up and down on the gentle swells of the cove. Sin Washer gave small blessings to go with great burdens, he supposed.

"So, no news is good news, yes?" he asked, still watching the shore, but turning so that he could see his companions as well.

Mahault nodded, but Ao shook his head.

"I'd be happier if they were shouting it from rooftops," the trader said. "It's when bad news goes quiet that it's worst news of all. It means that if they catch you, they don't want anyone to know that they have you, or why. The charges were brought up so quickly, and the accusations confirmed without any real proof, no chance for your master to hear of it, much less defend you. They want to keep this quiet."

Jerzy had no response to that.

"You think the Washers are involved in whatever is happening?" Mahl perched on an overturned cask next to Jerzy, her skirt, bedraggled and water-stained, gathered around her knees without shame. She was barefoot again, for better footing on the deck, the same as Jerzy, and her toes curled under against the slats of the cask as she split her attention between her companions. "Washers are Sin Washer's heirs; they're meant to ease pain and sorrow, not cause it."

"I don't know," Ao said. "We've been over it again and again, and I don't know. They have nothing to gain on the surface, but the Collegium is deep, and anything could be happening below. If this were a negotiation, I would count all my fingers and then count all of yours, and I still wouldn't swear we had them all still in our palms."

"So what do we do, Jerzy?" Mahl turned to him, her brown eyes intent. "We took on enough supplies today to last us another tenday, if we're careful. Do we head back toward The Berengia? Or do we keep heading south? Or west?"

"We can't go west!" Ao protested. "Once past the tip of the Outer Lands, there's nothing for weeks, and this ship isn't made for that kind of travel."

The ship was a sleek, sweet vessel, just as the previous owner had promised, but they had already pushed her limits just coming this far. Ao was right: more would be folly.

Jerzy shifted on his perch, uneasy with the way the question again weighed on him, the others looking to him to make a decision. Ao had more knowledge of sailing and foreign lands; Mahl was the more practical one, with better understanding of how the world worked. He was bare removed from a slave, torn too early from his training . . . and useless without his spellwines, his quiet-magic weak and suddenly strangely unpredictable. Panic threatened to rise up and engulf him, as it had while he was in the water, not allowing him to think, only react.

And into that swirl of panic came a stone-cool voice. *You Are Vineart.*

The Guardian could not reach him over this much water; he had, reluctantly, accepted that. Even in Aleppan the stone dragon's voice had been muted, its range limited beyond the borders of Master Malech's vineyards. And yet he heard the Guardian's advice, its cool reminder, and it settled him, allowed him to think clearly, without panic.

Even as an echo of memory, the Guardian protected him.

"If the Washers are involved, we will need proof that someone has been stirring trouble. Proof that even the Collegium could not deny."

The three looked at one another, all at an obvious loss.

"Let me see the map," Jerzy said, and Mahault went to the wheelhouse, where it was tacked to a post, and brought it back. Jerzy skimmed it, trying to fix locations in his mind. "If we continue south, we pass Atakus." Something about the name stirred his memory and made him uneasy. It was an island principality, he knew that, and home to a powerful Vineart, in addition to being one of the safe ports for ships traveling to the Southern Isles. But what . . .

Jerzy closed his eyes, trying to remember. He did as his master had taught him, opening all his senses, letting taste and smell and sound bring forward the missing memory the way a decantation pulled the magic from *vin magica*.

Something had happened in Atakus. He remembered his master speaking of it: They had closed the port, withdrawn? That was the sort of mischief and out-of-ordinary occurrence he had been sent to Aleppan to discover. It did not matter now, save that they would avoid Atakus. They needed to find the source, not where it had already done damage.

"Traveling farther south leads us to the desert lands." His master hailed from there, before the slavers had taken him up and left him with Master Josia in The Berengia, decades past.

"Is that good or bad?" Ao cocked his head, waiting for Jerzy's response while seated next to the Vineart; Mahault did the same, making them look like a pair of inquisitive cats.

Jerzy considered the question, looking down at the map again, comparing it to his memory of Master Malech's maps, and his history of the Lands before the Breaking. "The grapes there took a full dose of Sin Washer's blood: firevines and aethervines, fierce and bitter." He tasted firewine in his memory, tried to remember what he knew of aethervines. "The taint . . . yes. It might have come from there."

"Might . . . and might not." Ao sounded dispirited. "Either way, I don't think this girl could make it there, Jer."

Ao was right. There was no way their little ship could make it to Atakus, much less past there, even if the harbor were open. They would have to take larger transport, which meant interacting with others . . . and where would they find the money to buy passage for all three of them? Not even a master trader could transform this ship into that much coin, and Ao had been third in his delegation, a self-described fetch-and-carry boy, before his actions had cast him in with Jerzy's fate.

"We could go east," Mahault said doubtfully. East was back to Corguruth. Aleppan was only one city-state; there were others who had no ties to Aleppan, no obligations—and who would in fact be just as happy to shield someone or several someones running from Aleppan's maiar. But Corguruth was a Vin Land.

"If we go east, through Corguruth, we would reach Altenne," Jerzy said, thinking out loud. "The city of scholars, they hold the entire history as we remember it, the study of the First Vine and all its legacies. They might protect us . . . but Altenne is also home to the Collegium. Rot and blast."

He got up and started to pace, feeling the deck move under his feet and noting again how his body adjusted to match it, smooth and steady, the same way Mahl and Ao seemed to have picked up after their first day. Had it been his dousing in the seawater that had accomplished that? Or was it related to his sudden use of magic, that soaring into the air? He still had no idea how he had managed that, and no resources or time to study it, to understand the structure of the magic the way a Vineart should.

Priorities. In a storm, the vines were protected first. In this storm, he needed to ensure his safety—and the only way to do that was to wipe clean Sar Anton's accusation, and the Washers' penalty of death.

"We don't know what's happening," he said finally. "We don't know if they're still looking for me—if they're looking for all three of us. It doesn't matter. My master sent me to discover information, track down some truth in the rumors, a source to the trouble. That hasn't changed. If I can't return home, then I need to follow the taint. So that is what I will do."

"Then we will go with you," Ao said, and Mahault nodded, her face set in determined lines. "We will see this through."

Jerzy should have felt satisfaction, or relief, but his stomach roiled in a way that had nothing to do with the motion of the ship underneath him. It all came back to the taint, the odd, unpleasant scent of magic that seemed to underlay every attack, every oddity, every uncertainty they had encountered, the way the taste of the soil ran through every spellwine, identifying its origin.

Jerzy had sensed it first in the flesh of the sea creature that had attacked the Berengian shore—the flesh that Master Malech said was spelled into life, but by no winespell he could identify—and then again in the court of the lord-maiar of Aleppan, Mahl's father. There, the taint had been centered in an aide, a man of no importance, no status within his own right . . . no magic within his soul. In order for him to carry it, the way the serpent had, someone had imbued him with it. Someone, or something.

Merely the thought of that moment when he had tasted the taint, as others argued his fate around him . . . it took him back in the swirl of fear and anger and despair. Of being dragged by the arm down corridors, others stepping back and staring at him, whispering; the fear when the servant had attacked him, trying to steal the mirror that was his one connection to Master Malech; the confusion when Sar Anton killed the servant to save him, then warned him to stay silent; and the realization that it was not he they were after, but Vineart Giordan, for reasons he still did not understand . . . and then Giordan's raising a storm within the council hall itself, and Ao dragging him to safety, and flight . . .

The sound of Ao's voice, normal and steady, was a path out of those dark and unnerving memories, and Jerzy followed it gratefully.

"Follow it? You can . . . sniff it out? Like a dog?" Curious as always, Ao looked at Jerzy as though he might suddenly have grown a longer nose, and a tail.

"Like a Vineart," Mahl told Ao, rolling her eyes at him. "The way they know when the vines are ready, the grapes are ripe. Right?"

"Something like that," Jersey acknowledged, clinging to the familiarity of their voices to keep him anchored in the present, letting their trust restore some of his own confidence. In truth, he did not know how he had found it or, absent a direct source, if he might ever find it again. He had been hoping for some message from Malech, some sign of what he was to do, even hoping silently, secretly, that the Washers would find them, give him no choice. In the end, though, there was no choice. If he did not want to be useless . . . he had to be useful.

And he knew what the taint tasted like. Not Master Malech, who had only tested the dead, near-rotted flesh of the serpent, had not touched it in living, breathing form. Only him.

Jerzy faced into the wind, and his nostrils flared, trying to take in as much information as he could, although it wasn't a smell he was seeking, exactly. The taint could be found only with the Vineart's Sense, something that was neither taste nor smell nor sight, but something combined and beyond.

A Vineart was both born and made, Malech had said. The skill, the Sense, had to be there, honed by the harsh conditions of slavery, enhanced by the constant exposure to the vines themselves, the Harvest and the pressing, until it expressed itself somehow, enough that the Vineart noticed and brought the slave forward. Jerzy had known that the mustus, the juice of the press, was off. He had not reacted when the vat overturned, when every other slave scurried to salvage some of the spill. Master Malech had seen that and taken him in, tested him.

Jerzy lifted his left hand. Where once there had been a slave-mark on the inside of his wrist, placed there by Master Malech when he bought Jerzy as a child, now the top of his wrist bore a smaller, darker red stain. Malech had not put it there; it had appeared after his second testing, when he had not drowned in the mustus but breathed it in. Only by relaxing and letting the mustus enter into him, allowing it to blend with his own body, was he able to survive. When he had emerged, the mark had been there. Sign of a Vineart. Sign of the quiet-magic resting within him.

The deep sea, so far from the root of the Vine, was unkind to Vinearts. Master Malech could not find him here. And yet . . . the taint came from beyond The Berengia, traveled throughout the Vin Lands . . . the sea serpents had swum through this sea, through waves that passed from shore to shore. Had they left their mark? Could those same waves and winds help him now?

The thought stirred the faintest flicker of hope. Help. He had spent time among Giordan's weathervines, yes, at the Vineart's invitation. The act Sar Anton and Washer Darian had used to accuse him of in their plot to snare Vineart Giordan . . . he had sought to ask the vines only if their master was tainted. Had they known he sought to clear their Vineart? If he had not taken but been given . . . if the quiet-magic were freely offered . . .

And if they had let him in once, would they allow him use once again?

Jerzy went back to one of the new water casks, dipping his hand in and wetting his tongue with the handful of fresh water, trying to summon the wind-driven magic. Caught up within his own senses, it took him a moment to realize that there was something else in his awareness. Like the smell of distant smoke on a clear day, or the taste of rain in the wind: quiet-magic, so quiet he had not even sensed it rising to his summons, natural as breathing.

He turned back to the railing, his face lifted to the afternoon sun, his mouth open as though tasting *vina*, letting it settle on his tongue and touch the roof of his mouth, drawing air in to spread the sensation through all of his senses. There was no space for distractions or doubts. A Vineart must never show weakness, his master said.

"There."

"Where?"

Jerzy was only vaguely aware of Ao now standing behind him, turning as he turned, trying to catch sight or sound of what the Vineart was following. Mahault stood very still, just watching.

"That way." Jerzy followed his instincts, walking forward and to his right until he was up against the railing once again. "That direction. Faint, so faint . . . but I can . . . that way."

"Are you sure?"

Doubt entered, and the connection broke, the quiet-magic fleeing. Jerzy felt his shoulders sag, his head dipping forward so that his chin rested on his chest, his hair flopping into his face until he shoved it back with a distracted gesture. "No. I'm not sure of anything. But there is no taint to the east, nothing I can detect. It's west and southward, like a . . . like the trail a snail leaves. I can see it glisten."

"In the air?"

"No. Not . . . I don't know. I just know it's there. Or I could. It's gone now."

Mahl was obviously dubious, but a glare from Ao kept her silent.

"Can you follow it?"

"No. I can find it again, I think." The feel, the Sense of the taint lingered within him, a deep hole filled with an impossibly smooth darkness pressing against him, like being surrounded by mustus, but slicker, heavier. It was as familiar as the feel of earth under his fingers, and as foreign, as unthinkable as . . .

His imagination failed him. Like the feel of rot in the vines, or a blight in the grapes, he simply knew that it was *wrong*.

"We need to go west," he said finally. "West and then south."

"West . . . past Ifran? Jerzy, do you have any idea how long that would take us?" Ao had a trader's memory for maps, and his normally sleepy-looking eyes were wide as he calculated the distance in his head. Ifran was a place shrouded in mystery and legend, populated with wild beasts and nomadic people who ate their elders and sacrificed their young, and other impossibly wild tales. While Iajan sailors, noted explorers and cartographers with a powerful prince funding their discoveries, had ventured onto Irfan's coastline in recent decades, none penetrated deeply. It was an entire land outside Sin Washer's solace, untouched since the days of the ancient Ettonian Empire—and even then, the Emperor took tribute in the form of exotic animals and precious stones, and left the people unconquered, and unknown.

"The westing wind brings the taint. West, and south. I don't know more than that."

Ao looked at Mahault, as though hoping for support, but she was merely watching Jerzy, waiting. A soldier's patience, Jerzy thought suddenly.

"It's almost dark. We should stay here for the night," Ao said, giving in without much grace. "Get a good night's sleep, all three of us, instead of one person keeping watch."

"Someone would have to keep watch anyway," Mahl said. "In case someone came on us, or came up from shore, or—"

"We need to go," Jerzy interrupted. The taint lingered under his skin and made him itch. "We need to be under sail." He didn't know why, but something told him that it was not safe to remain here any longer— they had lingered in one place too long already. The wind pushed at him, willing them to be gone, promising to fill their sails and take them where they needed to go.

Magic, even quiet-magic, did not work like that, but he felt the truth of it nonetheless.

"All right, then." Mahault heard the urgency in him, and gave way, shooting a look at Ao that made him back down as well. "Is everything secured down below?"

"Tied and stashed," Jerzy replied.

"Then let's be off. I'll take first stand at the wheel. Ao, you're best at maps, can you plot a possible course?"

"Aye, Captain," the trader said, bowing with only slight mockery before going to unlash the sails, while Jerzy leaned over the rail to pull up the weigh-anchor. The weight had gone over easily enough, but his arms ached by the time the heavy clay forms cleared the railing. He managed to get them onto the deck without dropping them on his toes, and coiled the rope carefully on top so that it didn't catch or snag, before going to help Ao with the sails.

"Haul out there," the trader told him, "the way I showed you— careful!"

Despite his help, they managed to get the triangular sails raised without mishap. There were long oars stashed belowdeck, to be used if the ship was becalmed, but they required more arms than they had onboard. Thankfully, the winds cooperated just as Jerzy had felt they would, filling the sails and moving the ship forward at a slow but steady pace.

By the time the sun dipped below the watery horizon, leaving the sky around it streaked with reds and blues, they were in open water. The sky behind them was already blue-black, the sweep of stars spreading as the daylight faded. Jerzy stood at the prow of the ship and breathed in the air, trying to recapture a feel of the taint—but it was gone.

"You've finally got your sea legs," Ao noted, his sharp gaze taking Jerzy in from head to toe, as though assessing a horse or crate of goods.

"Perhaps." He thought about telling Ao of his experience in the water, but the words wouldn't come. He couldn't speak about any of it: the freedom, the sudden fear, the quiet-magic itself. He was still not accustomed to sharing things with another person; a slave kept to himself, and a Vineart . . . he listened and learned, he did not tell others or share his thoughts. Vinearts were meant to stand alone; that was the cost of their magic. Jerzy was only now beginning to understand that the rest of the world did not live that way.

Maybe that was why he felt so comfortable with Mahl. She, too, understood the importance of keeping your own thoughts. Ao, on the other hand, used words to disarm and provoke. Like the drinking trick he had used on Jerzy when they first met, pretending to match him sip for sip of ale, while actually dumping his mugs onto the floor. Not out of malice, but because he was curious to see what Jerzy might say when drunk. The fact that Jerzy said very little had made Ao respect him more, not less. Jerzy still found that odd—that Ao wanted information and yet was pleased when he didn't get it.

The world was a confusing place, and Jerzy wanted only to be back in his vineyards, on familiar ground, doing familiar things, where the lessons he needed to learn were already known, the risks and rewards established. Tradition was safe. The cycle of the vines was security, knowing your place in the world at all times.

He did not know his place at all now, only where he wished to be, and where he was.

"Where do you think we're going?" Ao asked, leaning his elbows on the railing and staring out across the horizon. The wind was just enough to tangle Jerzy's hair, and he wished briefly that he had replaced his kerchief, to keep the strands out of his face. Perhaps he could cut it short.

"I don't know," Jerzy said, amused at how the trader's question matched his own thoughts. "I don't have a map, clearly marked out. I don't even have a picture or a name. Just a sense of . . ." He couldn't describe it, not to Ao. To Malech, or Giordan, or another Vineart, maybe. They had the language to understand him. Ao, untouched by the Sense, unmarked by the mustus, could not understand how Jerzy thought or saw.

"If we keep heading in this direction, we'll be past Iaja and into the open ocean in . . . oh, a week or so. I don't suppose you could whip up a wind that would move us along faster, the way you summon fire?"

Vineart Giordan could have. Sailors paid solid coin for his spell-wines, to raise winds and calm seas. Farmers used them to bring rain in drought, and dry the skies during floods.

They were delicate, stubborn grapes, requiring that Giordan literally give his own blood to tame them into accepting incantation. Only aeth-ervines were more difficult to work. Jerzy had tasted the mustus, had sunk his fingers into the soil around their roots and heard their whispers in his head. He could taste the wind . . . but he could not control it. Without a spellwine, with its specific incantation, he could not decant anything useful.

"No," he said in response. "No, I can't."

He could, a voice like a soft breeze whispered to him. He had lifted himself out of the water, hovered in the air, and done it without spell-wines. He could fill the sails with wind and speed them on their way. . . .

No. Jerzy refused the temptation. His master lit flame with a touch of his fingers, closed wounds by merely pressing on them. But that was after a lifetime of working with his legacies of firevines and healvines, of letting their essence blend with the magic within him. Someday, Jerzy, too, would be able to do that, and he would welcome it.

The magic he had worked that afternoon with a legacy he had not been granted? It scared him down to his bones, and he would not willingly do it again. There were Commands and traditions for a reason. Breaking them . . . no. He was *not* apostate.

"I don't think I'll need magic," he said suddenly, distracted. "Look ahead."

The sky, clear only moments ago, was filling with dark clouds, blotting out the bright stars.

"Storm," Ao said, destroying Jerzy's hope for fair winds. "Bad one. Damn it, I knew we should have stayed in the cove."

"Storm ahead!" Mahl called out from her post at the wheel, and Ao raised his hand to let her know they had already seen it.

"You're the Vineart, Jer, you know the weather better than us. What do you think?"

Jerzy stared at the clouds, trying to sense their mood. Was this just rain coming toward them? Or a hard blow? He couldn't tell.

"Let's try to ride it out," he said finally.

That, Jerzy decided a little while later, had been a very bad decision. The ship crested over another wave and plunged back down, bow first, even as she tipped back and forth. He would throw up, save there was nothing left in his stomach. His right hand was wrapped in a lead rope, while his left braced him against the wheel-cabin, and the wind and rain hammered at him from all sides. Mahl was at the wheel just ahead of him, a rope tied around her waist to keep her there, both hands clenched around the wheel, while Ao braced her from behind. Every time the ship jolted, they staggered together, two soaking-wet figures occasionally outlined by the crack of lightning that came down from the sky.

He could feel the timbers shake under his feet, the wood shivering as it was pressured from every side. He had no affinity for its dead wood, no sense of its nature the way he did living vines, but even he could tell that the ship would not last much more of this storm.

His mouth was dry with fear and the residual bitterness of his vomit, but he sucked his cheeks in anyway, ignoring the bitterness, searching for some moisture to draw on. If he could bring enough saliva onto his tongue, he could summon quiet-magic, and . . . .

And do what?

Even Giordan could not calm this storm; not even Master Vineart Conna, renowned for his weatherspells, could still the fury that had been unleashed. It was a wild creature of wind and rain, raging down from the skies with the full force of Nature and magic behind it.

That much Jerzy knew: this was no purely natural storm. Under the salt of the wind and sea, and the sweet taste of the rain, there was a scent of magic that he recognized. Here, the nose of it was thin and stretched, enough that he thought the storm was merely a side effect of something else, spun out by actions elsewhere and crashing into a natural storm. Somewhere, someone was using a windspell; sheer bad luck that they were caught in it.

That was the danger and the delicacy of a weatherspell, and why Master Malech preferred not to use them himself; such a decantation did not stay in one place but raced with the wind from one field to the next, across entire lands . . . and across the sea as well.

There was a sharp crack and another bolt of lightning cut through the dark, this one heading straight for the mainsail. Jerzy flinched, warned by some instinct even as the smell of burning wood touched his nose.

"Fire!" he yelled, hastily untangling his hand from the rope. "Fire!"

Another wave came over the side of the boat, swamping the deck and hitting against Jerzy's knees hard enough to make him stagger. The rain might have put out the fire under ordinary circumstances, but the wind whipped the white-hot flames into greater fierceness, and it leaped, like a living thing, the sail catching in an instant, sparks dropping down to the deck, cinders that sizzled and caught, tiny fires springing to life.

A firespell could counter those flames, control them. If he had just one mouthful of a firewine, if he had a few more years' experience in his blood, he might be able to save the ship.

He had neither.

The ship rose and fell again, and Jerzy raced forward, grabbing at Ao's shoulder and shaking him. "Fire!" he screamed in the trader's ear, and Ao looked back over his shoulder, the firelight great enough now that Jerzy could see his face, rain slicked and set in grim lines. His lips moved, and although Jerzy couldn't hear him through the wind, he suspected it was a particularly pungent swearword. Then Ao turned back and got Mahault's attention, even as Jerzy was moving around, crouching low and reaching for the knife at his belt to cut the rope away from the wheel.

Master Malech had given him a proper knife before he left for Aleppan, a handle of polished horn, the blade the length of his longest finger and sharp enough to make short work of wax or twine—a proper Vineart's tool. "No Vineart should use another's knife to open his spellwines," his master had said, making him swell with unexpected pride. That knife should have hung from his belt, with a tasting spoon and small waterskin, identifying him to any with the wit to look. But his belt had been taken from him in Aleppan, when they brought him up on charges before the maiar, and all his tools as well. He had acquired another knife before they set sail, but the blade was too large, the handle wrong in his hand, and he felt keenly the loss of his master's gift every time he touched this replacement. Still, this blade did what was required.

Another rise over a swell, and Jerzy felt his stomach heave, but he kept sawing at the rope, even as he could hear and smell the fire spread, swirling with the wind, the thick wet smoke beginning to choke him.

The ship jumped, and a crack sounded underneath, deeper and more ominous than even the crackle of flames.

"She's breaking up," Ao said, and this time Jerzy heard him. "We have to get off the ship."

Off . . . and go where? The sea below them was wild as the storm, and there were things under the waves, things with teeth and hungry maws. Jerzy's imagination brought up images of the sea serpent he had seen killed, only three times as large and without armed soldiers or spellwines to help destroy it this time. Or a kraken, less fantastic but no less dangerous, its long arms and sharp beak reaching up to snap off his limbs and tear at his flesh . . .

"Jump!" Mahault, freed from her post, grabbed at Jerzy's arm and forced him to the railing. "Jump!"

He didn't think now was the time to tell them that he couldn't swim. Odds were they would be eaten or drowned in the waves before he could have made more than a few strokes, anyway.

The fear left him at that, and he stood up against the wind, his hands clenched on the railing. He should not try to call on weatherspells; they were not his to hold, and the challenge to keep one steady within the storm already brewing was beyond his skills, would tear him apart for his arrogance. Yet . . . If he was going to die, what did it matter? What did any of it matter?

His tongue licked the roof of his mouth and then opened as though to pull in the aroma of grapes. Sea air surrounded him, but the rain brought not salt but the sweet fruit of spellwine.

It was his imagination, fueled by panic, but it was enough.

"Above water, above wave. To safety, bring us, please."

It wasn't a proper decantation, but he had no idea what he was calling on, to focus it better. He was flailing, desperate and reaching beyond his grasp, beyond his rightful domain. Yes, he had worked with weathervines, knew the taste and scent of its fruit, the gritty feel of its soil, but it was not enough to fight a storm of this nature, even without another Vineart's spell behind it, building it to this fury.

He was not strong enough to control what he had raised.

So he merely let the magic within him rise as it would, whatever came to his summons, and asked it to save them.

THE STORM HAD come out of nowhere, giving Kaïnam barely enough time to strike the sails before it hit. He could have retreated to the cabin and stayed dry and warm, but the *Green Wave* was his ship, and he would not leave her alone to face this. So he wrapped himself in a cloak that had been treated for storm use, and went upside to stand by the wheel. The small shelter overhead was enough to keep the worst of the rain from his eyes, but the visibility was terrible anyway; he could barely see an arm's length past his nose. The ship swayed and rocked with every wave and gust of wind, but her timber was well seasoned and her construction the best that could be bought, and she slipped through the storm like a dancer following a steady drumbeat. He leaned back into the shelter, worrying briefly about where he actually was, but trusting that the spells built into the *Wave* would keep her from crashing into an unexpected spar of land. One of Master Edon's students had crafted that spell, and made his fortune off it, and every year gifted a new cask of it to the royal family, in gratitude for his training.

But nothing would keep even the best-protected ship from being overwhelmed by a storm, if it were bad enough. After his experience with the sea creature, Kaïnam could not help but worry.

Because he was worrying, and watching, he spotted the glimmer of light off to his port side and did not dismiss it entirely as a storm-born hallucination. Fire, raging even through the rain and wind.

"Firespout," he said immediately, his skin pricking with fear. Firespouts occurred naturally, dangerous eruptions from the ocean floor, but magic caused them as well—and he had last seen them appear without warning outside his own home during just such a storm, destroying the Caulic fleet that was searching for Atakus's hidden harbor.

Such out-of-place apparitions were the bastard creations of firespells and weatherspells, turning water and wind into deadly upward explosions of briny flame. If they had any use save destruction, he had never heard of it.

"No," he decided, scouring the rain-thick night for another blast. "No." It was a steady flicker, too high to be rising from the water. "Something is burning."

The only thing that could be burning out here, this far from land, was a ship.

"Blast and brine," he swore, hauling on the wheel to try to turn the *Wave* toward the flame. She hauled about sluggishly, fighting the order to go into the wind. No sane man would go near a fire at sea, not under these conditions, but if there was a ship, then odds were there was crew as well. He would not leave men out there to die.

The flames were flickering out as he came closer, the *Wave* not moving quickly enough to suit him, when there was another burst of light— not lightning, but colder, and appearing in midair just off his bow. There was a shriek, like a woman's scream, and then a heavy thud and splash.

There, his sister's voice said to him. *There*.

With a despairing glance at the still-burning ship, Kaïnam fought to turn the *Wave* around again, circling back to where he had seen the splash. Grabbing a spell-lamp in one hand, he went to the side and looked down into the water.

Three bodies, limp and water slick, clung to a piece of wrack, appearing and disappearing as the waves knocked them about. Instinct and training took over; Kaïnam set the lamp down on the deck and grabbed a towrope, coiled neatly in its proper niche by the railing for just such a purpose. Tossing the weighted end over the side, he called out to the bodies, hoping that one of them, at least, was still alive, and alert enough to hear him.

"Grab the tow!"

There was no response, and the line started to drift away from them, almost out of reach. Kaïnam hauled it up again, desperation making him clumsy, and yelled again. "Towline! Grab it!"

Something reached them, thank Deep Proeden, because one of the figures stirred, lifting his head as though to look for something.

"To your right!"

The figure turned and spotted the brightly colored rope shifting with the waves. As Kaïnam waited, his heart beating too fast with concern, the wrack victim reached out, fingers grasping for the lead. Kaïnam could do nothing more than hold the line steady, and wait, and hope. Hope that the figure could reach it, hope that no wave came up and swamped them, hope that nothing lurked below the surface, summoned by the turmoil and looking for an easy meal . . .

"Catch it," he chanted softly, trying by sheer force of will to connect the gasping hand with the towrope, its brightly dyed fibers visible as it bobbed under each passing wave and then surfaced again, tiny air bladders keeping the entire length afloat. "Catch it catch it catch it . . ."

Fingers connected with the rope, and Kaïnam swallowed hard, resisting the need to wipe rain from his eyes, watching and waiting until there was a tug on the line that indicated the man below had gotten a firm hold.

And there it came, and Kaïnam was hauling on the rope, hand over hand, hoping that the figure below had the sense to hold on to the wrack as well, to bring all three of them in safely.

A soft thud of the spar hitting against the *Green Wave*'s side indicated that he had. Kaïnam snugged the rope around a wooden bolt set into the deck and looked around for the rope ladder that should have been stowed in the niche next to the towrope. But it was not there, and he swore in anger. He should have checked before he took the *Wave* out and not trusted to others that it was fully prepared.

He turned back to the side, to see if the figure was able to use the towrope to climb to safety, and was greeted by a hand, glowing with the same clear white light he had seen earlier, reaching over the rail. He took a step back, as startled as he could ever remember being, and found the words to an ancient prayer rising to his lips.

"Deep Proeden, protect and defend us from the creatures of Your depths. From the deep-swimming children and the night-glowing wraiths . . ."

But the glow faded as the rest of the body crawled over the edge, its arm extended behind it, as though pulling something up by sheer force. Kaïnam, his paralysis broken, rushed forward, one hand gripping the first body by the scruff of its sodden shirt, even as he reached down to wrap his other hand around the arm of the second body clinging to the rope, hauling it over the side, and then a third figure, wet as fish and heavy as stone, until all four of them were sprawled on the deck of the *Wave* like so many oversized spearfish.

"Next time, Jer," one of the figures said weakly, "just let me drown."

*   *   *

THE THREE FIGURES turned out to be two youths, one lean and pale, the other stockier, with the dusky-skinned, round-faced look of the trader clans from the Greater Plains, and—to Kaïnam's surprise—a woman, tall and regal even when soaking wet. She had a gash on her head, and the red-haired boy, the one who had hauled them up the towrope, was so exhausted he could barely rise from the deck, but the third, the one who had spoken, seemed unharmed. The storm, as though realizing the damage had been done, was starting to fade. The wind no longer buffeted the *Wave* quite so much, and the rain, while still pelting down, no longer stung when it hit unprotected skin

After ensuring that the *Wave* was in no danger of capsizing, Kaïnam enlisted the dark-haired figure to help get the others belowdeck, where he could better judge the extent of their injuries.

"My name is Kaïnam," he said, lowering the woman down onto the single bunk as carefully as he could. Her long blond hair tangled around his wrist like a living thing, and he peeled it off carefully, not wanting to tug at it and give her any more pain.

"Mahault," she said, reaching up to touch at her forehead, where the blood was still seeping from the scalp wound. "That's Ao, and Jerzy. Thank you."

Jerzy, the redhead, collapsed onto a chair and was shaking as though chilled to the bone.

"There's *vina* in the cabinet," Kaïnam told Ao. "And a goblet on the table. Pour him some to warm him up, quickly."

"*Vina?*" The redhead looked up quickly, his dark eyes surprisingly alert. No shock, then. Good. "Do you have spellwine onboard?"

"Yes," Kaïnam said, and a thrill of unexpected anticipation that he could not explain shivered down his arms. "Not much, but some wind-call, and a bottle of bloodstaunch." He had thought to use it on the woman, Mahault, if the gash was deep enough.

"Bloodstaunch." The redhead—Jerzy, he was—sighed, but it was a sigh of . . . not relief. Pleasure? "May I?"

Kaïnam looked at the other youth. "The shelf above the *vina*. In the—"

"It's probably in a gray flask," Jerzy directed Ao. "With the darker seal on the side."

"Yes." This youth knew the Vineart's seal. Not that bloodstaunch was unusual, and if he were a sailor he likely would have been injured before, but . . .

Jerzy took the flask from Ao's hand, his arm shaking with the effort. But rather than opening the flask immediately, he instead let his fingers run over the surface of the flask, lingering on the seal in a way that suggested a fond memory associated with it. Then he uncorked the flask one-handed and lifted it to his nose, breathing in the aroma rather than drinking it directly.

The combination of actions explained everything to Kaïnam, and the shiver deepened, until he expected the Wise Lady to whisper in his ear again.

"You're a Vineart."

The youth—man, Kaïnam supposed, although he looked dreadfully young, waterlogged as he was—nodded, then brought the flask to his lips and drank. He did not sip, did not take the required mouthful onto his tongue and mumble the words of the decantation—he drank it, three long swallows, the precious liquid sliding down his throat as though it were *vin ordinaire*.

Kaïnam would have protested but something held him silent.

The reaction was almost immediate: the youth's skin flushed with a healthier color, and his shaking ceased. He sat up a little taller, and his frame seemed stronger, more filled with vigor.

"My thanks," he said, stoppering the flask, again one-handed, and with the ease of long practice. "I will see to it that you receive full measure and more, in repayment."

He stood then, and with surprising grace for someone so recently near-drowned, made a shallow bow. "I am Jerzy of House Malech."

Malech. The bloodstaunch was of Master Vineart Malech's making. No wonder the youth—the Vineart—had recognized it.

"I am Kaïnam of Atakus," Kaïnam said, returning the formal bow, peer to peer. "It is my honor to be of service." The echo of his sister's voice came to him, her warning to come this way to find his answer, and the shiver of anticipation he had felt on hearing Jerzy's voice, and he looked again at the young Vineart, this time with more interest.

"Although it may be that we meet not by coincidence," he said thoughtfully. "In fact, there is no coincidence here at all."

Chapter 4

From that beginning, relations between the refugees and their rescuer did not improve.

"You owe me your lives."

"That does not give you the right to order them around to your whim." Mahault was in a fury, her earlier gratitude long gone. Even wrapped in a blanket, after shedding her soaked-through clothing, she still projected a regal stance that would have had Jerzy backing away quickly. The princeling didn't seem to even notice; he was more occupied in not looking directly at her, as though he had never seen a female body before.

Ao, Jerzy noted, had no such hesitation, casting sideways glances at Mahault, especially where her legs showed underneath the blue woven fabric. Jerzy shook his head. They had seen Mahault's legs often enough, on shipboard. They still looked the same.

"It is no whim." The princeling made an impatient gesture, then looked away, toward the door of the cabin. "I must check on the ship's progress. I will be back." He made a curt incline of his head to Jerzy, and left, the door closing firmly behind him with the audible snick of a latch.

"How dare he . . . Who does he think he is?" Mahault asked, her voice high and thin with annoyance.

"The man who pulled us from the sea before we drowned?" Ao suggested.

Mahl stalked back and forth in the narrow cabin, her hair, now dried and pulled back into its usual long braid down her back, flicking between her shoulder blades as she moved. "He is a princeling. Worse, the son of a princeling! He has no right to order a Vineart like that!"

Jerzy sat on the bunk, his knees pulled up to his chin, and watched the two of them go at it. Mahault had a point. If Vinearts were enjoined by Sin Washer's Command from holding sway over men, then equally men of power were forbidden hold of magic—and by extension forbidden hold over those who worked with magic. Separate and distanced, to prevent the rise of another generation of prince-mages that so troubled the Lands Vin two thousand years before.

The Washers would doubtless have a few things to say about this princeling's demands. A pity they couldn't go to them to complain.

Their clothing was spread out over a wooden rack against the far wall, drying. He could feel the healwine he had drunk warming his belly, settling into his limbs, connecting him once again with the vines that had claimed him. Bloodstaunch did more than stop bleeding, although most used it for that purpose. It strengthened the blood as well, gave it vigor to speed healing throughout the entire body.

What had happened in the water, both times in the water, gave him pause: Dare he? If he was in truth tainted, if he were apostate, would summoning quiet-magic do more damage than good? Would he still be able to command it?

The fear was worse than knowing could possibly be. The taste still warm in his mouth, Jerzy brought up enough of the clean, fresh taste to rinse the salt from his tongue, and summoned a flicker of quiet-magic.

It came quiet as its name, obedient, waiting for decantation. While the other two argued over whether they should listen to the princeling's demands, Jerzy considered the still-wet clothing, and asked the quiet-magic to take the dampness from the cloth.

It was nothing he had not done a hundred times before, to the point where the act had been less than the physical act of wringing cloth out by hand. Yet this time, feeling the magic do his bidding, sensing the firespell consume the moisture, leaving their attire dry and ready to be worn again, filled him with an exultation similar to the first time he had tasted spellwine.

He might still be apostate. But the quiet-magic obeyed him.

Obeyed, but drained. Jerzy leaned back and considered his surroundings, while he tried to follow where Ao and Mahault were in their argument now.

COMPARED TO THE ship they had been on, this one was positively luxurious, although it was of a similar size. The wood gleamed with polish, the furnishings were crafted rather than simply built, and the bedding was of a finer, softer material than the scratchy blanket Jerzy had been resting on for the past tenday. He could very easily have curled up, rested his head on the feather-stuffed pillow, and slept until his exhaustion left him.

He didn't have that option. Not with this Kaïnam wanting—*demanding* that Jerzy lead them to the person or persons who had attacked his homeland.

The fact that they had been planning to do exactly that, somehow, before the storm wrecked their ship, didn't seem to deter Mahl's annoyance, and Ao's casual comment that the princeling was better suited to fund such a voyage simply made her angrier.

Jerzy had a suspicion that her annoyance was due less to the princeling's suggestion, and more to the way he had reacted when he realized that she was female. Once he had taken note of her hair, and her form, he had draped a blanket over her shoulders and turned his back on her, as though she no longer existed. Of course, he had not treated Ao much better, once the trader had identified himself by name and clan connection, focusing all of his attention on Jerzy, as though he were the sole person worthy to speak with.

Or, Jerzy thought with a touch of his master's dry humor, the only one worth using.

Ao finally shrugged, refusing to argue with Mahault any longer. "I don't like him, either. But he has the ship, and the means, and we'd be fish food if it weren't for him—and Jerzy's getting us off the ship. How did you accomplish that?" he asked, turning to Jerzy with a return of his usual impossible curiosity.

Jerzy didn't know. The entire time, from calling the magic to hearing the voice call out to them was a blank space in his memory. Flush with his smaller success, he didn't want to think about how he might or might not have used a forbidden legacy. "Our clothes are dry," he said, using that as a distraction.

"Already?" Mahault went over to touch them, to determine the truth for herself. "They are! Thank you, Jerzy."

She glared at Ao, who finally got the hint and turned around, while Jerzy merely closed his eyes to allow her privacy to re-dress herself. There was the sound of cloth moving against skin, and then her satisfied grunt. "All done."

Before Jerzy could find the strength to open his eyes again, there was a soft thump on the cot next to him, and when he looked, his clothing, in a neat pile, was waiting for him.

Heedless of the others in the room, he unwrapped himself from his blanket and dressed himself, feeling an ache in his body as he did so that suggested the morning would bring colorful bruises as well as exhaustion. He was adjusting the tunic over his shoulders when the door to the cabin swung open.

"The storm has let up." The princeling himself stood in the doorway, looking at them. His long black hair was slicked back, and the cape around his shoulders glittered with rain, the moisture beading off it, suggesting that it had been treated somehow to repel water. Not a spell,

Jerzy thought, but almost as expensive. The princeling slipped it off and hung it on a hook beside the door, coming all the way into the cabin.

Suddenly the space, no matter how luxurious, was too small. It had not been designed for four people to be in at once. Jerzy felt the press of too many bodies around him, reminding him of night in the slaves' sleep house, memories he had thought dead and gone. Uncomfortable and feeling crowded, he decided that there were too many pillows on the bed, and shoved them to the far end, resisting the urge to use them as a wall between himself and the others.

It was too much: he was too raw from the magic he had drawn on, too battered by the storm and the stress, and the press of the others breathing the same air, disturbing his thoughts, grew until Jerzy felt that if he did not find quiet space somewhere, he might lash out, shove them away physically.

But there was nowhere, shipboard, that gave him room to breathe, not unless he went up into the rigging, and the one time he had tried that the heave and toss of the ship had made him splatter the contents of his stomach all over the deck below—and his companions. They had not been pleased.

"We look to be nearing the Balears," Kaïnam said, as though he had been there all along. "The storm pushed us exactly in the direction we needed to go." He shook his head. "It was as though the hand of Deep Proeden carried us."

"*We* needed?" Exhausted or not, Jerzy found himself torn between annoyance at their rescuer's high-handedness, and an unwelcome relief that someone else was taking control, making decisions.

"I don't think any of the silent gods had anything to do with that storm," Ao said, trying to play the Washer and sooth ragged tempers.

"No?" Kaïnam tilted his head and looked inquiringly not at Ao, but Jerzy, who squirmed under the observation, not sure what any of them expected him to say.

"There was a taste of magic to the storm," he answered finally, speaking as much to Ao as Kaïnam. "We realized that, before our ship broke up, but I was unable to do anything about it." Best to let the princeling know, from the beginning, that there were limits to what his rescued Vineart could do.

"You use weatherspells, you know that they can often spread far beyond the intent, if you are not careful, or use too much force," he continued. "I think that someone decanted a powerful spell and we were caught in the backwash."

He did not share the fact that the "feel" of the storm had the same feel as lingered on this ship. Some magic Kaïnam had used, or been used on him. No need to feed the princeling's feelings of destiny, or fate. He did not distrust this man, had no reason to distrust him, especially since they owed him their lives, but he had no reason specifically to trust him, either. And Mahl was right: his attitude was insulting. Jerzy received respect as befitted his status as Vineart, even if it was because the princeling sought to use him. The others he treated not quite as servants, but not equals, either.

Jerzy supposed that to the son of a man of power, a trader—especially one without his clan, without official trade status—was not his equal. And Mahl, for reasons of her own, had not given her family connection with her name. Still, it rankled, for his companions to be so dismissed.

"Ah." The princeling nodded at Jerzy's words, as though he understood. No, not the princeling: Kaïnam. Master Malech might speak scornfully of men of power, but he, still a student, far from the protection of his Master's House and with a death sentence on his name, could not afford to be so dismissive.

Especially while on that man of power's ship, in the middle of endless waters.

"You planned to head north," Mahault asked, her pique forgotten with this new information. "Why north? What is there, to interest a prince of the Atakian Islands?"

Kaïnam did nothing to refute Mahault's first impression of him, addressing all of his comments to Jerzy, even when the others spoke originally. "My direction was not chosen by whim. Vineart, I ask again. Will you aid me in my journey?"

Behind Kaïnam, Ao rolled his eyes up to the heavens dramatically, and Jerzy almost laughed, schooling his features just in time. He suspected that Kaïnam would not find laughter an appropriate reaction.

The Atakian's voice was stiff, formal, but Jerzy could hear a note of desperation behind it, and if he could hear it, then certainly Ao and Mahault could, as well. A man who was desperate could be dangerous, too.

"Why north?"

"My goal is to seek the island of Caul. My home was attacked by ships of their fleet, and I would know why."

"Perhaps because you have used magic to hide yourself from the rest of the world?" Ao asked, and they were rewarded by seeing Kaïnam flinch, as though the words had been an actual physical blow. When Mahault and Jerzy looked at Ao, he shrugged. "It is my business to hear things," he said. "And the disappearance of a major port? Word travels quickly. The entire Principality of Atakus . . . disappeared. Shipping routes were thrown into chaos. Rumors flew—and the price of ship-bound goods trebled." Ao frowned in disapproval. "You don't suddenly take away a major port. It's bad trading." His gaze rested on Jerzy. "You weren't surprised—you knew, already."

"My master had also heard," Jerzy admitted. "As you said, word traveled quickly."

"The entire island?" Mahault, clearly, had not heard. "Gone?"

"Hidden," Kaïnam said. He shifted, finally addressing Ao's comment directly. "Yes. Word spread, as it does. As was inevitable. And . . . perhaps you are correct, Trader, that we brought it upon ourselves. The decision to mask our whereabouts was . . . made against my advisement." Oh, how it hurt him to admit that, Jerzy could tell. "The ships . . . the Caulic ships came near to our harbor, though we were hidden, under the cover of night, in a storm much as the one last night—and were destroyed by firespouts."

"There are no firespouts in the Atakua Sea." Ao shook his head, trying to puzzle it out, then his face cleared with comprehension. "Magic?"

Kaïnam's sharp-nosed features tightened, as though fighting an internal battle. "Not by our Vineart. He swears that, and I must believe him. It injured him to admit that such a thing was beyond his abilities."

"A Vineart who could make an entire island disappear, and yet can't cause a firespout?" Ao looked at Jerzy as though seeking confirmation.

"A firespout may occasionally occur naturally," Jerzy said, trying to remember his lessons. "Islands with active volcanoes are prone to them, as are shorelines where there are frequent quakes or great tides. To cause one to occur elsewhere requires two different spells, twined together to force contradictory elements, fire and water, to blend. It could only be done with two Vinearts working together, and that is . . ." Jerzy paused, remembering his own attempt to amend a spell in progress, cast by another, and the scolding he received from his master, after. "That can be very dangerous."

"So you are going to Caul to discover . . . what? To find this master Vineart with a grudge against you? To ask why someone might destroy their fleet to protect you? That makes no sense at all. Caul has no magic; they despise Vinearts." Mahault sounded disgusted. Jerzy had quickly learned that she had no tolerance for things that did not make sense.

"I want to know who sent the fleet," Kaïnam said, still looking at Jerzy, although the sideways tilt to his head when Mahl spoke told Jerzy that the princeling was quite aware of her, at least, even if he would not respond directly. "Someone sent them against us, gave them some sort of magic to find us, for only an aetherspell could have done so. It had to be someone they trusted, someone who convinced them they were in danger, to break their bias against magic. I cannot identify such a person—but a Vineart could.

"Finding you, in your moment of need . . ." He paused, and Jerzy had the feeling that he was reconsidering his words even as he spoke them. "I cannot believe that is coincidence."

"And if I were to go with you, and I could do this thing . . . what then?"

The two stared at each other, sizing each other up. "I believe that if I can identify that person, I will be able to trace back to whoever ordered my sister's murder and, with that knowledge, put right all that her death sent awry."

That silenced the others for a moment. Kaïnam took a deep breath, then let it out in a long sigh, the arrogance he had been displaying now tempered with a rueful charm that Jerzy felt himself, unwillingly, respond to.

"And I bring you into the middle of a longer story. My apologies. It has been . . . a difficult voyage. Let me begin from the beginning. Please, all of you. Sit down. This may take some time, and you have been through much in the past few hours."

Ao pulled forward a small, ornately carved stool from under a desk and sat down on it, looking up at Kaïnam expectantly. Jerzy recognized that look; the trader had shown the exact same expression when he tried pumping Jerzy for information, early in their friendship. Clearly, Ao was less swayed by the princeling's charm than Jerzy.

Kaïnam stared at the far wall, then began to speak, not focusing on any one of them, as though they might distract him from his words. "Earlier this year, we received under flag of parley a Negotiator from Ekai. He had come to my father's court asking for assistance with a matter . . . several ships under our protection had been destroyed, and they wished our aid in discovering the cause."

Kaïnam spoke so carefully, Jerzy suspected that there was more to the story than that. A quick glance at Ao showed only the same rapt expression, and Mahl's face was perfectly still, giving nothing away, but her gaze was intent on Kaïnam's face, like a raptor watching a snake.

"The day the Negotiator was due to leave, we discovered him dead, by his own hand, in his quarters. With him was my sister, our most trusted, most beloved voice of wisdom and caution, his blade hilt deep in her chest."

Kaïnam's tone was matter-of-fact, refusing any sympathy before it was offered.

"My father . . . went mad. There is no other way to explain it. A madness born of grief and displayed in cunning, but madness nonetheless. He saw danger and treachery in every step, and not even our Washer could talk sense back into his eyes. When Master Vineart Edon offered him a way to protect our home from further betrayal, he took it, without thinking through the repercussions. Or, perhaps, without caring."

He looked at Jerzy then with clear eyes. "Like spells, politics often have swells that reach far beyond that of the original casting.

"As the trader said, our island disappeared from the eyes and ears of the rest of the world. We could come and go as we pleased, but none might enter our harbors or sight our cliffs, and the magic worked to push ships away from us, keeping them from crashing upon our shores." His lips firmed, and his face could have been carved from stone as he said, "We had no desire to harm others, only to protect ourselves."

"And what of the ships that used your harbor as a waystop on their journey?" Ao asked, his own voice tight after hearing that dry recital of events. "My people trade regularly with the desert lands. Without safe-harbor along the way, the safe-harbor only Atakus could provide, that journey becomes more dangerous, and to go over land would triple the time such a journey would take and cut our profits near to nothing." He stood up as he spoke, moving forward so that Kaïnam had no choice but to answer him directly.

To his credit, Kaïnam looked at Ao without flinching. "I do not defend my father's actions," he said. "Merely explain the reasoning behind it."

"But you left," Mahault said. She had seated herself next to Jerzy on the bunk, as though either to take comfort—or to protect him from Kaïnam's importuning. Unlike Ao, her voice was soft, almost consoling. If Jerzy had not known that she had sipped intrigue with her dinner spoon from birth, from both her mother's and her father's lives, he might have been fooled into thinking she was displaying a womanly concern for the princeling's well-being, rather than challenging his words.

"I . . ." For the first time, the Atakian looked nonplussed. "I had my reasons to believe that this was an ill-chosen direction for my people, one that would reflect badly on them."

"You were afraid, once the entire island disappeared, that people would think that you were responsible for . . ." Mahault hesitated, not sure how much she should say, how much this stranger knew of the events that had brought them out into the sea.

"That we were responsible for the attacks on other nations? Yes." Kaïnam nodded. He looked at Mahl directly at that, with a dawning respect. "It may be that Caul came for that reason . . . or it may simply be that they were outraged at being denied our ports. Or . . . Caul is not of the *Lands Vin*. Their ways of doing things, their views of the world, are not always as ours."

"My weapons master was Caulic," Jerzy said, finally taking part in the conversation. "He was proud of the fact that they did not need spell-wines to make their way."

"Oh, aye, they're a proud people," Ao said. "Proud and arrogant."

"You would recognize that," Mahl said, unable to resist the barb.

"We're not arrogant," Ao retorted, falling into their usual back-and-forth. "Arrogance is bad bargaining. We're just naturally competent."

Kaïnam looked puzzled but then, when Jerzy indicated he should continue his story, went on. "I felt that, as my father's representative, I could make a case for our reasons for our actions, and perhaps discover who had set that first assassin against us."

"You, alone?" That surprised Jerzy.

"I am not alone." He drew himself up, his stare cold once again. "I am Kaïnam, Named-Heir of Erebus, Principal of Atakus. When I speak, I speak for my father and the island itself."

"Even if he didn't authorize your words?" Mahault looked scorn-ful. "If you were speaking for your father, you would travel with a full guard and retinue. Or he would have sent a Negotiator, rather than sending his heir, who might be held hostage, into the potential home of enemies."

Jerzy hadn't even thought of that. But then, Mahl had lived her entire life in a political nest; the sleep house was a tangle of petty fears and rules, but a slave did not need to think about things beyond his own survival, and a Vineart concerned himself only with his vines and his wines. Even Ao thought not in terms of a dozen yards to be cultivated and harvested, but of a hundred different markets, all connected. They could spot the flaws in what the princeling said, catch him out in lies and omissions.

Once again, Jerzy longed to feel solid, fertile earth under his feet instead of restless water, to be surrounded by the quiet murmur of living vines and taste the shimmer of magic in the air.

If he could not be Vineart, though, Jerzy thought, he could still be his master's ears and eyes. He would watch, and listen, and learn. But even as Jerzy made that determination, Ao's face nearly broke apart with a huge yawn, and then Mahault followed, unsuccessfully trying to hide it behind both her hands, and Jerzy felt his eyelids begin to weigh down, until it was a struggle to keep his gaze focused.

The princeling laughed, a low, surprisingly gentle sound. "Near-drowning, I'm told, is an exhausting thing. There are blankets in that cupboard," he said, indicating a delicately carved fixture against the far wall. "We will continue this discussion in the morning."

"But—"

"Sleep," the princeling said to Mahault, when she would have protested. "I've trimmed the sails; we won't go far off anyone's course until morning."

Ao was already pulling blankets out, and Jerzy slid over on the bunk to make room for Mahault to curl up next to him. They had slept side by side on the trail, shared the close space on their now-drowned ship; it seemed perfectly natural to share the bed.

Ao, though, took two of the blankets and one of the pillows and curled up on the floor in a makeshift bunk.

The last thing any of them were aware of was the princeling extinguishing the spell-light and closing the door softly behind him, taking up the long night's watch.

Ao woke as the first touches of dawn came through the cabin's sole window, and had his blankets rolled up and stowed before the others managed to pry their eyes open. Mahault stretched, kicking Jerzy in the process. There was a brief scuffle, and she shoved him off the bunk, taking his blanket and huddling under both it and her own.

"Still tired," she said, muffled. "Ache."

"Best to move, then," Jerzy said without sympathy. His muscles were sore, too, but nothing compared to mid-Harvest, when every inch of his body had felt as though the overseer had beaten him with a heavy stick. He stood and stretched, his hands lifting to the ceiling, and heard something crack back into place. "Where is our host?" he asked Ao.

"He shoved his head in a little while ago, said there would be food and water to wash in, when we were ready."

That got Mahault moving, sliding off the bunk, still wrapped in a blanket, and out the door.

"Best follow, or there won't be anything left for breakfast," Ao said.

There was, as it turned out, enough, plus the inevitable tai, although sweetened to make it palatable to Jerzy's tastes.

"He kept to his word," Ao said quietly. He and Jerzy were sitting on a low, carved bench running the length of the cabin, looking out across the waters as they moved swiftly to the north. "We haven't gone too far, to refuse to go along with his plans. But I still don't trust him."

The sun was bright, the sky was a clear, almost blinding blue, and Jerzy hadn't felt even a twinge of seasickness. He wasn't sure if he had indeed finally adjusted to the feel of the water beneath him, or if the bloodstaunch he had consumed was responsible, but despite their situation he felt better, more optimistic, than he had since . . .

Ever, actually. It was an odd feeling, like expecting a bruise and touching healthy skin, instead.

"Well, he doesn't trust us," Jerzy said in response. "He thinks he needs me to help him find the Vineart who cast the firespouts, and who enspelled the Negotiator to murder his sister and then kill himself. But he does not trust me . . . or any Vineart, I would suspect." Not even the one hand in glove with his lord-father. Perhaps not especially him, for all that Kaïnam claimed he did not blame the man. There was a bitterness in the princeling, a sorrow that had festered. Jerzy could almost taste it, the way he could taste the ripeness of a grape.

"And yet, you are willing to go to Caul with him?" Ao said "you," but Jerzy heard "we." Whatever Jerzy decided, Ao—and Mahault—would agree to. The loss of their ship had not changed that.

"I'm not about to leap over the side and try to swim for home," Jerzy said. "Are you?"

Ao stared out across the water and didn't answer, not directly. If the trader could barter up a new ship for them, he would. But they were caught.

"I don't like the way he speaks to Mahl."

Jerzy glanced at him, then turned around to look at where the other two were standing near the bow, Mahl with a map unrolled in her hands, fighting against the wind to keep it open long enough to read from it.

"She seems fine."

"First he ignored her as a mere female, and now—"

"And now he discovered that she has thoughts in her head, and he enjoys hearing them," Jerzy said. "And she likes that."

The Vineart felt the urge to take his mug of tai and beat Ao over the head with it. Mahault might be interested in him, or she might be interested in the princeling, but even now she had her eye on the solitaire's star-brand, and a life of the road. In that, the two were well matched; Jerzy couldn't imagine Ao staying in one place for long, either. But they would have to work that out for themselves, if at all, and whatever Kaïnam added to the mix. . . .

Just then, something made him whip his attention back around to the seascape. The wind had changed, or a current of the sea had twisted. His nostrils flared, and his mouth opened as though trying to drink from the air.

"What is it?" All other thoughts were forgotten as Ao stepped back, as though trying to give the Vineart room to work.

"There. The tang, the taint . . . I found it again."

KAÏNAM SET HIS temper, forcing his fingers to rest lightly on the wheel, not clench it. "I am going to Caul."

The Vineart's tone was cool as the breeze, and just as salted. "If you do, you lose your best chance to discover who is behind all of this. You lose your chance for revenge."

"Caul is—"

"Caul is not where the answers are."

Kaïnam glared down at Jerzy, still vaguely disconcerted that this youth was a Vineart. Master Edon's students had always seemed . . . older. He might almost have thought his three rescuees were lying, save the way the boy handled the flask—and the way the other two deferred to him, even when they argued. Kaïnam was the son of the Principal of Atakus, trained and set against his brothers to constantly prove his worth, and he was accustomed to reading the manners and voices of those around him. Mahault and Ao gave way before Jerzy, even though he was younger and weaker. Therefore, they believed that he was indeed a Vineart.

And now this Vineart was telling him to abandon his plans.

Only a fool asked for help, and then disregarded the advice from that quarter. Kaïnam did not wish to be a fool. Yet he had placed so much on Caul being the source of answers that to abandon it now left him feeling hollow and lost. He waited, hoping that the Wise Lady's voice would whisper into his ear again, telling him what path to take. But she was still and silent as the gods themselves, and he felt the loss keenly.

"And you know where the answers are," he challenged Jerzy, to cover his hesitation.

"I think so." This Vineart might be young, but his voice had a tone of command that made Kaïnam listen, even if he was not yet ready to agree. "My master," and there was a faint hesitation, as though he were about to say one thing, and then changed his mind, "sent me on a mission to find answers. I am still on that mission."

Truth, but not the full truth? No way to tell, and certainly the Vineart would not tell him. Vinearts did not meddle in politics, but his companions would surely have advised him well; they, too, were young, but not fools. Kaïnam did not press. "And your thoughts say we should go . . . where?"

The Vineart's dark gaze flickered from one companion to the other, then back to Kaïnam. "I don't know our destination. Only the trail I follow."

Mahault came forward with one of the maps she had taken from his chart case, and placed it down on the map desk, securing the edges of the map with the ivory clips set into the tablet for that purpose.

"We are here," she said, her voice cool and soft, but determined.

Her voice reminded Kaïnam of his sister's voice, and he steeled himself against it, against reacting to the memory rather than the reality. The girl was quick, and brave, but she was not his sister—her goals and means were not bent toward Atakus, but her own purposes.

"Jerzy thinks that the taint is coming from the west."

"South and west," Ao corrected her.

She nodded agreement. "West, and south."

"Into Mur-Magrib?"

Jerzy looked at Ao. "On the northwest coast of Irfan. A few trading ports, not much else inland except mountains and desert."

"No. I don't think so." Jerzy frowned, rubbing the back of one hand against his cheekbone, as though the red blotch on his wrist itched, and stared at the map, his other hand tracking the line they were sailing. "The taint is so faint, it comes from farther away."

"My *Wave* can't take us farther," Kaïnam said firmly. "She isn't built for the open seas, and with four of us, there's no way to carry the proper supplies. Besides, even if we had a full complement and spellwines to speed us along and protect us, I would not take my sail into a storm on a whim."

He realized, as the words left his mouth, that these three had done exactly that. Still, he stood by his words. Without his sister's whisper goading him on, he would have put about and waited the storm out, not plunged in. And then these three would have died. Did they not owe him some consideration for their lives?

"What if you had a larger ship?" Ao asked suddenly.

"You think you can barter for a wide-sea vessel?"

Kaïnam noted that Mahault was not incredulous, merely curious.

"I won't know until I try," Ao said, looking pleased the way only a trader could when confronted by such a challenge. "This ship is sleek and pretty enough to bring a good price, and if we're not too fussy about the looks of what we're bargaining for, it should be seaworthy enough."

"There is no such thing as seaworthy enough," Jerzy objected, looking a little green. Kaïnam guessed that he was not a natural-born sailor.

Kaïnam raised both hands as though to block any further discussion. "You're asking me to sell the *Green Wave?*" The thought was deeply offensive, as though being asked to hand over a child, even as he understood the logic behind it.

"Not at all." Ao now looked offended. "I'd do the selling. You would come back with a lake skimmer and an ancient goat."

Kaïnam blinked at that, and then the absurdity of the situation—the entire situation—finally caught up with him. He wanted to laugh but feared that it would be taken the wrong way. Whatever the Wise Lady had led him to, it was up to him to manage it to satisfaction. He was his sister's brother—but he was also his father's son, and mad or no, the Principal of Atakus knew how to work things—and people—to his own ends.

"We all want the same thing," he said carefully, making an effort to speak to all three of them, as his earlier assessment was clearly in error. The Vineart led, yes, but only with the approval of the others. Kaïnam had to win all three in order to gain his way. "To discover the cause of the suspicious events of the past year. The attack on my home, our ships, your villages and . . . all of it, you say, can be traced back to this . . . taint."

The Vineart nodded. Kaïnam studied him carefully. No longer half drowned, his form was solidly muscled, his forearms sinewy, and his shoulders slightly bent but strong. When he stood, he leaned back, as though contemplating something just out of sight, but when he sat down, he leaned forward instinctively, ready to work. Had they met in a social setting, Kaïnam decided, he would have known Jerzy for a Vineart. Take away thirty years and Master Edon's cane, and Atakus's Vineart would have looked much the same.

That did not mean he would trust Jerzy. He did not entirely trust Master Vineart Edon, after all, despite the Vineart having proven his dedication to Atakus, over and over again. Vinearts were independent creatures, and they did not often mingle with others—and certainly did not travel away from their vineyards, save in the greatest of emergencies. Jerzy might yet be malleable . . . but what game was his master playing, to send him thus?

And yet, his sister's ghost voice had sent him to find these three, to continue his quest. He had followed her, trusted her, all his life . . . could he stop now? Could she have meant for him to rely on them? Or to use them?

He needed to decide.

"Master Vineart Malech is well known to us," Kaïnam said finally. "His healwines are noted throughout the Lands Vin, and I have never heard it said that he was anything other than thoughtful and wise, if unsociable."

The Vineart ducked his head as though to hide a smile at that description of his master, and it was that simple movement that decided Kaïnam. He looked at the map, and then placed a finger over one marker.

"We will make landing at Tétouan, in the Mur-Magrib," he said. "There, in their marketplace, we will find a buyer for the *Wave*."

* * *

XIMEN, PRAEPOSITUS OF the Grounding and outlying Households, was furious. His jaw ached from being clenched, and the sides of his head throbbed as he stared at the latest missive from the vine-mage.

Two more of my pets have approached the Iajan Islands, to strike fear into their vessels and villagers.

That was all, the single line on a scrap of paper, as though the detail were an afterthought, barely worthy of notice. Ximen took a deep breath and was pleased to see that his hand did not shake with the rage he felt. Handing the missive back to the messenger, whose fault it was not, he managed a reassuring smile. "There is no response," he said. "Go down to the kitchens; they will feed you before you return." The boy, a scanty thing barely ten years young, bobbed his head and fled.

Ximen took another deep breath, then turned on his heel and walked briskly down the hallway to the solar where Bohaide sat, working on the Household accounts.

"Walk with me," he said, reaching for her hand. Well trained, she did not question but abandoned the ledgers, and placed her own slender hand in his own, allowing him to draw her up and out of her chair.

He had not said anything more as they left the main building, and she knew better than to initiate conversation. Striding through the fields, Bohaide at his side and the sun warm on the back of his neck, he felt the muscles in his jaw—as well as those of his shoulders and back—start to unclench.

Getting out of the House had been a good idea, as had stealing Bo. Walking with her could soothe even his worst moods, and this morning had been the father of all black tempers.

"The vine-mage will be the death of me," he said finally. "The fool. I warned him against such arrogance."

"You let yourself worry too much about such things," Bo said calmly, although she had no idea what the vine-mage had done, nor did she particularly care, save that it upset him. She did not look up at him, as was only proper, but kept her gaze on her feet, watching where she placed them in the soft dirt. Her feet were high-arched and delicate, but the flesh was firm and strong, and he delighted in watching her wash them before bed each evening, as she told him of the events of the day, the small and large matters that made up a Household.

"It is my responsibility to worry about such things," he responded, but his tone was softer than his words. She was correct, even without knowing the specifics; the thing had been done, and he could not undo it, not with all the foul temper and scathing words at his command. You did not argue with a vine-mage, not if you wanted—needed—his help. The fact that the rope pulled both ways, the vine-mage knew as well. If Ximen were to send back a scathing reply, asking him if he had finally gone mad . . .

Ximen let out a deep sigh. If he did, the vine-mage would likely laugh. Damn the man—if he were not irreplaceable . . . But he was. There was no other vine-mage; the bastard had made sure of that ten years past, and none of his slaves had been chosen to take up the vines should he meet with an unfortunate accident of his own.

Ximen was slightly more expendable—he had cousins he had allowed to live, since none of his sons were of age to inherit, yet. A man might be forgiven for caution, but the Praepositus had an obligation to his people not to leave them without a leader. Thankfully, none of those cousins had proven themselves of interest to the vine-mage. That fact kept Ximen healthy—and his own wits kept him in power.

A drop of sweat ran down his cheek, and he brushed at it with the back of his hand, surprised. It had been too long since he walked outside in the light of day, too often busy with matters of the Grounding, and now, this Agreement he had forged with the vine-mage. Bo, wiser, had a scarf draped over her head, and her blouse was loose enough to let the light breeze dry her skin. He had left his surcoat tossed over the back of the chair in his chamber, but the shirt underneath was still too warm. He briefly considered unlacing it and tossing it aside as well. The thought of his people's reaction to the sight of their lord running about bare-chested like a weanling made his mood lighten even more. He would never do such a thing, of course. His people expected dignity and control from him at all times. But the thought lightened his spirits nonetheless.

"It is my responsibility," he said again.

Bohaide shrugged, her sleek body giving the gesture a grace akin to the strike of a great cat taking down an ebru. "You are the praepositus."

Yes. He was. The burden of that was there when he woke in the morning, and when he lay down each night, and often even as he slept. The only thing he had no say over were the vineyards, and the man who controlled them.

"He understands nothing but his own twisted mind," Ximen said out loud, here where only Bo and the plants could hear him. "We had an understanding: he was to use the sea beasts as strategic weapons, and keep them contained, otherwise. Allowing the beasts to attack on impulse increases fear, but it also allows our enemies more time to study the attacks and muster a defense. If we are to keep them off-kilter . . . I do not care what that bastard son of a catamite says, there was no benefit to his actions."

He knew that Bo had no idea what he was speaking of. She was a good woman, gentle with his children and fierce with the Household workers, but she did not poke her straight nose into matters of governance. She had not been raised to it; women were too few, too valuable to be risked in the games of men.

Decade after decade, his family had watched, waited while others grew complacent, forgot where they had come from, what they had been. And they did forget, a little more with every generation. The people clung to rules to appease the dangers of daily life—the wild dogs and vicious, solitary cats, the poisonous snakes and deadly crawling things—even the shallow waters could be deadly. Ximen wanted more. For himself, for his children . . . his people.

"We are almost ready, he tells me. Justice will be meted out, the sins against our fathers washed clean, our honor reclaimed. That is what I must focus on, not his mad games. Leave the vine-mage to his work, and be ready. That is how I will win."

"And then you will leave us, sire?"

Ximen lifted his face to the sky, drawing in a deep breath of the warm, dusty air. Leave. His grandfather's great-grandfather had landed on the shore of what would become the Grounding that fateful night, when the sky opened in flame and the waves rose up in turmoil, and the Betrayal was made clear. Four ships' complement and cargo, and only six score had survived. Had it not been for Bo's people taking them in, the story would have ended there.

The Praepositus was responsible for them all, from the youngest child in the crèche to the oldster on his final walk. From those who served to those who ruled, the ones who survived, and the ones who went to feed the Harvest's need.

His family had ruled the settlement for three generations, but their blood and bone were bound deeper to the soil than that, seven generations since they came to this place as unwilling settlers. His forefathers and Bo's had not been of the same people, but time and hardship had bound them together as vines were bound to stalks, growing together in one single purpose. Survival.

"Sire!"

He turned and saw a servant running toward him. A girl-child, barely at puberty, her long dark legs flashing through the lengths of fabric around her waist, her bare torso gleaming with sweat from her effort under the warm sun.

He held up a hand to keep Bo from going farther and waited for the servant to catch up with them. He identified her as she came closer: Suraya, the daughter of his stableman.

"Sire, my father sends me summon you. A horse has come in, lathered and sore rode. The ear-markings are those of the outlaying House-steads, but there is no rider, only a message tube strapped to its back."

The messenger might have encountered mischance during the day's journey, or they might have had no one to spare. Either way, it boded ill, and he needed to know what the message said immediately, to prepare his response, be it with words, medical aid, or weaponry.

Thankfully his head was clear and his temper calm now, so he could hopefully deal with whatever crisis had occurred without misjudgment.

"Continue without me," he told Bo. "You deserve a long walk, away from the clamor of children."

She shook her head, amused, but started walking again, obedient to his order.

Bo taught the children how to be strong, how to be brave, readied them to be warriors, no matter what their final place in life, but they were a drain on her position within the House. He should stop bringing them to her, should keep his seed confined so that there were not so many children to bring. But he did love the sound of young laughter in the house, and so many of them still died so young; the thought of being left without suitable heirs sent a chill down his back. Even now that his eldest was of an age to sit with him while he heard petitions, he still feared the sudden chill of illness, or the scream of a keyrack come in from the wilds, looking for food.

This land was strong and fierce and beautiful, but it was deadly as well, and demanded too much in the way of sacrifice for the rewards it doled out. Bo was right. He would take his people—all those who would follow—and leave it behind without hesitation, when the time came.

Chapter 5

Dawn *shipboard was* one of Kaïnam's favorite times, when there was nothing but his hand on the wheel, a breeze rising in the sails, and the clear light of the sun just hitting the waters.

"Beautiful, isn't it?"

"It's . . . yes, it is," Kaïnam replied, resisting the urge to snarl at the interruption. He had not heard Mahault come up alongside him, rapt in his enjoyment of the moment. If she had been an enemy . . . but she was not. They were all allies on this ship, and he need not tense or guard his back around them.

She was looking not at the dawn but the coastline drawing into sight. Personally, he thought that the endless line of coast was incredibly boring—he preferred the open sea to this narrowing body of water—but when he looked again, pushed by Mahault's enthusiasm, he could admit that the rocky, sloping hills on either side of the Strait were a pleasing, if somewhat stark, view—certainly more interesting than the magic-caused blur he had been surrounded by before taking on his three rescuees.

Two full days of sailing under fair winds had brought them here, just outside the Strait itself. At night, Kaïnam had insisted that Mahl take the bunk in the cabin, while the other three slept their off shift in the practice area toward the bow. They had shared the cabin that first night because he had not the heart to move them in their exhaustion, but his sense of decency would have been offended had she slept among them after that. She seemed to realize that and acquiesced with grace.

Ao seemed able to sleep anywhere, merely wrapping himself up in a blanket and snoring the moment his eyes closed. The Vineart, however, slept but briefly, often sitting up through his off shift, staring at the sky. Kaïnam wondered what he was thinking, watching the constellations whirl through the early-morning hours, but did not ask. Despite the two Jerzy traveled with, Vinearts were solitary creatures. Of all on the *Wave,* in fact, only Ao seemed in need of conversation; the others were content—or not upset—to let the sands slip past with a minimum of discussion. They picked up on what the ship needed and performed their duties without fuss. Kaïnam found it oddly restful, having companions, and yet not needing to speak to them.

And so that second day rolled peacefully into the third, and on the fourth day after their rescue, with Ao at the wheel, Jerzy sleeping, and Mahault practicing fighting moves in the space he had originally cleared for his own sword practice, the *Green Wave* slid through the narrow pass, the great cliff rising up on one side and blocking the wind so that they slowed to a crawl. Then they were through, the wind catching up their sail again, and the port of Tétouan came into view.

Ao took it in stride, the pose of experienced voyager well ground into his trader bones, but Mahl and Jerzy crowded to the bow of the ship, jostling each other for a better look. There were a hundred or more small ships like theirs anchored in the blue waters outside the port itself, with tiny narrow boats darting between them, rowers ferrying passengers to and fro. The port itself was a sloping curve surrounded by an ever-rising crest of white buildings spilling over with a profusion of greens and reds visible even from that distance.

"Can we all go ashore?" Jerzy asked wistfully. It should be safe: the Washers would not think to look for him traveling with a princeling.

Kaïnam shot him a startled glance, then looked back out over the port, imagining how exotic it must seem to those two, bred in cooler, less colorful climates.

"You'll need to clean up, if you're to travel with me," he said. "There are fresh clothes in the cabin that should fit you, Vineart. Ao . . ." The trader looked at him with an amused expression, well aware that he would not fit anything Kaïnam might have in his wardrobe. "We'll make do."

"And me?"

Kaïnam looked at Mahl carefully. She was wearing a pair of trousers under her plain, ankle-length skirt, and her arms were bare. The port was not known for modesty or a particular sense of fashion, but her exotic paleness might cause trouble among the more opportunistic sorts unless she indicated by her attire that she was above such rough handling. "There will be proper woman's clothing in the far closet," he said reluctantly. His sister had sailed with him a few times, when she was not otherwise called away by their father. None of her belongings had been touched since her murder.

He turned away then, not willing to speak to them any longer while his sister's memory was fresh in his mind.

Her voice had directed him to these three; they were part of his plan. And yet, by agreeing to their direction, giving up his original goal, he felt as though he was abandoning his own quest for answers. Not for the first time he felt keenly his lack of years and experience.

"Thaïs, I miss you," he said into the faint breeze, hoping that the words would be carried to her, wherever she waited. "Tell me what to do."

He waited for a response, alone on the foredeck, but no whisper came out of the breeze.

Whatever advice she had to give, she had given. The Wise Lady was gone, and by the time the three travelers had reemerged, he had composed himself, able to face the result of their wardrobe raiding with a calm and serene manner.

As he had expected, the Vineart's build and coloring were suited by his own clothing, a pair of loose white trousers and a dark blue linen shirt with white embroidery picked out along the laces making him look older, more dignified. He had added a pair of low leather boots, and wrapped a narrow length of leather twice around his hips as a makeshift belt, a small unsheathed knife hanging from the side. The only thing lacking was the silver tasting spoon most Vinearts carried; Kaïnam suspected he had lost it when they went overboard. No matter—he led this expedition, not the Vineart. There was no need to advertise his presence, unless it was required.

The trader, Ao, had found a dark green sleeveless tunic that fit—barely—across his broader shoulders and fell to midleg. He wore his own trou underneath, and a pair of low boots that had seen better days. The trader clearly understood the nature of these sun-heavy lands, as he had taken a wrap of cloth and tied it around his neck, knotted in the front in the fashion of Kaïnam's own people, to use as protection against the sun and to stop sweat from running down under his shirt.

Overall the look was rough but quality, as though he were a younger son gone adventuring. It would do.

Mahault was standing in the doorway of the cabin, not uncertain but waiting for a moment to announce her presence. Bracing himself, Kaïnam looked directly at her.

He needn't have worried. Mahault's stern good looks were different enough from Thaïs's beauty that the softly draping blue robe did not look at all as he remembered it. Mahault stepped forward, her hands holding the sleeves properly, the golden belt at her hips making a delicate chiming noise, exactly as it was supposed to. Cloth sandals peeped out from under the hem as she walked, and the draped neckline showed off the proud carriage of her shoulders and chin.

"A goddess come back to human form," Ao said in admiration, and the moment was broken when she tilted her head, a long curl of blond hair falling from her topknot and sliding over her shoulder, and she made a face at the trader, scrunching her eyes and wrinkling her straight, slender nose. The trader tilted his head right back and made an even less attractive face back at her in response, and Jerzy clouted them both, gently, on the back of the head as he walked by.

The pain Kaïnam felt in his chest watching them startled him, and it took a second breath to understand the cause.

They were playing with each other, similar to the way he and Thaïs had once played. The way he would never again tease and be teased by his sister.

He turned away from the memory, and the stranger in his sister's clothing, looking instead at the Vineart. Jerzy's dark eyes were focused on the port—no, on the flit ship that was being rowed alongside the *Green Wave*. Excellent. Exactly who they needed.

"Travel to port side? Coin for all of you, one single kehma!" the rower called up, his Ettonian fluted with the native accent.

"Half a kehma," Kaïnam responded before the trader could respond, and the rower screwed up his face and spat into the water in dismissal of the counteroffer.

"One kehma, and not a hem of the lady's gown will be wetted."

"If so much as a drop touches her, half a kehma."

"Done!"

THE PORT'S WATERS were as noisy and crowded as Jerzy had imagined. He sat, carefully, in the rowboat as their guide took them in through the dozens of other boats, avoiding the small naked children swimming and diving in the clear blue waters around them. It smelled strongly of fish and salt and flowers, and new wood and the pungent stink of something being charred off in the distance.

All of his conscious memories were of The Berengia: the mild winters and breeze-filled summers, the sky overhead a gentle canopy, not this hard, overbright glare. His birthright was the Seven Unions, according to Mil'ar Cai's assessment of his looks and his faint memory of that language, but he had been a child when taken up by the slavers; he knew nothing save random memories of being carried on the back of a racing horse, the hard wind in his face and the smell of snow in his nostrils. Even his trip to Corguruth had been within a familiar enough landscape, although the language and customs were different. This, the exotic smells and sounds, and the heat making his armpits sweat as though he had been working all morning rather than merely sitting in a boat while another man rowed? It was all new, and not a little overwhelming. He wanted both to soak it all in, the way he would a new spellwine, and to hide somewhere dark and cool until he could better understand it all.

But there was no respite; their little rowboat slipped into a spare slot among the boats heading for shore, and their guide leaped out with surprising agility, knee deep in the water, reaching back to tow them onto the creamy golden sands. Once the hull of the rowboat scraped dry ground, they scrambled out, Mahault lifting the hems of her skirt over the wooden edge. As the rower had promised, not a drop had fallen on her.

Kaïnam paid him his coin with good grace, and Jerzy saw him slip another, much smaller, duller coin into the man's hand as well.

Jerzy had never seen such glittering golden soil—the shoreline of The Berengia was hard rock and scrub vegetation for the most part—and he bent down to touch it, wondering if it felt as soft as it looked. No sooner had his bare skin touched the tiny granules, though, than a sudden, tingling shock ran through him, making him forget everything else.

"Jer?"

Ao was there, immediately, helping him stand up when his body seemed to refuse orders. "Jer, are you all right? Are you seasick again? Is the sun too much for you? Here, Kaïnam, get him some water!"

Jerzy missed the princeling's reaction to being ordered about like that, still caught up in the sensations coursing through his body. It was totally unfamiliar, the shivering sensation, and yet he knew, immediately, what it was.

Master?

No, not quite right.

Guardian?

His thoughts went from chaotic, disordered, to a sharp-edged clarity. No matter what he had told himself about the reach of magic, and the diluting effects of the expansive sea, Jerzy had never quite believed that there was anything Master Malech could not do. All the days at sea, the nights he had spent staring up at the stars, the fear had come that, perhaps, Master Malech and the Guardian were not searching for him, had—he could acknowledge the fear now—abandoned him for his failure. Not so. It had merely taken his touching land again—land where the roots of the vine still grew—for the connection to be regrown.

MALECH.

It was rare the Guardian used his name, rare enough that Malech paused midpour and looked up at the stone dragon perched in its usual place over the doorway, its long gray tail curling just over the frame.

Jerzy would reach up and touch the pointed tip of its tail when he came in, like a good-luck charm. The Guardian allowed the liberty, which always amused Malech. He would never have thought to do that, never had the thought to treat the dragon as some sort of pet. Jerzy . . . the boy and the Guardian worked differently together, and Malech was not certain yet what, if anything, that might mean.

It had been nearly a month since Jerzy had disappeared from Aleppan. None of Malech's contacts had seen or heard of him, no dose of the powerful, expensive Magewine had found trace of him, no messages had come from him. And the Washers who were still camped in the field behind his House had not heard anything of his missing student, either—at least, not that they were sharing with him.

A vague and cautious truce had been issued between them in recent days; the Washers had pulled back their demand for Jerzy to be handed over to them, under Malech's assurances that the boy would come home without struggle, thereby proving his innocence. The fact that Malech did not know where the boy was, or how he fared, was the only rot in that crop. That, and he was not sure he could trust the Washers to keep their word to leave the boy alone . . . but what choice did he have?

Malech.

"What is it?"

The boy.

The Vineart placed the flask of *vina magica* he had been testing down on the desk, almost knocking an expensive glass goblet off the surface in the process.

"You have found him?"

The Guardian was linked to every member of the Household, by some extension of the magic that animated it. The range was limited, though—the dragon had been able to reach the boy but briefly, while he was in Corguruth—and since Jerzy disappeared, there had been nothing the dragon could report.

I have found him.

The Guardian was incapable of sounding smug. It was purely Malech's own imagination that put that tone of self-satisfaction into its mental voice. That made it no less annoying.

"Where is he? No, never mind, is the connection solid? Can you reach him?"

Barely. But I have touched him. He lives.

Malech had not allowed himself to seriously consider the possibility that the boy had been killed, but the Guardian's confirmation made his eyes close in an instant of relief. A Vineart did not form attachments beyond the vines . . . but it was good to know the boy yet lived.

The desire to know where the boy was, what he had been up to, what he had learned, all crowded like butterflies in his mind, and he waved them away with an effort. Only one thing mattered right now.

"Tell him to come home."

"Guardian?"

The others stopped what they were doing and looked at him. Jerzy knelt on the sand, not caring that his borrowed clothing might be getting wet, or that people were staring at him. The touch had been so faint, he almost thought he might have imagined it, save that it felt more

real, more solid than any memory of that voice. He could not have explained it to another person, but he knew that the touch was true.

"Vineart, is there a problem?"

Kaïnam's voice, officious but without the coldness he had first projected. The days at sea had shown a different side to their rescuer, and
Jerzy could hear the compassion underneath—arrogant, yes, but also
kind. The princeling would have been a good ruler, someday. Might still,
if his quest to restore his people's place in the world was successful.

Jerzy knew he should respond to the question, but he could not form
the words. His mouth was heavy, as though it were carved from the
same stone as the Guardian's muzzle.

"Is he having a fit?" That was a voice Jerzy did not recognize, worried
and apprehensive.

"No." Ao that time: familiar and confident. The trader might not
have any idea what was happening, but he would take control until
Jerzy could explain. That was what he had been in training to do, as part
of his trade delegation: to observe, and cover, and gain—or keep—the
advantage. "Give him room, step back, leave him be. He'll come back to
us when he is done."

The bodies shifted away from him, and Jerzy focused again on that
touch of stone-cool voice. "Guardian?"

He was flesh and wind, and yet heavy and solid as stone, wrapped
in misty clouds and touched by warm sunlight. Not-he and he merged
and tumbled, and he could not tell what was true, and what was magic,
faint and dizzy with sensations. The connection wavered, was almost
lost, and he almost cried out in pain. Then a swift dive, wings folded
underneath him, breaking through the mists and into the familiar stone
encasement of the Guardian's voice.

You are to come home.

"But . . ." The longed-for instructions came, and he rebelled, his mind
stuttered over all the reasons why he was where he was, what they were
planning to do, the trace he was trying to follow . . .

Home, the Guardian repeated. There was an odd echo to its voice, as though something else was underlying it. Jerzy sucked at his cheeks, trying to pull up enough saliva to touch the bloodstaunch, using it to force a connection with the Guardian—both spellwine and the spell animating the Guardian were Master Malech's work, and there should be a link he could use. . . .

His tongue collected a small pool of spittle, and swallowed it again. The taste of the bloodstaunch was faint now, four days later, but the quiet-magic within him recognized what was being summoned, and made the leap from his tongue to his throat to the Guardian's touch; as quickly as that he felt Master Malech's voice, pushing through the stone conduit of the Guardian. No words, but a sense of relief, and urgency, and yet through it all the confirmation of the order, and a sense of something that Jerzy could not recognize; the feel of solid ground underfoot, of a warm bath, a comfortable bed . . .

Reassurance. Security. Safety. It was safe to come home. More, it was important that he come home.

"But we . . ." He tried again to explain what he had intended to do, but the stone's voice weighed heavily on him, a command, until he gave in.

"All right."

Then the connection was broken, and he was able to open his eyes to the crowd of people determinedly not looking at him.

"I need to return to The Berengia," he said. "Immediately."

Ao, in the middle of negotiating with a young boy to arrange lodging for them, threw up his hands in exaggerated dismay, while Kaïnam merely looked thoughtful. "Your master calls you?"

Jerzy could see no way of denying it, not if he wanted to ensure Kaïnam's assistance, and the use of his ship. Else he would have to hire passage home on another vessel, and that would cost him time and coin he did not have. "Yes."

"Ah." Kaïnam did not look angry or frustrated, but merely turned to Ao, removing a small leather bag from the inside of his tunic. "If we are to set to sea again, bound for The Berengia, we will not need a larger ship, but we will need more supplies. Water, food—and clothing for all three of you to replace what was lost. If you are as good as you think you are, this should suffice."

Ao took the bag, weighing it with his hand, his eyes thoughtful. "It will take me several hours," he said, speaking to all three of them directly, rather than replying only to Kaïnam, a small rebellion against the princeling's manner. The assumption that they would all go with Jerzy passed unchallenged, as though there was no other option, and Jerzy was still too fuddled to think beyond the need to be home as quickly as possible.

"I will go with you," Mahault said. "Not that I do not trust you to choose clothing you think suitable . . ."

Ao looked her up and down with a considering eye. "A sahee, perhaps? Or a—"

"Off with you," Kaïnam said, flicking his hands at them in dismissal. "Suitable clothing. No sahee. Cover her arms and her legs; The Berengia is a more sober place than this port. Be wise in your choices!"

Once the two of them had started off up the sandy slope toward the brightly colored awnings that heralded the marketplace, Kaïnam turned to Jerzy. The Vineart had regained his feet, and his composure, and was brushing at the sand clinging to his trou's legs.

"It will be some time before they return, even if your trader is as good as he thinks himself. There is no point to our waiting here, in the direct sunlight, and even less to returning to the ship so quickly. A short walk from here I remember a stall where we could purchase something to eat . . . and perhaps visit a wine seller's stall, to see if there is any whisper of news from that quarter."

Jerzy paused in his brushing and considered the suggestion. Wine sellers were merchants who bought *vin ordinaire*—and the occasional spellwine—from Vinearts, and then resold them at a markup in places where no Vinearts lived, or where they could not trade directly. Jerzy had never seen one of their stalls, and wasn't sure he enjoyed the thought of paying for his *vinas*, but he saw no way around it. If he was to be useful at all, he needed at least a basic winespell or three on hand, and not rely on Kaïnam's sparse supply if he needed anything on the journey home.

Jerzy had had enough of being useless. No more.

So he nodded agreement, and the two of them set out, heading in the opposite direction from Ao and Mahl's path.

"You fought us to go to Caul, and yet now you agree without hesitation to change course again. No questions, no arguments. Why?"

Kaïnam chuckled. "You will never be a Negotiator."

Jerzy waited. He might not be subtle, and Ao despaired of teaching him how to get answers without asking questions, but he had the patience of stone when it came to waiting.

"Your master spoke to you," Kaïnam said finally as they walked across the sand, avoiding the sailors, porters, and occasional child running messages from town to shore. "Through magic. I did not know that there was a spellwine that could do such a thing."

Jerzy looked sideways at Kaïnam, but the prince's face showed only casual interest. Was this a trick question? Or merely an intelligent and educated man's curiosity? A slave learned not to trust anyone, and recent events had made him even more cautious

"There isn't," he said. "My master . . ." Tricky, this. He could not deny it had happened, obviously, but neither could he give away any of his master's secrets, nor was he willing to start rumors of a spellwine that did not exist. He did not think that Kaïnam would use the information badly, but it was still not information that he should have. Bad enough that Ao and Mahault knew as much as they did . . .

Then again, Jerzy thought bitterly, he had already been judged apostate, for no crime at all. What was to stop him from being so, in fact? Nothing . . . save the fact that he did not know Kaïnam. The fact that they had the same thirst did not mean they were drinking from the same flask.

Caution won. "My master has his ways," was all he said. "I am not yet so wise, and can only respond to his summons."

And with that, the princeling had to be satisfied. But Jerzy suspected, from the look in Kaïnam's eye, that it would not be the last time he asked Jerzy about it. When it came to curiosity, Kaïnam could give even Ao a challenge.

It would be a long journey back to The Berengia.

Those worries, even the Guardian's summons, could not stand up to the wonders of the moment, however. Once away from the sea of boats, the port of Tétouan showed a different face from the crowded, noisy, smell-filled harbor, and Jerzy almost broke his neck trying to take in every flash of color and sound possible. White blocks of stone made for streets that were smoother and easier to walk on than the cobbled stones of The Berengia, and the buildings, made of similar material, cast surprisingly cool shadows, keeping pedestrians sheltered from the blazing sun. The doors were not blocked or barred, but rather open to the breeze, occasionally filled with strands of beads that stirred musically as people walked by. There were no horses being ridden, or even led through the streets, but rather small carts drawn by short-coated goats, their horns covered with a dark resin at the tips, or filed off entirely, leaving only a finger's-length stub. The dizziness he had felt when the Guardian contacted him was nothing to the swirl of amazement that swept over him now, and only Kaïnam's presence by his side kept him moving forward through the streets, rather than stopping to gape.

They turned down a narrower street, the bright-colored awnings of the stalls more crowded together, and Jerzy stopped to sniff at the air, trying to differentiate the sweet aromas floating past him. Some were from the oversized red flowers blooming everywhere, and a strand was from a bakery somewhere nearby, the unmistakable smells of fresh bread and warm honey, and the ever-present tang of the great sea surrounding them, but there was something else in there as well that he could not place, and it tickled at his mind the way the Guardian's voice did until he tucked it away to puzzle at later. The area of the city Kaïnam was leading him through might be less crowded and confusing than the marketplace Ao would be trading in, but it still required that he keep his wits about him. The portion of The Berengia where he had grown up was countryside, where things happened slowly, in tune with the seasons, and Aleppan had been a civilized, sophisticated city. This, by contrast, was chaos: filled with people intent on greeting each other, hanging out of windows and pausing midstreet, their hands gesturing as they spoke, heedless of who might be trying to pass them unscathed.

Men and women alike wore long robes similar to what Mahl had been wearing, or long tunics over trou like Kaïnam's, and Jerzy intercepted more than one sideways glance at his own attire, the gawker looking away again quickly when they came to the double-wrapped belt at his hips.

He had been so pleased when he found the length of leather in the wardrobe. He should, as a student, wrap his belt only once . . . but the second twist came naturally under his hands, and the buckle, a simple hook, had slid into place with a pleasing snick, and so it remained.

Only Vinearts and Washers wore their belts double-looped, by centuries of tradition, and only a Vineart carried a blade too short for fighting and too large for eating. Hence, he assumed, the stares and the second looks and why, when they reached the wine seller's stall—a deep crimson canopy over a row of wooden stools pulled up to a cloth-draped counter, and casks set behind, well out of the sun—the seller himself, a tiny, dark-skinned man with an easy smile and constantly moving hands, came out to greet them.

"Good sirs! Noble sirs! Sin Washer's peace upon you! Please, you honor my small stall with your presence; come in, come in, away from the sun and the press of lesser beings. . . ."

The flattery seemed over the top, even for a merchant, and Jerzy looked sideways up at Kaïnam to see how he should respond. The princeling seemed amused by it, gesturing with one hand for Jerzy to follow the older man into the cool depths of the shop.

They were seated at the far end of the cloth-draped bar by a scurrying servant, and two goblets were placed in front of them. Jerzy picked his up carefully, turning it around in his hand to better admire it. The glass was almost clear, if slightly clouded, and there were only a few crackling lines ruining the design. Unlike the goblets in his master's House, these had no stem, but were rather small, deep bowls, meant to be cupped in the palm of the hand.

He did not think his master would approve, but it doubtless made them easier to craft and transport. The Glassmakers' Guild was far away, and their work was too fragile to travel easily, making it expensive . . . were these the work of local craftsmen? If so, the guild should keep an eye on their own worth, or risk losing custom. The realization that he was thinking like a trader made Jerzy blanch slightly. Politics, and now trading . . . what else was happening to him?

"For you, good sirs, my finest. Yes, just the thing on such a warm day." The wine seller, without hesitation, reached behind him and pulled out a small clay flask, the wax seal around the edge already cracked open. There was moisture on the surface, indicating that it had been kept chilled somehow, despite the sun's heat. Jerzy was intrigued. Did they have an icehouse behind the counter? That would be expensive, in this warm land. Or were they using a weatherspell to maintain its cool temperature? If so, small wonder a thunderstorm had not broken out under the tent by now!

The wine seller poured the liquid into the glasses, and Jerzy's breath caught. The wine—a *vin ordinaire* that did not catch at his mage-sense at all—was a deep golden color, thick and rich-looking. To be certain, he glanced at the seal on the side of the flask. Yes, he was correct. Gilded *vina*, from Master Bartlet. Not a *vina magica*, but just as precious. He had never tasted this *vina* himself, but his master served it for special visitors. It was truly an honor, being offered it.

Jerzy lifted his glass, once it was poured, and raised it to chest level, letting the edge tip toward their host. The Vineart's toast was "warm days, cool nights," but he was not sure that was appropriate here. Instead, he used one he had heard from Ao: "Health and wealth." When Kaïnam echoed him, and the wine seller beamed, he relaxed slightly and lifted the rim of the glass to his mouth.

Smoothly ripe, intensely bright fruit filled his mouth and nearly overwhelmed his senses; only the sure hand of a Master Vineart had kept
the *vina* in check, wrapping it around a structure of cool stone and dry
earth that tempered it into a refreshing drink, rather than a cloying one.
Magnificent.

Kaïnam did not seem to notice anything special in the wine being
poured, even as it slipped down his throat, and Jerzy pitied him.

From the gleam in the wine seller's eye, he knew the impact his offering had made on Jerzy. "So. Gentlesirs. What service may I offer to
you? Or are you perhaps looking to offer your services to me?" The
wine seller looked so hopeful, Jerzy almost wished he could say yes. He
waited for Kaïnam to respond, then realized with a start that the prince
had ceded the conversation to him.

"I am here only to taste, and perhaps to acquire," he said, thankful
that Ao wasn't with them. The trader would doubtless attempt to work
some deal for Jerzy's services, regardless of the fact that he was not, in
fact, a Vineart yet, and had no yards of his own to plant, much less
harvest.

"Ah. Well, gentlesir, I will do my very best to accommodate you. My
vins ordinaire are excellent, as you yourself have tasted, and I have a
small selection of spellwines you might perhaps wish to sample? Not
so many, these days, I am afraid. Our shipments have been . . . lacking,
lately." He paused, and seemed to be waiting for Jerzy to say something.

Beside him, Kaïnam stirred, as though wanting to join the conversation, but he remained silent.

"You have not been able to come to Agreement? I know this is a difficult land to work, but there is . . ." Jerzy had to think a moment, thankful that Master Malech had taught him the map of the Vin Lands,
annotated with the names and specializations of as many Vinearts
as Malech himself knew of. They were still within its boundaries, if
barely, and while the coastline was not suited to vines, surely there was a
Vineart or two near enough . . .

"What of Vineart Poul? He surely could supply you with the basics."

The Vineart was not a master, but he had inherited vineyards farther inland that were known for a rare variant of weathervines that could be incanted to find hidden stores of water, deep underground. He would be considered a master soon enough, Malech had said in passing. All he needed was the confidence to claim the title, and it would be his.

The wine seller looked surprised, then assumed a sad expression. "Vineart Poul died months back," he said. "A terrible, terrible thing."

"Illness?" Kaïnam asked, in the tone of a man making idle conversation.

"No. Or if so, one that came suddenly, and left no trace—nor infected others around him. He lay down to sleep one night, in the prime of health, and never woke up."

"And he had no student, past or present, to inherit?" Jerzy felt himself tense, although he was unsure why.

The wine seller shook his head. "And none have come to claim his lands, either. They have lain fallow since then. A few brave souls have harvested what they could, but their *vin ordinaire* was . . ." He made a face and shook his head. "It needs a Vineart's touch, those vines do, before they are lost to us." He looked carefully at Jerzy, who tensed. "You are young yet, gentlesir. Might you be looking . . ."

Something surged inside Jerzy, but he forced it down harshly. That was not how it worked. A Vineart did not acquire lands that way. This merchant should know that; any who dealt with Vinearts should know that.

Jerzy thought of Mahault, of her cool demeanor no matter the affront, and his voice showed none of his disgust or dismay when he replied. "Alas, my friend, I am bound to another yard, yet. But I will let my master know of your dilemma. Perhaps something may be done."

Letting a producing yard revert to the wild was a waste. It happened, occasionally, that a Vineart died without a student, and no slaves showed the Sense beyond what first attracted a Vineart to buy them, but it was rare. The slavers were very good at their job, and it was unheard of for a Vineart with Poul's reputation to have no student at all.

"What happened to his slaves?" Perhaps Jerzy could investigate, or . . .

"Ah. They ran off, after his death."

Jerzy looked at him, both his earlier tension and the surge of greed banished by an utter lack of comprehension. "Ran off?"

"Yes. He had, hrmn, twenty, perhaps? Maybe half again that. All gone, by the time someone came to see what had happened to the man."

Impossible. Even if their master was harsh, they would not abandon the vines. One, or two, perhaps. But not all. Even if they lacked all sense of magic in their bones, they would not abandon the vines.

Vineart Poul's death might have been from natural causes. *Might.* But Jerzy did not think so. Too many things were off; he could feel the tainted hand of their enemy pressing down on the land, plucking off another piece from the game board. Jerzy kept that fear to himself, for now. That was Vineart business, and none of theirs. Master Malech would know what it all meant.

Kaïnam seemed to sense his distraction and, with gentle maneuverings, turned the discussion to more commonplace matters, of weather and the arrival and departure of trading ships, and what news was heard from Mur-Magrib's ruling family, and the taxes they demanded. Jerzy understood little of it, and it was a relief when, their glasses empty, the wine seller invited him to look over the stock available for sale. Kaïnam indicated that he would remain there, and so Jerzy followed the wine seller back behind the bar to a cool, stone-built storeroom. The smell— a slightly dusty, cool scent—made his chest clench again with longing, but he hid it, looking over each offering carefully. Finally, he found a half cask of healwine—not his master's, but acceptable—and two flasks of firewine to replenish the lighting of the ship, and allow their food to be heated, rather than relying on cold meals midday. There was also a flagon of Master Giordan's weatherwine that tempted him, so much that he found his hand on the clay surface without consciously meaning to.

"And that, gentlesir?"

"No," he meant to say, but his voice said, "Yes."

Vineart Giordan had betrayed him, but his vines had been

magnificent, his skills undeniable. Giordan had no slaves as part of his Agreement with Mahault's father, the maiar of Aleppan; if the Washers had executed him, would that spellwine disappear from this world the way Vineart Poul's would? A tragedy, if so. There were not so many Vinearts that the death of even one without a successor would not be a loss. Two, in such a short time . . . and a wine seller who seemed in ignorance—or not to care—about the Commands that ruled what a Vineart might or might not do?

His last reluctance to obey the Guardian's order faded. Master Malech needed to know of all he, Jerzy, had seen and heard, and it was too hard, at this distance, for the Guardian to give him more than vague instructions, much less convey anything this complicated. No—the sooner he was home, the better.

After they agreed on a price, the wine seller had his assistant select the wines and bring them to the front, where Kaïnam waited. The Atakusian was not quite as calm as he had been earlier, and refused the wine seller's offer to have the wines delivered. Jerzy started to protest, then shrugged, tucking the flasks over his shoulder and lifting the cask into an easy cradle carry while Kaïnam paid over the required coins.

For someone who had spent half of his life hauling casks and bushel baskets, the weight was nothing unusual. The pace that Kaïnam set when they left, however, quickly left him breathless.

"What is wrong?"

Kaïnam scanned the crowd, his taller height an advantage. His stance was still tense, but his hands rested loose by his side, his shoulders open, not hunched as though expecting a blow, the way Jerzy might have expected, the way he was acting. The lessons from his own weapons master came back to him: someone had taught this princeling to fight with more than words . . . and he was expecting to use those skills.

"While you were in the back, one of the customers near us left."

That could not be what had set his companion off, so Jerzy waited, shifting the cask in his arms to ease the strain on his muscles and ready himself as well. Mil'ar Cai had spent more time teaching the young student how to escape a fight without injury than how to start one, but, if need be, Jerzy could place a blow well enough.

The thought came that, with the spellwine he carried, he could do significantly more damage, but it would take too long to ready himself, and he dared not use quiet-magic here, where anyone might see and wonder. Kaïnam, suddenly realizing how fast they were wending through the slower-moving crowd, slowed his steps, as much to avoid curious notice as for Jerzy's comfort.

"He came back, not a moment later," Kaïnam went on, still looking over Jerzy's head, his gaze restlessly watching the crowd around them. "And he was not alone. Two men, and neither of them had ever done an honest day's work in his life, I vow that. They were speaking intently, and looking in my direction too often for comfort. I do not think they were interested in me, however."

Jerzy hesitated, then shared his thoughts. "The Vineart Poul. His death was not natural." The switch in topics seemed unrelated, but his companion followed without hesitation.

"Men do die, without seeming cause," Kaïnam said, but he sounded as though he were arguing counterpoint, not because he believed it, but because he had been trained to do so.

"Men do. But a Vineart's slaves do not run off in the night. It is not how we are trained."

"If he was a harsh master . . ."

Kaïnam didn't understand. He couldn't. Jerzy remembered Cooper Shen, who had also misunderstood what it meant to be a vintnery slave. Yes, it was a harsh life. The Master's word was life or death, his whim the difference between a good day and bad. But . . . there was nowhere else Jerzy could imagine being, nowhere else he would have wanted to be.

A Vineart chose his slaves for the Sense he saw within them, the touch of mage-magic in their bones. Not all developed into Vinearts, but all responded to the vines. They all were in thrall to the magic that surged in the soil, grew to expression within the fruit.

They would not have left.

And so they must have been taken.

Nothing came at them from the crowd, no attacks manifested while they walked, and Jerzy relaxed. Perhaps Kaïnam had been mistaken.

If Poul had been murdered, that was another crime to lay at the feet of their unknown enemy. But for the slaves to have been taken . . . no, it made no sense. Who would steal slaves? Another Vineart, only. One who could not afford his own? But how to transport so many, so quietly? Had a slaver's caravan been through, to sweep them up and resell them?

Kaïnam steered them down a different street, this one less crowded, with fewer stalls. Deep in thought and burdened with the casks, trusting his companion to lead the way, Jerzy didn't see the other man until they knocked shoulders.

"Ho, sorry there, my friend." A hand reached out to steady him as Jerzy staggered, but kept hold of the half barrel. He nodded his thanks, but the hand did not release him.

"Kaï—" he began, nervous. He instinctively sucked at his cheeks, trying to dredge moisture to call the quiet-magic to him, but fear made his mouth too dry to cooperate. Kaïnam's presence at his side disappeared, and for an instant Jerzy had the wild thought that he had been abandoned, that the princeling had somehow betrayed him.

Then there was a snicking noise of metal clearing a sheath, and his assailant suddenly had six inches of shining blade pressed, edge first, under his bearded chin.

"Drop hands and back away," Kaïnam said. His voice was sharper and more frightening than the blade he held, and the stranger did as he was ordered.

"I am wise to you, my friend," Kaïnam said in that same frightening voice, his hand not wavering, the blade pressing ever so slightly into the soft flesh of the stranger's neck. "And so are our companions, who have been shadowing you as you shadowed us. So I would advise you tell your employer that this Vineart is not for the taking."

The man, his eyes wide, dared not nod, but the princeling seemed satisfied that his message had been heard, and relaxed the pressure just enough. The man backed up and then disappeared back into the swirling crowd, which seemed deliberately unaware that anything odd had happened.

Perhaps, Jerzy thought, dazed, it wasn't odd at all, here.

Kaïnam sheathed his blade, pushing Jerzy forward with a firm hand on his shoulder. "It will take them time to determine I lied," he said calmly, only the strength of his grip indicating his anger—and his concern. "We need to be back on the ship before then. The others will have to catch up with us when they are done."

Jerzy, shaken and still not quite sure what had almost happened, could find nothing to disagree with in that plan.

PART 2

Factor

Chapter 6

The Berengia

*T*he *week of* hard sailing after they left Tétouan was quiet, each of the four caught in his or her own thoughts and plans, going about the ship's routine as though they had been sailing together for months, standing watch and sleeping in alternating rounds. There had been no unusual storms, no sudden appearances of sea serpents or firespouts. Even the wind seemed to be cowed, filling their sails and speeding them on their way, day and night, as though it, too, was eager for them to return to The Berengia. Jerzy halfway suspected windspells, but each gust smelled perfectly natural.

"Maybe it's all over," Ao said on the fourth morning, when Jerzy mentioned how calm things had been. "Your master is smart, yes? Maybe he called you back because he knows who is behind all this, and . . ."

Jerzy stared at Ao, waiting. "And . . . ?"

The trader slumped down onto the barrel opposite Jerzy, looking defeated. "I have no idea. I only wish it were so, that we were free of it."

Ao hadn't been the only one with wishes. Jerzy had begun to hope that his master's summons meant that whatever had been happening was done, that he would be able to return to his normal studies. Perhaps Ao was right, and while he was at sea, Master Malech had uncovered the truth, had convinced the Washers to take the matter on themselves, and . . . his imagination failed him as well. The Collegium was powerful, but Washers were but men—what could they do against magic that could create monsters out of dead flesh, or close a man's mind to reason?

And if Washers were, as he feared, involved in this somehow . . .

Ao wanted things to return as they were, the adventure over and order restored. Jerzy was beginning to suspect that would not happen.

And so the *Green Wave* sailed into the shallow waters along the coast of The Berengia, and tied up at the shoddy wooden wharf of a small fishing village barely large enough to claim the name. They could have sailed into one of the larger towns, farther down the coast, but that would have involved waiting for a berth and paying the harbormaster, and, as Ao pointed out, they had a ship that could slip into more quiet coves, so why not make use of it?

The fact that it was closer to home appealed to Jerzy. The fact that it would be less expensive pleased Ao. The fact that it would not take them out of their way convinced Kaïnam, who had the final say.

Only Jerzy and Mahault were leaving the *Wave*.

When Ao had announced his plans the day before, Mahault had been furious. "You're doing what?"

"I'm going with Kaï." Ao looked worried, but defiant.

"Going where?" Mahault glared at him, her hands knuckled at her waist, her entire body fierce. "Ao, we promised to see this through."

"I know. But we aren't, are we?" Ao looked at Jerzy then, as though asking him to say otherwise. "Your master called you home, and,

I'm sorry, Jerzy, but there's nothing for me there. You don't need me anymore."

There was nothing Jerzy could say to that; Malech had his own Agreement to sell his spellwines, and he could not think of anything else in the Valle of Ivy that might interest a trader.

"And you?" Mahault turned on Kaïnam, including him in her ire.

"If you are not following up on this taint, I will return to my original plan," Kaïnam said, directing his words not to Mahault, but Jerzy.

"Caul?"

"Caul."

Unlike Mahault, Jerzy did not take the switch of allegiances personally. Ao's goal had always been to return to his people with something equal in value to what he had cost them when he helped Jerzy escape. Only that way would he be forgiven. Ao's people had little knowledge of the Caulic markets, what would sell well there, and what could be acquired. Proof that the lords they bargained with were influenced by external forces, or new markets ripe for trade—they were both of value. And Kaïnam . . . he would follow his duty, just as Jerzy did. The Vineart understood.

"We'll keep ears pricked," Ao assured Jerzy. "For news or gossip you might use. If we hear anything, we will send a message-bird or if there's a *courien* heading your way . . ."

Courien were too expensive to hire for anything of the sort, but Jerzy appreciated what Ao was trying to say.

Ao looked over at the fourth member of their crew. "Mahault, you may—"

"I will go with Jerzy," she said, to Jerzy's surprise.

"Are you sure?" Ao looked crestfallen; clearly he had hoped she would accompany them. "There are many solitaire in Caul, in hire to the king there . . . surely one of them would be willing to sponsor you."

Her anger deflated, Mahault shook her head. "It's . . . it's not that simple a choice, not now." Once they left the port she had reverted back to her shipboard attire, and now sat with a distinct lack of modesty on one of the now-empty water casks, the trou showing underneath her skirt. "Without a dowry or family name, no recommendation or true training . . . I need more, or they will not accept me."

Jerzy finished coiling the rope in his hands and stashed it properly, not saying anything now, only listening.

"And you think a Vineart can help you? No offense intended, Jer."

"Master Vineart Malech is well known throughout the Vin Lands," she said. "If he is willing to lend his name to my petition, that could make them overlook . . . all else."

Jerzy suspected that a pack of spellwines as dowry would make them overlook everything, and determined to convince Master Malech—and Detta—that it should be done. He owed her that, and more.

"And if not . . ." Mahault made an elegant gesture indicating an abundance of choices. "Perhaps it was not meant to be. I made my choice and do not regret it." She looked at Jerzy and smiled, a small, almost shy smile that was more in her eyes than her mouth. "Sometimes, you do not know what you are meant to do, until you are already doing it. Choosing to go with Jerzy, hearing and seeing what I have seen . . . maybe that was what I was meant for, not the life of the road. Or maybe there is something else waiting for me." Her smile grew a little more rueful. "Who knows, perhaps I will find life in a Vineart's House to be to my liking."

Ao snorted but, with a sideways look at Jerzy, who met his gaze evenly, said nothing more on the subject.

That night was awkward, none of them quite sure how to act or react, and it was with a palpable relief that they reached their destination midway through the next day.

By the time the *Wave* was anchored within the little cove, they had been noticed, and several adults—accompanied by a few flat-tailed dogs—had come out of the village to watch them. Interestingly, no children were to be seen, although they should, at that time of day, be helping their elders mend nets and pots, or scraping the hulls of the small boats pulled up on the beach.

By the time Jerzy and Mahault's belongings were off-loaded onto the rocky shore, a sober-faced man bearing an old fish spear with a newly sharpened point gleaming at the end came down to meet them. The man's face and stance lightened only when Jerzy identified himself, and showed him the token with his master's sigil on it, still tied on a thong around his neck.

"We've been watchful along the coast, young sir," the man said. "Anything odd, we report right away. But it's been properly quietful; you tell your master that."

"I will." Jerzy nodded, even though he felt anything but certain. Had things become so much worse, since he left, that his master was organizing patrols? Or was it the other way around—that the villages were reporting to him of their own accord, rather than their land-lord? It was not the proper way of such things, and did not speak well of Ranulf, the prince of their region, whose men were supposed to patrol the shoreline and watch for the occasional raiders and pirates. Did Master Malech fear that Ranulf, too, had been influenced by the taint? But no, how could he; he did not know what Jerzy had learned.

The urge to be home grew until his body practically shivered with it.

"Looks as you'll need transport," the fisherman said, casting a knowing eye over their belongings. "Happens I can oblige you. S'not grand, but it will carry you safe and sweet."

His solution was a small cart, just large enough for two riders and their belongings, and a spavined and ancient, if good-natured, pony to pull it.

"What do we owe?" Kaïnam started to ask, and the fisherman looked shocked. "Nah, the young sir's sigil's good enough for me. His Master will return what's ours, and make good the claim when we call it due. That's how it works, hereabouts."

"You had that, why didn't you use it before?" Ao asked as Jerzy replaced the token around his neck, plainly outraged that his companion had kept something of value from him, bargaining-wise. "We could have gotten whatever we needed, and not had to rely on Kaïnam's goodwill."

Jerzy looked at the trader sideways. "Even if any had taken the token, beyond The Berengia, we were trying not to be noticed," he reminded his friend. "Waving Master Malech's sigil about? Not exactly subtle."

"Hah!" Ao crowed loudly, clapping him on the back, his previous outrage gone and replaced by determined cheer. "You learn! Slowly, it's true, but you do learn!" When they first met, Jerzy would have likely floundered, using the token too soon, or forgotten to use it when he could. The trader gleefully took credit for his friend's new sophistication. "Now make sure that you do not forget what I've pounded into your skull, and all will be well."

Jerzy gave the trader an elbow to the rib, and the two tussled for a moment by the side of the dirt road; Jerzy had the upper hand, for all that he was slighter in build than Ao, and they quickly fell apart, panting and grinning like idiots at each other, while Mahault leaned against the pony's side, patting its neck gently.

"Ao," Kaïnam said, coming up to them from where he had been speaking with the fisherman, looking solemn. "If we're to catch this tide, we need to leave now."

An awkward silence fell, the four of them looking at one another. They had known this moment would come, had lived with it overnight, and yet still none of them were sure how to manage it. Jerzy had never had to say good-bye before, not truly; he didn't know how it was done.

"The sea is wide," Kaïnam said finally. "And yet, the waves return each tide to the shore. May it be so with we four."

With that, he took Mahault's hand, raising it and bowing slightly, even as she dipped her own head in recognition, the courtly movements too formal for the rough countryside. Then he turned and clasped Jerzy's hands between his own, the features that had once seemed haughty and cool now bright with concern.

"Be careful, Vineart."

"And you, Prince," Jerzy said, making a slight bow as Cai and Detta had taught him, one peer to another.

Kaïnam returned it, then turned and left. Ao stared at first one then the other before lunging forward and taking them both into a quick, hard hug.

"Watch yourselves," he said, his voice cracking, and was gone, following Kaïnam back down to the sea.

Jerzy swallowed hard, then shrugged and loaded their few belongings into the cart. He climbed up on the hard bench alongside Mahl, who took up the pony's reins, and they set off.

Jerzy looked behind once, but Ao and Kaïnam were already on their way back out to the *Wave*, and neither of them saw him lift his hand in a final farewell.

Beside him, Mahault kept her gaze upon the road ahead and did not look back.

THEY RODE IN silence, only the heavy clop of the pony's hooves and the rattling of the wheels to keep them company, and Jerzy was struck by how similar those sounds were to the slap of waves and creak of ship. The landscape seemed both familiar and utterly foreign as they passed through it, as though he had been away for years rather than months, and he wondered, but did not ask, what Mahault must think of this rolling green countryside, so different from the hills and stone-walled cities of Corguruth.

"What is your master like?"

"What?" Jerzy was startled; they had gone half the day without speaking, and Mahl's voice seemed to come out of nowhere.

"Your master. What is he like? Is he like Master Giordan?"

"Sin Washer, no." Vineart Giordan was—had been—an ebullient, overfriendly, garrulous man, subject to loud laughter and fits of energy, as well as sudden periods of morose thought. "Master Malech . . . he is stern. I was terrified of him when I was a slave. Not that he was cruel," he hastened to add, seeing a look of doubt cross her face. "Only that his word is law on the vintnery, and to fail him, to disobey, is death."

The day he had been found and chosen, Malech had ordered a slave killed for tipping over the precious mustus, the unfermented juice of the spellgrapes. It had been a just punishment; the mustus was worth more than any slave, but Jerzy had learned since then that the outside world did not see things in quite the same light. To be proud of having been a slave . . . it made others uncomfortable, or angry, and so he did not speak of it.

Jerzy did not understand their reaction. It was tradition, handed down for generations. If not for slaves, how would new Vinearts be found? The world wanted spellvines, and yet, as part of their Agreement, Mahault's father had forbidden Vineart Giordan from having his own slaves—and therefore prevented him from finding students, as well.

Giordan had claimed not to care, and yet he had given Jerzy his master's sketchbook, filled with detailed, beautiful drawings of vines and roots, birds and small animals who lived among the vines, not wanting it to fall into outside hands after his death. . . .

The sketchbook was still back in Aleppan, in the rooms he had been given. Jerzy hoped that nobody had destroyed the book; that they took care of it, or even overlooked it, thinking it of no value. Maybe someday he would get it back.

He didn't think so, though. The Washers had probably burned it when they killed Giordan. Sin Washer demanded that they destroy everything belonging to an apostate Vineart . . . even the vineyards. Maybe it had been best, after all, that Giordan had no slaves. Jerzy stared at the passing countryside, barely noticing as people working in the fields stopped and stared as they rode past. Strangers were not so rare on this road; why was the sight of their small wagon worth notice? They could hardly be thought a threat.

"And your Household?" Mahault asked, not knowing where his thoughts ranged. "What is it like?"

It struck Jerzy, suddenly, that she was nervous. He studied her carefully. Her hands were steady on the reins, and her face was as composed as the first day he had met her, when he mistook her for a junior Housekeeper, but he knew what else to look for, now. There was a fluttering in her neck that said her heart was beating faster, and her gaze was too determined to stay on the wide-open road ahead of them, refusing to even glance his way. Fearless Mahl was not always fearless. It was an odd feeling, wanting—needing—to ease her concerns.

"Detta is our House-keeper," he said. "You will like her." Mahault reminded him of Detta, in fact, although the two looked nothing alike. "Nothing shakes her, nothing startles her. I believe Master Malech would be lost without her to run things. And then there's Lil, who runs the kitchen, and Roan and maybe others by now, Detta is forever taking in new ones to train. And old Per—you won't ever see him, though. He keeps the stable clean and the outsides neat, but Master Malech says he doesn't much like people."

Talking about home made it seem closer, somehow, and also more distant, as though he had dreamed all of these people, once.

"And . . . the slaves?"

There it was again. She hesitated over the word, as though it were impolite. Jerzy shrugged. He didn't know what she feared and so did not know how to reassure her. "They keep to the sleep house and the yards, mostly. You'll see them working, but I doubt you'll run into any of them."

"Don't . . . don't you see any of them? Or is that not allowed, once you became Master Malech's student?"

"See them?"

"Yes. Stop by to speak to them, to . . . I guess not much changes in the life of a slave. But didn't you have any friends there?"

"No."

The lot of a slave was to be tested: grapes did not flourish in rich soil and easy conditions, and neither did the Sense. Stressed to greatness, Master Malech said. That was how it had been since the Breaking of the First Vine, when the prince-mages were undone, and Vinearts raised up. Once the fruit was ready, the empty skins were discarded.

"You don't make friends in the sleep house," he said, trying to explain. "And once you leave . . . you can't really go back."

Mahault thought about that as the wheels turned, the pony plodded, and the fields passed by on either side, and then finally she nodded. "I suppose I understand that."

After that, they fell into silence again, until the sun sank into the fields behind them, and the moon rose, thick and bright, lighting the way. They did not stop, the pony contentedly walking on and on, until the fields became as familiar as Jerzy's own limbs, the stone barns and quietly sleeping villages bringing him closer and closer to home.

"Turn there," he said, and Mahl clucked the pony onto the left-hand fork, and then, suddenly, they were on the cobbled road that led to the vintnery, and then they were there.

Word must have gone ahead, or perhaps the Guardian sensed them, for they were greeted in front of the green archway fronting the House by Master Malech, a teary-eyed Detta, and a delegation of three Washers, somber-faced and disapproving. Jerzy almost bolted and ran, and only Mahl's hand clenched in the back of his tunic kept him steady.

"Master Malech." Jerzy slid from Mahault's grasp and climbed out of the cart to stand before his master, suddenly aware that the ground was rocking oddly, as though he were still on the *Wave*, the sea moving under his feet. "It is good to be home."

He thought it would be good to be home, anyway. The sight of the Washers, their faces grim, their robes fresh and clean, as though they had been waiting long enough to wash and prepare, did not fill him with confidence. Still, Master Malech would not have summoned him home if they were simply to drag him off again. Would he?

Giordan would have. Giordan *had*. Yet . . . His thoughts tumbled madly, and he tried to order them into the calm required of a Vineart. Malech was his master. Jerzy belonged to him. What happened to Jerzy happened to House Malech. His master would not betray him.

Malech did not say anything, but merely took Jerzy's hand in his own, turning it so that the red mark of the mustus was visible.

"Welcome back, boy," he said, and released his hand, nodding slightly toward the other men, who were waiting.

"Sar Washers," Jerzy said, bowing slightly, slipping without noticing into the common trade tongue of Ettonian, rather than the Berengian he had used to greet his master. "Sin Washer's solace upon you."

"And upon you as well, young Jerzy," the oldest of them said, and made the offering of the cup with his hands. At that, Jerzy breathed a little easier. They would not bless him if they thought him apostate, surely.

"And your companion?" Master Malech asked, one graying eyebrow twitching upward in a manner that was soothingly familiar even as it rebuked his failure.

"Oh. Master Malech, my apologies. Mahault . . ." He paused there. She had not given her *nomen familias*, her Household naming, to Kaïnam, so he was not sure if he had the right to share it. "Mahault of Aleppan, who has chosen to travel with me."

"Indeed?" Malech looked surprised at that, but the Washers nodded.

"Former daughter of the maiar Niccolo," the younger Washer said, and beside him, Mahl stumbled slightly as she stepped forward to greet Master Malech, and the Washers in turn.

Former . . . the maiar had disowned Mahl, then. No doubt under pressure from the aide who had poisoned him against so much, including his own city council. Jerzy still did not know that man's master, but guessed the purpose of the tool's being there; to undermine the maiar's standing in his own court, and grow suspicion and distrust throughout the city. But to what ultimate purpose? And who was the master behind it all?

They, the four of them, had been given a chance to discover who incanted those spells, who directed those actions. Jerzy could have led them to the source; he was certain of it now. A sense of indignation at being summoned back, to be dragged before the Washers when he had done nothing wrong, rose in him, making his stomach churn the same way it had when he was seasick.

But Master Malech had his reasons, and it was not for Jerzy to question, only to obey. That was what he had wished for . . . wasn't it?

The Washers disregarded Mahault; her father had disowned her, and so she was unimportant. Instead, they focused on Jerzy, intently enough that he felt their gaze like flame on his skin.

"Where have you been, young Vineart?" the oldest one asked. His voice was not hard, but neither did it allow for lies or avoidance. He expected an answer, given easily and without delay.

Jerzy looked to his master.

Malech's expression was as hard as the Guardian's, his beaked face as though it was carved from stone as well, but he nodded.

"At sea, Sar Washers." The Sar was an honorific used in Corguruth, given to a man of standing or honor, but not noble birth. There was no equivalent in The Berengia, that he knew.

"Indeed. And—"

"No." A voice broke into whatever he meant to say, and Detta bustled forward then, pushing aside Master Malech with the casual arrogance of long familiarity. She placed her round form between the Washers and Jerzy, hands on her ample hips, graying curls tousled as though she had been roused from sleep, daring them to challenge her. "Enough of this. Both of these children look near to falling over, and no wonder, considering the hour. They will be here in the morning, and whatever questions you mean to ask can and will wait until then. Now, off with you, all of you, and let me settle them down right and proper."

Jerzy had forgotten, somehow, what a power Detta was, like a storm or spell. The Washers backed up, reluctant but obedient, and the two travelers were whisked under the arbor arch and into the House proper.

Hello, the House seemed to whisper, the gathered voices of the grapes growing on the vines, the roots deep in the soil, the spellwine waiting in the storerooms . . . *welcome home*.

Pure exhausted fancy, of course. But the thought still made Jerzy smile.

THE MOMENT THEY entered the building, there was a flurry of activity, with a sleepy-eyed Roan preparing a cold meal for them in the kitchen while a cot in Detta's room was readied for Mahault. They ate without ceremony, cramming the bread and meats into their jaws, washing it down with goblets of *vin ordinaire* warmed to ease both digestion and sleep. No one asked them further questions, for which they were grateful.

Jerzy's own room waited for him, looking exactly the same as it had been when he left. He shed his clothing onto the floor and slid under the blanket, luxuriating in the way the thin mattress seemed to match his spine perfectly, the hard pillow holding his head just right. The blanket had been aired recently, and everything felt right. Proper.

Home.

The last thing before sleep claimed him was a gentle nudge in his mind, and the sense of something heavy and cool sliding in, reclaiming a space he had not even realized was empty until then.

"'lo, Guardian," he mumbled.

There was no response, but the weight of stone remained.

MORNING CAME BEFORE Jerzy realized he had fallen asleep, the sun streaming in through the window. His feet were flat on the braided rug and he was reaching for his clothing before he remembered that this was not a normal day, and he was not late for anything.

Or, if he was, no one had told him he needed to be there.

Then he remembered the Washers, and everything that waited, and his stomach tightened with nerves again.

He dressed quickly but carefully, wrapping his belt around his hips once and finding a new buckle waiting for him—a dragon, styled after the Guardian, the sigil of the House of Malech. He had lost his original dragon buckle, along with the rest of his belt back in Aleppan. The dark red metal was a satisfying press against his hip bone when he slipped it onto the leather, reminding him of the press of the Guardian's thoughts against his own the night before.

He stopped, and *felt* for that presence. The merest touch, and the weight returned, forming a question.

"Glad to be home," he told it, and it disappeared—but was not gone. The weight remained: a steady comfort against his uncertainty.

Master Malech was undoubtedly waiting for him. Jerzy hesitated at the knife, then decided against hooking it onto his belt, adding only the normal student's waterskin. The loss of his master's gift still stung, and he did not want to use the lesser replacement a moment longer than needful.

Satisfied with his appearance, he went down the narrow wooden stairs to the kitchen, where he was set upon by Lil, who hugged him as though he had been gone a year.

"Look at you! You've grown again! Not tall, you'll never be tall, but such muscles! And you've gone darker, just as Detta predicted!" Lil's familiarity, which had once annoyed him, was like warm water on a cold morning. She lifted a lock of his hair, admiring the dark auburn sheen to it. "And we'll need to have you trimmed . . . still not growing a beard, I see. All to the well, you'd only forget to trim it, not being such a peacock as the master. Come, your companion's already to table; we saved you some tai, special like."

He disliked tai, which Lil knew full well, but he took it anyway. The thick, noxious brew would help him think faster, and he feared he might need all the help he could find, today. And, now that he knew sweetener helped the taste, he could add honey when Lil wasn't looking.

Mahault was already sitting at the table, dressed in a dark blue gown similar to the ones she had worn back in Aleppan, probably Lil's best dress, from the way it almost but didn't quite fit her taller form. Her blond hair was once again coiled back sleekly, and she was quietly eating everything that Roan served her, smiling polite thanks every time another item was offered. Roan hovered as though the Aleppanese woman was one of the silent gods come to visit, her eyes wide with awe and fascination.

"I think she likes you," he said to Mahl quietly.

"She's young. She hasn't ever seen anyone from more than two days' journey from here, at least not a woman." Mahault was matter-of-fact about it, biting into the crisp slice of pork with obvious relish. "I was like that the first time I saw a solitaire."

Before Jerzy could respond, a deep raspy voice interrupted.

"Ah, you're both awake. Good."

Master Malech joined them, taking a mug from Lil with a nod of thanks, then pulling a chair up to the table and leaning intently in to talk to both of them. "I have no idea how much time we will have, so I will make this quick. Lady Mahault, you have already learned that your father has disowned you. I am sorry."

She nodded, not showing any emotion behind her composed exterior. Jerzy, who had no memory of his parents, wondered if she regretted it, or if she had resigned herself the moment she left Aleppan. She had not seemed close to her lady-mother, particularly, but he knew that her father's change in behavior had dismayed her, yet Mahault had not mentioned her family even once in their travels; he had not thought to question that then. Had she known, or at least suspected?

Malech was still speaking. "However it happened, whatever happened there, and in the time since then, you have aided my student, and for that I am in your debt. Anything I can do, I will, but I do not know how much help I can be, right now."

She nodded again, and what looked like real sympathy crossed Malech's stone-cut face, and then was gone. He shifted his attention to his student. "Jerzy, they will want to question you. They dare not use spells, not here, not against a Vineart, but do not let that disarm you. Answer them truthfully, but briefly, and volunteer nothing! Do you understand?"

"Yes, Master Malech." He exchanged a look with Mahault, who gave him an encouraging smile. Had it been Ao, he would have leaped in with advice, but Mahl merely engaged Detta and Malech in conversation about their washing room versus the hot tubs of Aleppan, leaving Jerzy to eat—and worry—in relative peace.

With impeccable timing, the youngest Washer appeared in the doorway just as Jerzy was finishing the last of his meal. He washed down the bit of egg with the last sip of tai, grimacing at the now-cold liquid's taste, and stood. The memory of the last time he was taken by Washers shook him, the feel of hard hands and the metallic tang of swords and blood, Sar Anton standing over him, a serving boy dead at their feet, then the raised voices and magic-raised wind as Giordan tried to defend himself....

No. Jerzy refused the memory. That was then. He was home, in his master's House, and nothing would happen that Master Malech did not allow. His master would not allow harm to come to him. Malech would not have summoned Jerzy home if it were not safe.

But the utter certainty Jerzy had hoped for did not come.

"Vineart-student Jerzy of House Malech." The Washer was only a few years older than himself, his belt single-wrapped, and his voice quavered a little.

"I am ready," Jerzy said, as much to himself as the Washer. The other tried to escort him, reaching for his arm, but Jerzy shot him a look that made him step back, his hand dropping.

"This is my own home," Jerzy said. "I know the way to the front door."

That bravado lasted until they came to the back field, where the Washers had erected a large tent in the same shade of red as their robes. Inside, three rope cots were tied up and out of the way, along with three travel packs and a variety of leather saddlebags. In the center of the tent there was a long wooden table that looked as though it folded for travel, and a single chair.

And the two other Washers, waiting for him.

The tent flap dropped down behind Jerzy, and he was alone with them.

"Please," the older Washer said, "sit down."

Not knowing what to expect, Jerzy sat down. The older Washer circled in front of him, the younger one remaining behind, barely within his peripheral vision. The mid-aged Washer stood behind the table, and picked up a stick of ink.

"You are Vineart-student Jerzy of House Malech," the older Washer—he had not been given their names—said.

"I am."

At the table, the Washer wrote down his response.

"The beginning of last spring, your master, Master Vineart Malech, sent you to study with the Vineart Giordan of Aleppan. To what purpose?"

"My master told me to learn what I could of Vineart Giordan."

"To what purpose?"

Jerzy kept himself still, focusing on the Washer's face, reminding himself to speak only of what was asked, and no more. "To learn."

The Washer sighed. "Jerzy, your master has given you into our holding. You may answer our questions freely, with no fear of harm."

That was almost funny. No harm, no. Only apostasy, and death, if they were to discover that Malech had sent him to spy on the court of Aleppan, to learn of the doings of a man of power with the intent—if needful—to interfere with the actions of a man of power.

That last was forbidden by Sin Washer's Command, even before the thing they had accused him of already, the attempt to interfere with another Vineart's wines. The fact that Master Malech felt it needful, that it was a lesser of evils to allowing the force that was moving against them free rein would not save him, if they discovered the truth. Although he had, in fact, not interfered at all, it was merely that he had not been given the chance to do so, before being taken, and then rescued.

Jerzy took refuge in a lesser truth. "He believed that Vineart Giordan had a special skill with the crafting of his spellwines, and that I might be able to learn from that, and bring it back to our vines, to add to our abilities."

Not forbidden, that. Merely not done. Vinearts kept their secrets to themselves, by tradition centuries old, and difficult to break.

"And when you were there. What did you learn?"

Jerzy widened his eyes, not having to work hard to feign shock. "Washer! You know I may not speak of that to you!"

The Washer's eyes narrowed, then he nodded, accepting the rebuke. "Tell me of the trader, Ao. How did you become friends with him?"

Admitting that the trader had caught him, ineptly trying to eaves-drop on courtiers, would not go over well with the Washer. Jerzy improvised.

"He had never met a Vineart. His people do not use spellwines." That was a fact the Washers would know already, and would support his story. "And Ao was curious." He allowed humor, and a little exas-peration, to fill his voice. "He is always curious, especially if he thinks that he can make a profit on the information somehow."

Ao was off with Kaï, by now in Caul and therefore out of the Wash-ers' reach. Throwing a little suspicion on him couldn't hurt.

"And he helped you escape . . ."

"Because he believed I was not guilty."

Actually, Jerzy suspected that Ao did not understand the accusation, and would not have cared if Jerzy were guilty even if he had understood.

"And the girl, Mahault?"

Jerzy opened his mouth to respond, then shut it.

"Vineart?" The Washer learned forward, as though scenting rot.

These were not his secrets to tell. More, he was not sure how much of what he knew was safe to share. If Washer Darian had been involved somehow in what was happening in Aleppan, would these Washers believe Jerzy, or would they assume he was hiding something to protect himself?

"Lady Mahault believed that her father was not entirely himself." In point of fact, she was convinced that he had been under the influence of another person for months before Jerzy arrived, although she did not know who, or why. "She believed that whoever had caused the accusa-tion against me had also worked against him."

That should set the cat in among the doves, he thought, watching the Washer behind the desk pause to take in his words, then continue writing.

Plots driven by plots. Players playing one another. Like Kaïnam's conviction that someone in Caul would be able to explain why his sister had been murdered. It made no sense . . . and yet there were roots, if you looked, connecting it all. Were the Washers aware of that? Jerzy did not know, and could not ask. He could not even ask his master, not without disclosing Kaïnam's own story, and Jerzy did not know if speaking of it would help or hinder the princeling's mission. Not knowing, he would say nothing. Unless his master asked directly, he would share no confidences.

Thankfully, the Washers seemed to accept Jerzy's answer. The questions continued, polite questions asking who he spoke with, and why, and what they discussed. For the most part Jerzy answered without hesitation: he had spoken to very few people in the time he was there. Vineart Giordan, of course, and Ao, and the occasional guard or servant, and then Mahault. But that was it.

"And Sar Anton, of course," he added with a touch of malice well hidden from his voice. Sar Anton and Washer Darian had been the ones to accuse him, using him as a way to get at Vineart Giordan. It could have been as simple as internal politics—Anton fearing Giordan's influence with the maiar, but then why would Washer Darian be part of it—unless it was, as they half feared, part of some greater plan of the Washer Collegium. And that made no sense at all. But he had no hesitation giving Sar Anton to these men.

"Sar Anton."

The Washer's voice made it clear he had not expected that.

Jerzy nodded, trying to shape his features into what Ao had once called his "innocent dolt" expression. "Oh, yes. Sar Anton spoke quite often with me. He came with Vineart Giordan to meet me, when I landed. And he was most curious as to what I was doing there—he and Washer Darian."

"You are accusing us?" the Washer behind him burst out, and Jerzy jolted forward at the noise; he had nearly forgotten the younger man was there. "You dare to—"

"Oren." The older Washer's voice grew hard and cold, as it had not been during the questioning, and the man behind the desk lifted his head as though watching players perform for his amusement.

"He accused no one of anything," the eldest Washer went on. "Merely answering a question I put to him. Taking offense at an honest answer is not the mark of a clear mind, and none are above suspicion. Be still."

Jerzy tried to force his heart to a calmer beat, and the Washer turned his attention back to him. "You say Sar Anton took an unusual interest in you?"

"I do not know what would be unusual," Jerzy answered. "Only that I noted it at the time."

The Washer at the table let out what sounded like an amused grunt, and his inquisitor went on to the next question. The matter of Washer Darian's intent was left untouched . . . but not, Jerzy suspected, forgotten.

WHEN THE WASHER finally released Jerzy from his questions, the light outside the tent had taken on the pale purple light of dusk, and the slaves were being served their evening meal at the long tables beside the sleep-house kitchen. The sight made his stomach rumble, reminding him that he had eaten nothing since dawn, and suddenly he was starving.

He walked back to the House, stretching his arms overhead and feeling his spine crack pleasurably. Washer Neth, as he had finally learned the older man was named, had been calm-voiced and polite, and rarely asked the same question twice, but he had been thorough; Jerzy felt as though he had been put through one of weapons master Cai's more intense lessons while Master Malech asked him detailed questions about how to temper a new cask. All Jerzy wanted now was to eat something that required as little effort as possible to chew, not think about anything at all, and then sleep for an entire night. And possibly half the next day as well.

When he walked up to the House, however, Detta was there, inspecting the dark red flowers blooming on runners against the far wall. She took one look at him, sniffed the air, and then shook her graying head in mock dismay. "Bathing room for you, my boy, before you go in among civilized folk. And then Master Malech wants to see you."

"Food, before I die," he begged, not having to fake the pathetic expression on his face.

Detta wasn't impressed. "You'll never be dying from not eating, you. I'll have Roan fetch you something and bring it to the study. Now go, hurry!"

In truth, he did not need all that much encouragement. The first time Jerzy had seen a washtub, he had to be ordered in, and the water had been near-black when he emerged. Now he slipped into the water with a blissful sigh.

Despite the seductively warm steam coming from the tub, he could not forget Detta's urgency—or the thought of food. Once the water cooled, Jerzy made quick use of the soap and brush, and then took a rough towel from the pile on the shelf and dried himself off. He made use of the chamber pot, then reclaimed his clothing from the bench where he had dropped them, dressed, and did his best to untangle and smooth back his hair, finally tucking it behind his ears in disgust. He would either need to cut it short, or begin wearing it in a queue the way his master did.

He stared into the mirror that hung on the wall, remembering the first time he had seen himself in it: shorter, scrawnier, with hunched-over shoulders and a look in his eyes better suited to a rabbit than a Vineart.

The person who looked back at him was taller, and not only because he stood upright now, the way Cai had beaten into him. His hair was a darker red, his skin weathered from the wind and sea, and the look he gave himself was steady, considering.

He did not feel all that different from the slave called Fox-fur. And yet . . . he did not feel the same at all, as though that self had been a lifetime past, not a simple cycle of seasons.

It made no sense, and Jerzy didn't let himself linger on it, aware that Malech still waited for him—and would be growing impatient, by now.

While he no longer feared his master would toss him back into the yard, he had no desire to be cuffed across the ears again, either.

He left the bathing room and headed across the open courtyard to Master Malech's quarters, but the moment he entered the courtyard, Jerzy stopped, his rush forgotten. Mahault sat on the low wooden bench under the single tree growing off to the side, her head tilted back to admire the blossoms. Jerzy had taken lessons from Mil'ar Cai in this courtyard, crossed it hundreds of times to reach his master's study, had helped Roan and Lil fetch water from the well set in the center of the courtyard, and never, in all that time, had he noticed that the tree had tiny white flowers hidden among the dark green leaves.

"It's lovely here," Mahl said when he came to stand next to her, without so much as a hello to greet him. "I understand why you love it so much. But . . . I'm not staying."

Even when she had announced her intent to travel home with him, he had known that she would not stay. He had not expected her to change her mind overnight, however.

"But—"

"I had thought, maybe, there would be a place for me here. That I could . . ." She let out a small laugh. "The moment I walked through the door last night I knew . . . this House is complete within itself. I have no reason to be here."

Jerzy had no response to that. In truth, he could not imagine her here, either. Everything in the House turned to the need of the vines, and she could not feel them, not even as Detta and Lil did, from years of service.

Unlike Kaïnam and Ao, whose thoughts were still a mystery, Jerzy thought that he understood Mahault. It was not profit or power that drove her, but the desire to *do*.

He sat down next to Mahl on the bench and stared up at the cloudless sky. He had missed an entire season, between the city streets and the featureless tides. When he left, the ground was only slowly waking up from its winter rest. Now it was time for the vines to flower; the slaves were working the yards, making sure that the plants were free of pests or blights, the roots healthy, the leaves unfurling properly. The urge to get his fingers into the soil, to hear the hum of the vines as they grew, was a physical pain.

Master Malech wanted to see him. Once he answered his master's questions, he would be allowed to return to the vines, where he belonged.

But Mahault needed him, too. She had followed him, hoping to find a place to fill her ambitions, and he had an obligation to her. And he did not like seeing her look so sad.

"Have you talked with Detta? Maybe she—"

"After breakfast, yes. She did."

Of course. Detta handled all of Master Malech's interactions with the outside world, including the incoming flow of orders and the flow of spellwines. She would have a solution.

"She has a friend who has a sister," Mahl said, plucking at the fabric of her gown, a plain gray castoff of Lil's. "The sister's a solitaire, just re-tired, living a ways east of here, near the border. Detta thinks that the sister would be willing to foster me. I'm too old for it, but I'd be able to learn from her, and . . ."

And perhaps the woman would be willing to sponsor her to the solitaires. Jerzy understood. The recommendation of a former soldier would overcome everything else in Mahl's past, even her disowning. He felt a guilty relief that nothing more was required of him. But if she had what she wanted, why was Mahault not happier?

"So much has changed, Jer," she said. "I know that this was what I wanted, but now . . . I don't know anymore. What if I'm not supposed to be a solitaire? What if . . ."

What if I fail hung unspoken between them.

"If it's meant to be . . . it happens," Jerzy said slowly, thinking his words through before he spoke them, trying to feel for the right thing to say. "We find the place we're meant to be, the master we're meant to follow."

Mahault laughed a little, but not happily. "When magic's involved, maybe. It doesn't always work that well for the rest of us."

He had no answer to that.

"The Washers said they'll be leaving soon," he said instead. "You can travel with them, if Detta hears from her friend in time. Or ride with one of the wagons when they take a shipment east." Going alone was not an option; Mahault was fierce, but not a solitaire yet, and a woman alone without the protection of their sigil-marked leathers and sword? She would be easy prey for anyone. Detta would not allow it.

She made a face, either at having to travel with the Washers, or the speed of leaving, but did not argue with him. There was no point in delaying; it would change nothing. As suddenly as Ao and Mahl had entered his life, they would be gone.

Boy.

The Guardian's cool voice in his head made him sigh. "I have to go—Master Malech wishes to see me." He wasn't sure what else to say, finally ending with, "I will see you at dinner?"

With her nod, he took his leave.

HIS MASTER WAS waiting in the study, clad in a dirt-stained trou and vest, his wooden-soled, dirt-covered shoes left by the door for cleaning. Even grubby, Master Vineart Malech was still an imposing sight—tall and thin, as though a strong storm might break him in two. His long hair was even grayer than Jerzy remembered, and the cool, dark blue eyes set in his narrow face seemed even more deeply hooded. But the gray-brown beard, trimmed to a point, and the long, elegant hands that moved as he spoke, the single ring glittering in the spell-light, remained the same; and his face, rather than being the stone-hard features of yesterday, was softer now, more welcoming.

"Your answers have done what my words could not," Malech said as Jerzy came in through the door, his hand reaching up to touch the tip of the Guardian's tail where it hung down. It was not there at first, and Jerzy frowned, then the cool stone flicked down into his palm, as though greeting him.

"Yes. They believe I am innocent." It was a relief, the weight that had been between his shoulders, waiting for an arrow or sword or heavy hand to hit him there, suddenly gone.

His master snorted, a rude sound at odds with his normal dignity, and gestured for him to take the stool that was drawn up in front of the Vineart's desk. "Innocent? I don't think they believe any of us are innocent, boy."

Jerzy sat, frowning at how uncomfortable the familiar seat had become, even as he considered his master's words.

"You've grown again." Malech had noted his fidgeting. "I have Per making you a taller stool, to better suit those legs of yours. Meanwhile, no, I do not believe the Washers are convinced that the claims against you were false; they simply cannot prove that they were true. To continue with punishment, in this climate, with all that is occurring, no matter the cause . . . would be dangerous. We are all agreed upon that. So for now, you are left unmolested, free to continue your work."

"Too late a reversal for Giordan," Jerzy said. Washer Neth had confirmed his fears: the Vineart had been killed the very day of the trial, and his vines forfeit. The flagon he had carried with him might be the last he ever saw of Giordan's spellwork. That thought left a leaden pain in his chest.

"He played in politics," Malech replied, his voice hard. "We are commanded to abjure power that none might claim that very thing, that we have abused our magic to control others, or interfere with the greater play of lords.

"Giordan thought his Agreement with the maiar was harmless, and in another lifetime doubtless it might have been. But we can none of us chose the time we must live in. And in this life, we have a task set before us that none other have faced. Your information, the news from Atakus, from Mur-Magrib, it all ties together, somehow. We must determine the connection."

He looked at his student, his hooded eyes cool but patient, waiting for a response.

"Mahault is leaving." It seemed important to say it.

"Yes. Detta informed me she spoke to the girl. Good. We have work to be done, and the sooner all these disturbances are gone, the better."

His master was correct. And yet, another weight joined the first in Jerzy's chest. Giordan, Ao, and now Mahault . . .

The feeling he'd had in the courtyard returned. Even on the ship, when he had been alone for the first time in his life, he had known they would return. They had become . . . expected. Now his companions had scattered, following their own lives . . . and despite Ao's breezy assurances, it was likely that he would never see them again.

Jerzy felt his throat convulse in a tight swallow, and he forced the weight away. He was not alone. He was home, among his own vines, studying with Master Malech. That was all he had wanted. That was enough.

THE GROUNDING

Fallowtime

THE ABANDONED LAND was well named; it was a harsh place, and men had to fight for dominion every day, every season. Some of those battles were visible, and some . . . less so. The vine-mage watched as three slaves worked to clean the floor, getting the blood out from the edges of the mosaic before it could dry and crust. His shoulders and knees ached in distant sympathy: he had done the same, once. Years ago, in this same hall, as his own master did what was needed to ensure that the wild vines were tamed, made obedient to man's needs, to ensure their survival. The ritual Harvests were done in the public eye, to remind the people of the cost of their safety, and to honor the sacrifice their loved ones made. But more was needed, to achieve their goals. More blood than the people—or Praepositus Ximen—would be able to accept.

It had always been that way, from the moment the first shattered, abandoned sailor had set foot on this soil. Sacrifice, in order to survive. From the very first days, when the settlement was nothing but a cluster of shacks build from driftwood and salvaged timbers, when Washer Patrus had discovered the wild vines growing, untended and unshaped, and searched for those among the survivors who might be able to harness the magic within . . .

From that very first year, there had always been more demanded than could be borne—and so some of it was always done out of sight, and so out of mind. That was how mortals survived: forcing the strongest to bear the burdens, carry the weight of responsibility.

The Harvest was a matter of ceremony and public occasion, a reminder of those responsibilities, without the force of true sacrifice. What happened within the vineyard was pragmatic, practical, taking every drop of blood, rather than the ceremonial tipping-bowl's worth collected from the chosen ones. While the Harvested Ones were cleansed and returned to their families with honor, these bodies, unnamed and unmourned, would be tipped into a ditch behind the vineyard. None ever went there save slaves and wild dogs, and they all knew—and would never tell.

Leaving the slaves to their cleaning, he left the hall and went out into the sunlit day. The air was dry and dusty, and he breathed it in with relief; inside the hall the smell of blood became overpowering, and the single door at either end was not enough to let the breeze flow through and clean it out, save during the winter storms.

He had no fondness for blood, no pleasure at the letting of it, despite what Ximen and his ilk thought. But neither did he flinch from it; it was the path to power, and he had been born and bred to follow no other way.

A wild dog pup nosed at his heel, and he shoved it away, striding away from the low, long wooden hall, and toward the yard. Unlike the descriptions he had read of vineyards in the old world, his vines were no tidy, tended things. Each cluster was a thick tangle of vines, strong and well fed, and the fruit they gave reflected that in a fierce burst of power that made him shiver simply thinking of it.

The Harvest was nearly done; the last of the dark red fruit was being stripped even as he watched. Storms could come up quickly off the coast, or down from the mountains; the slaves did not sleep until the last grape was taken and the mustus was in its wooden tanks.

The vine-mage watched the wind move the leaves softly, their colors already starting to shade from deep green to paler reds and browns. Sheer luck that this unknown land, so far beyond the Vin borders, grew vines at all, much less usable ones. When Washer Patrus had chosen potential vine-mages from the survivors of the wreckage and set them to working the soil, hoping against all sanity for a viable harvest, the newly made slaves had added a splash of their own blood to the soil in a superstitious ritual to appease the gods of this land. Over the generations, the tradition had continued—only for reasons far from what those ignorant, fearful wretches could have foreseen. As Sin Washer's blood changed the First Growth, so did vine-mage blood somehow change Patrus's wild vine, shifting it into domestication.

As a slave he had seen two slaves killed in a fight. It being planting time, their bodies had merely been plowed into the soil. He alone had noted that the vines there grew stronger that season, their fruit holding more potential than before.

Thinking to test his observation, he had first let his own blood drip directly into the winter-sleeping roots of a selected cluster, then killed a fellow slave and drained him for another. The change in the fruit the next season from the latter cluster had been startling, and consistent.

Nothing, after that moment, would stand in his way, holding the secret close to him, keeping him company during the long hard days and nights until it was time to strike, until he had the power to do what needed be done.

Now, twenty years later, he could sense the power in the grapes even before they were ripe. They had always been strong, the wild spellvines his cursed forefathers had found when they came to these shores, but now they were massive, almost beyond control. The incanting was like breaking wild dogs to leash—difficult and dangerous, but once it was done, you had a tool well honed and worth using.

But there were only five vineyards planted and maintained: in all that time, only five.

The old world might be able to fritter away their magic on petty spells and casual drinking. Here, where the Praepositus dared not send his men to hunt beyond the foothills, much less beyond them to the inland regions from where not a single exploration party had ever returned, in a land where even men who did not believe in gods huddled by their fire and hid when ice storms or blazes of lightning hurled down from wrath-filled skies, possession of spellwines was equal to survival.

Common folk might starve or be used as tools by those above them, but a vine-slave was protected for what he might become, and the vine-mage . . . the vine-mage was the only god his people needed.

Only magic kept them safe. And only he controlled access to the magic.

Ximen might look to the past, to reclaiming his position, his family name, and abandoning this rot-blasted coastline. He had larger plans.

Turning away from the yard, he continued with a steady stride across the courtyard, away from the main building. His workroom was a low stone structure set into the hillside: to outsiders it might look more like an animal shelter, with its double door, barred from the outside, and its single window set up high for ventilation rather than view. But inside, the floor was smooth-planed planks, and the walls were plastered and lined with shelves that were filled with pots and flagons made of dark green clay. Here the true secrets of power hid. He ignored the waiting spellwines and *vina*, going to the far wall, set against the earth of the hill. There, a manikin was chained to the plaster, its face roughly carved out of that same green clay, its body dressed in a length of brightly colored cloth. A scrap of dark skin was fixed to the left cheek, and a hank of hair was worked into the scalp. There was a leather collar around its neck, and two more, smaller, around its wrists. From each band, a length of copper tubing ran, connected to three different flasks of the same metal, green-dappled with age and use.

In poor light, a newcomer might at first think it was a human form that hung there, its life's essence being drained. In fact, it was much the reverse.

The vine-mage studied the manikin, then turned to choose three new flasks from a shelf, carefully replacing each one, one at a time. He made sure that the seal on each new flask was tight to the tubing, at no time allowing the flow to more than one band be interrupted.

The spellwine flowed into the manikin. Far away, the owner of that skin and hair coughed up blood each morning, the spellwine replacing it, drop by drop.

An incantation of his own devising and perfected over the years, over a dozen different subjects. Difficult, time-consuming . . . but through it, he had hands where he could not be, reaching places even his spells could not, managing indirectly what could not be done directly.

Sea beasts and storms were the least of his tools, despite what Ximen thought. He was far more subtle . . . and more dangerous.

"And how are you today, poppet?" he asked, his tone gentler, softer than any around him had ever heard. "Are you ready?"

There was no response, and yet he nodded as though he had heard something. "Excellent. You have served me so well; today, I will give you something in return. The day you have been waiting for, poppet. The day your dream is handed to you . . . so long as you, in turn, do this for me . . ."

"Vine-mage."

The voice came from outside the workroom, a cautious distance from the door. He turned to confront the slave, who bowed quickly, averting his gaze as they were trained. "The Praepositus has arrived, Master Magus."

The vine-mage nodded once, and the slave turned and ran back to the main building.

The mage touched the poppet once. Ximen could wait. This was a moment he had worked for his entire life, the moment five generations of vine-mages had worked for. And it was due to his magic, his Harvests, his incantations.

"Your instructions, poppet," he said, and leaned forward to whisper into the clay ears.

Vine-mages were not meant to feel pride. They carried no names for that very reason; their entire existence bent toward the crafting of spell-wines to keep their people alive. And yet, pride swelled within him as the poppet carried his words to his tool in that distance place, like juice scarce contained within the skin of his fruit. Vinearts dead or disabled, the tendrils of paranoia pricking at the souls of land-lords and Washers alike . . .

Soon, the old world would remember those they had forgotten. Remember . . . and beg for mercy that would never come.

Chapter 7

Caul was a cold and bitter place, even in the warmer months; the buildings huddled in on themselves as though perpetually miserable, and Kaïnam would have traded everything on his person to be back on Mount Parpur, in the gardens of the royal residence, with green grass under his feet, blue sky spread out overhead, and sweet-scented air like silk, not this harsh, biting wind.

"It's not that bad," his companion said, when Kaï commented on that desire—not complain, he refused to complain, merely mentioning the wish to be home. Easy for the trader to say such a thing; his skin was thicker, his body built to withstand temperature extremes. Kaï did not think he would ever truly be warm again, even wrapped in a thick woven wrap, and with newly fitted boots on his feet.

"No wonder these people are such fierce voyagers," he said instead. "I, too, would take every chance to leave."

They were in the city of Áth Cliath, the main city of Greater Caul and, according to those in the harbor where the *Green Lady* rested, the only truly civilized city in all of Caul, Greater and Lesser.

The bay itself was too shallow for the greater war vessels of Caul, which sailed from port a day's journey south, but the *Lady* had sailed in as though she owned the waters, sliding up the river into the city proper and finding dockage among the flat-bottomed barges and shallow-water pleasure boats of these mad northmen, who thought it great sport to test themselves in winter seas, to find and plunder, arrogant beyond all belief.

No, Kaïnam had no fondness for this land or its rough-dressed, harsh-spoken people. But they were here, for now, for a reason. He watched the others on the street with a cautious eye: ruddy-skinned and fair-haired, for the most part, their locks plaited with beads and their clothing trimmed with ribbons and fur, as though to brighten the dreary stones of their city. He did not underestimate those he saw, but he could not bring himself to admire them, either. Even Jerzy, with his odd ways and secretive manners, had seemed more comprehensible to him than these people.

"Next street over," Ao said, checking something against a sheet in his hand, then looking around at the curving, unmarked street they were on as though disbelieving his own notes.

"You are sure this man will help us?"

"I'm never sure of anything," the trader admitted with annoying cheerfulness. "It is a calculated risk. He may turn around and hand us over to his king, who may in turn reward us with great riches, or have us for dinner. It's the not-knowing that makes the negotiations so interesting. If we know how every journey would turn out, why bother taking it?"

"For profit?" Kaïnam had always assumed that was why traders did everything.

"Of course for profit," Ao said, dismissing that as a given. "But any fool can make a profit." He was counting off buildings as they passed, the cold stone and timber fronts as dreary and forbidding to Kaïnam's gaze as the heavy gray sky overhead. "But if all you worry about is the counting-up at the end of the day, you might as well stay home and send others to do your work for you."

"The travel?" Kaï assayed. "The learning?"

"The experiences," Ao said, as though it should have been obvious. "To learn, to see, to understand . . . and, by understanding, make better bargains. And learning, unlike a thing, can be passed down to every child, not only one."

Kaïnam tucked his chilled and damp fingers more tightly into the wool wrap and almost smiled, despite the weather and his greater concerns. "I would that my sister might have met you," he said. "I think you two would have had much to speak of, together."

"Ah, here we are." Ao did not respond to Kaïnam's comment, but the princeling thought that perhaps his companion's shoulders pulled back a little more, conveying a quiet pleasure. Or it might merely have been the fact that they had finally arrived at their destination.

A small wooden sign by the door read: MIL'AR ATAN, SHIPPING & SERVICES.

"Services?"

"A simple word that covers a multitude of meanings," Ao said. "What, you expected him to say 'spymaster' for all to see?"

Kaïnam would not have been surprised, in truth. This land seemed to know little of subtlety.

Inside the stone and timber building, there was a fire in the hearth that warmed the air, and Kaïnam let the plaid fall away from his shoulders gratefully. A huge shaggy dog, lean and golden like the sands of Atakus, raised its head from its paws and observed them with patient brown eyes, even as a young man came forward to greet them.

"I am Ao of the Eastern Wind trading clan," Ao said, making a formal bow to their host. "This is my patron, Kaïnam son of Eerebus." They had agreed not to use his formal title; if any recognized the name and connected it to the hidden island of Atakus, then that would be significant information. Otherwise, Kaïnam was simply to play a wealthy son looking to invest in something with enough risk to tempt his jaded appetites.

"Of course, good masters," the man said, giving the impression that he had been waiting all day, indeed all his life, for the chance to take their wraps and usher them into the inner rooms where his master waited. "If you would follow me, please?"

Kaïnam let Ao go first, shifting slightly to ensure that his longknife was still comfortably set at his back. On Ao's advice he had left his blade on the *Lady*, not wanting to risk any hothead Caulic warrior seeing the weapon and deciding he would make a good challenge, but he refused to go into the unknown unarmed.

Especially not as he entered the offices of the man who might tell him who had sent the Caulic fleet to his home land.

HOUSE OF MALECH

Late Spring

DESPITE THE WORRIES that rode him, the awareness of the taint still winding its way through the world beyond, the vineyard reclaimed Jerzy quickly, and a month later he could barely remember what riding the sea had felt like, now up to his wrists in mud. Although the sun was not yet at summer warmth, his shirt was abandoned over a nearby bush, sweat gleaming on his skin and running down the line of his spine, dripping under the waistband of his trou. His bare toes flexed, feeling the soil underneath him, even as his fingers dipped deeper, searching for the roots stretching far below.

"A little to the left," he instructed one of the slaves holding the canes upright, and they shifted obligingly. They wore straw hats to keep the afternoon sun off their heads, and Jerzy wondered briefly what insanity had possessed him not to have taken one for himself. The red kerchief around his neck chafed the skin raw, and he could already feel the burn on the tips of his ears and between his shoulder blades. But all that faded to insignificance when his fingers came into contact with the first tendril of root.

"Ah, there you are," he said to it, his attention entirely focused. "Now where's the trouble?"

The vine they were working on was from Master Malech's first planting-year, a small plot on the upper ridge, near where the ancient trees grew. The vines there were a firevine legacy, slower to return from winter's dormancy than most, but the flowers had begun to drop, and there was scarce fruit to be seen.

In Aleppan, Giordan's weathervines had already fruited, green nubs the size of his fingernails. He wondered if anyone had thought to protect them from the early spring frosts, at that altitude, or if they had frozen and died without Giordan there. If the vines yet lived.

Here and now.

The Guardian's touch brought him back to what he was doing. The dragon was right; he could do nothing for those vines, but the ones here required his touch. This vine, and all its cluster-kin, looked more like the spelled vine covering the entrance to the House, all dark leaf and no fruit, than a working vine. It was Jerzy's duty to discover *why.*

There was a balance to be kept between a vine that produced too much fruit, diluting the magic within the vines and requiring more work for less result, and a vine that produced too few to make a vintage at all. A vine that did not produce would be pulled up and replaced . . . but they needed to be sure, first.

Master Malech was cautious these days. They both were, waiting to see if another attack would come, if the Washers would return, or some dark news would arrive bearing the tale of another Vineart dead, or a harbor closed to outsiders, or . . .

Once, Jerzy had no knowledge of the world beyond the vines, no sense of the tangles and knots that bound civilization to its own follies. He wished, some mornings, he still did not know.

Once you learned, you could not unlearn. Once tangled, forever entwined.

His fingers, coated liberally with his own spittle, closed around the root, inching along to take hold of a thicker strand, trying to sense if anything was awry.

The first planting-year was a tradition and a test: a Vineart-student's ability to transplant his master's vines, and have them root in the soil of his preparing, to grow to his command and not his master's. There was no judgment as the guilds had it; the vines were the sole judge of his worth to be considered a Vineart, just as the mustus had judged his readiness to move from slave to student. Mastery was not conferred, but established.

Without the tests, one remained a student forever.

"Talk to me," he coaxed the vine, the way a farrier might a skittish horse. "Tell me what's disturbing you."

Oddly, he got no sense of distress, no tinge of rot or pest. He thought at first that the vines were ignoring him, but that wasn't it, either. The vines were . . . content.

He sat back on his heels, his hands coming free of the soil, dirt deep under his close-trimmed nails.

Content?

Vines were not meant to be content. That was the first thing he learned: stressing the vine, making it work a little harder to survive, made the fruit more intense, the magic stronger, just as a slave, forced to survive each day by the quickness of his wits and the sharpness of his mind, developed the magic within him, enough to recognize the magic within the vines, within the mustus, and become a Vineart.

Still, a content vine was not a vine under attack. That had been the fear, that whatever power they were seeking had turned its attention to them once again. A year before, the rot known as root-glow had appeared out of season, attacking the oldest of the vines near the house. Malech had suspected intent in that attack, had started connecting events, seeing a pattern in the waves of disruption moving through the Vin Land.

What Jerzy had seen since then . . . he did not think the root-glow had been directed at the House of Malech specifically, but rather loosed upon any vines it could find. Bad luck they had been in its way.

Bad luck for their enemy, as well. Had it not struck Malech's vine-yards, his master might never have been pushed to investigate, and in in-vestigating, become suspicious, and in his suspicions, be driven to break tradition and send Jerzy off to another Vineart's lands.

The memory of Giordan's vineyard returned to him, the taste of the spellwines he crafted: deep green, clean, with an underlying tone of bitterness, like rain on the sea, or wind in the morning. Jerzy shook his head, focusing again on the sense of firewines. The memory of the sea, the mountain air of Aleppan, the look of Mahault, so serious even when pleased, the sound of Ao's laugh or the touch of Kaï's hand on his shoulder, solid and warm—they should not haunt his thoughts, nor fill his dreams. And yet they did, distracting him from what was real and true and important. The treacherous thought—that this was *not* impor-tant—wormed its way in and would not be plucked, no matter how he tried.

You could not untangle, once bound.

"All right. Let it down," he told the slaves. "Replace the soil that we disturbed, and . . ." He paused. How would one stress a content vine?

"Add more crackstone to the soil," he said. "And mark this entire row to be left untouched."

"Master?" the oldest slave, a bald man with sun-kissed skin and a bulbous nose, asked hesitantly, clearly speaking for the other two with him as well.

"No weeding," he told the slaves, exasperated at having to spell it out. "No ashing, after Harvest." Ashing was compost made of pruned canes, collected pigeon shit, and debris from the crushing, sifted together and left until it was a thick black mass used to feed the soil.

He left them to it, reclaiming his shirt and tying the sleeves over his shoulders as he stalked down the narrow furrow, the pale green leaves of the vines brushing at him like a kitten's questing paws. They were too close together. He would have planted the vines farther apart, the way

Giordan had, giving the slaves more room to work. It wasn't as though Master Malech had any lack of land to work in....

Not now, a cool voice came, and Jerzy sighed, letting his annoyance and irritation slide over the implacable sense of the Guardian, and fade into the air. Giordan's ways were Giordan's ways, and what had that earned him? The dragon was right—again. Now was not the time to bring anything new into the yards. The Washers had left, but their suspicions were assuaged, not put entirely to rest, and the enemy they still could not name lurked, his plans unknown, his means undetected. Master Malech spent his days following on news and rumor, while he . . . he did what he was meant to do. More, he kept suspicion from falling back on them, presenting the façade of everyday activities.

He knew all this, and still it itched.

Every day, he went about the routine, took care of the budding vines in the field, and the spellwines in the vintnery that were almost ready to be shipped to buyers throughout the Vin Lands, and beyond. To all intents and purposes, sunrise to sunset, it was life as ever in the House of Malech.

Beyond those borders . . . the attacks went on. Not serpents, not so far as the guards along the coastline reported, but two more Vinearts dead in other lands—one possibly from old age, another thrown by a trusted horse—and there was no way of telling how many men of power were, like Mahault's father, under an evil sway.

No telling how deep and wide the roots of the taint had spread, or what it might mean.

Master Malech was looking into it, but he was not bound to it. He did not understand, in his flesh, the fear that grew, the tension rising . . .

Return, the cool voice said, and then disappeared from his mind.

Jerzy smiled ruefully. The Guardian had taken to ordering him around the way Detta did the House-servants, as though he were merely an extension of its own stone-carved body. His first day within the House, the stone dragon had flown up to his window, Detta letting him in through the casements, and—silently, with a gentle tug of cold stone claws—taken control of the still-shocked slave boy. They had roamed the House together that day, Jerzy slowly losing his fear as they poked into corners and nobody hauled them out or lit into them with the lash. He slowly, with the Guardian's silent encouragement, began to believe that his life had, truly, changed.

How much, the slave-turned-student could never have understood, that day, or the days to follow.

Even now, looking out at the main field, and the shadow of the sleep house, he felt an odd sense of unreality, as though the slave called Fox-fur had never existed, or was perhaps still down there, weeding and sorting, careful hands touching the vines only when needed, fearful every moment of doing something wrong, of being singled out by the overseer and killed for his carelessness.

Fox-fur could never have imagined the things Jerzy had seen.

Leaf to flower, flower to fruit, fruit to mustus, and mustus to wine. Jerzy reminded himself that the cycle continued, even now. The slaves knew what to do, and so did he.

Returning to the House, he ducked into the bathing room, hoping to get the worst of the dirt off his skin and out from under his nails, but even the bar of harsh soap could only do so much. "Vineart's blush," Detta called it, the grime that worked its way into the whorls of his fingertips and the edges of his nails. Once presentable, he detoured again into the kitchen, where Lil was in heated discussion with the lad from the butcher in the nearby village. She saw him, but did not pause in her tirade to do more than nod in greeting.

"Anything to eat quickly?"

Roan waved a hand at the table behind her, as she stirred something in the great pot over the fire. Once, these females, brusque and caring, had awed him, with their sassy words and clean, neat manners. Now they were as familiar as the Guardian, if usually more outspoken.

There were soft brown rolls piled on a wooden trencher. He took two, wrapping one in his kerchief and looping it over his belt and taking a careful bite out of the other. Lil was a good cook—better than

Detta had been—but she liked to use spices that sometimes scalded the tongue, and he had learned to taste carefully, until he knew what she was serving. But the meat inside the roll was warm, not too hot, and only tingled his tongue pleasantly.

Eating the rest of it, he crossed the courtyard and went in through the door at the other end, heading not to Master Malech's formal study but down the stairs to the cool stone-lined workrooms. His master was there, but the Guardian was not.

"Jerzy." His master did not look up from the ledger open on his desk. "Report."

"The only thing wrong with the vines is that there is nothing wrong with them. I've ordered the slaves to put more stress on the roots, so that they will feel threatened and produce more fruit."

"Ah. Good, good."

Malech had heard his report, and acknowledged it, but Jerzy had the sense that his master wasn't really listening.

"You have received more messages?" Jerzy asked, seeing the small, rectangular scraps on top of the ledger's pages, their edges curling in a way to indicate that they had been rolled into a pigeon's leg case.

"Yes. But not as many as I sent out. Seven, out of nearly thirty."

Jerzy frowned. "Might your messages not have reached them? Could they have been intercepted?" They had been waiting nearly a tenday for any response, which was unusual, and they had to consider the risks. Pigeons were the best way to send a message over distances—faster than a horse and rider, and less expensive than hiring a *meme-courier*, but there was no way to verify that it had reached its destination. Their birds were bred for speed and smarts, but a falcon could take one from the sky in the time it took to blink, and a storm could blow it off course, or unfriendly hands could divert it. Master Malech had wagered that small birds would attract less notice than any other method, but although they knew the direction of their enemy now, they did not know his name—or his reach.

Jerzy sat down, and then stood up again. The old stool that he had used before leaving for Aleppan was gone, replaced by a taller stool that suited his now-longer legs, but the seat had not been worn down properly yet, and Jerzy found that he preferred to pace while he thought, rather than sitting. It made for an interesting dance, since his master often did the same, and the space in the workroom was limited.

"Possible, but the sheer number of them, to have gone astray . . . unlikely." Master Malech, indeed, stood up and paced to the left, so Jerzy changed his direction to pace to the right, noting as he did so that his strides were longer than his master's. That seemed wrong, somehow, especially since the Master Vineart was still considerably taller. "No, I suspect the cause is less violent and more predictable: fear."

"Master?" That made Jerzy check his step, and turn to look at the Vineart. Malech's long hair was as neatly queued as ever, his clothing clean and unwrinkled, his hands and voice steady, and yet Master Malech seemed . . . distressed.

Jerzy felt an odd twist in his gut, similar to the sickness he had felt while at sea. He had seen his master angry, and worried, and even upset before. But this distress was new, and worrisome.

"Master?" Jerzy had been willing until now to remain quiet, doing as he was told, but his earlier thoughts were crowding at him, not letting him stay still any longer.

"Thirty messages I sent, asking not for money, or requiring them to divulge any secrets of their yard."

After what happened to Giordan, none would offer, anyway. Earlier correspondence brought via bird and villager proved that word had spread—courtesy of the Washers, no doubt, using the Vineart's fate to rein in any others who might tread beyond the constraints of tradition and Command. No matter that Jerzy suspected the game in Aleppan had originally been Sar Anton's, the Washers owned it now. None would step forward as Giordan had, and risk the same result.

Malech stopped his own pacing, staring at the doorsill where the Guardian normally rested. There was a smoke-black smudge against the wall, as though its carved body had left a stain, somehow. "I asked no secrets," the Vineart repeated, "merely requested that they tell me of any oddities, any strangeness, any thing off season or out of place. Of any strangers in their lands, wielding more influence than their status would indicate."

He sighed, turning to stand face-to-face with his student. "These are things that should not terrify a Vineart. And yet . . . they have. Terrified them into retreating behind walls. And not only Vinearts—the messages were sent to princelings and maiars, land-lords and reeves. It is perhaps ironic that of my seven responses, three were from reeves."

"Ironic?" Jerzy wasn't sure what his master meant.

Malech turned, returning to stand behind the desk. Jerzy relaxed: the lecture pose. This was something he knew, and knew how to deal with.

"Reeves are limited in scope—their sphere of influence is no greater than the village they live in. They have no power, no status beyond those boundaries. The games of land-lords and princelings rage over them, and all that may change is who they give tribute to, and under what name. A jaded view, perhaps, but no less valid. They are, I suspect, in our enemy's mind too small to cause great trouble and too weak to be useful; if they stayed quiet, it is likely they would be left alone . . . and yet it appears that they are the ones who are most willing to speak out." Malech stroked his beard with one hand, and sighed. "Perhaps ironic is not the correct word. Perhaps it is merely sad.

"If this continues, more lands will follow Atakus's lead, if perhaps with less drastic measures. Already dialogue ceases, Agreements either unsealed or abandoned as each man of power looks around and sees only suspicion and potential threat."

"The same as in Aleppan," Jerzy said, remembering the fear and worry that filled the Aleppanese court, courtesy of the maiar's aide, a man of no particular name or importance, according to Mahault: years loyal and yet filled with a tainted magic only Jerzy could connect to the magic that animated the serpents as well.

The Washers had heard Jerzy's report of the matter, but neither he nor Malech thought they would act on it. Even if the Collegium itself were blameless in Darian's actions, they had no reason to trust the word of a student already brushed with suspicion on his own, and the thought of a nobody, a minor court functionary, having magic . . .

Impossible.

If Jerzy hadn't seen it himself, hadn't tasted the magic in the man's soul, he would not have believed it, either. Only a Vineart could hold magic within himself, wield spells without spellwine. That man had been no Vineart. And yet . . .

Only Jerzy had sensed it. Only Malech believed him.

"It is the remaining four responses that concern me right now," Malech said, sitting behind the desk and spreading his left hand over the papers, pressing them flat. "Only one from a Vineart—Rosario, from the coast of Iaja. I had not thought to hear from him, in truth. He is isolationist, even by our standards, and intentionally unpleasant to be around. Were his spellwines not so potent, he might be ignored completely, but they are strong—perhaps the best for preventing child loss ever incanted. We buy a cask every year, ourselves."

"What does he say?" Jerzy was curious about the spellwine, but more so about the message.

"That he has been approached by not one but two maiars of cities within a day's travel of his yards. Each requested dialogue with him, the implication being that they wished to form an alliance."

"But that is what caused Vineart Giordan trouble," Jerzy said, startled.

"Worse, boy," Malech said. He had not called Jerzy "boy" since his return, and the old usage felt less like a rebuke and more like affection. "Giordan only bartered first pick of his spellwines in exchange for the use of the maiar's lands. These requests—and from Rosario's words, I think they were phrased more as demands—were for Rosario to turn his skills over to them, and their land, exclusively."

Jerzy felt his legs give under him, and he dropped onto the stool, not minding the uncomfortable seat so long as it supported him. Sin Washer give grace to them all. And the Washers had accused *him* of apostasy?

"That is . . . The Washers will never stand for that."

"No," Malech agreed, sitting in his own chair, lacing his fingers together and looking at Jerzy over their tips, his dark blue eyes cold and brooding. "No, they will not. They cannot. And the maiars must know this, as they know their own names . . . and yet still they proceed.

"Two questions that leaves me with, boy. One: What will—what *can*—the Washers do, if Vineart and men of power combine their strengths, as was forbidden by Sin Washer? And two: What purpose does that serve our enemy? What benefit might he find, in driving us back to the dark times, when too much power was held by too few men?"

Jerzy stared at this master, then realized the older man was expecting him to reply. He cudgeled his brain, trying to come up with something that might be, if not useful, at least not useless. "Sin Washer broke the First Growth because it was too powerful," he said slowly, feeling his way along the thought. "He broke the prince-mages likewise—that power never be centered all in one place. He did it because the prince-mages abused their power, and mistreated their people . . . and the gods would not stand for it. But the gods have been silent ever since. Perhaps . . . someone wishes to make the gods speak again?"

It seemed outrageous to him, but his master nodded his head thoughtfully. "A possible scenario. Unlikely, but possible, and in truth a crazed mind could believe such a thing, and take steps to cause it. It is also possible that this Vineart, whoever he is, wishes not to rouse the gods but destroy them. But what purpose that might serve, when they are already silent, and few believe, much less worship their altars any longer . . ."

"Not the gods," Jerzy said quietly, the realization unfolding in his head like new leaves uncurling. The bindings that tied it all together, the knots and snags, the memory of what he had seen and heard: the merchants in Aleppan, worrying about ships lost and taxes due; Kaï's voice breaking as he spoke of his sister, his father's madness; Mahl's sadness looking at a rosebush and speaking of the ones her father had uprooted;

the voice of the shopkeeper suggesting that he, Jerzy, take over another Vineart's yards . . . it all unraveled in a sudden understanding that made no sense at all. "Us."

He lifted his gaze to his master's, and saw no understanding in that granite-sharp face.

"A chip here, a crack there, piece by piece, until it all comes apart and shatters in fear and distrust. He seeks to destroy the Vin Lands."

EVEN ONCE MALECH understood, and accepted it as the only explanation that fit, they still had no idea who might wish it, or how to prevent the suspicion from becoming truth.

Master Malech had dismissed him after their discussion, the Vineart mumbling over the map on his desk and stroking the tip of his beard the way he did when he was hard-pressed on a thought. Much as Jerzy wanted to stay, he knew that he could offer no more assistance in the matter. And he was not entirely useless—while his master worried about the world around them, there was still work to be done here. The vines were healthy, and the weather was holding, but yards needed constant vigilance during the growing season, and there were yards beyond the House that needed to be checked.

And yet, two days later, Jerzy found himself unable to settle back into that daily, necessary work. Without other, more specific orders, he decided to ride out to visit the southern yard's overseer.

It had been good to reacquaint himself with that yard, planted only ten years back with firevines, but the journey meant too many hours on the back of a horse, returning only that morning after a few hours of sleep in the overseer's cottage.

He still did not enjoy traveling on horseback, preferring to use his own feet when possible, but the old gelding and he had ridden this road often enough that he trusted the horse to find its way along the hard-packed dirt, and not shy when a villager drove his sheep across it, or a flock of birds erupted from a grove of trees, or a fox came out of the ditch in the early-morning light and watched as human and horse went by, its red plumed tail the same color Jerzy's hair had been when he was young.

The memory brought back others, and for once, soothed by his exhaustion and the slow steady rocking of the horse below him, both like and unlike the feel of the *Green Lady*, Jerzy let them come.

The slaver's caravan, packed leg to leg with other slaves as they were taken from market to market, offered not on a public stage with the livestock but set apart where others need not see them. The men who would come, one at a time, quietly, looking and never speaking, choosing one or two, sometimes three but never more. And those slaves would be gone, and the rest would be loaded back into the wagons, brought to another town, another land. The languages changed, but all else remained the same. New slaves were added, some others were removed, either from death—tossed to the side of the road, left for the carrion eaters— or because they had grown too old to be purchased, and were unwanted and abandoned with a set of clothes and a coin, to do as they might in the whatever land they were in.

For the first time, Jerzy remembered, and wondered what happened to those slaves. Were they taken in by the local villages or towns, seen as new blood, new backs for the working? Did they turn to theft, ending their days on the end of a rope, or the edge of a lordsman's sword?

Had Master Malech not chosen him in that market, years before, what might have become of him? What had become of the slaves of Vineart Poul, who would not have run and yet were gone? What happened to them when there was no need for them?

Without planning to, Jerzy sucked at the inside of his mouth, drawing a flood of saliva onto his tongue. The tang of firevine grapes filled his senses, the mixture of fruit he had tasted the afternoon before blending with the finished wines, the smell and feel of the soil under his hand and the touch of the leaves against his skin . . . and the undercurrents of something else, more acidic, cooler, with a hint of stone and salt . . .

Weathervines. The memory still within him, the pull of the sun-drenched soil of the Aleppan hills, of cool sun and freshening winds like those that filled the sails of a ship when it turned and ran with the prevailing breeze. Things he should not know, would not know, save for his master breaking tradition and sending him away. And he did not have the strength, in the early-dawn hour, to push it away, but instead let the two blend in his mouth, not thinking, not directing the quiet-magic, but letting it rise within him almost curiously, to see what it might do.

It was wrong, this blending. His master had warned him to never try to mix spells; Sin Washer's Command forbade him to use another Vineart's vines, but to step back, keep his distance, use only the finished *vin magica* of another's work, the same as anyone else. Was this wrong, this thing that made his heart beat faster, his limbs shiver in anticipation, until the gelding stopped underneath him of its own accord, aware that something was happening, that something was not right.

And yet Jerzy felt nothing but that anticipation, a surge of satisfaction; none of the black taint that had buried itself in the dead flesh of the sea serpent, or flowed from the mouth of the aid in Aleppan. It could not be wrong, not the way that had been . . .

He urged the gelding forward again with his knees, his hands slack on the reins as he tried to follow the feel of the quiet-magic, subtle and fresh within him. He cast his memory to that taint, to confirm that they were nothing alike, in no way the same.

The first blow was an utter surprise, nearly knocking him off the horse. Only instinct made him close his hips and legs to stay upright, dropping a hand to the gelding's neck to reassure it, even as Jerzy tried to determine what had hit him. He looked around, expecting to see a branch that had somehow fallen from a tree, or a cudgel thrown by a would-be brigand, and he reached back for his own, strapped across the back of the saddle.

Shifting, the quiet-magic shifted within him as well, and the lash of taint slapped across his awareness even as another blow came, this one aimed not at his torso, but the horse beneath him. The horse let out a scream that sounded like a woman in agony, and lost its footing, struggling and then collapsing on his side. Jerzy was able to swing free of the saddle just in time not to be crushed underneath, pulling his foot free of the horse's bulk at the last second and scrambling to the side of the road as though there would be safety there.

He spit into his palm, dirty from hitting the ground, and saw the red-tinged spittle mix with the dirt to create a smear of mud. In another place, that might have worried him, but not here, not in The Berengia, not so close to his own yards. Here, that dirt would not weaken the spellwine, but strengthen it.

When the next blow came, sweeping low over the dying horse, Jerzy was ready.

"To the defense, rise," he cried, lifting his spittle-covered hand, palm out as though that alone could stop the blow. Now, looking, ready, Jerzy almost saw the attack, as though the wind had shaped itself to the great paw of a catamount, white claws stretching for his face, ready to rend open his face the way it had the side of the gelding, breaking his neck as easily as it had broken the horse's.

Instead, the quiet-magic he called stopped the paw midswipe, holding it in place. Jerzy's arm trembled from the strain, as though he were wrestling with some physical beast, and sweat ran on his skin, dripping down into his eyes, his own body fighting against him, willing him to fail.

"Not here. Not on my soil," Jerzy said, and his toes curled within his shoes as though to make contact with that dirt, trying to feel the roots of the vines that spread not so far from here.

Hold.

Here, the Guardian could reach him easily, and although the creature did not leave the confines of the House grounds, Jerzy felt its cool weight settle on his shoulder, the stone claws gripping his flesh as it had that very first morning, claiming the slave Fox-fur for the House of Malech.

"Begone!" Jerzy yelled, and thrust his arm forward as though flinging a weapon from his empty hand.

And the wind died, the giant paw was gone, and he was left in the road with only the carcass of the gelding to prove that anything had actually happened.

Jerzy waited, breathless, a moment, and then another, until his heart stopped pounding and the wetness on his hand dried to a sticky mess. The tainted magic did not return, but he did not trust himself to move until a tarn flew overhead, calling softly as though to sound an all clear. He stood then, feeling his knees crackle in protest, and made his way, carefully, to where the gelding lay, having bled out into the road.

He did not want to leave it there, abandoned like an old shoe, but he had no choice. Stripping the saddle and bags from the animal's back, he patted its thick neck softly, the cool heavy feel of the flesh such a change from the usual warm liveliness that he shuddered. He had seen men die, watched them be eaten by a serpent, beaten to death by the overseer, broken in two by a broken wagon, and yet the sight of this simple beast turned to so much useless weight made his throat swell from the inside, as though he had something caught within.

"Thank you," he said, feeling foolish, then hoisted the saddle over his shoulder and started walking for home.

By the time he walked up the cobbled-stone drive to the House, Jerzy felt as though he might as well have dragged the horse's body home, he felt so weary. Summoning a slave from the garden, he handed over the saddle and bags, and told the boy to tell the stable master what had happened to the gelding. If the carcass was still there, it would go into the stewpot for the slaves that night. To the end, everything served the House.

Everything served....

That thought bore him company as he entered the House through the side door only he and the Vineart used, taking the stone steps down to where his master waited, in the workroom cellar where *vina* became *vin magica*.

"Master Malech."

The Vineart looked up, taking Jerzy's muddied and torn clothing, his exhaustion, in one evaluating sweep from head to toe. "The Guardian said something happened. A beast attacked?"

Jerzy shook his head. "No beast. Magic. The taint."

That got his master's attention. "How? What happened? You are unharmed?"

"I . . ." Jerzy hesitated. He should tell Malech everything, what he had done, what he had been thinking. But the words caught in his sore throat, and he dropped his gaze, staring instead at the polished stone floor. "I don't know." He shifted, swallowed. "I was riding back this morning, and thinking about the slaves that went missing, Vineart Poul's slaves."

"Yes?"

The ability to lie had never been bred into him; he might say nothing, he might avoid answering, but he could not lie, certainly not to his master.

"I was thinking of the slaves, wondering what had happened to them, and of the taint, and I called the quiet-magic. I did not mean to, but I did, and I think it found me that way; because I was thinking of it, using magic."

"Like gazes meeting across a room," Malech said, leaning back in his chair and steepling his fingers the way he did when deep in thought. "If our enemy can do this, yes. It would explain . . . it would explain why some have been targeted merely for mischief, and others for devastation. Sionio . . ." The Vineart who had disappeared, a year or more before, leaving his vineyards untouched. "He was powerful, and brash, and would have gone after any attacker, be it mortal or magical. The ones who have gone missing, they must have done as you did . . . but you held it off."

"I knew it was an attack," Jerzy said. "They did not."

"Yes. But you must do nothing more to rouse its attention, Jerzy. Not until we are ready. Do you understand?"

Jerzy had no desire whatsoever to face that taint again. He nodded.

"Good. Now go, put on fresh clothing and eat something before you fall over. And speak to no one of this, do you understand? No one."

He headed immediately for the kitchen, hunger driving him more than the need to bathe and change. The House was filled with the smell of something roasting in the fireplace. A small child, one of Detta's newest kitchen children, was sitting by the ledge, conscientiously turning the roast slowly on its spit. Jerzy had offered, once, to craft a spell that would do that for them, but Lil had refused, claiming that no spell could ever tell when meat was properly cooked.

Detta, who was sitting at the table talking to Lil as the cook directed events, scowled when Jerzy walked in, but did not comment on the state of his clothing, merely telling him that he was not eating near-enough.

"Detta, he eats everything in sight," Lil protested, but she was laughing, most of her attention on the action in the kitchen.

Detta scowled, and broke off half the loaf of bread Roan had just placed on the table to cool, pushing it across toward Jerzy with an air of finality while Lil put together a plate for him.

"You've grown a handspan high and another handspan in the chest since you left on that foolish quest of his. Do any of your clothes still fit you?"

"You made 'em large," he said around a mouthful of the warm, crusty bread. Detta glared at him, and he swallowed the rest before speaking again. "They're fine. I'm not going to get much taller. Not like Master Malech."

"Hrmph. No, you won't. But you're already broader than he, and no mistake. You're built like one of the Riders, out Seven Unions-way. Which makes sense, your looks and that name."

Jerzy took a sip of tai, wincing as usual at the taste but relishing the surge of energy he felt returning to his aching body. Guilt swept through him again, at allowing the gelding to be slaughtered that way. If he were in truth Rider-born, they would have cast him out for that; they valued their horses above children, stories said.

"Cai said as much, about me being from the Seven Unions. I even remember a few words of the language." He missed the Caulic weapons master, who had taught him how to, in Cai's own words, "move like a man, not a slave." The weapons master had gone on to other students when Jerzy was away, and the House seemed somehow quieter, and more drab, without his beaded mustache and colorful attire.

He wondered if all Caulians dressed that way, and what stories Ao would come back with, when he returned. . . .

Assuming he returned at all. Why should he? It was a wide world, filled with more things to do than backtrack his steps, and if Ao did indeed find a new source or contact that would convince his clan to take him back—why would he even think twice about one Vineart?

Jerzy was surprised to find that thought hurt. Ao and Mahault, even Kaïnam . . . he missed them.

A Vineart stood alone and showed no weakness to outsiders. But were they outsiders, truly? He might have asked Master Malech, but it seemed too small, too petty a thought to bother his master with, right now.

"We had two orders come in yesterday," Detta said, apparently satisfied that he would continue eating. "Both for basic healwines. You'll check with Malech and make sure we'll have enough to restock? If not, I'll be raising the prices on future orders, to make them think twice."

"Raise the prices anyway," Jerzy said, without thinking.

"Oh?" Detta tilted her head at him, the short gray curls bounding along the side of her round face as she did so. She wasn't doubting him; she had been the first to require him to make decisions in Malech's absence, treating him as his master's voice in all things, even when Jerzy wasn't certain he should. He was certain about this. But he wasn't sure he could explain to her why.

"By how much?" she asked.

Jerzy shrugged, using a chunk of bread to sop up the last of the sausage grease from his platter and cramming it into his mouth so that she couldn't expect him to answer. He was merely the Vineart; she was the House-keeper. Matters of business were her domain, not his.

He left her to pondering, scratching numbers into a sheet of re-scraped parchment with the nub of a pen, then crossing them out and refiguring them. Detta had been running the House since Master Malech was his age—she would do what was best, leaving them to do what they did best. That was how the vintnery worked.

Once he had thought the entire world worked like that—everyone knowing what they were meant to do, the days moving on an orderly basis. Then he had gone to Aleppan, before seeing how different things were there, in the port towns and villages of The Berengia, and Mur-Magrib. The world beyond was chaos and confusion, a constantly shift-ing landscape of power and entanglements and desires. Vinearts were sheltered, protected . . . isolated.

Jerzy frowned. It was Sin Washer's Command, the price of having magic. They traded their work for others to use, but they themselves might not have or hold power beyond the confines of their vineyards. Order, trust, the proper place of all things in the world—all the things the Washers preached, when they spoke of Sin Washer's solace.

Jerzy had asked if Sin Washer had known about the quiet-magic, the residue of spellwines that built up within a Vineart over the years. Master Malech had not been able to answer him; had never, it seemed, considered the question one worth asking.

It made Jerzy uneasy when he asked a question his master could not answer.

The quiet-magic, more than any Command, was what kept them isolated; the need to keep it a secret. The rest of the Vin Lands—and beyond—believed that magic could be used equally by all, so long as they had the spellwine and the decantation to open it with. The truth—that a Vineart could use magic without a decantation—could draw upon the magic within him, could cause outsiders to distrust Vinearts, wonder what other secrets they hid. Master Malech said only that he would learn more, as his training progressed, and to keep close what he did know.

Jerzy had not spoken to Master Malech of that moment on

shipboard, when he used the quiet-magic without volition, nor had he admitted to using it where Mahl and Ao could see. He had wanted to return to things as they had been, not shake up what was known.

Only now did he admit, to himself, that that would not happen. If someone meant to destroy the Vin Lands, break Sin Washer's Commands, and turn two millennia of order to dust, then Vinearts would be the first wall to breach. But if they fought back, revealed their hidden secret, the power they had not shared . . . what would happen then?

You would be powerful . . . and hunted. Feared . . . and abused. The structure would break, and chaos would rule.

The dragon was never that eloquent, and for the first time, Jerzy thought he felt emotion with the Guardian's words, Sadness. And . . . fear?

The thought that the dragon might have emotions startled Jerzy enough that he almost walked into a doorway, rather than going through it. "What do you know, Guardian?"

There was a silence, an absence of the weight of the Guardian's voice that made Jerzy feel suddenly dizzy, and then the dragon returned.

Ask Malech.

THE NEXT MORNING, Jerzy woke to orders, sent via the Guardian, to check on another vineyard's progress. This was a two-day trip, with an overnight at a wayhouse where Jerzy slept in an alcove over the sheep, and came away feeling as though he were wearing wool himself, his skin was so itchy. Jerzy managed to keep himself focused on what he was doing, not allowing a hint of either quiet-magic or what might be happening beyond the low stone walls of the vineyard to distract him. To anyone looking on, he was the perfect ideal of the student-Vineart, his master's well-trained factor, concerned only with matters that properly concerned him.

The vines here were healthy, the clusters of grapes progressing properly, but the overseer was ailing, as much from age as any ailment. Jerzy did as much as he could, and promised to arrange for a replacement to be chosen before Harvest came around.

On the third day, finally back home, a late rain came in, tiny hailstones pounding from the sky. Jerzy had heard the first sound as he was finishing breakfast, and headed for the yard at a run, ignoring the stinging feel of the icy pellets on his skin. Every slave—and the entire Household—was needed to cover the vines as best they could, setting up tarps on wooden stakes and placing smudge pots underneath to keep the plants warm.

The storm lasted, off and on, for most of the day, and everyone was too busy to think of anything beyond protecting the grapes. On the fourth day, in the aftermath, Malech and Jerzy walked the rows, determining how much damage had been done.

It wasn't until much later that night, when everyone else had collapsed, exhausted, into their beds, that Jerzy had time to wonder again at the Guardian's words, to go beyond the immediate concerns of the day. He lay in his own bed, staring at the smooth stone ceiling overhead.

Ask Malech.

Ask him what? What the Guardian knew? What his master knew? What did his master know that he had not shared, and why had he not told Jerzy? A sense of anxiety unfolded in him, his certainty in Malech shaken again by the realization that he did not, entirely, trust his master.

A question he had not allowed himself to consider before rose to the surface, as though the Guardian's words had lifted it. Why had Malech called Jerzy back when he was ready to start the search? To calm the Washers? That had been done; they were calm, as calm as they were like to be, and yet the taint still spread, a more subtle damage than sea serpents or flamespouts, but, like root rot or leaf powder, more dangerous the longer it went unchecked.

Why did Master Malech not do something?

What *could* Master Malech do?

Unable to sleep, Jerzy threw off his blanket and pulled on the pair of trou he had shed a few hours before. Barefoot, bare-chested, he went down the narrow stairs to the main level of the House and out into the courtyard.

The moon was a bare splinter overhead, but the stars splashed across the sky bright enough to light his way. The stones here were cool beneath his feet, while the air was moist with night dew. A dove hooted somewhere on the rooftop, and the scent of the flowers in the front yard drifted on the slow breeze. Jerzy breathed in deeply, and felt a softness creep into his limbs. On a night like this, there could be nothing bad, nothing violent, happening anywhere.

A flash of memory: the sight of the sea creature, rising up out of the waters, a hapless villager caught in its maw. The sound of the wine seller's voice as he told of the Vineart dead, the slaves gone without a trace. The look in Kai's eyes as he recounted the fate of his sister and the attacks on his homeland.

The tainted magic, creeping through the corners of the Aleppan court, touching the edges of the Tétouan marketplace, wafting over the sea from somewhere unknown: able to cross any boundary, creep unseen into any House.

Feared, or abused, the Guardian had said. A Vineart freed from Sin Washer's Command could control a seaport or empower an army. He could pick and choose who received his spellwines, without fear of reprisal or rebuke.

Or a man of power might overwhelm a Vineart, take control of his yards by force, his work gone to one man's whim only, never shared save at another's direction. A slave, once again.

Impossible. For nearly two thousand years, unthinkable.

The structure would break, and chaos would rule.

Spellvines were creatures of order, pattern. There was a time and a place for everything, a reason for each action, a result from each action. Tested, consistent, known.

Would chaos destroy the spellvines . . . or change them once again into something else? What would Vinearts become, in the aftermath?

Suddenly, the quiet night seemed ominous, not peaceful.

"Jerzy?"

Malech's voice made him start, leaping up from the bench in a reflexive motion. For that instant, he was once again a slave, nameless and disposable, without value.

"Boy? Jerzy? What is wrong?"

"I . . . was startled." His heart slowing back down to a normal pace, he saw that his master, too, looked as though he had dressed in a hurry, wrapped in a deep green robe with a pattern of vines embroidered along the sleeves and hem. Jerzy noted almost absently that the vine pattern glowed with a faint green light, under the cool white light of the stars. A year ago, he would have been intrigued; two years ago, he would have been awed. Now he recognized it as a variant of Malech's own spell-lights decanted into the threads, and returned to his master's question.

Caught off guard, he asked not the question he had meant to ask, but one that rose from him, unbidden.

"Master . . . what is the Guardian?"

MALECH OPENED HIS mouth to respond, and then looked more closely at his student and closed his mouth, thinking carefully. He called the boy a boy, but in truth Jerzy was a young man—grown and no longer so green. There were things he needed to know.

Things that needed to be passed on.

"I spoke to you once of the Iajan foreseer wine, yes?"

Jerzy nodded, sitting down again as though sensing another lecture. Instead, Malech sat down on the bench next to him and looked up at the stars overhead. Sin Washer's Pour splashed across the dark blue backdrop, and off to the side was the Great Ship, and the hindquarters of the Bull . . .

Aware that he was avoiding the question, he closed his eyes once, and continued speaking.

"Foreseer wine is a tricky thing. It will show you what is to come, yes, but magic does not speak in human tongues, for all that we use our words to incant our desires into the wines. What is shown must be interpreted, adapted to what is already known, or suspected.

"I prefer, generally, to let events come as they will, to face them when they arrive, and not worry overmuch over the inevitability of hard times, or rejoice too early for good times. What will, will." He smiled ruefully, as though remembering something that did not entirely please him. "We can only harvest what grapes have been grown, not those still to come.

"But my master Josia was of a more . . . mystical bent, or perhaps more anxious about my place in this world, what role I might play. He paid dear coin for a hand flask of foreseer, and had me drink it all in one long pull."

Malech still remembered, vividly, how the smooth, silky liquid had swirled within his mouth, almost as though alive, and then slithered down his throat, leaving a trail of tingling warmth behind.

And then, how the vision had hit him.

"I fell to the ground as though felled by one of Mil'ar Cai's backhand cudgel swings. When I awoke, all I could remember was a wave of red, sticky and slow, washing over me, filling my mouth and lungs with a taste I'd never encountered before—or since. I retained nothing more— save a weight, heavy as stone, on my chest, not weighing me down but lifting me up, whispering to me that the world would need healing.

"I did not understand the whisper, but the feel of the weight, the shadow that fell over me, remained in my mind, even after the rest of the vision had dimmed and been near-forgotten.

"Josia took the whisper to mean that I should focus on my healwines, even to the exclusion of the other vines he had cultivated, all his life. He also arranged for me to receive training from the local physick, an old man who had seen more lives come and go from this world than the Old Woman could count."

Jerzy made an involuntary warding gesture at the mention of the guide of the dead. It was a silly superstition, as though a hand movement might ward off death's attention, but he did it anyway, and Malech's long fingers twitched in a similar fashion.

"All well and good, but the weight was unexplained, digging at my mind until it was a shadow with me, every day, haunting my steps and crowding my breath. And then Josia fell ill, suddenly, when I was bringing healing spells to a distant village, and it came to me: if Josia had died while I was away—farther away than our own yards—the vintnery needed protection. From what, I was unsure—but the need was urgent in my mind.

"My kinfolk were stone carvers. I had some memory of them, faint but true, whenever I passed my hands over the stone walls of the House, and it seemed proper, somehow, to create the House Guardian from that same material. Josia and I worked together to craft the spell, his knowledge and my skills, blending carefully, cautiously, to bring life to my work, awareness. . . .

"I could not do it on my own, could not replicate it now, even if Josia had written down what he did. My share was minor . . . but when we were finished, the Guardian lived; more, it was linked to the lands, to the House it was carved from, and to every creature that is affiliated with these vines, and lives within this House. It can reach any of us, if we are within The Berengia, and even beyond, as you discovered, although greater waters confuse it. It is loyal the way only stone may be, forever a part of the House, forever bound to its borders, to protect the House and all within it if its master was called away."

Malech fell silent, and in the quiet that surrounded them, the cool darkness of the starlit night, he could hear his student breathing quietly beside him, slow and steady, as though he might have fallen asleep.

In truth, Malech had no idea of the depths of the stone dragon's connection to the vineyards—or what the Guardian was capable of. He had taken a quiet comfort in that lack of knowing, as though if he did not know, he did not have to worry.

"All those years, I assumed that the foreseer wine had shown me the coming great death, the rose plague. I was ready for it, prepared as few were, and we lost few souls, compared to other lands that were hit. But now, I wonder."

He did not look at Jerzy, but kept his gaze on the great wash of stars that made up Sin Washer's Pour.

"I wonder if perhaps it foresaw not me, but you."

He let that fall into the air around them, and then reached over to touch Jerzy's knee, allowing himself this one moment of affection. "Go back to bed, boy. No day will be easier, and I suspect they will only become worse. Best to get rest while we can."

He got up, hearing his knees crack with the effort, and shuffled off to his own quarters, leaving the boy sitting there, silent and still.

Chapter 8

You should not.

"Hush," Jerzy said, shooting an annoyed look over his shoulder at the stone dragon.

The first day or so after Malech's revelation, Jerzy had been uneasy around the Guardian, watching it as though it might suddenly do something, or say something, or—in truth, he didn't know what he thought, or expected. Then one day passed, and another, and Jerzy found himself reaching up to touch the Guardian's tail as he passed through a doorway where the dragon was perched, just as he always had before, and nothing had really changed.

The Guardian was special magic. Important. Jerzy had always known that, even if he didn't know why, or how unique it was. There were more important things to take precedence in his thoughts right now. Malech's words to him lingered in his every action, kept him company when he slept, and ate at his brain until he thought he might go mad.

"I prefer, generally, to let events come as they will, to face them when they arrive, and not worry overmuch over the inevitability of hard times, or rejoice too early for good times. What will, will."

His master considered the vineyard, the House, and the villages surrounding, and only then the rest of the Vin Lands. But Jerzy knew *people* there. Vineart Giordan had not been a name, but a person. Ao and Mahault, Kaïnam . . .

What will, will. The cycle moved forward, one season following the next. But like the wind carrying a storm, like fire unchecked, a bad season could cause the next to fail as well. People starved, if crops failed. People died, if winters were too harsh, or the rainy season too wet. The Guardian warned of chaos, and Master Malech feared the destruction of the world as they knew it . . .

If things were to get worse, what was his master waiting for? Jerzy felt the tension grow in him until he could no longer contain it, not without bursting.

You should not, the dragon repeated, not moving from the wall niche where it had settled. Its sightless stone eyes stared down at Jerzy, gray and unblinking, and at the assortment of flasks and vials spread out on the table in front of him.

"I have to."

Jerzy had woken that morning to the sound of a soft rain on the roof of his bedchamber. Not more hail, just a normal, refreshing rain. There was no need for him to go outside today. No need to throw himself over a horse's back or into a jolting wagon, no need to get wet and muddy . . . and nothing for his body to do, no exhaustion to keep the worry at bay.

Master Malech had already been in his study when Jerzy came down to receive his orders for the day, a smear of ink on his angular face and a crease between his brow that meant, Jerzy knew, that Detta had finally cornered him with the House accounts. The day-to-day running of the House was her domain, but the Vineart still had to place his seal on certain orders, and approve her plans—although Malech had merely nodded in approval when Jerzy told him of his own decision to raise prices.

Master Malech needed not only to consider what they had in the cellars, but what they would need to craft from this year's harvest. If men of power were suspicious of one another, there would be a need for more bloodstaunch, of a certainty, and purges. Blended together, cirurgiens used them to ease fevers, but they had to be made fresh each season or else the spellwine faded and was useless.

It had been that casual mention of blended spells by Master Malech that had given root to the thought Jerzy was now contemplating, and sent him down into the cellar, to his current course.

The one the Guardian was warning him against.

"I'm not going to test it on anyone," Jerzy said in response, defending himself. "I just want to see what it would take."

"It" was an incantation that would prevent a hailstorm like the one they'd just had from doing quite so much damage. But it was what such an incantation might mean to a Vineart that had Jerzy fascinated. If you could protect a vine from storm damage, then a major risk would be averted from the early growing season. But more, if it could be used to further protect travelers on the road, caught away from shelter . . .

Someone like Mahault, or Ao.

You should not.

"I know what Master Malech said about mixing spells." When a fishing village along the coast had been attacked by a sea creature, months before, Jerzy had been sent with a spellwine to help cure an odd melancholia afflicting villagers in the aftermath. But another creature had attacked while he was delivering the spells, and Jerzy had added his own decantation to the princeling's counterattack, not truly thinking about what he was doing save that the spell needed to be reinforced.

He had been right: it had worked, and the beast was defeated. Master Malech had not praised him when Jerzy admitted what he had done, but rather had warned him about the dangers of using spellwines in concert with another, especially without more training.

This was not that. He was not trying to force two different spells to work at the same time, but to incant them together, to be greater than their individual strengths. He knew how to incant safely, and he knew how to handle both healspells and weatherspells.

It is not done. You should not.

Tradition. Habit. Must nots and should nots.

He sighed, letting the small clay vial of Giordan's weatherwine rest back in its holder on the table. "That it has not been done does not mean it should not be done. I am not going against any Command, Guardian. No more so than Master Malech was when he sent me to learn from Giordan."

The spellwine he was experimenting with was the one he had bought in Tétouan. It was a basic weatherspell, useful for lifting a light wind to fill a sail, or clear away the stench of illness. At worst, he might make a storm in the area slightly worse—or even cause it to lighten up slightly.

There was no hesitation in his mind. He knew these wines better than anyone else still living; he had worked in their soul, been there when Giordan shared his own blood with the mustus, forcing the stubborn, difficult weathergrapes to accept incantation. He knew what to do, and how to handle them.

Or at least he thought he did. The worry flitted into his brain and would not leave. Giordan had thought that Jerzy could handle that full-strength spellwine in Aleppan, too, and look what had happened there—he had accidentally called up a full storm where he had meant only to bring a slight rain, and the precious vines had been damaged. Knowing the vines made his touch more powerful, more uncontrollable, not less.

Jerzy bit his lip. No. He knew more now. He understood what he was trying to do, and what the dangers were. Plus, he was using a spellwine of his own, one he had helped cultivate and harvest. He had pressed the crush and worked the mustus. He could control this.

The Guardian merely looked at him down that long stone muzzle, and Jerzy could almost see impossible wafts of air rising from its nostrils.

Some of Jerzy's confidence deflated. "What else am I to do, Guardian? Malech is busy with cellar work, there is nothing to be done in the fields except wait, and if I sit here and think about what may or may not be happening in the rest of the Lands, I will go mad."

The Guardian had no response to that. If Malech's words in the courtyard were true, if the spelled vision he had been given years ago had not been about the rose plague, but rather the illness they faced now, this creeping fear . . . then shouldn't they be doing something? Something more than waiting, and listening, and . . . more waiting?

"It keeps my hands and my thoughts occupied," he said again to the Guardian. The stone figure did not speak again, but curled its long narrow tail around its dog-sized body and rested its head on stone-clawed paws, watching as Jerzy picked up the vial once again. It was not approval, but the Guardian was not stopping him, either.

Left to his own thoughts, Jerzy acknowledged that there was more to it than he was admitting to the Guardian. That small taste of discovery he'd had with Giordan, the feel of the windspell in his blood, the oddly greenish fruit in his hands, in his mouth, had triggered something inside him, restless as the wind itself. Something that not even the firespells of House Malech could match. What happened on the ship merely proved his suspicion, that those vines had touched him more than should have been possible.

A slave was sold to the vintnery he was intended for. A Vineart became one with the vines he worked. Those were truths that had never been questioned, never doubted. There had been no reason to doubt them.

Master Malech was a healer; it was his very nature to make broken things whole. But the spellwines that grew for the House of Malech did not speak so loudly to Jerzy. The healing of flesh, the sparking of purifying fire, those spellwines touched him, gave him satisfaction to craft, yes, but carrying Giordan's work with him, remembering the moment in the workroom where he had watched the Vineart give a few delicate drops of blood to the mustus, to better bind it to his commands, shivered against his spine like the rising wind itself, and made his pulse race like . . . like the sail belling with a freshening breeze.

Jerzy should never have touched the windvines, should never have let their leaves brush against his skin. But he had, and he would never be the same. Magic brought slaves to where they belonged . . . but maybe

Mahault was right, and it wasn't that simple. Maybe, sometimes, there was some other place to be.

The thought rocked Jerzy back onto his heels, and he paused.

Tradition, order, they had kept the Lands Vin strong for two thousand years. Vineart Giordan had broken tradition in a handful of ways, and that had gotten him killed, but it also meant that his work had not entirely died with him. Jerzy had no access to his vines . . . but he had the mustus within him, the smell of the soil, the touch of their leaves and roots. He had heard the whisper of the weathervines, and they knew his name. Tradition tied him to healvines and firevines, as his master and his master's master worked . . . but the weathervines had spoken to him, although they were not his, and he could not let the knowledge of them die.

Jerzy's head hurt as though he were back under the blazing sun, assaulted by the endless cries of seabirds. His thoughts were too busy; he needed to calm them, to focus on the wines, not things he could not control.

He breathed in once, letting it go, letting the thoughts come and go, draining from him until his mind was clear and steady once again.

You are Vineart. The Guardian, neither supporting nor protesting.

Jerzy lifted the vial of weatherwine and poured it, slowly, into the cup that held an equal amount of heal-all, the most basic—and easily mutable—of Malech's spellwines. The more specific—melancholia, for example—the more specific and rigid the incantation, the less it would yield to later influences.

He tried, first, with a *vin magica* from the cellar, a deep red liquid he had helped craft the season before. It had not yet been given a specific incantation, and so he thought that it might be more malleable. But Giordan's incanted wine overwhelmed the *vina*, and the magic went out of them both like water quenching flame, leaving him with an odd-tasting *vin ordinaire.* Thinking it a matter of blending, the second time he added them together gradually, alternating small doses, but with the same result. It was odd; an alternating or joint pouring seemed the proper way to blend them, just as Malech did for fever purges, but . . .

Jerzy sat back and stared at his gathered tools, thinking hard. If he could use two *vinas*, prepared but not yet decanted, it might work, but he did not have access to any unspecified weathervine *vina*. If, however, he were to use two incanted wines, equal in all other respects, then it should work. The flagon he had bought was wind-rise, the most basic of Giordan's spells, and so he selected an equal measure of heal-all, the most basic of Master Malech's work.

Equal . . . but not crafted in the same way. Giordan had shared the secret of his craft: the weathervines were stubborn, and needed a sacrifice from the Vineart to bind them to his will.

Could it be that simple? No other spellwine was prepared that way, according to Giordan, and yet . . .

Jerzy picked up his knife and pricked the tip of his finger. There was no pain, the blade nicking a bit of flesh away easily, the bright red welling to the surface, so similar to the shade of an incanted firewine it nearly took his breath away.

Holding his blooded finger away, careful not to let the blood spill, he grasped the two flagons, one in each hand, and slowly, carefully, poured them in equal measure into a third, empty vessel. As the two spellwines merged, he tilted his injured hand so that the welling drop of blood fell downward, into the waiting vessel.

The drop hit the blending liquids, and the two spellwines swirled together as though an invisible finger stirred them, the way the river Ivy rippled when passing under a bridge, turning and turning around the immovable object.

He held his breath and waited, then lifted the cup toward his face, breathing in the scent of the liquid. It was . . . odd: familiar and yet unrecognizable. Stone and soil from two different locations, and a sour floral scent like a bloom turning brown. Not pleasant, but not off-putting, either. And the tingling sensation that alerted him to the presence of magic, the gentle, inexorable pressure in his chest, rising as the two *vinas* mingled and combined, the blood forcing them to do his bidding.

Jerzy took a deep breath and focused. Decantations were simple, if you knew what you were doing. Like riding a horse. Incanting, however, was more like breaking that horse to saddle, after it had run free all its life. Since an incantation, once specified, could not be stripped out of the wine, he needed to convince the two spells somehow to work together, to join their magic to a common end.

Others, non-Vinearts, thought that the decantation was the most important part. When Jerzy had been tasked to deliver spellwines, the first thing asked was, "How is it decanted?" In truth, it was the incantation that mattered. To take the wild potential of mustus and make it express your intent, to craft the intent so that it controlled the magic; that ability was what made a Vineart. All else was merely knowledge and training.

"Air and flesh combine, to give protection against harm." As he spoke, he visualized what he wanted the *vina* to do, asking it with as much force as he could gather to do this thing and only this thing.

The liquid shivered, still swirling, and then it stilled. The surface shimmered, as though glowing with its own reddish light, and Jerzy could sense something happening inside the cup, some change occurring in the spellwine. It was not quite the same change that he felt during an original incantation, though. This was deeper, heavier, building pressure like a storm about to break. Jerzy leaned forward, drawn by the sense of something tremendous happening, something new, and then he felt the cool, hard voice in his head again.

Run.

The Guardian's voice never raised or lowered, it did not change in tone or inflection, but there was something in that cool hard word pressing into his thoughts that did not allow Jerzy any chance to hesitate or question. Something had gone wrong.

Not bothering to put his tools away, thinking only to grab the flask of Giordan's weatherwine, he bolted off his stool, and out of the cellar, the Guardian a wingspan ahead of him, its heavy stone body moving through the air, not even bothering to flap its unneeded wings in its urgency. Jerzy slammed the heavy wooden door behind him and, driven by the Guardian's word, kept moving up the narrow stone stairs to the main level of the House.

"What rot chases you, boy?" Malech met him in the circular hall-way, coming out of his study, Detta hard on his heels. Then Malech's face changed from annoyance to concern as the Guardian's warning reached him as well. He grabbed the front of Jerzy's shirt and pulled him forward, his other arm shoving Detta backward, all three of them retreating back into Master Malech's study while the Guardian took up a defensive posture in front of the open door.

"What?" Detta started to ask, then subsided, clearly deciding that she could get answers after whatever had them so worried was dealt with.

"Master?" Jerzy had been braced for something to happen since the dragon had warned him, but there had been no blast, no thunder, no upswing of magic that could have been the cause of their flight.

"Hush, Jerzy," was all Malech said. "Listen."

The way he said it told Jerzy that his master wasn't talking about a sound that might be heard with his ears, and so he reached inside, instead, to where he sensed the vines whisper to him, where the Guard-ian's voice echoed. And there, quiet, almost hidden under the sound of his own heartbeat, he found it. Like the slither of a snake through ground cover, or the whisper of wind in the trees, it was soft and seem-ingly harmless . . . until the underlying tone rose into Jerzy's awareness, and he almost gagged.

Something terribly, terrifyingly deadly was filling the room where he had just been working. Something he had caused, or created.

I hold.

The cool words were as reassuring as its earlier one had been alarm-ing. The Guardian was containing whatever it was below them, within the room it had been born in.

"How long?" Jerzy asked, not sure if he was asking his master, or the dragon.

"Until it dissipates, hopefully." Malech's voice was thin, strained.

There was also, Jerzy noted with resignation, a sharp undercurrent of anger. Deserved—his actions had caused a danger of some sort to be unleashed within the House, and for that . . .

For that a slave would be killed, and no one would gainsay the judgment. Endangering the vineyard was the sole unforgivable act.

Jerzy did not think that Master Malech would kill him. But he did not doubt that there would be punishment. He held that thought, uncomfortable and yet reassuring; the order of the House restored. Detta, unable to sense what was happening, went back into the study and, with the faith of a lifetime of service, returned to the ledgers. Jerzy envied her that stoic calm; his own body was so tight, he thought the wrong word or movement might cause it all to come apart in a violent blast. Master Malech appeared to feel the same, still caught in his listening pose, his sharply pointed beard practically quivering with the intensity of his concentration.

And then it came, the blast that Jerzy had been braced for. Not a physical blast: the solid stone of the House barely trembled, and Detta merely paused as she sorted markers into piles. To Jerzy, it was as though a giant wind had tried to pick him up and shake him, and an equally powerful hand held him firmly in place, causing him to feel as though he were covered in bruises without having moved an inch. Then the blast moved beyond them, spreading out like ripples from a rock tossed into a stream, and was gone.

Clear.

Malech sighed, a long, tired sound; his narrow shoulders sagged, his bearded chin tilting down toward his chest.

"We are safe?" Detta asked, resuming her counting.

"We are. For the moment." Master Malech turned his cold blue stare at Jerzy, and even expecting it, Jerzy quailed at the anger in that look. "What rot have you been up to, boy?"

"WHAT WAS THAT?" A Washer lifted his head from his studies, his face alight with curiosity as a deep wail rose and fell through the hall of the

Colloquium. They were in the Library, where all sounds were muted, so the wail was particularly disturbing. Two students, their pale blue robes and shaved heads marking them as such, broke from their quietly intense debate over a passage and lifted their heads as well, to better listen and identify the noise, then looked toward the two Washers to see if a response was required.

"It is the alarum," his companion said, rising from his seat. He saw the students watching him and made a gesture with his hand, to indicate that they should continue with their studies. He replaced the protective cover over the age-delicate pages he had been reading, the purported journal of a contemporary of Sin Washer, and shook his head sadly. "The House of Malech has broken the seal we placed on them."

"So you were wrong, Brother Neth," the first Washer said, not without a tinge of malice.

"It appears," Neth agreed calmly, "that I was. Come."

The halls of the Colloquium were aware of the alarum—it was impossible to ignore—but most of the brothers they passed in the hall seemed to be doing exactly that, secure in the knowledge that someone somewhere else was dealing with the cause. That was as it should be, and Neth would not have wished for disorder, but a part of him wondered if that security, that arrogance, was not about to be sorely tested in the coming months.

He did not speak any of this to his brother Washer, sure that his thoughts would not be taken well by that particular worthy.

Still, the fear lingered, even as they arrived at the commons room to see three of their brothers already gathered there, and the discussion in full swing. The alarum still rose and fell, louder here than in the hushed sanctum of the Library or the tapestry-shrouded halls, and their voices rose to compete with it.

"It is proof!" Brother Roderick. He was hot-tempered but not unreasonable, normally, but the way his face was red-mottled suggested to Neth that he would not be swayed from his stance this time, would not be forced down from demanding that the boy and his master be punished, to set an example.

"It is proof of nothing!" Brother . . . Sin Washer, what was his name? Neth couldn't remember. The newcomer had been promoted only the season before, but that was no excuse. "We have no ideas what triggered the alarum," the nameless brother reminded them.

"Magic," Roderick said, in the tone of someone presenting the killing blow.

"And what else would you expect a Vineart to be doing—baking pies? Writing poetry?" Neth couldn't help himself; the words simply fell out of his mouth, causing his companion to snort in reluctant amusement.

Brother Ranklin came in on the heels of that retort, attended by an aide and followed by two other Washers, Omar and Matthias. The council of the Vineart apostasy was now fully, if not officially, convened.

"This was not crafting," Roderick protested. "This was—"

"What was it?" Brother Ranklin asked gently, disarming Roderick's frustration with his very presence. Ranklin was nearly ninety, and needed his aide's help to perform his daily physical functions, but his brain was as keen—and his tongue as sharp—as when he had taught most of the Washers in this room their first lessons.

"We do not know what it is." Neth stepped in, hoping to direct the conversation where he wished it to go. But gently, carefully. "That was what the seal was placed to identify—anything that we could not recognize. Anything that might indicate a deviance from Vineart tradition—and a path toward apostasy."

The rest of the Lands Vin might assume that Washers merely counseled and consoled. They did not need to know the vast amount of research accumulated over the centuries, the layers of information gathered . . . or the size of the spellwine cellar that lay underneath the Collegium grounds, filled with the work of the finest of Vinearts, including many spellwines now lost to the rest of the Vin Lands.

Most spellwines did not age well, their potency fading over the course of a year or more. Brother Adem, over a hundred years past, had found a way to enhance a spellwine so that it would retain its potency, so long as the bottle remained unopened. The Brotherhood kept this a secret, known only to a select few—many of them in this very room. Some were ordinary spells, the work of Vinearts dead and disappeared from the Lands—and some were terrible things, entire casks bought and stored merely to keep them from the grasp of others who could not be trusted with such power. The Brotherhood would use those spells if it were needed, with due consideration and lasting regret. Sin Washer had given unto the Washers the responsibility of maintaining the balance . . . and so they would. By whatever means available.

"You think Malech is crafting a new spellwine?" Matthias asked.

"Master Vineart Malech," Brother Ranklin said, correcting him sternly. "You will show him respect, even here."

The reprimanded Washer, a burly man in his mid-years, looked as abashed as the student he had once been, ducking his head and mumbling an apology.

"I do not believe that Master Malech is the source," Neth said. He had been the one to place the seal, so the others let him speak, even before Ranklin gestured for him to continue.

"It was my opinion that Master Malech acted as he did, sending his student beyond his House borders, out of concern for recent events and a need for more information. He now has that information, and knows that further incursions will not earn him anything other than trouble. More, he must know that we would not leave him entirely unguarded. No, he would not cause this sort of commotion."

"The boy, then? You questioned him, Neth. What is your take of the lad?"

This had all been in his report, but Ranklin often asked for second or third iterations, less for himself than to force the speaker to reconsider initial judgments. Therefore, Neth did not take offense, but answered carefully.

"He is young, headstrong, but not stupid, and not foolish. Master

Malech thinks highly of him, but has not in any way coddled or spoiled him. In an ordinary lifetime, Vineart-student Jerzy would have grown to be an unexceptional Vineart, crafting spellwines that would have profited both his House and the Vin Lands entire."

"And in this, unordinary lifetime?" Brother Omar hailed from the same desert lands as Master Malech, his skin nearly ebony to Malech's olive, but their elongated build and sharp features were otherwise similar.

"The boy has been exposed to the things we guard against. I believe he was an innocent, meaning no harm . . . but there is a reason Vinearts are limited to their own yards, and he has broken that. A blast of magic of this sort? Something new, unexpected? It bears the imprint of his hand, yes." Neth regretted that; he had liked what he had seen of the boy, liked what Brother Darian had reported back in Aleppan—even if Darian himself had not been charitable in his assessment—and felt the loss of the Vineart the boy would have become. But there was no other choice.

An apostate Vineart could not—would not—be allowed to live.

Chapter 9

he next morning, there was still a tension in the House that had nothing to do with the toxic fumes yet lingering in the lower workrooms. When questioned, the boy had admitted attempting to combine spellwines of two different Houses—not merely decanting them together, but attempting to reincant them!

Malech was not sure if he was more horrified by the idiocy or the arrogance of the attempt. While he calmed his temper, he set Jerzy to the task of airing out the space. If he had his way, the boy would have been doing it by hand, with one of the wooden fans Lil used in the kitchen, but that was not feasible. Instead, he had given the boy one of the weakest aetherwines they had, and told him to keep at it until the rooms were habitable again. Aetherwines were rare and expensive, and the thought of using it . . . still there was nothing to be done for it.

At best, the effort it would take to cleanse the air of all the poison would exhaust the boy to the point where he would not be able to even think of another such folly for at least a day.

By then, Malech hoped that he would have come up with a plan to deal with the inevitable repercussions of this disaster.

He is young.

"And stupid." All his hopes for the boy seemed rotted, now. Even if they were to survive their enemy's plans and Jerzy avoided the most dire of punishments from the Washers, which seemed unlikely now, he would never be allowed to come into his full power. Would never follow Malech in crafting the spellwines of this House. The Collegium would never allow it, not with that stain on his reputation.

He is frustrated. As you would be, hedged in such a manner.

It was unlike the Guardian to take a side, so much so that Malech stopped what he was doing to consider not what the dragon was saying, but what it wasn't saying.

"You think that I am at fault? For not constantly reminding him that the Washers would still be observing us, waiting for a sign that one of us was not . . ." He could not think of the word he wanted, and so settled for "obedient?"

Ser veh.

It took Malech a moment to identify the phrase. Ettonian, an older dialect, formal. "What was, continues." In this context, it suggested an air of inevitability, of fate set in motion.

"I don't believe in fate," Malech said irritably. "We make our own choices, and the various gods can keep up as best they will."

The Guardian had no response to that, but stared down at the Vineart. Fate—forecasting—had brought it into being. How could it not believe in it, as much as it could believe in anything?

"I hold no faith in fate," Malech said again, stubborn in the face of his own past, and then an idea glimmered in his mind. "But coincidence . . . that's a fruit I can work with."

There was a symmetry to it that appealed. He had called the boy off his search in order to show his innocence, and to protect them all from the Washers' ire. Now, to protect them again, he would send the boy back. What was the saying his master had used? "Once the cup was lifted, the draught must be drunk." He, Malech, had started this, merely by noticing things beyond his walls . . . and now he must finish it.

Jerzy'd had the right of it, originally; if they were to find the source of this rot, the origin of the attacks, the Washers would have a new target to throw themselves at. All other transgressions could be forgiven, after that. His House would be secured. Assuming they survived the battle, anyway. The thought was a grim one, but Malech had stood in the middle of a plague house, and come out whole. He would not flinch from this.

Reaching for a scrap of parchment and his inkpot, Malech dipped a pen, and began writing. The note was a quick one, and while he waited for the ink to dry, he withdrew a small vial from a small, hidden drawer in the desk. The identifying seal on the side was worn down to an unrecognizable scarring, but the color of the flask was unmistakable: that particular reddish clay was used only to make a particular flagon, and those flagons were used only to carry a particular spellwine—ones that required quiet-magic to properly decant.

Magewine. He had used it most recently to identify a legacy, the type of grape used, but it took its name from a more specific use: the ability to identify a particular Vineart's work—or to find the Vineart himself.

Working the stopper out carefully, he sniffed at the contents once, to make sure that the spellwine within had not turned. He had last used this vial months before, when they tested the flesh of the sea beast, and spellwines did not always age evenly. There was no off-note in the nose, however, so he hoped that it was still intact. There was, as always, only one way to know for certain.

Lightly blotting the ink to make sure it would not smear, Malech let a drop of the liquid fall onto his tongue, feeling the slightly acidic liquid burn the flesh. Unlike most spelllwines, it was not a pleasant sensation: the fruits this wine came from were harsh and bitter, less crafted than beaten into submission, and the taste showed the process. Anyone without quiet-magic would taste only a bitter, spoiled *vina* that would beg to be spat from the mouth.

When the wine had blended with the spittle on his tongue, leaving a cooling sensation behind, Malech picked up the scrap of paper and visualized the person he needed to read it.

"From page the words, words onto page," he instructed the magic, and then with a gentle breath, issued the command: "Go."

If the spell worked, they would be re-forming elsewhere, on something his target was looking at. If not, well, he had no way of knowing. He needed a second plan, in case that one failed.

"Guardian, call Detta in. I need to speak with her about Household matters." If the Washers did come again, the House needed to be prepared. He did not think they would harm the servants . . . but one of the forfeits of apostasy was the burning of the yards.

The thought gave him pause. Would they do so, if the convicted one was student, not master? Would his own reputation protect him and his lands?

He thought that the Washers would not dare risk destroying him as well, but the fact that he did not know was proof, if he needed it, of how far into chaos the world had already fallen.

If they did—would he allow it?

Was that—Washer against Vineart—what their enemy was hoping for? The thought darkened his brow. Land-lords in disarray was bad enough; bringing magic against religion would be the death knell for the Lands Vin, indeed.

"When Jerzy is done with his cleanup, perhaps I will send him out to the North Yard." In addition to keeping the boy busy and out of trouble, it seemed unlikely that their unknown enemy would be able to strike at him there, in one of Malech's oldest, best-established yards. More, if the Washers were on their way even now, they would come here first. That would buy him more time to consider his options.

Malech stared at the now-blank parchment in his hand. It had been scraped and reused so many times that the surface had taken on an almost translucent appearance. It was still useful, but not for much longer.

Ser veh.

He did not believe in fate, and he would not believe in omens. But you could not be a Vineart and fail to understand that all things had their seasons, and even order occasionally fails in the face of disaster.

"Not in my lifetime, Sin Washer," he asked, not even aware that he was speaking the words out loud. "I beg you, not in my lifetime."

"It stinks down here."

Jerzy paused, the cup of aetherwine half empty in his hand and a headache throbbing across his forehead.

"I had noticed that," he said, irritated. The smell was less than it had been, and nowhere near the deadly levels his spell-attempt had first created, but Lil's face was scrunched up in an expression of distaste, and she had taken her red kerchief off her hair and was holding it over her mouth and nose, so he thought he might merely have gotten used to the worst of it, in the time he had been down here.

A full day, and everything still stank. It would take at least another day to make the rooms usable again, if that. And neither Master Malech nor the Guardian would speak to him until it was done.

"What did you do?" Lil asked, not coming any farther into the rooms. It wasn't merely the smell; the House-servants were not allowed down here, unless specifically summoned—or sent. "Master Malech is still furious. He yelled at Detta, just now. I heard it even in the courtyard."

"You did not." The walls of the House were thick stone, the same sort that the Guardian was carved from. Sound did not travel easily through them, and the door to Malech's study was always closed.

"I did. That's why I came downstairs. I figured it would be safer here. Although maybe not. What did you do, Jerzy?"

For a moment, indignation held Jerzy speechless. For all that she was cook now, Lil was only a House-servant, not a Vineart. She had no right to be here, no right to be asking questions.

The indignation passed, driven by a weary sort of resignation. Lil had been senior to most of the kitchen children when Jerzy was first taken from the sleep house, had seen him stumble and fall, and succeed. She was asking not to mock him, or to take advantage of him, but because she was curious. Because whatever happened in the House, to the Vinearts, happened to her as well.

Survival alone did not give her the right to question him. But it wasn't merely survival behind her worried expression. She was concerned . . . for him.

Jerzy didn't understand it. But he had seen it before, on Malech's face when Jerzy had undergone his testing with the mustus; in the way Ao had half carried him out of the meeting hall, when they escaped from Aleppan; the time Mahl had asked him if he would be all right, without spellwines.

Lil cared.

Like the feeling of loneliness he got when he thought of Ao or Mahl, this made him uneasy, so he shrugged and turned back to the work at hand.

She waited. Lil was patient; she could set a roast to cook and not touch it before it was completely done, or prepare bread dough and then leave it to rise perfectly. Waiting out a reluctant boy was nothing.

"I shouldn't be here," he burst out suddenly. Talking to Lil wasn't the same as Mahl, or Ao—or even the Guardian. But she was all he had, right then, and he found that the stoic silence he had perfected in the sleep house no longer satisfied.

"What? Where else would you be? Oh, you'd rather be in the field? I suppose I can understand that. It would certainly smell better."

"No. Not . . ." Jerzy shook his head and lifted the cup to his mouth, taking a small draught of the spellwine into his mouth to keep from having to respond further. It wasn't the same. This wasn't Ao, or Mahl. Lil didn't understand. She didn't know what was happening. She didn't know he was a danger to the House. Not the Washers—Master Malech could handle them. But their enemy . . . nothing had happened since that attack on the road; he had no reason to believe that he would be a target here, through the Guardian's protections, but . . .

Once he had decanted half a dozen times, the words were no longer needed; like the candle-lighting quiet-magic his master used with merely a twitch of his fingers, Jerzy could raise a breeze merely by exhaling with *vin magica*–scented breath.

A faint, fresh wind started around Jerzy, swirling around to gather the lingering spell-fumes and carry them out the door. Lil gagged as they passed her, moving aside to avoid the smell, the kerchief clutched to her face. "It's safer upstairs, even with the yelling," she managed, and fled.

Safer. What was safe? Jerzy had thought he knew, once: safe was not being noticed by the overseer. Safe was doing everything perfectly, so that Master Malech would keep him. Safe was running, so that the Washers could not take him. Safe was returning home . . .

None of those things were safe, anymore.

Lil didn't understand. Detta couldn't understand, no matter how she fussed over his needing new clothing, or how dark a red his hair was becoming. Master Malech understood, but he didn't *know*.

The thought stopped him, the spell-wind swirling and fading as the decantation wore out and the air became still again. Master Malech did not know. *He* had been the one sent out, sent into the world, not his master. *He* was the one who had worked the *vina* of another Vineart, had crossed the lines Sin Washer had laid down, had felt the taint of an unnatural magic against his thoughts. *He* was the one who could not fit himself back into the comfortable Jerzy-shaped space of House Malech.

The frustration he had been feeling surged again, until even the familiar, comforting sense of spellwines and *vina* casked and waiting around him failed to soothe it. Like a toothache or a cramp, only the feeling spread from his chest out toward his knees and elbows, his fingers tingling, the headache from the noxious fumes twisting his thoughts into puzzling, tantalizing shapes he could neither understand, nor forget.

He felt prickly and uncomfortable, twisting inside his own skin.

"Guardian?"

The cool, hard awareness of the stone dragon was in his head, immediately.

"What's happening to me?"

The Guardian did not respond, but the weight of its presence grew stronger, as though trying to enfold Jerzy within itself, giving him something familiar, something reassuring to lean against.

For the moment, it was enough, and he could feel his nerves settle back down, regaining the cool, measured temperament required of a Vineart.

Finish the cleaning, the Guardian told him. *Help will come.*

WHEN THE WORKROOM was usable again, Master Malech sent Jerzy off to check on progress at one of the older, more established yards. The trip was blessedly boring, and he returned four days later, falling into bed too exhausted to eat, waking too exhausted to wash.

The next morning, rather than setting him to a new task, or picking up their lessons, Master Malech sent him out to work alongside the slaves, weeding. At another time it might have seemed like punishment, and Jerzy knew that a few months ago he would have resented the mindless, muscle-aching work, wanting only to learn more of magic.

Master Malech was wiser than he, though. The feel of the soil under his fingers, the touch of the leaves against his skin and hair as he moved among the vines, calmed him even more than the Guardian's cool presence in his mind. The rote activities, the silent synchronized movements of the slaves, even the occasional roughhousing of the younger ones and the irritated shouts of the overseer as he cracked his whip to bring them back to order, all these were better than a healspell to his exhaustion and worries.

He was a Vineart. Whatever tension, whatever restlessness he felt now, it was only due to the uncertainty . . . this was where he belonged. He wanted nothing else.

He believed that, until he heard Ao's voice drifting through the vines. "Ho the House!"

Help will come. The echo of the Guardian's promise, days before. Jerzy had thought the dragon meant . . .

Jerzy didn't care what he had thought. The surge of pleasure at hearing Ao's voice caught him by surprise, as did the urge to abandon the weeding and run to greet the trader.

You never abandoned the job before it was finished, not unless the overseer told you to do so. Jerzy was not a slave any longer; as Vineart he had the right to tell the overseer what to do, and only Malech could reprimand him. And yet his training had fallen over him like a comfortable blanket, and it was only with difficulty that he walked away, handing his wooden hoe to a slave and brushing the dirt off his hands, painfully aware that his shirt was soaked in sweat and his feet were bare and dirty. Hardly the way he should appear, to welcome guests to the House of Malech, but the thought of avoiding Ao long enough to make himself presentable was not one he wanted to consider, either.

All this went through his mind as he walked up to the cobble-paved road, where two horses were being led off by a slave barely tall enough to reach their reins. Ao and Kaïnam were standing by the side of the road, two horses waiting beside them, heads low and sides dark with sweat. They had come in a hurry, then. But how? And why?

Master Malech had already responded to their hail, dressed casually, with the laces of his shirt untied, his hair tangled as though he had been pulling at the brown-gray strands again while he worked. Seeing that, Jerzy felt a little better about the state of his own clothing, and the dirt ground under his nails.

"Ah, Jerzy. We have guests."

Master Malech did not look annoyed at the interruption. Jerzy wasn't certain—his master was difficult to read, even now—but he thought the Vineart looked satisfied, in fact.

"Ho, Jerzy!" Ao looked much the same as he had when they last parted, although his clothing was of a flashier sort: a pale blue smock over green pantaloons that reminded Jerzy of Mil'ar Cai and his oddly flamboyant attire. Kaïnam was dressed more soberly, but the cut of his jacket, and the blue and green beading on it, indicated a similar source. Clearly, they had been to Caul. And now were here?

"Thank you for responding to a stranger's summons," Malech was saying as Jerzy joined them.

"Jerzy's master could not be a stranger," Kaï said.

"We were already on our way back," Ao added. "The messenger caught us just before we set sail, so we"—and here Ao paused, grinning a little in memory—"we put on a little extra speed."

Messenger? Master Malech had summoned them? Jerzy was puzzled, and then hurt that his master had not said anything to him. Clearly, the Guardian had known . . .

Jerzy cut that thought off before it could grow into self-pity. The Guardian knew everything; that was why it was the Guardian. And Malech was still Master Vineart Malech, *his* master, and Jerzy had best never forget that.

Instead, he turned to Ao, masking his hurt with a welcoming smile, and grasping his friend's arm in greeting. "Extra speed?" That could mean only one thing, when sailing. "If your people hear how much magic you have been using," he scolded, "they'll never take you back."

"So we won't tell them." But Ao looked briefly uncomfortable at the reminder of yet another barrier between himself and his clan. The Eastern Wind trading clan was perfectly willing to carry and sell spellwines, but they scorned the use of any magic for themselves, claiming it might injure their reputation for honest, unbiased negotiation.

"I shall take full responsibility, Trader Ao," Kaïnam said, oddly formal. "As your patron, you could do nothing but heed my desires."

Patron? Jerzy couldn't wait to hear the story behind that, as the last he knew, Kaïnam had cast himself off from his family and title, choosing to go against his father the prince's orders. Had Kaï suddenly come into some new wealth since they parted? Jerzy supposed it was possible. . . .

"Hah," Ao said. "The *Vine's Heart* is as much mine as yours, lordling!"

"The . . . what?"

Even Malech looked taken aback.

"Our ship," Kaïnam explained, his normally solemn expression breaking enough to show a hint of humor, although Jerzy thought you needed to know the man to see it through his normal solemn mien. "After discovering what we discovered—more of which, later—Trader Ao and I were able to . . . combine our skills and use our various connections to acquire a Caulish ship for our travels. The name seemed appropriate, all things considered"

"She's a sweet thing, Jer," Ao said enthusiastically. "You'll love her."

Jerzy's head hurt. He didn't love any ship. Why was the name appropriate? Why were they here?

"All of you, come," Master Malech said. His stern face looked out over the vineyard, toward the south and then back up the slope to the east, as though expecting something to sweep down from the skies, or crash down from the forested fringe of the low hills bordering his lands. "Come inside, where we may speak freely."

The four of them walked up the path, under the leafed archway. As usual, Jerzy felt the cool touch that he could now identify as the Guardian as he walked back onto the House grounds proper, but neither Ao nor Kaï seemed to notice anything out of the ordinary.

The great doors stood open, as they had when Jerzy first saw them, and he was pleased to note that Ao, at least, was as impressed by the House itself as he had been. Not to the standards of Aleppan, perhaps, or Kaï's home, but the golden stone façade, and the narrow, colored-glass windows at either side of the door, had a beauty of their own, and Jerzy felt a twitch of pride.

Inside the hallway, Detta waited for them. "Master Malech. Two more joining us for the eve meal?"

"In my study, I believe," Master Malech said, and the House-keeper nodded, as though this were the normal turn of events.

Jerzy was still trying to comprehend what had obviously happened. Master Malech had sent a message. To Kaï and Ao. Who had come, who had already been on their way, with a ship named the *Vine's Heart*.

The confusion and worry chewed at him, even more than curiosity, but years of obedience kept any of it from showing on his face as he made a gesture with his right hand to indicate that the newcomers should follow Master Malech to his study.

"Young Jerzy." Detta held up a hand to stop him, when he would have followed them into the Master's wing of the House. "I presume the gentles will be staying, at least the one night. Shall I place them in your chamber?"

The House was not set up for overnight guests; the few who had been there before had been Master Malech's guests, and were settled in the Master's rooms, and Mahault, who had slept in Detta's chamber. The Washers had set up camp outside, the battle lines drawn even then. These visitors . . . no matter that Malech had summoned them, Detta was saying that he, Jerzy, was their host.

His room was large enough to add two mattresses without trouble, although Jerzy suspected he would end up giving his bed to Kaï. "That would be best," he agreed. The only other option would be to move them into one of the kitchen children's rooms on the other side of the House, or set them to sleeping out of doors. The Washers had come with their own encampment; he had seen no such equipment on the horses that had been led away earlier.

"And Ao does not drink *vin ordinaire*," he added. "If we have a cask of ale, somewhere?" He remembered seeing Roan drinking a tankard of it not too long before, but had never thought to inquire. His one encounter with the brown, surprisingly filling liquid had not ended well.

"As you say," Detta agreed, and she left him, heading under the main staircase to the hallway that led to the kitchen, no doubt to issue Lil her changed orders for dinner.

Jerzy stared after her, his thoughts still in an uproar, then headed in the other direction, toward Master Malech's study.

"THE CAULIC NATION is in uproar. Their king is demanding more and more ships be built, taxing the abilities of their shipwrights and depleting their forests at a terrible rate."

Kaïnam was standing before Malech's desk, tall and elegant even in his gaudy Caulic attire, his hands behind his back, his voice clear as a soldier giving his report. Three glasses of a fine *vin ordinaire* and a polished wooden mug of something that met with Ao's satisfied approval were half consumed, the others listening intently to the princeling's report. Even Ao, who had been there while they gathered the intelligence, seemed fascinated.

"He seems convinced that there is a plot in the wind, steered by Vinearts, to invade Caul, depose him, and take his daughter as the prize for whoever would hold the throne next."

Malech's eyes narrowed at the suggestion that Vinearts might do such a thing, but merely asked, "How old is the girl?"

"Twelve. Young still, but fair game if such a plot were in truth in play."

"You were not able to have an audience with this king?"

Ao shook his head. "I have not the standing, Trade-wise, and Kaïnam . . . we thought it best not to identify him, at that point. Not with so much suspicion running wild."

Jerzy frowned, remembering the look in the maiar of Aleppan's eyes, the feel of the tainted aide who had whispered poisoned thoughts into his ears. If they had been able to see the man, would they have been able to tell if he was so influenced? Would anyone in the court be able to recognize a spell, if it had been cast?

One of Master Malech's lessons: there were no vineyards at all in Caul; although the First Growth had thrived there once, none of its broken variants had survived, and no Vineart had ever succeeded in replanting—none tried, now. Caul now took pride in allowing no vine-magic on their lands, relying only on their mighty navy to keep the island safe. They claimed that no spells were allowed within those protected walls, and had executed those who thought to break the ban without compunction.

If there was no magic being used . . . "Could the Caulic king be faking his madness, using it as some sort of plot of his own?"

Malech raised an eyebrow at the suggestion, while Kaïnam looked at Ao, who shook his head.

"Interesting—you're getting sneaky, Jer—but I think not," Ao said. "Our informant believes that his king is truly frightened—or mad, and not the madness of a fox. The fear seeps through all levels, until trade is affected. The gossip in the taverns and port offices is that people are hoarding, not buying or selling, and the only guilds doing well are shipwrights and fight masters."

"That was my conclusion as well," Kaï said, turning back to Malech. "Merely mentioning the fleet that came to Atakus made the people I approached—men with knowledge of the sea, and ships—pull into their shells and refuse to speak further. They are afraid—and hiding something."

Jerzy picked up a goblet and ran his finger along its lip, still frowning. What they were describing was similar to what he had overhead beginning in the streets of Aleppan as well. Fear: beginning at the head of state and slithering its way down through the trader clans and local merchants. Jerzy might not know battles or politics, but he knew rot when he saw it.

Kaï moved his jaw as though he were chewing on something. "It was odd, actually. The man we spoke with is accustomed to being privy to his king's mind . . . he would not have spoken to us at all if he were not deeply concerned at being shut out. The king's military advisors have all but pushed him away, and made decisions he cannot fathom. I could find no one who would speak of why the ships had been out there, save that the king had sent them, prepared to do battle with whatever they found."

"It would make sense for them to wish to discover what had become of Atakus—but not to approach us the way they did, under the cover of a storm, and warships with them. That has the feel of a long prod from another hand, and it may be that something—or someone—has indeed driven the king mad."

"Like Aleppan," Jerzy said, and Ao, the only other who had been there, nodded, his round face as somber as Jerzy had ever seen it.

"You think he, too, has a whisperer in his ear? But why?" Malech seemed perplexed. "I could see them as the aggressor, for it has always been their wish to find some way to rise in power over the Vin Lands, but what use would there be to destabilizing Caul? How would that serve someone who sought to cause us harm?"

"To gain control of their navy," Ao suggested. "That is all I can think of—that is their sole source of wealth: their sailors and captains, and the groves of hardwood trees they use to make their ships."

"Sailors, and fighters," Kaï said. "Their navy could be a valiant addition to another force, if someone were to bring them to heel."

"Unlikely," Ao said, shaking his head. "As much as the factions brangle over internal matters, they would have no reason to follow an outsider, and it is a matter of pride to them that they cannot be bought."

"Not all purchases are paid for in coin," Malech said quietly. "But every man has a price."

"Someone set them against my country," Kaïnam insisted, his voice tight. "Someone warned them, even as my father was goaded into his ill-fated decision. That sort of manipulation does not occur quickly, or without long-term planning—and a goal in mind. Caul is involved, somehow."

Jerzy listened to the discussion going back and forth, and frowned. Ao was well traveled, Master Malech wise, and Kaï knew the ways of politics. Anything he might see or say would surely be without use. And yet . . .

He heard them discussing the situation in Caul, but he wasn't truly listening. Instead, he followed the niggling thought in his mind, like reaching for a root deep in the graveled soil.

What they were describing was familiar, if he stripped away the men and the ships, the causes or intents. Rot. Spreading from the leaf to root. The discoloration on a leaf was a warning signal: when the rot reached the root, it was too late. Caul and Atakus, the sea serpents' attacks, the rumors and fear sown in Aleppan and elsewhere, they were all discolored leaves. But why would someone intentionally give a warning sign, before . . .

"The best way to fight an enemy is to never fight him." It was something Cai used to say, usually after Jerzy had just landed facedown in the dirt, tripping over the weight of his own cudgel rather than any blow Cai had landed.

"What?"

Jerzy tried to recover, not having intended to speak his thoughts out loud. "It's a Caulic saying. Or one that Cai—my weapons master," he explained to the other two, "used to say."

"A Vineart had a weapons master?" Kaï looked slightly scandalized.

"It seemed a good idea at the time," the Master Vineart said without apology. Cai had told Jerzy it was to teach him to move like a Vineart, not a slave; to learn to defend himself when he left his master's lands. In light of Malech's revelations about the Guardian and the foreseer wine, Jerzy suddenly heard those words with a different, darker meaning.

"What are you thinking, Jerzy?" Ao asked.

"I don't know." He was no strategist, no man of power, to be thinking this way. He tended vines, not alliances. And yet . . . "Someone wishes to injure the Lands Vin. Only it seems to me that every strike we have seen is made not to be a killing blow, but . . ." His thoughts tangled together, and he couldn't seem to reach what he wanted to say. "But to cause another strike to fall. As though our enemy is not attacking, but leading us somewhere . . ." His thoughts were fractured but coming together as he worried at the memories.

"Cai had me do an exercise, over and over again, where he would attack with the staff, and I had to duck."

"Standard enough," Kaïnam said, nodding his understanding. "I learned similar parrying moves myself."

"But the purpose was not to evade the blows," Jerzy explained, standing and pacing as he spoke. "I was to duck under the blows, under and in, so that when we finished the pattern I was inside Cai's strike zone, and he was backed up against a wall or cliff. The goal was not to attack, but to create a situation where my opponent could not win."

"You think that we are being pushed to a cliff. All of us." Malech didn't sound disbelieving, but his voice did not sound convinced, either. His master thought like a Vineart, of root and stem, crush and magic, a direct line of cause and effect. This . . . this was not direct. "Again, boy: To what purpose? You can't—"

"Yes. It makes sense," Kaïnam said, nodding, overriding Malech's question in a way only a princeling would dare. He picked up Jerzy's vague thought and played it out, before Malech could respond to the insult. "To make us chase our tails, accusing each other, while the true enemy is . . . where?

"Where is a map?"

Malech pushed one of the scrolls forward, and Kaïnam unrolled it carefully, using the goblets and tankard to hold the edges down. "Here, my home. And there, Aleppan. And here, northwest of Tétouan, where the slaves went missing. Where else have attacks on Vinearts or vineyards been reported?"

"Vineart Sionio, in Iaja," Malech said, placing a drop of *vin ordinaire* on the map so that it stained the spot. "Also, Armanica, along the Great River." Another drop. "Perhaps others, we don't know. Some, like the Vineart outside Tétouan, may have disappeared and no one thought to report it. Who would they report it to? We are not a guild, not a merchants' consortium, to be counted off and remarked upon."

"Ducking under blows," Kaïnam said softly. "And then pushing . . . men of power misled and their power abused here, and here." Kaï touched places on the map, and Malech placed drops there as well. "Push, and duck. Duck, and push.

"A giant net, Master Malech. Do you see?"

Malech stared at the map, Ao and Jerzy trying to see what it was that had captured Kaïnam's fascination.

"Think of it. Vinearts—your fields attacked, your honor smeared. The lords—their people attacked, confidence in their advisors undermined. The common folk—unnerved by what they see as madness in their leaders, afraid that Vinearts might not be trustworthy . . . Push, and duck, and push. The net closes, and chaos falls."

Chaos echoed in Jerzy's mind, the feel of the Guardian's voice heavy in his memory. The Guardian had said that, too.

"And here," Jerzy said, leaning over to mark a point, "where the serpents were sighted."

Kaïnam jerked back, as though surprised. "Serpents?"

Jerzy had told Ao and Mahault of his earlier encounters, but the matter had never come up with Kaïnam.

"Sea beasts," Malech said. "Two, perhaps three, no more that have been reported. Creatures born of magic, to strike fear . . . yes. Another push."

"To what purpose?" Ao asked, looking at each of them in turn, his round face bewildered, trying to put together the pieces in an order that made sense. "What profit could come out of destroying the natural balance of things?"

Kaïnam rocked back on his heels, crossing his arms over his chest. "There are three sides to every balance," he said with the air of a man about to finalize an Agreement. "Three points in Sin Washer's Commands." One finger. "Vinearts." A second finger. "Men of power."

"And Washers," Malech finished, the words coming out on a quiet exhale, even as Kaïnam held up a third finger. "The one side that has not been attacked."

"That's not possible." Ao's objection was instinctive, the result of a lifetime of hearing Washer preachings, of being told that they were the balance-keepers, the easers of pain, the bringers of solace, in Sin Washer's name. "They could not be doing this."

Jerzy looked to his master, but said nothing.

"Everything is possible," Kaï said, his mouth set in a grim line. "Especially if the lure of power becomes too much to resist. Who else moves so freely throughout every land, has access to every House and council, is trusted without question?"

"They accuse Vinearts, to deflect suspicion from themselves?" Malech was not asking a question, but testing the idea out loud, his head tilted in a way that made Jerzy think he was listening to a response from the Guardian.

"But to what purpose?" Ao was still struggling to understand the logic. "They cannot rule, it is against . . . the people would . . ."

"The people would welcome them, if they were seen as taking down a corrupt lord," Kaïnam said with assurance.

"And magic? Washers, to work the vineyards?" Malech had followed Kaïnam's thought all the way to the end and was now shaking his head. "No. It takes more than knowledge of growing things to be a Vineart. It is impossible that they take over the vineyards for themselves."

"What if they had an ally?" Ao asked, his voice tentative, as though expecting to be slapped down for the suggestion.

"That . . . that would explain much, yes. A Vineart, unsatisfied with the Commands, with the way things have been. Hungry for more . . ." Jerzy saw his master's eyes close, his face creasing with age and sorrow. "It should be unthinkable, but the facts tell us otherwise. A Vineart, thus dissatisfied, could be bought with the promise of more land, more power . . ."

Master Malech stopped himself, slapping his hand down flat on the desk to make a sharp, hard noise. "All conjecture. It brings us back to where we were before: the need to find the source of the magic, to pull it by the roots, and stop its growth. Then and only then we can worry about the hands directing it."

"That was where we were heading when we received your summons," Kai said. "To continue my original plan."

"Your plan?" Ao snorted, his shock seemingly broken, and a continuing argument revived. "You keep saying that like it's truth. That was Jer's plan. He was the one who could scent the magic. Without him we were just going to point our sails half-winded and hope for the best." He grinned at Jerzy, for that moment all care and confusion gone. "We were coming back for you. With what we'd learned, we figured you'd want a share in the journey. Even if it was on water."

"Yes, you must take Jerzy with you," Malech said. "I had meant only to share with you our findings and set you to a goal, but this changes everything."

Kaïnam seemed surprised but pleased, while Ao's round face split with a relieved grin, his usual impassive trader's expression abandoned for the moment.

"Master?" Jerzy felt a twist in his chest, both excited to be set on the trail again, and wounded that his master was, to all appearances, rejecting him. "I know I failed, but . . ."

"Jerzy. Listen to me." Malech came around the desk and stood in front of Jerzy, closing them off to the others by dint of turning his back to the outsiders. They took the hint, and busied themselves over the map, discussing ports and the need for supplies. Malech's hand closed on Jerzy's shoulder, those long, strong fingers pressing into the skin, down to the bone, to make sure his student paid attention. "We can protect ourselves from this enemy—for now. But you have already been marked, and if what we suspect is true, if the Washers themselves are involved . . . you must disappear, boy. They must not find you. Do you understand me?"

Jerzy didn't. All he could understand was that he was being sent away from the vineyards. Not only his own, but any others', too. No hands in the soil; instead, sent away on a ship, to spend more time heaving his guts over the side into the deep briny waters, at risk for sea beasts and firespouts, Washers looking to burn him, and some unknown foe who might kill him out of hand . . . or worse.

So why did he feel this excitement growing in him, as though he had been granted a terrible, unexpected gift?

His earlier thoughts came back to him, not as restlessness but comprehension. He was the one who could recognize the taint. He would be Master Malech's hoe, to clear the soil, untangle the roots, and find the rot. Then Master Malech would be able to destroy it.

The thought—that it was not all dependent upon him, that Master

Malech must have a plan—should have made it easier to breathe, but it didn't.

"The three of us, alone?"

"Four of us, don't you mean?" a voice asked, somewhere between amused and annoyed.

They all turned to see Mahault standing in the doorway of the study, her blond hair bound up in a coil behind her head, her dark brown riding dress splattered with mud and dust, and a grim look on her normally calm face. "Or did you think that you were going without me?"

"I DID NOT summon you," Malech said, staring at the unexpected arrival. Off to the side, Ao made a face, preparing for the blast of annoyance Mahault could unleash when she felt slighted, but she merely stepped forward into the study, as gracious as her lady-mother back in Aleppan, even clearly road worn and tired. "No, you did not. And yet here I am."

You need her.

From the annoyed glare Malech gave the dragon, resting in its usual spot over the mantel, Jerzy assumed that his master had heard the comment as well.

"You? You called her back? How?" Master Malech was not pleased.

The boy. The girl. The man. They are all part of this.

The Guardian raised its head then, making Kaï, who had turned to see who Malech was addressing, take a startled step backward and raise his hands for Sin Washer's blessing in shock.

"Blood and vine," Ao swore, his eyes going round and his jaw dropping open. "That's not alive, is it? Jer, is that magic?"

Only Mahault seemed unconcerned by the stone carving that was leaning forward now, its gray stone neck dropping below the mantel so that it could keep its elongated snout even with Master Malech's gaze. It made sense, if she had somehow heard the Guardian's voice, to bring her back . . .

The Guardian was linked to every member of the House, but

none beyond its walls, and he spoke only to Malech and Jerzy. Master Malech's question was a valid one. How had it reached Mahault, days' travel away? And yet, clearly, the Guardian *had* done it, even as Malech was summoning the others.

From the look on Malech's face, he was thinking the same thing: there were skills the Guardian had that they had not known about. Unlike Jerzy, he was not pleased by that.

I know only what I must do to protect the House.

Mahault was unaware of what was happening, silently, among the three members of the House of Malech. "Weren't we all in this together?" she asked Jerzy and Ao. The trader dropped his gaze, shuffling his feet in discomfort. When her cool, assessing gaze met Jerzy's, he could only shrug helplessly. "You were the one who said that you had to leave," he said. "And it was only just decided that I should go. I didn't know anything about it, either." Ao and Kaï, and even Mahl, could choose where to go and what to do. He was bound to his master's decisions.

The explanation seemed to sooth her temper somewhat, and she turned then to Master Malech. "You and House-keeper Detta gave me the chance to study, and for that I am grateful. And yet the past weeks have shown me that there is something else I must do, before I can think to claim a solitaire's sigil, no matter who vouches for me. My father's actions have darkened our family honor, and though he may have cast me out, I . . . I cannot simply walk away."

Kaïnam nodded as though he approved of her words, striking so close to his own reasons, but Master Malech's face was clouded, as though he would refuse her.

"Master." Jerzy stepped forward, finding the courage in the Guardian's cool voice to intervene. "Master, if the Guardian was created, as you say, for the reasons you say"—he carefully avoided specifics, where the others could hear—"then we must trust it. It works only to protect us. So it believes that Mahl is needed, to protect me."

The Vineart looked away from the Guardian, down to Jerzy, and seemed suddenly to realize that his student could now look him in the eye without stretching. His thin lips did not quite curve into a smile, but there was a softening to them that told Jerzy all was, if not well, then accepted.

Mahault would travel with them.

TWO DAYS AFTER Malech broke the news to her, Detta was still unhappy.

"I do not like this," she muttered as she looked down the wooden table when they were gathered for the morning meal, on the day they were to depart. "I do not like this at all."

"What's not to like?" Ao asked flippantly, even as he was taking a bowl and sniffing at the steam rising from the porridge in appreciation. "We shall all die horribly, and have long laments made about our grue-some fates."

Detta hit Ao on the side of his head with the back of her meaty hand, hard enough to ring his ears but not actually hurt him. He merely grinned and sat down, spooning the porridge into his mouth. Their first meeting, Detta had taken the trader's measure, and now treated him like one of her own kitchen children—a rough, affectionate abuse he seemed to thrive on.

Kaï shook his head, as though despairing of Ao's behavior, while Ma-hault merely drank her tai as though she liked it, and finished braiding her hair back into the coil at the back of her head. They were all dressed for traveling in dark-colored trou and jerkins—even Mahl, although that was another thing Detta clearly did not like. Mahl was not a soli-taire yet, that she should mimic their attire.

Unknown to Detta, there was a short but deadly looking sword in a battered scabbard, tucked in among Mahl's belongings, warning to any who might approach that she was not to be trifled with. From watching her move during her exercises, Jerzy had no doubt that she knew how to use it. Detta might not like it, the solitaire might not formally claim her, but Mahault was not a pampered maiar's daughter any longer.

She was not the only one of their party bearing weapons. Kaïnam bore a fine-edged sword equal to his birthrank, and Jerzy, the memory of the attempted attack in Tétouan still clear, had a newly cut cudgel, magic-shaped and polished, to make a comforting weight in his hands. Only Ao was unarmed, but Jerzy suspected that the trader could have taught Cai himself a few lessons in quick moves and tumbling escapes, if need be.

They had maps, and supplies, and were well rested and well fed. They were ready, as much as they would ever be. The impossibility of their undertaking, to track the source of the taint and uncover it for all to see, seemed at once perfectly reasonable, and utterly impossible.

Jerzy dealt with it, as he always did, by focusing on the immediate needs. This morning he had come down early, leaving the others snoring—Kaï, as predicted, taking up the single bed—and broke his fast alone. By the time Ao, the last riser, had stumbled downstairs to join them, Jerzy had cleaned his platter and finished his cup of warmed *vina*. The banter at the table made him want to linger, but there was no reason to delay, and many reasons to hurry.

The five of them had spent much of the night before going over maps one last time, with Master Malech and Jerzy updating each as best they could with the names and regions of the Vinearts in the areas they might be traveling through, while Detta and Lil finished preparing everything Jerzy might need to bring with him, and whatever extras they decided the others needed, as well.

After a while, Malech had left the four of them to their discussions, Kaï marking down the political boundaries as best he recalled them, and returned in a bit with a large wooden box floating behind him, a handspan off the ground.

"You will need supplies," was all he had said. Jerzy, who could feel the soft hum of the magics within the crate, nodded solemnly. Healwines, to be certain, and firewines, so that they need not worry about open flames on the ship. And other things, no doubt, from Master Malech's storeroom.

Ao had been openly calculating the value of a crate that size, but Kaïnam stepped forward and made a deep bow to both Vinearts. "You honor us."

"You named your ship the *Vine's Heart*," Malech said, his voice softer than Jerzy could ever remember it sounding. "Should that heart not be well strengthened?"

Now, while the others filled their bellies, Jerzy went out to make sure that the crate was securely loaded and fastened, as befitted a Vineart traveling with spellwines. The horses the three others had come in on were saddled and waiting, plus the brown mare Jerzy had ridden, so many months ago, to investigate that first sighting of the sea beast. He went forward and patted her neck, pleased to see her. She had been steady and loyal even when frightened, and if he had to spend an entire day on horseback, she was better than most. He only hoped that he could keep her alive until it was time to board their new vessel. The thought—the memory—of that unexpected attack on the road made him shudder.

You are frightened.

"Terrified."

The mare flicked one long ear at him, as though to ask who he was speaking to, but did not seem at all alarmed when the Guardian flew down from the roof and landed, heavily, on the back of the cart where the crate, and their other supplies, were loaded.

Be careful. Trust those who should be trusted. None other.

Ao and Mahl and Kaïnam, obviously. But the feel of the Guardian's words implied future, not present. "How will I know who those people are?"

You will know.

If the Guardian meant to be reassuring, it failed, miserably.

Chapter 10

"*There she is.*"

Ao's voice was thick with pride, but Jerzy could not blame him. Unlike the small ship they had traded for in Corguruth, or even Kaïnam's sleek *Green Wave*, the *Vine's Heart* was longer and deeper hulled, better suited for the open seas, with two masts bearing angled sails that looked, even to Jerzy's unskilled eye, like they would fill easily with wind. Her hull was painted a soft, weathered gray, with a figurehead not of a woman's torso, but cupped hands holding a garland of vines in their wooden palms.

They had returned the horses at a small hire-stable, Jerzy's House token ensuring that his mare would be well cared for and then returned to her master. Ao and Jerzy had pulled the small cart the rest of the way to the docks themselves, with Mahl and Kaïnam walking alongside to make sure that no enterprising pick-it or thief tried to make off with any of their belongings.

They had paused for Ao to point out their destination amid the half a dozen ships tied up at the wooden pier—unlike the fishing village where they had come ashore months earlier, the port town of Brilan saw a number of vessels coming in and out on a daily basis, carrying trade shipments, messengers, and travelers. There was even a Brotherhood chapterhouse in town, which they had been careful to skirt around, just in case. Beyond the pier, another handful of larger vessels were anchored in deeper water, riding the soft waves as though impatient to be gone.

"She's, well, you don't care about details," Kaïnam said, "but she has room for all you're hauling and then some, and still moves like the wind. She would normally carry a crew of seven, but in a pinch can be handled by three."

"We had some trouble on the way here, with only two," Ao admitted, then shrugged when Kaïnam glared at him. The two had bickered—amicably but endlessly—the entire journey from the vintnery to the docks, on everything from the type of bird winging overhead to the distance they had traveled. Jerzy had finally decided that Ao simply wasn't happy unless he was arguing with *someone*. "Well, we did, and that was between Caul and The Berengia. Any farther, and we would have been stretched thin and raw. Three is the minimum."

"Well, it won't be a problem now," Mahault said with definitive practicality, as Kaïnam excused himself to speak with the shipyard guildsmen he had hired to watch the ship while it was in dock. "Four of us—well, three and Jerzy—can handle her."

"Master Malech gave me something in case the seasickness returns," Jerzy said, stung by the implication of uselessness. He hadn't been able to take his eyes off the *Vine's Heart*, but that didn't mean he wasn't listening.

"There's a spellwine for that?" Jerzy could almost hear Ao counting the coins in his head.

"There's a healwine for nausea," he told the trader, intending to cut those thoughts off before they could set fruit. "But no, he gave me a sugared root to chew that should keep me healthy." The root was a common trade item for disordered stomachs, not a magical cure, but Master Malech swore to him that it would work.

"Ho, good sirs, good sirs, need you help with the loading?"

Seeing them pause, laden with supplies, wharf-rats swarmed off their perches on the wharf rigging and barrels, calling out to offer their services unloading the cart and loading the boat. None of them were older than Jerzy, and most were in sad shape, underfed and unwashed. Kaïnam took a distinct step back, as though offended, and instinctively tried to shield Mahl from the sight of their bare, scarred limbs. She gave him a glare, and he relented, clearly remembering that she neither needed nor desired his protection.

Jerzy watched Ao, ignoring the wharf-rats, negotiating with some of the older, more well-muscled men who hired themselves out as porters, feeling his jaw clench in frustration. The entire flight from Aleppan, he had been more a burden than an aid, without spellwines, weakened by seasickness.

The time home had strengthened him, working with his own vines, feeling the soil beneath his skin, letting the scent of the vines fill his dreams. He might be leaving the vineyard again, but this time he could feel the quiet-magic in his blood, filling his flesh. It would be years more before he could claim anything close to even Vineart Giordan's abilities, but Master Malech judged him strong, and ready.

It would be a simple matter, this close to the ship, to use the quiet-magic and shift their belongings onboard. A manipulation of a wind-spell, to carry the boxes . . .

He dared not. Whether that quiet-magic was born of his own vines or his exposure to Vineart Giordan's weathervines did not matter. Master Malech's concerns, and the memory of what had happened the last time he was away from the Guardian's protections, and used quiet-magic, even briefly, came back to him. Then, a horse had died. Here . . . he risked the lives of his companions, and the safety of their venture. Only in the direst of cases could he use anything other than spellwines, and this was a matter best left to muscle, not magic.

Ao had just sealed his Agreement with the porters, calling to Kaï to open his wallet and pay the men, when Jerzy was sent to his knees by a sudden bolt of pain, an agony that went from the soles of his feet to the crown of his head, tearing sinew and splitting his head open like a shock of firewood.

He hadn't used quiet-magic, he thought, agonized. He hadn't done anything to call the cat's-paw back to him!

Before Jerzy blacked out, the last thing in his awareness not Mahault's sudden worried voice calling his name, but the slam of something cold and hard into his brain.

Danger!

WHEN HE CAME around, he could tell that they were on the ship, from the way the bunk underneath him seemed to sway back and forth, but the disorientation—not remembering how he got there, or why he was lying down—took a moment to clear.

"Master Malech!" He struggled to sit up, and a wave of dizziness swamped him, making him collapse back against the hard pillow.

"What is it? What happened?" Ao's voice, strangely pitched and scratchy.

"Ao, back off. Give him room to breathe." Mahault, speaking with the cool competence that had made him first think that she was a House-keeper. Her hands were steady as she lifted him to a sitting position, and her voice was worried but not panicked. Jerzy's eyes focused a little better, and he could see Ao and Kaï standing behind her, looking far more concerned but leaving room for her to work.

"The cargo . . ." he said, looking at Ao.

"Loaded," the trader replied, his voice still sounding strange. "Don't worry about it."

"What happened, Jerzy? You cried out and went down. Did the Master Vineart summon you again?" Kaïnam leaned forward, his face set in deep lines of worry. It seemed to Jerzy that the princeling had aged since they first met him; his skin had already been lined around the eyes in the manner of seafaring folk, and his eyes had held a deep sadness in them, even when he relaxed, but the shadows under those eyes were new since the conference in Master Malech's study.

"Something . . . is wrong." The awareness filled him as he remembered the feel of the Guardian in his mind, and panic and urgency returned. "I need to go back. I need to be back there now."

"Jer, Vineart Malech wanted you away—and even so, it's a full day's ride, and you cracked your forehead badly when you fell. There's no way you're getting back on a horse." Ao was logical and practical, and completely right—there was no way he could mount, much less ride, the way he felt—but that did not make Jerzy's sense of urgency any less.

"Can you magic yourself back?" Kaïnam asked, and when the others turned to stare at him in astonishment, he shook his head at their reaction. "No, I've never heard it done, either. But I never heard a spell that could hide an entire island from sight and sail, before Master Edon did so. Nor have I heard of any who could create a sea serpent from dead flesh, as Master Malech and Jerzy say was done. I do not wonder at anything that a Vineart might do, in need, now."

"No," Jerzy said, feeling completely useless all over again. "There is no spell that will carry me that distance." Not even with quiet-magic, none that he had heard of, and if Master Malech knew, he had no way to share it. . . . Or was there?

"Guardian?" He spoke into the air, unheard by the other three as they gathered a few steps away, casting worried glances back at him. The Guardian had called him; maybe it had an idea of what he should do, trapped here on this ship.

He got a sense of blankness in response, as though the Guardian did not understand, then a feeling of . . . change, like a ripple in stone. It made no sense; the Guardian did not shift or change, but: *Gather them.*

"Come here."

They didn't hear him, intent on their conversation, so he raised his voice, the sense of hard urgency from the Guardian pressing on him. "Come here!"

As a shout went, it wasn't impressive, but the sound echoed within the cabin's space, cutting them off midword. More shocked than obedient, they turned and moved back toward the bunk.

"What is it?" Mahl asked, reaching out to touch his forehead, as though to see if he were feverish.

The instant her hand touched him, the others crowded around closely, Jerzy felt the weight of the Guardian's presence increase from the pressure inside him, expanding outward until his entire body felt turned to stone as well. There was a shock of magic inside his mouth and throat unlike anything he had ever felt before, making his limbs stiffen and his headache treble in intensity. He heard someone—Ao?—cry out in surprise and pain.

And then the cabin, the others around him, the sense of the water underneath, any awareness of himself at all was gone.

THE FOUR TRAVELERS had barely been gone half a day when the Guardian gave Malech the bad news.

Riders coming over the ridge.

There was no cleared road through the forest that covered the ridge, intentionally so; the ancient trees had stood longer than the vineyard had existed, and Malech's master Josia had often gone in among them to clear his thoughts and find inspiration. Malech felt no such need, but he respected the memory. For riders to come through there, rather than using the easier, but longer road around, meant one of two things. Either they were in a terrible hurry, or they did not wish to be seen approaching.

Or both.

Rising from the workroom—the first time he had used it since Jerzy's misapplied attempt at spell-crafting and the resulting cleaning of the poisoned air—Malech went up the narrow stone stairs, moving quickly but without undue haste; his much younger student might take these steps at breakneck speed, but he had slipped and fallen on them some years before and had no wish to repeat the incident. Vineart heads were hard, but stone was harder.

"Detta!" His voice echoed throughout the House, suddenly so empty feeling, after the onslaught of youngsters. Malech pursed his lips, amused at the thought. The House had never felt empty—or quiet—before, but then, in all the years he had lived here, there had never been so many strangers coming in and out. Change, after so long. He wondered if the vines would sense the difference, if the Harvest would change as well, or remain the same.

The thought made him sigh. The Harvest would be difficult, without Jerzy's assistance, but the incipient guests proved that his decision had been the right one. Even if they were not part of the greater danger, the Washers were no friend to them now. Malech needed to keep them off balance and uncertain—at least enough that they did not strike against the House itself—and ensure that there *was* a Harvest to worry about.

"Detta!"

"She's gone out to the icehouse, Master Malech." Lil appeared, her pale skin flushed from the warmth of the kitchen, wiping her hands on the oversized apron tied around her frame. "Is there aught I can help with? Should we fetch her?"

"Straightaway," he agreed. "And bring the rest of your staff inside, out of sight. We have company coming." He paused, and said words he never would have believed could come from his mouth. "I do not know if they are friend, or foe."

That question was not immediately answered when the riders came into human sight: Washers, five of them in their red robes, and two solitaires riding with them, brown leathers and short swords strapped to their horses' saddles, their womanly faces grim even at this distance. No bullyboys this time, but impartial fighters. So impartial, they were often hired to carry out sentences of death among the highborn or important.

They had come for Jerzy, then.

Malech went to the front of the House and waited, deliberately forcing them to dismount and walk up under the archway to meet him, rather than the other way around.

"Where is the boy?" the leader asked, before Malech could utter a word in welcome. "Bring him here to us, for binding."

"He was cleared by one of your own," Malech said quietly. He had dressed himself in his most formal robe, taking the time to tie his hair back, and ensure that his tasting spoon and knife were properly hung on his belt, rather than hanging on the back of his chair. These Washers were strangers, not the same three who had visited before. Like the presence of the solitaires, Malech thought that was not a good sign.

"Events have countered that decision, as you are well aware, Vineart. Bring him here and do not interfere . . . or risk implication as well."

Malech sized the Washer up. Tall, burly, and young. All of them were young, and worried; they did not like what they were here to do. Not because they disbelieved the charges, but because they were frightened. Of him? Or of whoever had sent them? Or of something else entirely, perhaps. Washers, like Vinearts, rested in tradition. They did not enjoy change.

Was it possible they were guilty only of trying to resist the inevitable, holding on to the past even as it tumbled down around them? If so, Malech could empathize. But he would not falter. With a light touch, he gathered the quiet-magic from within his many years of exposure, holding it ready, just in case.

"My student is not here," he said, still quiet, keeping his hands clear of his belt, his palms forward. "You are welcome to enter my House and see for yourself. But remember"—he added, as the first Washer stepped forward—"that you are a guest within these walls. And that they are, by Sin Washer's Command, *my* walls."

Washers had no authority over Vinearts, and the same in return, unless a triad—Lord, Mage, and Brother—determined their guilt and bound them over for judgment. He had not been accused of any crime, merely suspected of a poor student. Any act against him was as much apostasy as what they accused Jerzy.

The Washer seemingly in charge nodded, then made a curt gesture to the solitaires, who came forward with him, while the other four Washers remained behind, making themselves comfortable on the deep green grass.

*   *   *

FEELING CAME BACK to Jerzy slowly, first pain, then a blessed numbness washing away the agony, and then a slow return to normal, with only a slight tingling left in his arms and legs to prove that he had not, in fact, been turned into stone. The newly returned awareness of his flesh also brought the awareness that he was facedown in grass.

It took some effort, but he raised his head, feeling the strain in his neck and back, and saw boots.

Boots that were attached to legs wrapped in dark red robes that were attached to a man's body that lay staring up at the sky through the branches of the fruit tree in front of the House of Malech. Another lay at an angle to him.

Both bodies were unmarked, but unmistakably dead.

Beside him, a woman groaned, more a noise of confusion than pain. Mahault.

Jerzy could not pause to wonder how he had been returned to the vineyard, much less why or how Mahault had come with him. He got to his knees, willing the dizziness to go away. "Guardian?" He wasn't sure why he was whispering: the body wasn't going to hear him.

Inside. The mental voice did not show emotion, but there was something in the weight of the word: worry, sorrow, rage . . .

His legs wobbly, Jerzy left Mahault where she lay and staggered inside, only to be met by Lil, wielding a massive wooden rolling pin, her pale face even paler than usual, her eyes wide with fear but her mouth set in determination. When she saw it was him, a little color came back to her skin.

"Jerzy? How—"

"What happened?" he demanded, ignoring her question. "Where is Master Malech?"

"He told us to stay in the kitchen. We heard shouting from his study, and then . . . nothing."

Jerzy's stomach sank, but he was already moving toward his master's wing of the House, his legs still uncertain with the aftereffects of whatever magic the Guardian had used on him—and it had to have been the Guardian, it was impossible but there was no other explanation, so he accepted it and moved on, barely aware of other people following. Lil, and Roan, and Per, the yardman who never, ever came inside.

There was no time to wonder at any of it. The door to Master Malech's study was open, and the Vineart was on the floor, staring up at the ceiling the same way the Washers out front had been.

"Master!"

The feel of the taint lay on his master's skin, mixed with the acrid stink of sweat and piss. Jerzy ignored it, going down on his knees beside the older man, looking anxiously for some obvious wound or sign of distress. There was no blood, no visible damage, and Jerzy had a moment of hope, but Malech's skin was waxy, and his eyes were not focusing.

"Master?" Jerzy's voice cracked the way it did when he was younger, and heat prickled behind his eyes. Malech did not respond, did not seem to have heard him, or be aware of anything happening in the room.

Outside. The word carried with it the rustle of leaves and the feel of dirt under his skin, and Jerzy knew what he needed to do.

"Outside. We need to get him outside." Even as he spoke he bent to slide his arms under his master's shoulders, Lil joining him to take those long legs, trying not to jostle him as they stood. Malech was tall but not bulky, but the years of working in the vineyards, first as slave and then Vineart, had given him ropey muscles that were surprisingly heavy.

"Back the way we came," Jerzy said. Roan led the way, shoving open doors and warning Detta and Per away when the two would have rushed up to check on Malech.

Outside, Mahault had recovered enough to stand, her color still ashen and her expression worried—a worry that only grew when she saw the burden Jerzy and Lil bore between them.

The entire Household followed Jerzy and Lil down the path and across the roadway, down the slight incline to the vineyard. Despite the shock of his master's condition, and the aches and disorientation of whatever the Guardian had done to draw him back here, Jerzy took a deep breath of the air and felt something inside him unclench, just a little. Part of him still believed that nothing bad could ever happen here, in the main vineyards. Nothing could ever happen to Master Vineart Malech in his own yard. It was impossible to imagine.

The slaves, seemingly unaware that anything had occurred across the wide road and sloping hill that separated them from the House, gathered to see what was happening, too shocked and too frightened to speak. The overseer, a burly man who had once terrified Jerzy, came up to demand an explanation for the slaves' behavior.

"Not now," Jerzy snapped at him, catching Lil's attention and indicating, with a jerk of his chin, where he wanted to go. They moved through the crowd of slaves, many of the younger boys dropping to their knees when they saw what—who—was being carried, so motionless. With a tilt of his head, Jerzy indicated to Lil where he wanted her to go, and they placed the Vineart gently on the ground in the nearest row of vines, Jerzy carefully lowering his master's graying head to the dark soil. Surely this would be magic enough.

The leaves rustled, although there was no wind, and far overhead a banded tarn soared, the sunlight catching its wings as it banked and turned.

"Guardian!" Jerzy cried the name like a decantation, the plea he had never let slip since he was taken into the slavers' camp finally escaping.

A weight of sorrow and loss lodged itself at the back of his throat, bitter as unripe fruit, and he tasted the dry flavor of cold stone and salt in his mouth. The Guardian could do nothing to stop the inevitable.

"Ahhh . . ."

The noise was barely a whisper, more an echo, but Jerzy heard it. "Master." He wasn't sure if he was asking a question, or demanding action.

But there was no response.

*   *   *

"You cannot stay."

"I must! There is"—

"Jerzy, listen to me!" Detta rarely raised her voice, and then only within the confines of the kitchen, where the din often required a loud tone. Here, in the stillness of Malech's study, where she had tracked him down, the noise practically rocked Jerzy off his feet. "There were five Washers, Jerzy. Five, and two solitaire." One of the women had been found in the courtyard. Unlike the others, her ribs had been crushed, causing death—but there was no sign of any other struggle, and the ties on her scabbard had not been touched, her sword undrawn. Whatever took her took her by surprise, and killed immediately.

"Where are the others?" Detta asked. "Two dead Washers, one dead solitaire . . . where are the others? Their horses are still here, none saw them leave. . . ."

"You think something took them." Disappeared. The same as the slaves, in Mur-Magrib. The same as Vineart Sionio, when this all began . . . He should never have left. His leaving hadn't protected anyone.

Detta had heard no sound of struggle; the Guardian could say only that magic had been done. Who or how . . . still unknown. The books and journals in Master Malech's study spoke at length about spellvines and legacies, but nowhere did they mention what might reach out and kill a Vineart without leaving a mark, or steal away bodies, living or dead.

All knowledge said that it was impossible to decant a spell out of line of sight. It was impossible to animate dead flesh to live again, as the serpents had been. Impossible to transport living creatures over a day's distance instantly. And yet their enemy had done the former, and the Guardian had done the latter. The impossible, the untraditional—nothing was certain anymore. Nothing was safe. Nothing was secure.

"I don't know what to think." Detta's eyes were red-veined and swollen, but she had not cried yet. "Master Malech is dead. He told me only a little of what he feared, of where you've been, but I see and I hear and I know something's gone wrong. Something the Washers are part of, maybe." She wasn't asking for confirmation, so Jerzy didn't say anything.

"I have to—" Jerzy stopped. He didn't know what he needed to do, anymore.

"He sent you off for a reason. You need to go, as you were, and find who it is. Stop them."

"Master Malech is dead." The words didn't feel real, not when she said it and not when he said it, not even with the body resting on the soil of the vineyard while the slaves built a proper bier. "I need to stay, to . . ." To do what? He was still a student, he had not learned enough. His head ached, his eyes burned, but the deep sense of loss, like a cut from a sharp knife, had not yet begun to hurt; he was only aware of it as an observation: my Master is dead.

"There will be no Harvest this year," Detta said, and the words were like another blow across Jerzy's shoulders, the taste of ashes in his mouth. "But we can survive that."

He wanted to protest, but she kept talking.

"I know enough after all these years, the overseers know enough, to maintain the vines for a season, to ensure that they are healthy for you when you return. But you must ensure that there will be a Harvest after that, and again after that, Jerzy. If this continues, the Washers: whatever else is happening, they will blame us for the death of their brothers; they will try to take the lands from us, salt the earth, and break the House of Malech. You must go and put an end to this before they do."

It is true.

Jerzy shook his head, refusing both her words and the Guardian's echo.

You must go. There was a sensation, like the lifting of heavy stone wings over the vineyard. *I remain.*

Only then did Jerzy, reluctantly, nod. The moment he agreed, only then did Detta's tears begin to fall.

*　　*　　*

BEFORE THE DAY had reached evening, word spread, via messenger pigeons and means more exotic, to those who had developed an interest in the doings of one Vineart, far away.

"The Vineart Malech is dead."

There was a pause while the man addressed tried to recollect who that was and why he was being informed. Ah. The troublemaker in The Berengia. "Good. Has the bounty been paid?"

The aide, a man who had been with the land-lord of Évura since he came to his title, shook his head, looking perplexed. "It has not been claimed, sahr."

The land-lord raised his attention from the parchments on his desk at that information. "Not claimed."

"No, sahr. Nor have any of the others reported a request for payment, with or without proof of the deed."

While some men might be pleased to keep their coin, the thought disturbed Sar Diogo. If the offered reward—a not unsubstantial sum— was not claimed, too often that meant another price would be asked.

Diogo did not like surprises. He leaned back in his chair, and thought. The others—land-lords from across Iaja—had joined him in offering the bounty, worried by the reports they had been hearing from trusted and valued sources. Whispers of a man who did not know his place within the Commands, who sought to take more power than he had been granted, who sought to meddle in things that were not his concern. They had known it was a Vineart who caused them such misery, but they could not determine who—not until they were approached by a Washer worried by the same things as they, who gave them a name.

House Malech.

Diogo had wondered then why the Washer had been so forthcoming—it stunk of maneuverings, for reasons unknown, and reasons unknown were reasons to worry about—but the intelligence was true. Master Vineart Malech had gone beyond tradition, was overstepping his bounded concerns.

It had seemed wrong, somehow; Vineart Malech was respected, valued by his people, and his own land-lord seemed to have no problems with him . . . but that in and of itself was also worrying. Was there collusion?

A bounty had been set—high enough to attract those who had an actual chance at succeeding, not so high that word might spread beyond the society of such folk who might be useful. He and his fellow lords all knew what they did was against the Command as well, to move against a Vineart . . . but had a Washer not given them the name? And were they not merely protecting themselves against one mage's arrogance and greed, not striking a blow for their own aggrandizement? Where one Vineart went bad, could not others—others closer to home?

It was only logical, and just, to act on the small problem before it became a larger one.

"You are certain he is dead?" he asked his aide.

"They are building a funeral bier even as we speak."

Then it was done. There were no second thoughts to be made. "Excellent. And even more excellent if someone has done our work for us, without requiring payment. Send word that the bounty is no longer open for the taking."

The aide saluted, and then paused at the door, as though struck by a sudden thought. "What about the student?"

His gaze was intent on his liege-lord, coaxing the proper response from him.

"Oh, yes." Diogo stroked his beard, as though checking that his man had trimmed it properly that morning. "The entire kennel should be emptied, should it not, else risk the pup growing up to bite us as well. Half the original bounty, then: for proof of the boy's unfortunate demise. And then step back, show no interest in what happens to their lands. Let the others squabble over it, if they will."

That should prove, if anyone connected him with the events, that he had acted out of concern for others, not himself. In truth, he had enough to do moderating his own lands, much less more farmland half a world away. The matter dismissed from his mind, he returned to his work, not even noticing when the aide left the room.

"Guardian."

Vineart.

That cool sense of the word in his mind made it real, suddenly. Never mind that he was half trained, or that he didn't even know if there would be a House to return to. His master was gone. Ready or not, he was Vineart Jerzy of House Malech. The sole Vineart of House Malech.

They stood in the courtyard, Mahault and Jerzy, while the Guardian perched on the rooftop, looking down at them. The rest of the House was in the vineyard, sitting vigil over Malech's body. At sunset it would be given back to the soil, as was proper. Jerzy would not be there to see it. His hand reached down to his belt, where an additional weight now swung. Malech's tasting spoon, taken from his master's belt before he was placed on the bier.

"How . . ." He let the question trail off. He had asked, already, how the Guardian had carried them from the *Vine's Heart*; asked, and gotten the same sense of loss and sorrow, of dry regret that had accompanied the Guardian's inability to heal Malech, the hint of something complicated that could not be explained, not because it did not wish to, but because it did not know *how*. The Guardian was magic, not a magic-user, and its creator was dead.

For the first time in his life, Jerzy was not willing to accept that he could not know something, but he did not know how to insist.

"Guardian . . . you will protect them." Detta, Lil, the House-servants, the slaves, the vines . . . all encompassed in that one word. *Them*. His, now. His to protect, to defend. To grow carefully, and harvest wisely.

There were no words then from the dragon, but a sense of assent, of agreement, of security that went from the bedrock of the vineyards to the roof of the room where Jerzy had slept, stretching beyond the edges of this yard and out across The Berengia to the secondary vineyards, the stone-built sleep houses, and low stone wall. All within the Guardian's touch.

It was foreseen, the dragon reminded him. It was why the Guardian existed: to protect the House when its master needed to be elsewhere.

Somehow, that did not ease the pain at all.

Are you ready? And then the Guardian's long stone tail twitched once, and Jerzy took Mahault's hand in his own, feeling her fingers tremble, and he felt the sensation again of being shifted into stone.

A breeze rose from within the courtyard, swirling dust into the air; they were gone, and only the Guardian remained.

PART 3

Fledge

Chapter 11

THE NORTHERN COAST OF IRFAN

Summer

The *Vine's Heart* did not sail; she danced. As the stars wheeled overhead, changing their formations as the *Heart* traveled farther south, Jerzy grew accustomed to the delicate sway of the deck under him, the sharp slap of the salt air, and the constant noise of the great white birds circling overhead. He was no longer ill, even when they ran into rough seas, and there was no panic when they were out of sight of land, the way they were right now.

He looked down at the rope he was coiling, down to his bare toes, as sun-browned as the rest of his exposed skin. He looked like a sailor; he was even starting to feel like one. The fact that he hated it, every minute they were under sail, mattered not at all.

Jerzy looked up again as one of the gray-and-white seafishers swung overhead, its harsh call falling into the open sky. Why had man not developed wings, rather than sails?

On the other hand, Ao, currently hanging overhead in the rigging, shouting something down to Mahl at the wheel, was clearly having a wonderful time. Jerzy couldn't find it in himself to be ill tempered; there was too little joy in the days, now, to begrudge any laughter.

There were footsteps behind him. "Ao has spotted another one."

"Is it doing anything?" he asked, storing the rope and taking a drink from the waterskin Kaï offered him, relishing the taste of the water down his throat. It was warm from the sun, but fresh, not salt.

Kaï had long ago abandoned his fancier clothing, and dressed like the rest of them in plain trou and a sleeveless vest. His black hair was no longer neatly styled, but tied back with a kerchief that Jerzy thought might have been one of his, once. Shipboard, clothing was washed and left to dry, and taken according to need, not original possession. "No," Kaï said. "Just swimming along. About quarter-mark, a full length away."

Jerzy handed back the waterskin, looking in the direction Kaï indicated. "Then we'll leave it be."

They had seen the first sea serpent a tenday after the Guardian returned Jerzy and Mahl to the *Vine's Heart*, and they had set sail—Jerzy a quiet spectre at the ship's bow, the other three moving quietly around him. They had just lost sight of the Iajan coastline behind them, the shadowed coast of Mur-Magrib distant to their left, when something had raised its monstrous head from the waters just off their bow and stared at them with those great, dead eyes. Kaï and Mahl had both lunged for their blades, slung from pegs near the wheel shack, and then stood there, uncertain of what they could do. The beast had simply blinked once, staring at Jerzy as though it knew his role in the death of its sibling, and then sank below the waves once again, neither attacking nor following them.

Since then they had seen three more, each time rising up to look at them, and then disappearing. There were subtle differences to each; one had a larger head; another a puckered scar across its terrible snout, as though it had tangled with something as deadly as itself. The fact that it was not a single beast, clearly tracking them, was a relief. The fact that there were three distinct beasts, plus the two he had seen dead, Jerzy found not at all comforting, since five seen meant more were likely roaming the waters, as yet unseen.

"Ignore it? You are certain?" Kaï was clearly unnerved by the serpents, particularly by the realization that his sword would be little defense should one of the beasts choose to attack.

"If it comes closer, I will warn it away."

One of the spellwines Jerzy carried with him at all times now was a firespell that could work through water. It had been crafted and incanted to repel smaller beasts that were occasionally drawn in by fishermen, attracted by their nets of fish into thinking they were an easy meal. If he decanted it at the sea serpent, it probably would not be enough to kill it, but it would remind the beast that they were not easy prey, and it should go elsewhere.

Probably. Hopefully. It might also simply enrage it. He did not mention that possibility to Kaïnam.

The truth was, with the spellwines they had to hand, and only Jerzy able to decant them with any skill, if the beast decided to come at them, they were dead. But it didn't hurt to pretend that they had a chance.

Ao swung down from the rigging, landing with a solid thud on the deck beside the two men. "Jer. We have company."

"I heard," Jerzy said, still watching the horizon where the beast had been sighted. He could tell from the way Kaï stiffened next to him that Ao was not pleased at having his news carried before him, and was glaring at the prince as the likely culprit.

Jerzy didn't sigh, but he wanted to. Another reason to be sick of life shipboard; there was no way to escape the others. Ao's need to argue was matched only by the pleasure he found in provoking the Atakusian, and despite their friendship, Kaï often reverted back to arrogance, especially when he was trying to make a point. Particularly when Mahl was around.

It was as though the fact that Mahault was female twisted both Ao and Kaïnam into knots, despite the fact that Mahault was not interested in becoming anyone's lady, and both Ao and Kaï knew it. It had become almost a game for them, a way to distract themselves from the impossibility of what they were doing. Knowing that did not keep Jerzy from wanting to throw all three of them overboard, save that he could not sail the *Heart* on his own.

"Would you rather he didn't tell me, and risk my not being prepared if it changed course and came for us," Jerzy asked now, showing only mild annoyance.

There was a surprised snort from Ao, and he leaned on the railing next to Jerzy. "You are never going to learn subtlety or an indirect jibe, are you?" he asked ruefully. "No matter how many times I teach you, no matter how many times we go over it . . ."

"I leave the parries to fighters and traders," Jerzy said. "Vinearts are not subtle creatures."

A lie: spellwines were infinitely more subtle, more indirect than even the wiliest trader. But there was no way Jerzy could explain that, and certainly not to a man who still insisted that he could manage just fine without relying on magic . . . if he needed to.

Jerzy fell silent again, his attention caught by a change in the wind from eastern to southerly, bringing with it a touch of moisture. There was no magic within the wind, but studying the play of patterns in the air was infinitely preferable to trying to explain himself to non-Vinearts.

Ao hesitated, then touched him once on the shoulder, his hand hard and callused from the ropes, and went back to work.

Jerzy shuddered, as though shaking off even that brief touch. He knew Ao meant well, was trying to apologize, but the contact felt like an imposition, instead.

Behind him, Kaï drew in a breath as though to speak, and Jerzy's entire body tensed, cursing silently as his hold on the winds was broken. The prince seemed to rethink his words, and released them unspoken with a heavy exhale.

Jerzy remained uneasy. His companions seemed to expect something from him that he didn't know how to give. Every mention of magic—every indirect reference to what had happened back in The Berengia, his master's death—made them feel as though they should offer a comfort he did not want, or need. He knew that he should be mourning. They clearly expected him to. But Jerzy did not know how, could not show the proper emotions that would reassure them, make them feel better.

Detta had understood; Detta knew Vinearts.

A Vineart did not show weakness. Jerzy needed to be calm and display only certainty when they questioned him. It was difficult: the press of their existence was always against his skin, the sound of their voices, the incomprehension . . . like now, it made him tense and irritable in the face of their concern.

It wasn't them. He knew that. The *Vine's Heart* was larger than their previous craft, so when he needed to be away from the others or risk losing his temper or doing something hurtful, he could find a quiet place where they did not disturb him, but space alone was not enough. There was no soil within reach for him to touch, to dig himself into, to hear the roots and leaves whisper his name.

Spellwines did not make a Vineart. Quiet-magic did not even make a Vineart. Vines made a Vineart. When Sin Washer had Commanded them to mind their vines to the exclusion of all else, he had set them on a path that did not allow for deviation.

If Jerzy did not get off this ship and onto growing soil again soon, he thought he might go mad.

"We are still on track?" Kaï asked, moving on to a topic they both could handle.

"Yes." Jerzy was certain of that, if nothing else. It drove him, the whip hanging over his shoulder, ready to flick out at the slightest sign of slacking. He woke in the morning, rising from his bunk already searching for the taint, and the last thing he did before falling asleep at the end of his shift was to taste the air one last time, to ensure nothing had changed. The feel of that magic, dark and potent and *wrong*, would not hide from him again.

It was not about avenging Master Malech, or making the Washers back off from their accusations, or even preventing the chaos the Guardian had predicted. Or, it was about all of those things, but a single thought kept Jerzy company when he woke, and when he went to bed, and when he breathed during the day and dreamed at night.

Master Malech was dead. The Guardian would protect the vineyards; Detta would ensure the House ran smoothly until he returned . . . but the Master of the House was dead, and the Washers who had come to take Jerzy into custody were either dead or missing.

If he did not find the source of the taint, their hidden foe, and expose him, Jerzy would have no home to return to. Ever. The Brotherhood of Washers would have their justice: the yards would be burned and salted, and the House of Malech would be no more.

His soil, his soul, would be destroyed.

"Vineart. If you let it eat you, there will be nothing left, after a while."

Kaï's voice was hard, as though he were speaking of something that made him angry, and Jerzy flinched, instinctively.

"You don't know . . ." he started to say, and then trailed off. Unlike Ao and Mahault, Kaï did know. His sister was dead, too, if not by the same hand, then directed by the same mind, and he, too, was outcast from the lands he had been chosen to protect and nurture. They were more alike than not; Jerzy was not so lost to self-pity and guilt that he could forget that.

Part of him wished that he could, that they would just leave him alone, and he felt guilty over that as well.

"I can't stop," he said instead, not looking back to see if Kaï was still there. "I keep wondering if, if I'd been there, if Master Malech would still be alive. If they would have taken me, and left, and . . ." He shrugged. "You can only harvest the fruit that's grown, not the fruit you wonder would have grown." The fact that the saying was true made it no easier to live by.

There was silence behind him, and when he did finally look over his shoulder, Kaïnam was gone.

Jerzy stayed by the railing, the shadow of the sail falling over him and protecting him from the sun's rays, letting the endless undulations of the waves soothe him even as he watched for another sign of a sleek, monstrous head or, worse, a hint of the neck, suggesting that it was about to rise up and strike.

"Although it could come at us from underneath, as well," he said to a large gray-and-white speckled bird that landed on the railing a span away. The bird folded its great wings and looked at him, cocking its head to one side and clacking its curved beak twice, as though in response.

"Fine help you are," he told the bird. "I don't have any bread for you. Go away." The birds were endless pests, lurking for food and leaving their filthy shit all over the deck. They weren't even good eating, according to Kaïnam, merely annoying.

The bird clacked at him again, then launched itself from the railing, in flight a much more graceful and attractive creature.

Serpents were not the only threat, nor the ever-present risk of a storm driving them off course. Twice they had seen ships with the red flag of the Brotherhood in the distance. Without a word from Jerzy, Kaï had ordered the *Heart* to change course, avoiding contact. They could not risk being found.

In the months since setting sail from The Berengia, there had been other ships, deeper out to sea: larger vessels bearing the trader-clan flags delivering their cargo from seller to buyer and back again, or Caulic vessels coming or going from their years' long ventures, exploring for new lands to claim. The *Heart* exchanged salutes in passing, but the hint of weapons arrayed along those ships were, according to Kaï, new, and made the princeling frown.

Heart was better suited for deep sea than the *Green Wave*, but Jerzy's sense of the taint was keeping them closer in to the coastline. Kaïnam charted a course that he said would minimize the danger from either coastal waters or unfriendly pursuit, but it was an uneasy compromise, and added to Jerzy's general feeling of discomfort.

The sound of metal on wood broke into his bleak thoughts, distracting him. Curious, Jerzy walked along the railing, no longer having to hold on to lines, to the middeck, where space had been cleared of barrels and ropes, to make a square large enough for a person to move freely.

Mahl, her long hair tied up at the back of her head and a dark green kerchief around her forehead to keep the sweat from blinding her, was doing sword movements. She was wearing a pair of trou and a sleeveless jerkin similar to Jerzy's, but there were soft leather boots on her feet and a leather bracer wrapped around her right forearm.

Even as he watched, she went through a series of poses, moving far more slowly than one would in an actual fight, bringing her blade up into readiness, then down again as though blocking something, and then up again and down in a swift and brutal-looking strike.

They were not, he reflected, entirely helpless.

Mahault paused, then retreated a step, and started the series of movements again.

Master Malech had hired Mil'ar Cai to teach him similar moves, only with a coarser, curved cudgel, learning how to judge what an opponent might be planning. Defensive fighting—to get out of trouble, not to find it, Cai had said over and over again.

The cudgel he had now, replacing the original that had been lost, did not have the same heft or balance, and Jerzy had not been keeping up with his practice. Cai would be annoyed with him, and yet practice had, before, seemed foolish. Vinearts did not carry weapons; there was no need, for who would attack one?

The idea of someone doing physical harm to a Vineart . . . unthinkable, even a year ago. Thinkable, now.

"Hai, Jer." Mahl saw him standing there as she turned into the final blow, and lowered her sword, using her free arm to take the headband off and wipe her forehead. Her face was flushed and her eyes bright, and she moved with an easy grace that made her normal smooth walk seem almost clumsy in comparison.

"You should practice with Kaïnam," he said. "Otherwise, he will forget all he knows, despite his pretty sword, and start to think he's only a sailor."

That made her laugh, as he'd intended. "No chance of that," she assured him. "He is out here every morning, working on his own moves when you're sound asleep." Jerzy had the last watch of the night, the quietest hours, and fell into bed after that in a dead sleep—or as deep as he could with Ao in the other hammock, snoring loudly.

"We sparred once," Mahl went on, "but two blades here . . . we were both too worried about damaging a line or canvas we would desperately need, later."

She looked him up and down, consideringly. "You could use a workout yourself," she said. "Ao climbs the ropes ten times a day, but you're starting to look a little soft."

"Soft?" He had never been soft a moment of his entire life. "Is that what you think?"

He looked around and saw a spar leaning against a barrel. Picking it up, he tested the heft experimentally, then nodded in satisfaction. As thick around as his wrist, the spar felt like seasoned hardwood, not the sort of thing to snap at the first or even second blow.

"With that?" she asked, her face expressing doubt and a hint of amusement.

"With this," he agreed, and stepped forward into the square.

The cudgel would not have helped him against the cat's-paw, or whatever came after Master Malech. But not all the blows had been magical.

MAHAULT PROVED HER point—Jerzy managed to hold off her attacks, but he was breathless, his arms quivering with exhaustion by the time they called it a draw. The exercise seemed to do some good, however, as Jerzy found his mood improved the rest of the day. After that, Jerzy made a point of joining Mahl for sparring practice some afternoons before his first turn at the wheel, and when they gathered for the midday meal under a spare sail slung overhead to keep the sun from baking them into a stupor, he tried to take part in the conversation, rather than merely listening. His thoughts still too often drifted into dark corners, but something usually brought him back into the daylight again.

Other than that, though, he still spent a great deal of time by himself, either leaning against the bowrail of the *Heart*, watching the waves flow under her hull as he looked for serpents, or counting the spinners as they leaped out of the waves, easily keeping pace with the ship.

Serpents and spinners seemed to avoid each other, he noted almost idly, and when the sleek gray hides of the smaller beasts disappeared from their wake, that was when Jerzy kept a sharper eye on the waters beyond.

The others, seemingly reassured by his renewed sociability, left him be. He wasn't brooding, or hiding: being alone felt natural to him, comfortable, and let him stay open to the next feel of the taint, drifting on the breeze. That was his responsibility, more than any time at the wheel, or in fighting practice.

Although he never lost it entirely, not even while sleeping, the taint seemed fainter now, as they slipped beyond the boundaries of the Lands Vin, and into the long shadow of the Beyond, the greater bulk of Irfan, largely uncharted and unknown. Yet against all likelihood, Jerzy remained convinced that they were heading to the source.

When he was off watch, and had taken as much of the bright sun and harsh air as his skin could bear, often as not Jerzy found himself drawn down into the hold, where the supplies they had brought from The Berengia were stored. Here he felt, if not at home, then *connected*. Here he could almost grieve.

It was there, one afternoon, that Ao cornered him.

"You should come upside."

"I'm comfortable here." Jerzy looked at Ao when he spoke, but his attention was taken up by the sound and feel of the cask he was sitting on. He needed to be alone—couldn't Ao see that?

Of course not. "It can't be healthy, Jer, you just sitting here with these casks and flasks, like they were talking to you."

Ao would never understand that they were. The soft, barely audible whispers were nothing compared to the murmuring of the vines themselves, but he could hear them, the liquid shifting as the waves moved the ship back and forth, the delicate nuances of each spellwine making itself heard, some of them fading, some increasing in strength as they aged.

Jerzy reluctantly disentangled himself from the whispers and turned to look at Ao. "Isn't this your off shift? Shouldn't you be sleeping?"

"Shouldn't you?"

"This is more restful." In sleep, he dreamed. Here, he could relax. As much as he could relax, trapped on a wooden tub on strange waters, surrounded by people who didn't understand him and expected him to have the answer for everything.

The thought brought a return of discomfort and irritability, and Jerzy breathed in deeply, willing the ambient magic within the hold to give him peace.

Ao, of course, didn't notice. "Jer, it's not good, you sitting alone. Not that you ever talked all that much, but you're too quiet, too . . . distant."

"I should talk nonstop, like you?"

The trader took the bitter riposte without flinching. "You couldn't even if you tried. I'm worried, Jer. About you." He softened his voice, unconsciously or not aping Mahault's manner. "It's been almost two months since. It's not good to—"

"Leave him alone." Kaïnam, his steps heavy on the ladder that led into the cargo hold.

"But—"

"Ao, leave him be." Kaïnam rarely used his princeling voice these days, but he did now, making Jerzy turn to look, as well. Ao bristled, drawing up to his full height—still barely to Kaï's shoulder—and stomped away, taking the stairs with far more energy than was required.

"He was only . . . He's right. I shouldn't spend so much time down here."

Kaïnam stood a careful distance away, his voice low and thoughtful, the way Jerzy thought a prince might speak. "You miss your home. Sitting here among the spellwines, it's a way to remember your master. We understand, mostly."

"Ao doesn't."

That won him a rare chuckle from the usually somber Kaï. "He does. He just can't believe it's healthy to suffer alone. Or quietly."

Jerzy let his hand rest on the nearest cask, listening to the healwine inside it hum contentedly to itself. He had helped harvest this, had worked with the mustus and punched down the skins, watching as it gained in potency until it was time to drain it off and set it to rest. It was *him* in a real sense, and spoke to him more than any of the humans on this ship ever could.

"Kaï? Jerzy?"

Mahault, her voice sounding worried.

"What did Ao do this time?" Kaïnam called back up the hatch.

"It's not Ao. Come up. There's something you need to see."

Her voice was concerned, but not panicked.

Kaïnam raised one of his dark brows and gestured for the Vineart to precede him on the steps. They emerged into a starlit night, the pinpoints of brightness in the sky reflecting against the glistening black waves, making it seem almost as though they were trapped between two skies, one near, the other far. Jerzy had been down there for longer than he thought. No wonder Ao had worried.

Ao had taken over the wheel, despite its being Mahault's watch, and Mahl was practically hopping up and down in her impatience for them to join her. She held their single, priceless spyglass in her hand, as though she had just been scouring the horizon.

"What is it?" Kaïnam asked, not seeing any immediate cause for alarm.

"There," and Mahl pointed off the bow of the *Heart*, her arm shaking a little.

"All the gods and their white-tailed ponies," Kaïnam said, grabbing the spyglass from her hand and raising it to his own eye. "What is that?"

Mahl shook her head. "I was hoping that one of you would know."

Kaï lowered the glass, still staring at the horizon, then handed the spyglass to Jerzy and strode to the wheel, Mahault easily keeping pace at his side. "More sail, Ao. Now!"

Ao was already at the rigging by the time the order hit air, pulling at the ropes. The sails jerked, filled with air, and slowly the ship turned starboard, toward the object Mahl had spotted.

Jerzy, left alone, slowly lifted the long spyglass to his eye and looked through it. It took a bit for him to focus, and then another long minute for him to realize what he was looking at.

A ship. It was a ship, but almost impossible to identify, as it seemed to glow with a thick blue light, from stem to stern, and all the way into her rigging and sails, full-bellied as though under a wicked wind. Jerzy tried to see what flags she was flying, but the blue light obscured any details he might have been able to make out, even the color of the fabric.

Sliding the spyglass shut carefully, his hands shaking, Jerzy went to join the others, handing Kaï back the spyglass.

"I don't know, and I don't care," Ao was saying. "Kaïnam's right—it can't be good, no matter what."

"But there might be people onboard," Mahl said, although Jerzy could tell that her heart was not in it. She didn't want to go anywhere near that strange ship, either. "We can't just abandon them, if they're in trouble."

She looked first to Kaïnam, as the only true sailor in their group, then at Jerzy. "Isn't there a rule about that?"

"There is," Kaïnam said grimly. "But there is also a rule about not endangering your own ship and crew, as well, and that one is more important than the other."

"Jerzy?" She appealed to him, her eyes red-rimmed with exhaustion. He had a sudden suspicion that she never truly slept; if she wasn't on watch, she was practicing, and if she wasn't practicing, she was poring over maps as though she intended to memorize each and every one.

Jerzy didn't want to answer her. "There's nobody there to save."

That got all their attention.

"What?" she asked, incredulous, doubting that he could be so cold.

"That blue glow," Jerzy said, holding his hands behind his back to hide how they still shook. "It's a warning."

Ao got it, immediately, and his face went ashen. "Plague ship."

Jerzy nodded. "There's a residue in the strongest healspells, so that when the illness reaches a certain level, a certain number of people dead, or if everyone has fallen ill, the glow is released to warn others away, to protect those who were not yet ill, who might have otherwise gone to help and died for nothing."

Ao and Mahl both made the cupping motion of Sin Washer's blessing, but Kaïnam merely stared at Jerzy, then lifted his gaze to the horizon, where the blue glow could be seen only faintly against the night sky.

"Is there anything you can do?" he asked, speaking as though the dying were there with them.

"Only speed them on their way," Jerzy said. "My master . . ."

His master had been the one to save entire villages, when the rose plague hit. But he had trained for it his entire life, driven by a vision.

I think it might have foreseen you.

"I am no healer," Jerzy said, responding to both the memory and the expressions of the three in front of him. "And we have no plague-wine with us. There is nothing I can do."

He turned away from them and walked back to the railing. The ship, with its pale blue light, bobbed up and down on the waves, at that distance looking like a child's toy.

He knew what plague did to its victims. How terrible the suffering was.

When he heard someone come to stand behind him, Jerzy shook his head before they could speak. "I can't heal them," he said again.

He looked down at his hands, where they gripped the railing. His nails were clean, even the faint whirls of dirt that were forever embedded in his fingertips had faded under repeated dunkings in the sea and constant work with the ropes and sails. There was not a touch of soil anywhere on his body, and the thought made hum unutterably sad.

"It's too far, too far away, and it's been too long."

"Jerzy." Kaïnam was using his princeling voice again, and he looked up, startled into obedience. The Atakusian's eyes were focused, not on Jerzy, but the distant ship. "Can you help them?"

Jerzy understood, then, what was being asked.

A moment of doubt: Could he? Dared he? There was no Command specifically against it; he had ended suffering once before, when there had been no hope. And yet, the scale of it, not one dying slave but an entire ship, still clinging to life . . .

"Jerzy?"

"Yes."

No hesitation, once the decision was made. Kaïnam stepped back, and Jerzy looked around, seeing the others waiting a few steps behind. "Mahl, bring us closer. Not too close—we don't want them to see us, if anyone is still alive, and think we're coming to rescue them. Desperate men can do desperate things, and desperation could get us all killed. Ao, in the hold, in the smallest of the crates. Inside, there will be flagons, about the size of a pitcher. Find one that is dark red, marked with a brighter red sigil, and bring it to me. Hurry!"

They went off to do his bidding, not rushing but moving swiftly, with a calm certainty. Action was better than standing around, waiting.

Ao returned with the flask, and Jerzy double-checked the seal to be certain, then used his belt knife to cut away the wax seal around the cork, letting the peelings drop onto the deck. Replacing the knife, he found his hand touching something else on his belt.

Master Malech's tasting spoon. His fingers closed on it, hoping to feel some rush of certainty, the sense that this was the right thing to do, that Master Malech approved.

The handle remained cool, his thoughts and feelings jumbled as before.

Whatever he did, he did on his own.

Aware of the others carefully not crowding him, Jerzy lifted the spoon clear from his belt, and, instead of pouring the spellwine into his mouth the way he had done previously, the way ordinary folk did, he filled the spoon, letting the liquid settle into the hammered silver surface. In the night, it did not glint, but instead shimmered darkly, as though it were one with the waves skimming below them, deep and full of mystery.

Allowing the air to touch a spellwine gave it a chance to open of its own volition. A spellwine allowed to open before decantation was more powerful. . . .

More powerful to a Vineart, specifically, when touched with quiet-magic.

A risk, if quiet-magic truly laid him open to being found, yet it would be required to counteract the healspell already in place. He had to trust Sin Washer and hope that the deep waters would continue to hide him.

He blew once, lightly, over the surface of the spellwine, and inhaled the aroma, then slid it onto his tongue, letting the deep, spicy liquid coat the surface, pulling in more sea air after, to intensify the effect.

Firewines especially needed to breathe, to pull air into them, for full power. Unlike a healwine, you did not decant the spell immediately on its touching the tongue, but let it rise from you, slowly. The more intense a fire needed, the more air was needed.

"Has a Vineart ever burned himself?"

"I have never seen it," his master replied. "But there are stories . . ."

Not letting himself worry about such a fate, Jerzy swallowed the mouthful of spellwine and raised his eyes to where the plague ship sailed, casting its warning light over the dark waters. There was no need to utter words: the magic knew what he wanted it to do.

A puff of red, barely; the spell touched, and a spark ran along the mast, almost hidden by the blue of the plague warning, and within the space of a breath, the entire ship was engulfed.

The four of them stood on the *Vine Heart*'s deck and watched in silence, bearing witness, until the night was still and dark once again.

XIMEN HAD THOUGHT that he knew the worst of what the vine-mage might and could do. Each time he let himself believe that, however, the older man came forward to prove him wrong.

Worse, the misbegotten creature was *proud* of it.

The air outside was chilled, but the room inside was far colder. Ximen stopped in the middle of his pacing, and resisted—barely—the urge to throw something, preferably something with a very sharp edge, at the vine-mage. "You did what?"

The mage almost smiled, as though knowing Ximen's internal struggle. Perhaps he did, rot him for his magic. "They were a threat. I dealt with it."

The two of them were alone in the study, the remains of a sparse meal on the table. It had been a formality more than hunger, the breaking of bread to establish that they had no intention of poisoning each other.

Not that it would be poison that took either one of them.

"You took Washers." Ximen was having trouble believing that part of the report. "Washers!" He was no slave to the gods, neither old nor new, but this was arrogance that could only bring disaster.

The vine-mage did smile then, a closed-lip twist, dry as the winter. "They were a threat, my prince."

"How do you know this, vine-mage?" Ximen's voice was coiled like a snake, warning before it struck. "You tell me who our enemies are, but how do you know? This I ask you, before all is lost in your foolish, misthought action."

The mage did not lose his smile, or his arrogant confidence in the rightness of his actions. "Washers are but mortal men, my Praepositus. They have no god-given skills, no magics within them, to find the one who stalks them."

Ximen threw himself down into one of the tall-backed chairs pulled up to the table and stared at the vine-mage, his face as hard and expressionless as he could make it, silently demanding a true answer.

The vine-mage sighed, his irritation barely masked in the sound of a disappointed father. "My sources came to me with warnings, of events happening that I had . . . not planned for." Oh, how it hurt him to admit that, Ximen noted, not without malicious satisfaction.

"Happenings?"

"There were whispers in the aether. A Vineart asking questions, making circles in the water, stirring doubt and worry. Others listened to him, were raising more whispers, casting suspicion not upon my pawns, but elsewhere—possibly even looking beyond the Lands Vin. I—we—needed for him not only to be silenced, but discredited."

The vine-mage smoothed the front of his robe with steady fingers.

"The Washers you speak of, they had visited that man, questioned him. The terrible deaths that occurred on their second visit . . . questions will be raised, whispers turned into shouts, blame will be placed square on the Vineart, drawing eyes there and leaving us to finish our work in peace. None will ever suspect, until it is too late."

Ximen frowned. He did not like it—he liked little of any of this. Slaves were not important; it was a Vineart's right to do as he wished with slaves, no matter who they had belonged to once. Vinearts—that was for the vine-mage to deal with, and Ximen would not interfere. Washers . . .

The sole Washer shipboard had died with the first generation, leaving the Grounding with only written teachings to improvise from, and Ximen had never found any of the silent gods worth more than a silent nod in return, but there were things that did not seem wise to meddle in. Still, the vine-mage was correct: any man who raised doubts, who endangered the blow they were to strike, had to be stopped. His people did not yet have ships that would cross the distance and allow them to fight honestly, hand to hand, so this was how it must be. Sin Washer would protect his own, or he would not.

Ximen leaned back in his chair, forcing his muscles to relax, or at least give the appearance of relaxing. "The anniversary is nearly here," he reminded the vine-mage; needlessly, he knew, but it brought to bear the original reason for the meeting. It was a symbolic celebration, perhaps, but symbolism was important: they had kept the colony living for seven generations on symbolism and hope. There would be the usual bonfire on the original rocky beach where the shipwrecked sailors had come ashore, and the burning of a derelict ship to symbolize the burning of their connection to the old world and the acceptance of their abandonment. This year, it would also be when Ximen, their Praepositus, announced their return to the world.

If all was ready.

"We will be ready," the vine-mage said, hearing the unspoken worries. "The final piece is being set in motion. All who might have defended against us are silenced or dead, and none think to look beyond their own countrymen to point a finger and shout accusations. Exactly as was planned." He smiled, and lifted his glass to the Praepositus. "At this time next year, my prince, you will be restored, and our people will be safe, no longer at the mercy of these fickle lands but masters of their own fate once again."

Ximen did not raise his glass in return, despite the insult that could be taken. Not for the first—or even the tenth—time, he felt the stirrings of foreboding. This could not end well, the means the vine-mage had chosen. But he, Ximen, had set his feet on that road as well, and must perforce follow it to the end.

Reluctantly, aware the vine-mage saw that reluctance, he lifted his glass and drank.

Chapter 12

erzy woke one morning, nearly three months into their journey, with a headache, bringing him to full awareness well before dawn, despite the fact that he wasn't due for a watch until then. Unable to fall back asleep, he emerged from the sleeping area and took a breath of fresh, salted air. Ao had the last night watch, but only raised a hand in silent greeting.

Jerzy moved quietly to the side of the ship and leaned against the railing, watching the distant shoreline pass by. Unlike the more populated, well-mapped shoreline farther north, this was a sparse, forbidding landscape of jagged rocks and overgrown beaches, without a single village to be seen. Once or twice Mahault or Ao claimed they had seen small boats, hugging close to the shore; fishermen, perhaps, or travelers, but Jerzy, who refused to climb the rigging, had only their word for it, and Kaïnam refused to let them take their only, irreplaceable spyglass up to take a closer look.

The taint dragged at him, reassuring him that they were headed in the right direction. More, now he was sure that it came from this coastline, the land Kaïnam's maps listed only as "Unknown Ifran." Outside of the Vin Lands, Jerzy knew nothing of who lived there or what they did, and even Ao, normally full of stories about lands so far away they seemed almost unreal, could say only that great treasures came from the depths of the land . . . but he knew no one who had ever seen them.

The sun rose enough that the shoreline was tinted with rose and purple shadows, and Jerzy's headache ebbed slightly as he watched fish swim along the bow of the *Heart*, shimmering schools of them like a herd of deer, turning and breaking when one of the birds, hunting in the dawn light, swooped down to catch one in its beak.

"Ifran," he said out loud, looking at the landmass as the dawn brightened to day, and someone—Mahault, from the tread—came up out of the sleeping quarters, splashing water from the wash bucket onto her face. "You, Ifran." As though he was calling it, or accusing it.

"Jer?"

He had almost gotten used to the abbreviation of his name; by now Mahault and even Kaïnam used it, as he used the shortened versions of their names. From nameless slave to the formality of the Vintnery, to the casual intimacy of life shipboard . . . there were times Jerzy could not remember who he was, or what he was doing, until the taint hit the roof of his mouth again, and it all flooded back.

"It's closer," he said suddenly. "There." Then, shouting, his voice thick from salt and too much wind, "Ao! Pull us landward and look for a place to shelter."

He had found the source of the taint.

IT WAS SEVERAL hours later when Ao finally found a place Kaïnam considered acceptable, with what they hoped was a village visible just beyond the ridge. The weigh-anchor was tossed overboard, and Jerzy and Mahault pulled the tiny sideboat out from under the railing where it had been stored, out of harm's way. Mahl inspected it dubiously, poking at the lightweight frame, even as Kaïnam pulled a dark canvas covering out from a storage bin and unfolded it, revealing a skin of sorts to slide over the frame.

"It's water-tight?"

"It will get us to shore and back," Kai said calmly, directing Ao and Jerzy on how to stretch the cover over the frame so that it fit snugly. "I paid solid coin for this; they're made in Ekai, near my home. And yes, Ao, if we survive this, I will introduce you to the makers so you may negotiate whatever trade Agreement your heart desires."

Jerzy wasn't as convinced of the craft's seaworthiness, and, from the look on her face, a line drawn between her brows and her brown eyes clouded, neither was Mahault. But when Kaï and Ao lowered it to the water, they allowed themselves to be coaxed down the rope ladder and to settle themselves onto the floor.

The craft dipped and swayed as Kaïnam pushed them away from the *Heart*, but it did not sink, and Ao's hand on the paddle carried them slowly but steadily toward the shore.

By now, Jerzy's headache was so fierce, his head felt as though his scalp had shrunk around the bones of his head, and the sway of the sideboat made him feel the first hint of seasickness he had suffered during the voyage. This close, they could see netting resting just below the surface. Jerzy poked at one, his hand dipping elbow deep into the water, distracted.

"Trap nets," Kaïnam said, seeing his curiosity. "Low enough to catch fish easily, but not tangle boats coming in and out. Whoever lives here are fisherfolk, experienced ones."

The small, sloping beach was cleared of debris, allowing them to paddle directly onto dry land. Ao stowed the oar, and Kaïnam jumped out to pull the nose of the boat farther onto the shore.

Jerzy got out as well, his boots sinking into the wet sand, and looked up. The village they had seen from the ship was now only just visible. He had to crane his neck back, up the jagged, rocky cliff covered with rough vegetation, to see rooftops patched here and there with black, and walls a paler red and dusty gray, with open windows set up high under those roofs. Other than the steady noise of the ocean at his back, the shore was quiet, no sounds of life carrying to them.

Behind him, the others got out of the sideboat, and he heard the sound of their packs hit the sand with quiet thumps.

"It's here?" Kaïnam sounded dubious.

"Not here, not the taint itself. It's beyond." Jerzy's gaze went over the rooftops, as though some light might come down through the now-overcast sky to guide them to their destination. But the air remained still, the low-lying clouds blue-white and featureless, masking the interior from sight. There were mountains there, he thought.

"How far beyond?"

"I don't know. Inland." Jerzy had been certain when he directed Mahl to change direction and head for the shore, but the closer he came, the less solid that certainty felt. What little confidence he had eroded like the dry sand under their feet.

He reached down to touch the sand, letting it crumble through his fingers. Not vineyard soil, but ground nonetheless. "Guardian?"

For the first time since Malech's death, he felt that cool weight slip into his awareness. Distant, so very distant, but present. Aware. No longer split between two Vinearts, the stone dragon seemed to have a greater range.

You are Vineart.

The reminder seemed less helpful this time.

Malech trained you. He believed you would outstrip him, in your prime.

Jerzy blinked and could almost feel the tips of his ears pink, even over the golden brown the sun had turned his skin. The Guardian neither lied nor exaggerated; it did not know how.

Be careful.

"Keep them safe," he said in return, and the stone weight was gone.

The others were waiting, Ao looking at the cliff rising ahead of them thoughtfully, the others staring back at the water and the *Heart* floating peacefully offshore, carefully giving him a sense of privacy and solitude. After the plague ship, even Ao had left him alone, although Jerzy occasionally wondered if it was not respect for his privacy they were showing, but something closer to fear.

The thought distressed him, but he had no idea what to do with it, or if there was anything to be done at all. He might, he knew, have misread things completely.

"All right." Jerzy stood up again, stretching his body, lifting his arms above his head until he felt something in his back crack and relax. The extra weight of clothing—boots and sleeved tunic plus a surcoat, at Ao's suggestion—felt odd after so long shipboard, but the air was cooler here, with a bite to it that suggested more Harvest than spring. Plus, he suspected that they would not be all too impressive to anyone who met them, looking the way they had the previous evening. Now, with the ragged edges of their hair trimmed, bodies washed and properly dressed, they had a better chance of getting people to speak with them. Assuming, he realized suddenly, that they could find a language in common.

"This isn't a Vin Land," Ao said, as though he had sensed Jerzy's thoughts. "Are you sure there are vineyards here?"

"Yes."

That much he was certain of. It was nothing he could explain; even more than the feel of the Guardian's voice, it was faint but real, and it was coming from these shores. More, the sense of the vines carried a similar feel to the taint he had sensed in the sea serpents, in the aide . . . not the same, not as distressing, or unnerving, but definitely the same legacy.

Master Malech had not been able to identify the vines from which the spellwine that animated the first sea serpent had come; the Mage-wine had not recognized it. If it came from a land that was not recognized as part of the ancient Lands Vin, from before the time of Sin Washer's touch on the land . . .

Jerzy's headache intensified at the thought; he couldn't begin to imagine what that might mean. The First Vine had been identified and the boundaries of the Lands Vin known and marked more than two millennia ago. Could the Breaking have scattered the pieces so far? There was legend of such things: wild vines, they were called—left to go feral, to forget all the cultivation, the connection to the Vinearts who had tended them. But how could anyone in this land have known what they were, and how to work them?

"The slavers travel everywhere," he said out loud, answering both his own question and Ao's. "They are supposed to take only children from within the Vin Lands—that is their charter—but I remember boys who spoke no Ettonian at all, who knew even less than the rest of us, and were chosen nonetheless."

Some of them had been bought. Some had not. There never seemed to be a pattern around who would be marked by the vines. If the slavers went this far in search of merchandise . . . might not a Vineart also come?

Master Malech might have known. Jerzy could only guess.

"So the magic has spread beyond the borders," Kaïnam said, following Jerzy's words. "Does that make this now part of the Vin Lands?"

Jerzy laughed, a harsh bark of amusement that startled him. "I leave that to the Vinearts of Altenne," he said, referring to the vine-scholars who reportedly held the knowledge of every grape that was created in the Breaking. "It will be their headache. Mine is more immediate."

Immediate, and worsening. He was curious; he did not deny that. The thought of wild vines, reclaimed, intrigued, but it did not matter. His purpose here did not allow for distraction. If those vines were the source, then the Vineart they searched for would be here, as well.

Jerzy's lips pressed together in an unconscious imitation of his master, and he rubbed at his forehead again, fingers catching at the salt-crusted tangle of his hair. If he was right, then Master Malech's killer would be here. Somewhere.

"That way." He pointed. "Farther inland."

"And we're to just leave the *Heart* there, unprotected?" Ao protested, even as the others went to pick up their packs. "I'm sure the locals are all perfectly honest," he went on, in the tone of voice that suggested that he believed anything but, "but leaving her without anyone at all to make sure things remain as they ought, with us heading off who knows where . . ."

"I'm not staying behind," Mahl said, before anyone else could speak. "Don't even think of suggesting that."

Ao looked at the other two, then looked at the ship again. "I suppose I should be the one, then," he said, and his disappointment was clear. "As we're not to leave Jer here, clearly, and I don't think Prince Kaïnam will agree to stay behind as guardsman."

Kaï didn't disagree with that assessment, but frowned. "I would prefer not to be without Ao's skills of discussion," he said, the closest he would come to complimenting the other. "Vineart, is there anything you can do, to safeguard the *Heart*?"

Jerzy squinted in thought, trying to will his headache away so that he could concentrate. "I don't know. I . . . no, wait."

When he had gone to Aleppan to study with Giordan, the casks of wine they were carrying had been out of his sight, when they overnighted at an inn, stored where anyone could reach them. Master Malech had enspelled the casks so that they would remain untouched. So it must be possible. The problem was in determining how.

"I don't think there's a spellwine we have that could do it," he said, thinking out loud as though he were back in Master Malech's workroom, being posed a question about the elements of a particular incantation. "Healwines would protect, but I don't know how well they would work on something that was not alive. Firewines . . . would repel an intruder, but how would it know?" He had brought an assortment of flasks and wineskins with him—not willing to rely purely on what he might find along the way to their destination—but it was limited to their available stocks and his ability to carry it with him.

There were other spellwines that might work, but Jerzy did not know them, had never worked with them, and most important, did not have them. There were a number of small flasks of water- and earth-related wines in his pack, most notably the growwine Master Malech used to work with healwines to ensure that wounds scabbed over properly, and bones strengthened after a break, but he could not see how they might meet what he needed.

"Jer?"

"Hush a moment," he said, flicking his hand at Ao. "I'm thinking."

With a bit of his awareness, Jerzy saw Mahl take Ao by the arm and lead him off a bit down the beach, the two of them talking intently. Kaï remained by his side, less a companion than a vigil-keeper, alert to any movement that might be a threat. Jerzy wanted to scoff, but the memory of those men in Tétouan came back. They still did not know who those men had been, who they had worked for, or why they had wanted Jerzy. It might be foolish, but Jerzy could not say Kaïnam's caution was foolish. Not with Master Malech dead, and the Washers after them.

"Fire, to repel. Earth, to protect. Water, because the *Heart* is a creature of it. . . ." He found his pack in the pile on the sand and knelt down beside it, undoing the straps and reaching inside the bag to find the flasks he needed.

Kaï spoke softly. "I thought that you said that was dangerous, mixing spells?"

"It is," Jerzy said. He had told them, one night as they shared histories, the story of the misincanted spell in the workroom.

"Oh."

Kaïnam did not take a step backward, but he obviously wanted to, and probably would have if he thought it would make a difference.

The first flask was a wavespell, similar to the one Kaïnam had used when he left Atakus, to speed his ship along. Jerzy poured a small dose into the tasting spoon, then placed it carefully on the sand next to him, where it would not be knocked over.

The second flask was barely the size of his palm, and it was covered with a pale green tracing. Growspell. Jerzy could practically feel the life pulsing within the spellwine, waiting for any excuse to go to work.

"Growspells are dangerous and difficult to control," he said, forgetting in the focused calm of his concentration that Kaïnam was not only not a Vineart, but the heir to a man of power, and should not be told such things. "The grapes are left to ripen until the very last moment, so they are powerful, the magic concentrated and rich. A strict incantation is needed, to keep it from doing too much once released. And the decantation must be performed perfectly."

"Is that why the price is so high?"

"That, and because the slightest failure of weather or timing, and an entire harvest is ruined." He opened the seal carefully and sniffed at the mouth of the flask, just to be sure. A bouquet of warm, rich soil met his nostrils, winding its way inside and making him smile in reflex. It was the most basic, most elemental of the growwines: root-strengthen. He had brought it on impulse; if these were wild vines, then he might be able to bring them back for replanting, to cleanse the taint and reclaim them and the magic they carried.

Inside him, Jerzy could feel something shift and stretch, much the way his body had earlier, only reaching downward, burrowing into the earth itself: the quiet-magic, waking to his call. Not fast or hard, the way it had been on the ship that day, but slow and natural, like the unfolding of a leaf.

"This is going to be tricky," he said, talking again to himself, his audience of one forgotten. Two spellwines in front of him, to be added to the two he carried within himself already . . .

His master would be horrified, would remind him that his quiet-magic had led the enemy to him, before, would forbid him from even trying such a thing, reminding him of the disaster he had caused trying to create the hailstorm-protection spell.

Master Vineart Malech had been wise, and beyond doubt talented. He had also been cautious, and careful, and he was dead.

The thought was hard, but it firmed Jerzy's resolve to do this thing. It was the only way to find his master's killer. The only way to clear his reputation so that he could return home and take up his work again. The only way for the House to be safe. Any risk, any cost, was worth that.

Pulling moisture from his cheeks and throat, Jerzy collected the spittle in the cup of his tongue, then with his free hand lifted the tasting spoon from the sand and let the liquid flow slowly onto his tongue as well, trying to keep it all balanced, not spilling or swallowing anything just yet. He had a passing heretical thought that this was forbidden not for the crossing of vinespells, but because the risk of a Vineart choking to death was terribly high.

Perhaps he was apostate after all. Perhaps the Washers were right. If so, they had driven him to it, and he would not apologize.

Placing the spoon down, he lifted the growwine flask to his mouth, and let a scant drop fall onto his lips.

The effect was as immediate as it was unexpected. Jerzy's entire body stiffened, his arms jolting forward to land palm down on the sand, supporting his body as his back arched and his knees locked and inside his body the magic swirled in dizzying loops, until his skin ached to break free with the power of it all. Through it all he remained still, his tongue cupping the liquid, pressing it slowly into the roof of his mouth, taking in all the magic contained within the wines and making it blend with the quiet-magic, adding the elements of each spellwine to his own abilities. He did not know how he was doing it, each next movement built on the last, following some instinct and the knowledge of what each wine could do.

All those hours of sitting in Master Malech's study, repeating the virtues of each spellvine, the aspects of each wine, the forms of incantations and decantations—it might not have been the purpose intended, but the knowledge allowed him to contain the magic, to control and direct it.

It was difficult to form the words, his mouth and throat almost numb with magic, but his lips moved to shape the words carefully, visualizing what he wanted while looking out to where the ship rested patiently, the masthead pointing toward them as though looking at the Vineart.

"*Vine's Heart*, safely keep. Stem to stern, mast to hull. Go."

He swallowed the warm liquid, and his body collapsed as the magic left him, flowing to follow his decantation.

"All the silent gods!"

The soft exclamation came from Ao, even as Jerzy moved back onto his haunches and tried to focus on the results of his spell-casting.

"Oh." Mahault, her voice round with wonder.

"That was . . . impressive," Kaïnam said. His voice was dry and distant, but Jerzy had heard that tone often enough from the prince, while sparring with Mahl, to know that it hid a very real appreciation.

His eyes finally cleared enough to see what they were talking about. The *Heart* still rested at anchor, rising and falling on the gentle swells of the cove. At first glance, nothing seemed to have changed. The sails were furled, the deck empty Then his gaze was drawn to the cupped hands of the figurehead set on the bow of the ship, and his breath caught.

The wooden carving was wood no longer. Rather than the weathered, white-painted wood of before, the hands were now a deep olive skin tone, similar to Master Malech's own hands, and they moved slowly, the fingers lifting and relaxing as though testing their own strength. The vine-wreath that had been clenched between those fingers was now thick green, not with paint but life, each individual leaf trembling in the sea-breeze.

"Sin Washer protect us," Jerzy breathed, staring at what he had done.

Behind him, Kaïnam let out a noise that might have been a strangled laugh. "I think, Vineart, that he already does."

"Nothing will dare touch her now," Mahl said quietly, having come back at some point to rejoin them. Beside her, Ao was silent and slack-jawed, looking from the ship to Jerzy, and then back again. "A pirate would wet himself rather than board her, and if the Washers come upon her . . ."

"They might board her," Jerzy said. "But they would not dare damage anything, nor take her for their own. Not with that, and her name clear on the side."

"Then let's get moving," Kaïnam said, shaking off the awe and fear of the moment and making his voice brisk and matter-of-fact. "Jerzy, are you able to walk?"

"I'm fine," he said, but remained on his haunches a moment longer, still staring at the masthead. He rubbed his own hands thoughtfully, the fingers of one hand unconsciously finding the red mark on the back of the other hand. A slave was marked by his master, on the inside of his wrist. When the vines accepted him as their own, it disappeared and reappeared on the other side of his hand, for all to see.

He wondered, even as he was standing up, not noticing the hand Kaïnam offered in assistance, if the hand on the masthead carried a similar dark splotch.

"Jerzy?"

"Yes. Let's go."

THE MOMENT THEY entered the village itself, climbing up a narrow path through the low, ground-hugging vegetation, Jerzy realized how very far from home he was. The first person they encountered was a young child, barely knee high to an adult, wrapped in a dark green waistcloth that made his ebony skin shine. His eyes grew wide at the sight of the strangers, and a bright smile flashed onto his face as he ran toward them, grasping at Mahl's hand and tugging at her fingers as though expecting them to come off, crying out something in a language Jerzy did not recognize.

"I hope he's saying 'pretty!' and not 'dinner!'" Jerzy said, and then flinched when Ao hit him, the flat of his palm connecting across the back of Jerzy's head.

"Never assume, because you don't understand someone else, that they don't understand you," the trader said, his voice and face as angry as Jerzy had ever seen him, even when they had told him about Master Malech's death.

"Do you understand him?" Mahl asked, bending down so that she was face-to-face with the child, and reaching with her free hand to tug at his other hand in return, linking them together in a sort of cross-handed game the child found irresistible, giggling and tugging even harder.

"Not a word," Ao admitted, and Kaïnam shook his head as well. "Perhaps we will have better luck with his parents," he said, indicating the small group of adults who were emerging from the houses farther down the street, clearly drawn by the child's call.

"Let me approach them," Ao said, and shot a pointed look at Jerzy. "You, stay quiet."

The trader took a deep breath, straightened his tunic, and then handed his pack to Kaïnam—not, Jerzy thought, without a smirk at making the prince act as his servant—and stepped forward to meet the locals.

Jerzy couldn't hear what Ao was saying, but there was a great deal of body language, exactly the sort the trader was always telling him to observe. So he observed.

Ao had his back to them, but his arms were moving—not the wild swinging he occasionally had when he was caught up in telling a story, but a more studied, almost graceful looping of his hands. Jerzy thought that it might draw the attention of the person he was speaking to, distracting them from his face. So they could not judge his expression? Or so that he could look around without being watched? It could be either, or both, or neither.

Three of the locals had stepped forward to meet Ao: two women and a man. The others, about ten or so, hung back slightly, while down the main street of the village Jerzy could see a few dark-haired heads leaning out of windows and standing in doorways, watching them.

The women wore skirts that wrapped low around their hips, in brightly patterned fabric, and their upper bodies were draped with more cloth, leaving their arms and necks free. The woman who was talking to—at—Ao now wore a cloth wrapped around her head, similar to women Jerzy had seen when they'd stopped in Tétouan, only her head cloth was more brightly colored. She held her body still, only her hands moving as she spoke; her gaze remained on Ao's face, no matter how his own hands moved.

The other woman's head was bare, her night-black hair short and curled, with glints of bright color as she turned her head back and forth. She was listening intently to both speakers, occasionally adding a comment of her own. Her face was unlined, and occasionally she would smile, a full-lipped expression that reminded Jerzy of the child who had greeted them. There was no artifice in her, only fascination.

"Her hair is beaded," Mahl said delightedly. "The same beads that she has on her clothing, I'd think. How beautiful."

The man who stood beside them was a solid figure, looking as much like a carved stone statue from the Aleppanese Garden as a living crea-ture. His arms crossed over a bare chest, he watched the dual-tongued discussion with the air of someone who was waiting for a decision to be made, at which point he would take an interest in the result.

"My father spoke of folk like these," Kaïnam said quietly. "When he was much younger, not yet Principal, and traveled more. A tribe of wild hunters, he called them, fierce and strong, and dark as the night. But that was far from here, on the edge of the Dry Sea."

"Mahault," Ao called, turning slightly. "Come here."

She exchanged quick glances with her companions, then walked forward. Like the others, she had changed her clothing to leave the ship, not certain of who they would encounter. She wore a coarse-woven blouse of linen, with full sleeves tied at the wrists, and a leather vest that would serve as protection against a blade, and her trou had been replaced by a simple brown skirt cut so that she could, in need, move quickly, without being hindered. Compared to the women in front of her, she looked drab, but the color of her hair, sun-kissed to an even paler gold, fascinated them. At Ao's instruction, she undid the knot at the nape of her neck and let the hair fall its full length, down to her waist.

What followed, Jerzy could only compare to two—or three—cats greeting each other, as the two native women touched Mahault's hair, stroking it carefully, and Mahl in turn was allowed to touch the beads in the younger woman's hair, and examine the head wrap the older woman wore, making sounds of delight that apparently crossed over any language difficulties.

"Trust a trader to find the mutual value," Kaïnam said, dryly amused.

THEY NEVER DID manage to learn more than the few words for hello, my name is, and good-bye, but Ao still managed to explain, with frequent turns to Jerzy for advice, that they were looking for a place where a certain type of plant grew. After long discussion, seated together under the spreading branches of an ancient tree that had clearly served as a meeting place for centuries, another man—this one much older, his night-dark features marked with scars, and his hair the color of frost—came forward with a square piece of tanned animal hide with a detailed map on one side. It was placed on the ground so that everyone could see it, and with a great deal of hand motions and nodding at each other, Ao and the older woman came to an agreement on what direction the travelers should take.

While the negotiations were going on, several of the children who had been gathering around, peering curiously at them, finally worked up the courage to approach the strangers.

The local adults, rather than shooing them away, smiled indulgently as they touched Mahl's still unbound hair and stroked Jerzy's own dark red locks. Kaïnam's straight black hair, like Ao's, seemed to intrigue them less, despite the contrast to their own curls. The color seemed to be what fascinated them.

Ao sat back during a break in the discussions, letting the locals talk amongst themselves. He looked first at Jerzy, then quickly away, directing his attention to somewhere between Kaïnam and Mahault. "They say if we take this route, it will take us four days to reach the place where the vines grow."

"Can we trust them?" Kaïnam had kept his hand clear of his sword the entire time, but he had been unhappy at the way the children crowded at him, touching his clothing and staring at his low leather shoes—when Jerzy had taken off his own boots to show that he did indeed have toes underneath, they had shrieked in glee.

"There's no reason not to trust them. Unless you sense something bad about them, Jer?" The question sounded awkward, almost accusing, and Jerzy frowned.

"No." They smelled of clean sweat and earth and a spicy, nutty aroma, but he knew that wasn't what Ao was asking about. "I don't . . . there's nothing to them at all, no more than any of you."

"Then we'll go. And the sooner we leave, the better. They're bound to offer us hospitality, after such a long sit-down, but without knowing their traditions, I don't think we should wait for them to offer."

"Why not?" Mahault made a play-face at one of the children, and he giggled and scooted away. "Isn't that rude?"

Ao rubbed the side of his face, as though suddenly very tired. "Some cultures, you're offered the finest beds in the village to sleep in."

"That sounds nice," Mahl said.

"And the most comely son or daughter of the village to sleep with."

Mahl flushed red under her tanned skin, and Kaïnam chuckled.

"Or, they might offer you their finest delicacy, which could be a part of the local herdstock you'd rather gnaw off your own leg than consume. Or—"

"We have the idea, Ao, thank you," Kaïnam said quickly, but from the tick in his cheek Jerzy suspected the princeling was trying very hard not to laugh. Traders, like Negotiators, might be comfortable with such things, and men of power might accept them as necessary to seal Agreements, but neither Jerzy nor Mahault was so inclined.

Ao leaned forward again toward the locals, to indicate that the discussions were open, while Mahault shot Kaïnam a sidelong glare, daring him to say anything more. Jerzy reclaimed his shoes from one of the children and the rawhide laces from another, already thinking ahead to how they were going to carry everything they needed for four days, and what might have to be left behind.

Once Ao finalized the negotiations and they stood to leave; however, they received two surprises.

The first came in the form of three odd animals, somewhat like a donkey, but with an oddly jagged pattern of black and white stripes, and short manes that stood up against their neck almost like a thick row of spines. They were each haltered, woven leads running from the halters, and led by a young boy of perhaps ten.

"*Zecora*," the boy said, indicating the beasts.

"*Seh-kor-ah?*"

The boy nodded, clearly pleased that he had been able to teach these strangers something, and offered the leads to Ao. "*Zecora*."

Ao looked at the others, then shrugged and accepted the beasts. "*Heyabu*," he said in thanks, and made a formal, shallow bow, which the boy, more awkwardly, returned.

"Well, that should take some time off our travel," Ao said, looking at the beasts doubtfully. Unsaddled, with expressions on their faces that did not look particularly docile, they did not look like comfortable riding creatures, especially when one of them bared its great yellow teeth at him and uttered an odd, almost barking sound.

Mahault took a step back in shock, and then, as though in apology, lifted her hand to one black-tipped muzzle. The beast dropped its head and let her pet it, contentedly. Tiny little bits of black-and-white fur rose in a dusty cloud as it leaned into the touch, and the other two crowded her as though looking for affection, as well.

"I am not climbing on the back of that," Kaïnam declared, offended by their awkward, shabby appearance. "And there are only three. Who is going to—"

"Ride in the cart? Ao asked, seeing the second of the surprises being brought toward them. The wooden contraption was not handsome, and it seemed oddly narrow, but there was a bench across the front where the driver could sit, and room for two or three others and their packs in the back, if they sat close together. Before Kaïnam could be offended at the idea of riding in a cart, Mahault stepped down hard on his left foot, and Ao shot them all a glare that defied them to open their mouths.

"*Heyabu,*" Ao said again, bowing to the adults who brought the cart. "Jer, is there anything we can do for them, in return? I dislike accepting gifts without giving something in return. It's bad luck, and bad trading."

Jerzy had already been thinking of that. He stepped back to reclaim his pack, his hands reaching unerringly this time for what he needed. "Mahl? Go through and find any children who look ill, or have injuries."

"Oh, yes," Kaïnam murmured, and Ao plainly let some of the stress that had fallen on him with the offering of the beasts fall away.

"They'll remember you as a magician," he said. "Will that be a problem?"

Jerzy shrugged. "I don't know. But it's the best thing I can think of."

Mahl came back in short order with five children, all of them very young, their parents trailing worriedly behind. They were willing to trust these strangers, but not too far, not with their children.

Jerzy removed the smallest healwine flask and checked the sigil.

"Do they need to do anything?" Ao asked.

"No. Just keep them there, and calm."

The children, fortunately, were fascinated, and clearly thrilled to be the center of attention. Mahl sat down and let them play with her hair, their thin fingers combing it, then lifting up sections and letting it fall again against her shoulders.

Jerzy licked suddenly dry lips and forced himself to relax. He had healed before, although never under these circumstances. The memory of the slaves caught under the broken cart almost a year ago was still a visitor in his nightmares. He had saved most of them, but not all. One had been caught in living death, and he had been forced to end the slave's life rather than allow him to linger endlessly. Like the plague ship, there had been no other choice—but he could not forget.

He did not let himself think of the plague ship.

These children were not in immediate fear of death, although he doubted the smallest child, his entire side withered, would survive to become an adult. In the slavers caravan, these children would already have been tossed to the side of the road and left to starve. But these children had family, people who cared for them. Who would rejoice to see them well, and whole.

He was not Vineart Malech, no true healer, but he could make a difference here. Not enough to replace the memory of the plague ship, no, but it would be a start.

The world will need healing.

He poured a scant mouthful into the silver tasting spoon and motioned the first child, a girl with terrible burn scarring on her face, forward.

"What?"

The vine-mage jerked awake, all of his senses straining into the still air. He had returned to his chambers, as was his habit in the late afternoon, when the sun disappeared early, to rest before evening meal; and he had . . . not fallen asleep, but found himself in a half-dozing stage, thinking of the work he planned to do once the moon rose.

"Master?" The slave who waited attendance on him stepped forward, anxious, thinking that he had missed some signal, forgotten something that was needful. The vine-mage waved the boy away, all of his concentration focused on whatever it was that had woken him.

There had been, as he dozed, the sense of something shadowing him, walking directly in his footsteps, breathing on the back of his neck. It had seemed like a dream—except that he did not dream.

"Someone following me," he murmured. Ignoring the still-attentive slave, he lay back on his pillows and opened his senses as much as he could, the way he would before testing a new vintage. "What's out there?"

It was possible, possible, that what he was sensing was the awakening of one of the slaves, that a suitable candidate to become his student had finally appeared. Despite what others thought of him—that he would tolerate no competition, that he slaughtered any slave with true potential—he rather hoped it were so, that another woke among the roots.

He was not ready to give over control of the vines, no. He did not expect to be ready for many long years yet. But the vines lived longer than even the strongest vine-mage, and there would have to be another after him, eventually, even after his plan came to fruition. He would rather choose one of his own, even from this benighted land, than leave it to chance, or be forced to give his knowledge to an outsider, one born of the old world.

His Sense stretched outward, but there was no whisper of that shadow within the sleep house, nor did it echo within the yards themselves. Letting his awareness stretch farther, secure that the slave would protect his body while he was otherwise distracted, the vine-mage looked further. Not to the south, where there was only wilderness and death. Not to the north, where the mountains held a different sort of death. Not to the west, the greater uncharted wilderness where no civilized man went. East, toward the sea . . .

He sat upright again, as his search was rewarded with an echo of magic. Distant, so distant, but clear.

Not a decantation. Not of the normal sort, anyway. Someone had done more than pour a spellwine and utter a few words. The magic had been *manipulated.*

This was not an awakening slave, no matter how talented.

There was another vine-mage on lands he, himself, had claimed.

Chapter 13

I *think Tag-ear is* going lame."

Ao, sitting next to Mahault, who was handling the reins, let out a short laugh, then winced as the wheels hit a particularly deep rut and jounced him into the wooden frame. "On this road? I wouldn't be surprised."

"When we stop next, you take a look at his leg."

"I'd rather let the damned thing go lame."

"Ao!"

Jerzy, taking his turn in the back of the rickety, uncomfortable cart, shook his head. He did not blame Ao. The beasts were sturdy, strong creatures who smelled of clean sweat and flesh, nothing rank, who pulled the cart over the narrow, rut-ridden dirt road without hesitation, and who required only a limited amount of sleep and were able to graze off the grass under their hooves, but they were foul-tempered animals when released from the traces, and while they enjoyed being petted, any attempt to groom them, or check their hooves, landed the offending person with a purple-and-red bite mark on their flesh to show for it. Tag-ear was the worst, but Blacktail and Barrel were almost as bad.

Not that he could blame the beasts for biting Ao. The trader had been acting odd ever since they set out—not the same annoyed exasperation he had shown on the ship, or even the unusual distance, but a series of sidelong looks and awkward fidgeting whenever he thought Jerzy wasn't paying attention.

If the others had noticed anything wrong, however, they were ignoring it, so he dismissed it as his own imagining. They were all stressed, in an unfamiliar land, with unknown enemies in front of them and the Washers hunting behind them. It would be more odd if Ao was not acting oddly, would it not?

That thought made his head ache as badly as his backside.

"We're almost there, according to the map." Kaïnam had chosen to walk alongside the cart while they went over a particularly rough patch, claiming it was to allow Jerzy more room to stretch out. His longer legs almost managed to keep pace with the cart, although on a flatter, more easy-traveled path, he would need to trot to stay abreast of them. "We should be there by nightfall."

The sigh of relief Jerzy let escape was echoed by a heartfelt "Thank the silent gods" from Ao, and Mahault flicked the reins again, urging the beasts—lame or no—to a faster walk. After three days, they were all tired of the road, with its utter lack of villages or wayhouses, no other sign of civilization to be seen, only the rising hills, covered with dry brown scrub and thicket. More, the strange feel of the air, cool and dry when it should have been soft with warming weather, and the strange sounds at night when they camped to rest—the yipping howls and low coughs—and the strange glowing eyes that would appear and disappear from the low growth, watching them, but never daring to come within reach of the firelight—were all wearing on them. This was not a civilized land, for all its beauty, and Jerzy had his doubts about what he would find at their supposed destination. Surely no vines could thrive here, so far beyond Sin Washer's touch.

He said none of this, however; the others needed him to be confident, to keep moving forward, and what purpose would voicing his fears serve? They had no choice but to keep going.

*   *   *

TAG-EAR DID IN fact pull up lame, and they were forced to camp overnight one more time, hoping that the beast would recover with a few hours' rest. Two could pull the cart, but short of abandoning the lame beast there, it would still have to keep up with them.

"We could eat it," Ao suggested, making a face at the dried meat he had been chewing on, trying to soften it enough to taste. "It probably tastes like horse as much as it looks like one. Or maybe goat."

"It would be a nice change from dried meats and fruit," Mahault agreed, holding her piece over her mug of tai, trying to let the steam do the work for her. "But who is going to slaughter and skin it? You?" She looked at the others. "Jerzy? I don't think our prince has the skills required, either."

"If it were a fish, we would be set," Kaïnam agreed, not taking offense. "But I am not a butcher, no."

"If it's not able to continue in the morning," Jerzy said, "we let it go loose. Either someone will find it and give it a home, or—"

As though on cue, there was another deep coughing noise just out of reach of the firelight; the humans jumped, while the beasts shuddered, crowding in closer to the fire and the relative safety there.

"Or something else will make use of it," Jerzy finished.

This close to their goal, he felt his stomach twisting inside him, the doubts he could not speak making their presence known in other ways. What would they do, on the morrow? What would they find? And what in Sin Washer's grace had made him think that he—that they had a chance against anyone who could work such magic, that could reach out and kill a Master Vineart in his own House?

That thought brought him square back to the question he had been avoiding since they left the *Vine's Heart*. All four were so focused on finding the source, revealing it as the cause of everything gone wrong, that they were not going beyond the idea of discovery. If the source was here, if the taint he sensed grew in this soil . . . what sort of vines had created that magic? A wild vine, a legacy that had gone feral . . . Jerzy identified the twisting in his gut was as much anticipation as fear; the idea that there was a spellvine that had not been identified, that was unknown to the Magewine, to the scholars in Altenne, to the rest of all Vinearts piquing his interest the way a woman or a man never could. If he could bring a cutting home with him, see if it would grow in The Berengia . . . try to erase the taint from its magic . . . or try to erase the taint already here . . . there was no Command against that.

Save that the Vineart here might easily kill them as share a cutting. Save that Jerzy might have no yard to plant it in, even if he were allowed to return. Save the Command that an apostate Vineart's yard be burned and salted, and Vineart Malech no longer stood in the doorway to stop them.

Guardian, protect them, he thought, touching the tasting spoon hanging from his belt, biting his lip hard enough to draw salty blood. He was helpless, trapped by his obligation, bound by the charge given him: find the source, bring it to light, save the House of Malech from destruction. Guardian, he thought again, reaching for the stone dragon's presence. There was a suggestion of cool weight pressing against his chest, and then it was gone.

"Everyone get some sleep," Kaïnam said. "I'll take the first watch, and we'll do shipboard rotation, and be on the road at sunrise, with or without all the beasts."

Holding on to the ghost-touch, Jerzy unrolled his blanket and found a comfortable place near the fire, to get as much rest as he could before his turn on watch.

THE NEXT MORNING, Tag-ear seemed to have recovered enough to escape becoming anyone's meal. After a deeply unsatisfying breakfast and the last of their *vin ordinaire* cut with water from the tiny stream, they packed up their campsite and kicked dirt over the remains of the fire. If anyone was following them, they wanted to leave as little trace as possible.

Mahl and Jerzy hitched Blacktail and Barrel to the harness, while

Ao, who had drawn the short twig, checked Tag-ear's hooves again, then tied the still-limping *zecora* to the back of the cart while Kaïnam repacked their belongings. By the time the sun had risen fully above the horizon, they were on their way, and by midmorning, they crested over a hill and found themselves at their destination.

The flat-topped mountain that had been their constant, if distant companion to the east rose more sharply ahead of them, forming jagged peaks, but the sloping hills directly below them were coated with plantings, twisted brown arms wreathed with leaves the shimmering brown and red colors of Harvest.

Vines.

Something caught in Jerzy's chest, and his fingers flexed inward, curling into his palms. Mahault touched his shoulder, and when he looked at her, she smiled, as though telling him that she understood he was feeling something, even if she didn't know what. He nodded back, not sure what to say, either, and then looked back down the road, trying to see the vineyard with less yearning and more the way he thought Mahault or Kaïnam might: distanced, evaluating what might wait for them.

Unlike the bunched rows Jerzy was familiar with, or the more extended lines Vineart Giordan had cultivated, these were a thickly gathered mass, so much that the eye tried to tell the mind that it was all one massive plant, covering the entire slope.

There were only a few bodies moving in the yard, weaving in and around the vines. That, plus the glorious leaf colors, told him that the Harvest had been completed. The air had not lied; the seasons were all turned around in this land, the way Ao had claimed.

"What now, Jer?" Kaïnam asked.

As quickly as that, the moment they saw vineyards, they were looking to him again.

Jerzy stared at the vines spread out below them, feeling the familiar hunger rise up again to be down among them, listening to them whisper. Not his vines; not his soil. He did not know these vines, and he feared what they were able to do. And yet at the same time, he wanted them, with a hunger that surprised and dismayed him more than a little. It could not be normal. Vineart Giordan's weatherwines had not effected this pull on him, not even when he had a taste in his blood.

Maybe it was not the Vineart who was to be feared, but the vines.

The thought was so startling, Jerzy almost tripped and fell.

"Jer?"

"I am thinking," he said.

"You're drooling," Ao retorted.

Reflexively, Jerzy swiped at his chin, then turned to glare at Ao when he realized what he had done—and that his chin was utterly dry. But it was good to see Ao grinning at him again, and, despite the uncertainty of the moment, he smiled back.

Mahault brought them back to the moment. "Do we sneak around? Go down and introduce ourselves? Go back to the *Heart* and pretend that we never found this place?"

All of those choices sounded equally appealing to Jerzy. But only one would accomplish what they had set out to do.

"We go down and introduce ourselves," he said finally. "That is protocol, when you enter another Vineart's lands. If we follow protocol, we will know what to expect."

Ao and Kaïnam both nodded, but Mahault shook her head, even as she was following them down the road toward the front gate.

"Only if they know and follow protocol, too," she said, casting a worried look up at the vast expanse of open sky, as though already expecting some sort of attack. "If they don't . . ."

If whoever tended the vines below did not, they were likely walking into a trap.

THE GATES THAT marked the start of the vineyard were made of a dark wood that arched over the road the same way the vine-twined arch did the entrance to the House of Malech. Jerzy braced himself for the same sense of gentle interrogation, if not the welcome he always felt when he passed under that arch, but there was nothing.

Whoever this Vineart was, either he hid his protections—or he did not have any. Jerzy wasn't sure which possibility made him more uneasy.

"Ah-ah!" They were greeted by a slave dressed in a waist wrap made of the same brightly colored pattern as they had seen on the villagers four days back. His skin was not quite as dark as theirs, but his hair had the same night-black tone and tight-curled appearance, although it was trimmed close to his scalp. He also wore a white metal necklet, the square amulet hanging against his bare chest. Jerzy felt the urge to touch the token still tied around his own neck for reassurance, although he doubted Master Malech's name would mean anything here, in this place.

Or if it did, it would be nothing good.

"Welcome to the domain of the Vineart Esoba of the House of Runcidore." The slave spoke near-perfect Ettonian, the trade-lingua remnant of the ancient Empire, with only a trace of an accent, and made a formal bow that would have been perfectly in place in the Aleppanese court. "You have come far, and will wish refreshment before meeting with my master."

It was not a question, and they were not given the chance to answer, as two more slaves, less brightly dressed and wearing no jewelry, came forward to take the reins from Ao and to help Mahault down from the cart, leaving Jerzy to scramble down on his own.

"Civilized men," Kaïnam said quietly, in halting but clear Berengian, and Jerzy nodded. They were almost too well mannered, considering protocol had already been broken; slaves had no business greeting visitors. Jerzy would have thought this man some sort of servant or aide, except that he was dead certain the man was a slave. There was something, a tingling of the hairs on his forearms, or an itch behind his ears—it was how a Vineart could choose whom to buy, out of a crowd of scared, filthy, untrained children. That knowledge came to him as though he had always known it.

Perhaps he had. Or it might have been the Guardian, even at a distance, giving him what he needed. Jerzy grasped at the second explanation and clung to it. Anything to not feel so ignorant and isolated here.

The senior slave clearly expected them to follow. Lacking any other options, they did so, entering the vintnery proper without fanfare or obstacle. House Runcidore was a simple structure; there was only one story, and the windows were open to the air, rather than being glassed in, but it was strongly built, with pleasing lines. The door was open, too, but when they entered, they saw that there was a heavy wooden door set inside, and at each window as well, to be fastened from within.

"Storm shutters," Ao said quietly, looking around. "They must have bad storms here, in season."

The main hall was exactly that—a giant open space, with two open, arched doorways at the far end. There were no tapestries on the walls, nothing but whitewashed walls and sconces where candles flickered with the clean, smokeless light of a well-crafted firespell. Despite the simplicity, there was an elegance to the building that had been lacking in the rough clay-brick structures of the village.

"I have never heard of Vineart Esoba," Ao said, still keeping his voice pitched low, to avoid the slave's overhearing.

"Nor have I." And that was more worrying. Mahl and Kaïnam would only have encountered the few Vinearts who did business with their homes, and Ao's people had no traffic with spellwines. There was little reason for them to have known the name of a Vineart so far away. But Jerzy had learned the names of many of the Vinearts of note, even the ones far away, and he had never heard of Esoba, or the House of Runcidore.

Name was everything; you were always the student of your master, and lineage mattered as much to the Vineart as the legacy of their vines. Even Master Giordan, who admitted that his master had not been a great Vineart, acknowledged his name and his teachings, even if he did not keep the House name for himself. The fact that Master Malech had so eclipsed his master had shifted the name of his House, but that was exception, not rule.

"Is there a market for an unknown Vineart's spellwines, Jer?" Ao asked, following some thought of his own. "I mean, if we are the first to encounter him, if I could broker an Agreement . . ."

It was reassuring, to hear Ao mutter to himself. The world could not be too odd, if Ao still had his eyes on the trade.

"Jerzy, how can a Vineart be, beyond the Lands Vin?" Mahl was still looking around, but she had edged closer to the other three as she spoke, as though afraid the walls themselves might take offense at her question. "I thought the spellvines only grew there, not anywhere else? And a Vineart does not go away from his vine. . . ."

"The traditional borders were designated by the First Growth," Jerzy said, keeping his voice soft as well, although he was saying nothing that was not known. "That is why even lands where the blooded grapes no longer grow, for whatever reason, are considered within the Lands Vin." He did not want to mention wild vines; they were rare and unlikely, and none of an outsider's concern, anyway. "It is possible to carry rootstock away for replanting. If, unlike Caul, the roots will take hold in this soil, this location seems to be well suited for the vines."

"Indeed it is," a voice said. "Indeed, most wonderfully suiting."

The man who greeted them was tall, taller even than Kaïnam, and broad in the shoulders as Ao, and dark-skinned as any of his slaves. A cloth of bright red and blue bands was slung over his shoulder like a cloak, falling to his waist over a short wrap of dark blue cloth. A double-wrapped leather belt encircled his hips, and a battered silver tasting spoon and a short, unsheathed knife hung from it, moving as he walked.

Vineart.

"Be welcome, brother mage!" he said to Jerzy, not waiting for introductions. "Oh yes, yes, I feeling you on the road, coming. And you are feeling me the same, it must be. Else there is nothing here—we are a young vineyard, only one legacy, and not many visitors, only the traders who coming buy my wine. So be welcome, and be at home."

The Vineart stepped forward and embraced Jerzy, not seeming to notice the way the other stiffened at the contact. Jerzy had not sensed the Vineart, only the taint. Was it the isolation that made the man's sense so keen, or had Jerzy failed somehow?

"Jerzy of House Malech," he said, and waited for some reaction.

"And these, your companions, you are welcome as well. My slaves will take most care with your belongings." Jerzy might have made up names, for all the notice the other man took of them, turning to greet each of Jerzy's companions, placing his hands in front of his body, palms flat together rather than cupped, and bowing slightly over them. He paused when he came to Mahault, taken aback slightly, and cast a sideways glance at Jerzy, as though to ask how he should approach this female.

Jerzy looked back at him, keeping his face impassive. In the Vin Lands, a woman belonged to her family name—or she was a solitaire. Mahault had neither protection, but he knew her well enough to know that she would not thank him for trying to offer it, himself.

The idea that, in these lands, a woman traveling with males clearly unrelated to her might be a problem occurred to him only now. Ao, on the other hand, appeared greatly unconcerned, and Jerzy took some comfort in that. If they had trampled on some local taboo, surely Ao would know?

"This woman is yours?"

Or maybe Ao wouldn't.

Mahl opened her mouth to say something, inevitably blistering, then her training took over, and she halted herself, even as Kaïnam stepped forward. "She travels with me," he said. "I am Kaïnam, Named-Heir of the Principality of Atakus."

"My prince," the Vineart said, his voice sliding back into a pleased tone, although Jerzy suspected that he had never heard of Atakus. "Of course. My people will make sure she is most comfortable, and that none give offense."

A woman stepped forward, presenting herself to Mahault. She was young, her hips wrapped in a dark red fabric, but the rest of her body bare, showing off strong, ropey muscles under dark skin. Her head was lowered, but she looked up at Mahault with clear curiosity in her gaze.

Mahault looked first to Jerzy, then, recollecting herself, to Kaïnam, as though asking permission. He nodded, and she followed the female slave through the hallway and out through the left-side arch.

"And now, my brother, your companions, too, to come with me, and we shall have talking, and seeing, and you will tell me where you have coming from, and telling me the news I have not been hearing . . ."

In actuality, Vineart Esoba seemed remarkably uninterested in any news other than his own. Since that suited Jerzy well, he let their host do most of the speaking, with Ao asking the occasional ingenious question that led Esoba down another trail of chatter. Once he started, Esoba's command of Ettonian improved.

"We are small, small yes, but much quality," the Vineart said as they left the House after a brief tour that showcased clean, whitewashed rooms and low, comfortable-looking furniture, but no tapestries or silver such as Jerzy was accustomed to in his master's House. There were slaves—no servants, only dark-skinned boys with the mustus mark on the inside of their wrists—and a handful of guards, who seemed to sleep while standing upright.

"And here is my joy, my heart." They stopped at the outskirts of the yard, and Jerzy blinked. He had been right: the vines grew in a mad tangle, barely any distinction where one began and the other left off, low to the ground like creeper leaf, not proper spellvines.

The fruit had been harvested, as he had suspected, and the magic within the vines had already begun to slumber in anticipation of the Fallow season, but the invitation to wander in among them was there, the faint whisper of welcome, and he was barely able to resist.

"They are lovely," Jerzy said, forcing his body to remain still. "You have finished Harvest?"

The question seemed to discomfort Esoba, who nodded after a brief hesitation. "Yes, picked and pressed and readying themselves.

We produce not much here; as I said, we are small. But we do well for ourselves."

"Vineart Esoba?" Ao asked, pointing down at the ground where something was half buried in the soil. "What is that?"

"Ah." Esoba sounded delighted to have something other than the vines themselves to discuss. "That is our irrigation plank. Here, let me show you. . . ."

"I CAN'T BELIEVE Esoba is guilty of anything other than mediocre Ettonian," Kaïnam said, several hours later, after the Vineart had brought them back to the House, personally showing them the rooms he had set aside so that they could freshen up before the evening meal. There was a main room, and three small bedchambers off it. Their belongings had been unloaded from the cart and placed in the center of the main room, to all appearances untouched and unsearched. Jerzy did a quick check of his pack and found nothing missing, none of the spellwines disturbed.

"He seems like a pleasant sort to me," Ao agreed. He had claimed the long, low seat, his legs up and his head resting against the cushion at the other end, a goblet of Esoba's *vina* in his hand.

Even Mahault, who had been waiting in the room when they were escorted there, having been given rooms in another part of the House, seemed to think well of their host.

"You're not annoyed, that you weren't allowed to join us?" Jerzy asked.

Mahault poured herself more of the *vina* from the chilled clay pitcher on the center table and took a sip, nodding her approval of it. "My father once hosted a delegation from one of the Highmark kingdoms, north of Caul. They were shocked that I was allowed to be seen in public at all. In their home, a well-born female was never seen in public rooms from birth until death—she remained in the family home until it was time for her to go to her husband's house."

She shrugged, and went to sit on another chair, this one round, without any arms or back. All the furniture was low to the ground, made of a simple dark wood, and covered with cushions of the same colorful fabric as the clothing they saw around them. The walls had no coverings, but the simplicity of their surroundings made the colors that much more vibrant, more exotic.

"If I had to live like this, I would throw myself into the river," she said. "For a short time, to see what we are seeing? I don't mind. But I agree with Kaï. I can't see Esoba as the source of the evil you've described."

"He isn't." If Jerzy had been able to sense even the faintest trace of that dark taint within either the Vineart or his vines, he would never have let them touch the wine, even an *ordinaire*. The truth was that, in their entire tour, Jerzy had found nothing to frown over, and much—especially the curved wooden planks they used to bring water to the vines during the dry season—of interest. And yet he was uneasy, restless.

He lifted his own goblet and took a small sip. The *vina* was bright and clear, the color a pale ruby red, and it splashed on his tongue lightly, bringing the aroma of warm spices and a soft, sweet fruit. "The vines we saw? They had barely any magic in them at all, that I could sense. Spellvines, yes. But not strong ones." That explained why Esoba had not taken care of the people beyond his House, the villagers. He did not have the ability to do so. Jerzy shook his head, feeling oddly saddened. "That is what happens when you grow vines outside the Vin Lands. The fruit may grow, but the magic is not there, the spells will not incant."

"So he is not a Vineart?" Ao asked.

Jerzy leaned against the wall and looked down into the cup. "He has the training, from somewhere." That much was clear from what they had seen; Esoba's vintnery was impressive, the details all correct. "And he does craft an excellent *vina*. . . ."

"In fact, I've never tasted a *vin ordinaire* like this," he said. The goblet was a thin-walled cup with a properly narrow lip, but Jerzy did not like that he could not see the clarity of the *vina* in the cup's depth. "Have you, Kaï?"

"No. But my father bought only spellwines, not *vin ordinaire*, preferring to drink those we grew within our own borders. It pleased Master Edon, and saved us considerable costs."

"It is good," Mahault agreed. "It has a lovely taste, crisp and clean, but with a great deal of flavor. But if he's not the source, why are we here?"

"Oh, the taint is here," Jerzy said. "It's simply not in his vines." It was the same as in Aleppan, the sense of it in the air around them, not a specific source. That meant the taint had already established itself within the House somehow, attacking the Vineart, not arising from him.

If the taint was coming from elsewhere, then Esoba was a target. Worse, he was a target who did not seem to know there was a danger.

He looked around, waiting for some reaction to his words, but the others seemed to be perfectly relaxed, accepting everything as though it was only to be expected. It made his skin prickle and his uncertain mood take a dark turn.

"We need to find out where the taint is," he said, fighting to keep calm, summoning the memory of the Guardian's cool stone against his fingers, his master's hard voice telling him to breathe and relax, to feel the mustus, the magic within.

"Of course," Kaïnam agreed, leaning back in his own chair, a narrower version of the seat Ao had claimed. His legs were stretched out in front of him, and he looked as relaxed as Jerzy had ever seen him, as though there were no worries in his life at all.

Their behavior puzzled Jerzy. "Are none of you worried?"

"Of course we are," Mahl said, suddenly glaring up at him. "I know what this taint can do, Jerzy. If this man is the target of it, then we need to find it and root it out before it can do to him what it did to my father. How dare you think that we don't care!"

Ao picked up on Mahault's tone and glared at Jerzy as well. "Is that what you think? Or is it because we're not magic, that we are missing something?"

Kaïnam sat up suddenly, looking between the two of them and Jerzy, his handsome face now marred with a frown. "Is that what you think?

That we are somehow less involved in this that you are? You aren't the only one with losses, Vineart. My entire land is at risk, my people, if I don't discover who is doing this. We will be forever cut off from all of the lands, if I cannot reverse what was done. You think I am not worried?"

"You are now," Jerzy said, taken aback by their sudden anger, and feeling his way delicately. "You weren't, just before. You each looked as though you had no worries in the world, relaxed when we should be up and doing."

"I was not," Mahl exclaimed, and Ao looked equally indignant.

"When was the last time you put your feet up, Ao?"

The trader looked at him as though he had lost his mind, and then looked down at himself, supine on the couch. He stared at the toes of his boots as though he had never seen them before. "You still have no right to say that—"

"That what? What did I say? If you really think that I think less of you because you can't sense magic, if you think I abandoned my yards, left everything I know and care about, because I don't care, why are you here? Why did you come back to The Berengia for me?"

Jerzy turned to Mahault, now angry himself, at their ingratitude and their lack of understanding. "Why did you come back? You'd gotten the connection you needed; you could have stayed there, could have earned your way to the solitaires. Your father disowned you; you had no need to set his name clean, or save him from his own mistakes. They abandoned you, cut you off. You owe Aleppan nothing."

Her face paled under the sun-coloring, and her eyes went wide, as though he had slapped her. He found himself panting, he was so angry, and his fingers clenched on the polished wooden stem of the goblet.

The goblet.

He looked down, and in that unguarded instant, everything changed, as though a firespell had suddenly illuminated the darkness they had been walking through.

"Put down your wine."

"What?" Mahault still stared at him, her anger slightly tempered by confusion now.

"Put down the wine," he snapped.

It should have been impossible. It was impossible, what Jerzy suspected. And yet, everything he had sensed, felt, since they walked under that wooden gate suddenly made sense.

"Mindspells. That rootless bastard crafts mindspells."

Chapter 14

I *thought that you* said this was *vin ordinaire*," Kaïnam accused Jerzy, tossing his goblet onto the floor in disgust. The liquid spilled onto the tiles, the goblet rolling away to rest against the leg of a table.

"I did. It is." Jerzy was certain of that. Mindspell or no, there was no way that magic could hide from him, not when he was drinking it. Was there?

He did not know aetherwines, save the single weak one Master Malech had given him to clear the air in the workroom with. A mindspell was an aetherwine of such potency . . . there was no way it had come from the vineyard they had seen that afternoon. Not unless Esoba had some way to mask his vines . . . ?

He instinctively reached out to touch for the Guardian, then stopped. If this Vineart could hide magic from him, then who knew what else he could do. It should not be possible for another to hear his link to the Guardian . . . but it was not possible to hide magic from a Vineart, either.

"What is a mindspell?" Ao asked, setting his own goblet down, more carefully than Kaï but with equal distaste. "Obviously, it affects the mind, but—"

"It can make us do something we didn't want to do?" Mahault had stood up and was pacing around the room, clearly agitated. Only Jerzy appeared calm, as he searched through his memory for what little he knew.

"My master told me that there is no spellwine that can make you do anything you do not want to do. The only spellwine that can affect a man in his thoughts is Lethá. It causes memories to fade or disappear entirely, and it is grown only in Altenne—the conditions are not right, here." Altenne was cooler, its yards higher up on the mountain slopes.

But it might be some variant? Malech had told him that vines, transplanted by students taking on new yards, often changed their properties as well, to suit the needs and the desires of the land they grew in. The Altennese scholars called it Sin Washer's Left Hand, that change. Could someone have planted Lethá here, and had it go left-handed? Could it hide its own nature even from another Vineart?

What sort of vine would do that? A dangerous one . . .

A Vineart crafts more than spells, Jerzy. He crafts solutions, possibilities. Some are good. Some are . . . not good. Some heal; some cause harm. None of them are anything more than tools.

His master's voice, from the first days of his lessons. Think, it urged him. Understand. The magic was in the mustus, yes. But even the strongest spellwines were only tools, the same as a sword or a hammer or a carefully chosen word. If this spellwine were grown from the same aethervine as Lethá, a change in growing conditions and a different incantation might . . . what? Make those under its sway forget why they were here? Make them less inclined to search?

Or make them inclined to argue amongst themselves, leaving them open to outside attack, or being wooed to another thought?

A chill settled in his spine, sliding all the way down to his fingers. Yes. It was possible.

But how could it hide its nature from Jerzy, standing there in front of the entire yard? Was he too weak to sense it, too ill trained to discern its nature? He needed Magewine. The single wine crafted for the use only of Vinearts, rare and tremendously expensive, it allowed the user to see into the heart of another spell, identify the legacy it came from. Master Malech had used it to try to identify the spell that had formed the sea serpent, the fact that it could not identify . . .

Jerzy halted his thought there.

The magespell had not been able to identify the legacy of that spellwine. That had been what had started all of this: the thought that there was an unknown spellwine, an unknown *vine* being used against them.

Jerzy felt like having Kaïnam beat him with his own cudgel for being an idiot, for not remembering that earlier, when he realized that they might possibly be dealing with a wild vine. Possible. Yes. Even probable. A wild vine could go left-handed, could have *started* left-handed. . . . Then his sense that the taint was around them, not within Esoba himself, need also be doubted.

"What should I do, Master?" he asked in a whisper, but the only answer he received was the blank looks of his companions. He could not predict what these vines might do, not without testing them himself.

The surest way to be sure would be to determine if the spellvines growing in the yard outside matched the one that animated the sea beast. But how? Without Magewine, and if this Vineart could hide the true nature of his legacy, then what could Jerzy—half taught and without the proper tools himself—possibly learn?

But the vines had whispered to him. He had thought that they were too dormant to speak louder, but perhaps he had simply listened the wrong way.

Jerzy placed his own cup down carefully on the nearest table, and stared down into the ruby depths, trying to not look for anything, but simply let the *vina* speak to him.

"Jer?" Ao asked, worried.

"Hush," he said absently. "I have to think this through."

This was different from what he had done—whatever it was that he had done—to protect the *Vine's Heart*. That had been relatively simple, a combination of preexisting spells: dangerous, but not difficult, in a crafting sense. This was purely quiet-magic, drawing on the Vineart's Senses to act as a sort of Magewine. Could he draw this out, without knowing the proper decantation? Or was he too young, still too green? Was it even possible? And if he managed it—would it call the taint directly to him? Or was the fact that it was already here protection of a sort? Too many questions and no answers at all.

No. No doubts.

He took a risk, letting out the barest tendril of thought. *Guardian?*

Silence. Not even the familiar brush of cool weight. Either the Guardian was dealing with something back in The Berengia, or the wards on this House kept them from contacting each other.

He did not dare reach for more, not until he knew for certain if Esoba was their enemy.

There was still a hesitation inside him to do anything involving the quiet-magic in front of others. But this involved them, too; he could not go elsewhere, or tell them to leave. They had the right to know if magic was being worked on them without their knowledge, especially if it was meant to harm.

"I think . . ." An idea stirred inside him, heavy and cool. Not the Guardian, not directly, but the feel of it Jerzy carried within him now. He was Vineart Jerzy of House Malech, and he knew more than he thought he knew.

"Are you—"

"Shh. Let him work."

Their voices faded away, still audible but not important as Jerzy sorted through the depths of the Guardian's knowledge, made three times more difficult because he did not know what he was looking for, and the Guardian did not know what it knew. Stone held; it did not understand. That was a Vineart's responsibility.

"I think I can do this," he said, more to himself than to the others. "It should be possible. . . ."

Should. A tricky word. Spells were specific, binding. Simple, but only on the surface. An incantation told the magic in the wine what to do. It held the magic to form, kept it structured and contained, usable by non-Vinearts. A *vin magica* that had not been incanted was wild, unpredictable, uncontrollable by any save a Vineart, and not to be opened lightly. A *vin ordinaire* was made from mustus that had not properly ripened into its magic, and could not hold an incantation, or respond properly to the decantation. Different ends, but drawn from the same fruit. That was basic vinecraft. The difference was not in the *vina*, but what the Vineart did.

He gathered spittle in his mouth, while he thought of what he wanted to do.

Basic. Simple. Go back to the source. *He* was the magic. *He* was the Magewine.

Jerzy stuck the tip of his forefinger into his mouth, then tapped the wetted finger against the surface of the *vina*. *Confidence.*

"What are you?"

Silence. No, a faint tingle, the distant sound of a pop, the sound a fish might make rising to the surface. A sensation within the tingle, deep along the spine of the wine itself, the light echo of fruit and spice . . . and nothing more. He had been right: the wine was merely *ordinaire.* . . .

No. There was more within it. And . . . around it?

He moved his finger so that it was not touching the wine, but rather the edge of the goblet itself.

"And you?" he asked the wood, drawing on the faint memory of the earthspell he had consumed earlier, to protect the *Heart*. Wood to wood, calling an answer out of it.

And he had his answer.

"The goblets were enspelled, to make the *vin magica* into *vin ordinaire.*" He should have realized: Master Malech had offered him such an enspelled goblet on his very first day as his student; it was a test, to see if he could identify *magica* from *ordinaire*, after seeing them poured from the same source.

Destroying precious *vin magica* was wasteful; more than that, it went against the natural order, and required great skill, something not to be done lightly, and certainly not merely to create *ordinaire* for guests to drink. But once stripped, there should have been no magic within it to influence them.

"So it was harmless?"

"There is no way to tell." The spellwine could have been anything, once. It could have come from anywhere, any Vineart, any vatting. The knowledge came forward again: the change within the goblets pushed the magic out, dispersing it back into the elements and scattering it. "The magic was stripped out by the spell, but there were still traces of it left." Just enough to affect them, when they drank deeply, unaware. No other explanation sufficed.

"You think that's why we were so angry with each other, so suddenly? It made us angry?" Mahault glared at the wine, as though it could feel her wrath.

"Spellwines can't do that," Jerzy said again. "Magic can't make you think something you don't think, or feel something you don't feel. This just encourages what is already there or possible." Faded, hidden . . .

"Like you tried to do to me, back in that tavern," Jerzy said to Ao, willing him to understand. "To see what I might say when I was off guard."

"So . . . we all thought the things we said. Even if we didn't mean to say them." Ao looked thoughtful, while Mahl's eyes went wide at the implications.

"That . . . is a very dangerous spell, Jerzy," Kaïnam said. "My father—any man of power—would pay dearly to have that in his cellar."

"All spells are dangerous," Jerzy retorted, irritated, even though he knew that it was likely the spell that made him feel that way. Kaïnam had not said anything more or less than the truth. Magic and Land-power had been Commanded apart for just such a reason. "If this is Lethá, or a root-legacy, then it's incredibly rare. If it's not . . . it's something new entirely."

They had no idea how much more dangerous that could be: a new, undetermined vine . . . no feral legacy, but truly unknown . . .

"But is it what we're looking for?" Kaïnam brought them back to the matter at hand. "Is this the place, the man we have been looking for, spelling us to think he is not?"

"It doesn't feel right." Jerzy stood up, fighting the urge to hit something, as though that would make him feel better. "And I don't believe that the vines could have hidden that taint from me, not entirely. But the fact that he tricked us, tried to enspell us—that makes me trust him not at all."

Ao, who had argued for Esoba originally, started to say something in his defense, then seemed to realize that there was nothing he could say. They had all been fooled.

Jerzy stared at the far wall, thinking. Had Esoba been the one to enspell the goblets? Or was the taint borne by another individual, one they had not yet encountered? The complexity swirled around him like the scent of fresh mustus, thick and undisciplined, disorienting.

He needed to test the vines. They would not lie to him. "I need you three to distract Esoba, keep him occupied." Decision made, he went to where his pack rested against the wall and knelt down to untie the top flap.

"Why?" Mahault leaned forward, intent. "What are you going to be doing?"

Jerzy found what he was looking for: a small leather winesack, worn, with a familiar sigil embossed on the front. It wasn't Magewine, but heal-all. Basic, ordinary . . . but when used by a Vineart, it could focus concentration and make him think more quickly—at least for a short time.

"I can't tell anything from this wine," he said. "His cellar might be better, but we don't know where it is, and I can't imagine he would let me walk in, unescorted, if at all." A Vineart's cellar would be warded twice as well as his study. "So I need to ask the vines directly."

"Ask?" Kaïnam jumped on the word like a hawk on a mouse.

Jerzy hadn't meant to say that. Still, no matter. The Washers would have purple fits, and Master Malech would—*might* have scowled, but Jerzy did not see the terrible harm. He had already taught these three more than they should ever have known; what was one more thing?

It was likely they would all die before they ever got home, anyway.

It was the first time Jerzy had ever let himself think that, not as a fear or worry, but as a likelihood. A fact. He wondered, briefly, if the others let themselves think of it, and if they did, if they would ever admit it.

"How are we supposed to distract him?" Mahl said, jumping to the other part of what Jerzy had said. "And for how long?"

"Think of something," Jerzy said, fitting the flask to his belt, next to the tasting spoon. "And for as long as it takes. I can't risk his finding me out there."

If the vines were different, and Vineart Esoba was not the one they were seeking, then there was only the insult to his hospitality to worry about. If the vines were the same, if the tainted magic came from them . . .

The vine was the source of the magic, and spellwines were the tool. But it was the Vineart who incanted. The fault, and the responsibility, would be within Esoba, not the vines.

Jerzy needed to know which their host was—innocent or villain— before he could decide what to do.

Behind him, the other three had started to argue over possible ways to distract Esoba, should he summon them before Jerzy returned.

"We could say he's sleeping," Ao suggested.

"Sleeping through dinner? That would be rude."

"Vinearts aren't social," Kaïnam pointed out.

"Esoba seems to be," Ao retorted. "Is that a point in his favor, or does it make him evil?"

Leaving them to argue schemes, Jerzy slid out into the hallway, and walked not back the way they had been brought, but away from the main hall, hoping that there would be a back or side exit he could use. There was no courtyard; the low building ran narrow and long, rather than square, with their rooms toward the front and the Vineart's study, where Esoba had brought them, toward the back. If he could find the kitchen . . . kitchens always had an extra exit. All he needed was for the Vineart—and any slaves who might think to stop him—to be distracted long enough. . . .

Luck was with him: the day was fine enough that someone had left a door propped open, and the scent of cool, fresh air cut through the scent of candle wax and wood, leading him directly to it. Not the kitchen, but the herbary; a female servant was there, hanging up tied bunches of flowers to dry, while a child sat on the floor, naked, and played happily with colored stones, pouring the polished bits from one chubby hand to the other. It was simple enough for him to walk past them both; the servant looked up, but while her expression was first startled, and then puzzled, she clearly saw no reason to stop her master's guest from taking a breath of air.

The door led into a small yard, where three small brown goats were tethered, contentedly chewing. Jerzy avoided around them and walked around the corner of the building to where the vineyard lay, spread out before him.

He paused, just luxuriating in the feel of the open air, the cool rays of the sun sinking over the horizon, the awareness of the vines spreading deep into the ground, and out into the world. He might have missed their Harvest, but the plants themselves were still awake, still aware, if barely.

Thinking about Harvest, Jerzy was struck again by the change in temperatures. On the sea, with the wind blowing steadily, it had been less noticeable, but the air was definitely crisper, cooler than it should have been. Ao tried to explain it to them, how the seasons shifted the farther one traveled, but Jerzy couldn't quite work his way around the idea.

Aware that he did not have much time, Jerzy went to the gate latch and let himself inside the yard proper. As before, there was only the faint sense of welcome, but he did not sense any of the taint, either, not even when he jumped over the low stone wall—something Esoba had not invited him to do, before—and knelt down, close enough to touch the leaves.

The unease he felt had little to do with being caught. His being here was wrong. Every inch of him understood that, trying to force his body into turning around and leaving. This wasn't like going into Giordan's yard—Giordan had invited him in, had given him permission, had introduced him to the vines, and allowed him access. Whatever Washer Darian and Sar Anton might claim, he had done nothing truly wrong, there.

Here . . .

If he did this, he would have crossed that line. Never mind that Vineart Esoba had tampered with them somehow, never mind that he had masked his spell in order to manipulate them. If Jerzy did this, he would have gone beyond all claims of innocence. If the Washers found out, his yards would be salted for certain, Malech's name tarred forever.

His throat felt sore, as though he'd swallowed too much seawater, and his shoulders ached from keeping himself standing there, and not fleeing back into the House.

"I need to do this," he said, as much to the vines as himself, to the memory of his master, to anything that might be listening.

This close, he noted that those leaves were smaller than what he was used to, and veined with a dark orange color, rather than the red he was used to after Harvest. There were, as expected, not many grapes left; the ones that had not been picked had overripened and fallen to the dirt, where they were eaten by animals drawn to their rich aroma and sweet taste. He went down on his knees, looking at the underside of the leaves, hoping to find at least one cluster that had been overlooked by both slaves and animals. It took him a while, his knees aching and the backs of his hands scratched from surprisingly rough vines, but finally his fingers closed on a small cluster, a handful of grapes. Moving carefully, he detached it from the vine, whispering an apology, and drew it back into the sunlight.

At first, he thought that these grapes had simply not ripened at all; they were still small, and a pale, almost translucent green, only lightly touched with red streaks. But the juice within stretched the skins near to bursting, and when he touched them, questing, the sense of magic contained was almost enough to knock him over. Oh, there was magic here, slippery and seductive, and not any legacy he knew, personally. It felt . . . unfamiliar, in a way that he could not explain, and he pushed deeper, trying to get some understanding of it.

The vines, although they should have been resting, in these days after the Harvest, shivered, as though sensing a Vineart, and under his gentle, questing touch, gave up their secret.

And for the second time that day, Jerzy understood.

"You're unblooded," he said, his voice barely above a reverent whisper.

"BROTHER NETH." WASHER Brion acknowledged the man coming up behind him on the forecastle without turning around; as usual the man knew who was within reach without any seeming effort.

"That is their ship?" They had been chasing the damned thing for months—if it was not their quarry, Neth was tempted to sink it, just for spite.

"The *Vine's Heart,* yes." Neth noted the scant smile on his second's face, but said nothing. Brion had come late to the Brotherhood, and he had his own way of looking at things, but his dedication was undoubted, and his skills were invaluable.

"They are aboard?" Neth took the spyglass from Brion and lifted it to study the tidy little ship, sliding on the waves like a restless filly tethered in a field of bluish green.

"It does not appear so," Brion said. "We will lower a longboat and approach. Do you wish to accompany?"

"I do not, as you well know." Neth would willingly ride the length and breadth of the Lands Vin, but he did not travel well on seaback; it was only his desire to end this hunt as swiftly as possible that had gotten him onto this sow of a ship in the first place. The idea of putting his person into the tiny longboat was not to be thought of, for fear of upsetting his digestion even further, with unpleasant results.

His second nodded, and shouted an order to the sailors who were fussing at the side of the ship. When they did not move fast enough to his satisfaction, he strode forward, clearly intending to light a fire under them. Brion had come from a family of soldiers, and it often showed. He had given up on his robes the first day at sea, and instead wore a vest of dark red over a rough cloth trou similar to those of the sailors, tied at the ankle and waist with cord, but otherwise loose and—Neth admitted—comfortable-looking.

"Rot you, ready on the . . . what?"

The brother's voice changed, and his head lifted at a shout from one of the sailors clinging to the rigging. That sailor shouted again, and pointed to where the *Vine's Heart* was turning slightly on the wave and wind. The bow came around to face them, almost as though she had heard them coming, and Neth almost dropped the spyglass in shock, only the expense of the thing keeping his fingers tight and preventing the piece from crashing to the deck.

"Sin Washer, defend us," someone cried, and there were several loud thumps as sailors dropped to their knees, raising their hands in cupped supplication.

"What is that?" Neth asked the man who had come to stand beside him. The captain of this ship, a grizzled Iajan sea dog who had been sailing for more years than Neth had drawn breath, took a pull off his pipe, which emitted a noxious stench as the weed burned, and grunted.

"Figurehead," he said.

"Thank you." The irony was thick, but unheeded.

Around them, the sailors were still muttering and praying, while the rest of his men gathered around Neth, waiting for direction.

He waited a few beats, to show them that he was in control of the situation, and then called his second over. "Brion."

"Yes?"

"You are seeing what I am seeing, yes?"

The younger Washer matched his laconic tone, a careful contrast to the simmering panic and awe around them.

"The figurehead appears to be made of flesh," he said calmly. "More to the point, it is moving."

"Ah." That was what he was seeing, yes. "Thank you."

Ships normally had a woman's figure carved into the bowsprit; or a fearsome creature designed to frighten other flesh-and-blood creatures away; or a coat of arms, if the ship were under sail from a House of power. The cupped hands and circle of vine was decidedly untraditional, and yet perfectly matching the ship's name, painted along the side in clear gold lettering.

This is a Vineart's ship, it announced. *Approach with caution.*

Never mind that Vinearts did not have ships, did not take to the sea. It was not forbidden, simply because it was not done to *be* forbidden. It was not tradition; it was not custom. Vinearts were creatures of the soil; they did not travel, they did not sail, they did not do anything that took them from their slave-rotted roots. . . .

But this boy, Jerzy, did.

Neth would have applauded that sort of courage . . . in anyone else.

The why of the boy's actions no longer mattered, to the Brotherhood. The fact that he so disrupted what was, leaving chaos and disaster in his wake, was cause enough to bring him in; the fact that he stepped so close to apostasy, even if he did not—yet—overstep entirely, was cause enough. In unsettled times, a man who did unsettling things was a danger. The deaths that occurred within the House of Malech . . . Some within the Brotherhood whispered that the boy went insane, killed his master and the Washers sent to take him, and fled. Some spoke, more loudly, of the boy not fleeing, but going to rejoin his true master, the source of the unrest itself.

Neth had met the boy, interrogated him. He did not believe him mad, nor evil. But facts remained: the Vineart was dead, two brothers were dead and the others missing, and the boy had fled on this ship.

On this ship with a figurehead made of flesh.

A figurehead in the form of Sin Washer's hands, cupped in blessing. Made of flesh.

The thoughts warred with one another in his head, giving him the beginnings of a headache to match his upset stomach.

Magic. Possibly. Probably. To a sailor, a superstitious lout, it could be magic . . . or a miracle.

And in truth, Neth was uncertain enough of the boy he was chasing that he was not entirely certain, either. The Brotherhood carried out His blessings, it was true. But Sin Washer had touched the Vinearts directly. His blood fueled their magic, directed their lives. If Sin Washer's gift were to cause such a transformation of wood to flesh . . .

Magic or miracle, this apparition needed to be treated with caution, and respect.

"Hold the longboat," he said, and heard another voice carry his order to the sailors waiting with towropes. "If they are aboard, we will know soon enough. If they have gone ashore, they will return, eventually. We will wait here and see what happens."

Chapter 15

*J*erzy knelt in the vineyard, hidden by the clustered vines, with his fingers cupping the fruit and his thoughts whirling with his discovery, until the sun sank behind the hills and the air filled with shadows. Only when a bat swooped overhead, off for its evening hunt, did he realize how long he had been gone. Placing the grapes carefully on the ground, he retraced his steps to the House, so wrapped up in his own thoughts he almost did not care who saw him— in fact, he was not aware if anyone had seen him, or spoken to him, or tried to stop him.

He made it back to the rooms, only to be greeted by a young slave waiting by the door.

"I take you," the boy said, his Ettonian rough but clear, with a respectful bow that almost brushed his flat nose across the floor.

Jerzy nodded, then went inside and shut the door in the boy's face. Moving quickly, he went to the basin, pouring water over his hands and splashing his face and neck to try to wipe every trace of the soil from his skin, all the while wanting nothing more than to keep it to himself, to lay claim to the vines from root to leaf.

They were not transplants. They were not wild vines, gone feral without a Vineart to shape them. They were . . .

They were not his vines. This was not his vineyard. He kept repeating that to himself, trying to make his still-quivering senses understand. But the way the vines had called him, until he could practically feel the tendrils curling around his wrist and ankle, the roots pulling him down into the soil, left him shaken and disturbed. Did Esoba know what he grew, isolated out here? Did he *understand?*

The effects of the heal-all was wearing off, and Jerzy could feel the lassitude creeping back into his mind, trying to convince him to relax, that nothing was wrong, that he should not worry about anything. If he wasn't aware, hadn't been able to sense the magics subtly influencing him, he would have thought that a perfectly reasonable suggestion. Jerzy took another sip of the heal-all, then a longer pull, careless of how much he used, trying to clear his mind.

Unblooded.

The First Growth had been, legend went, pale green even when ripe, their flesh full of magic. When Sin Washer broke the Vine, his blood spread through the roots of the world, changing the vines throughout the Lands Vin. From the Blooding came the legacies, the Second Growth, limited in what it could do. No more concentration of power, no more mages who thought themselves equal to the gods.

Some vines were deeper red than others. Master Malech had said that the less touched, the stronger—and less amenable to incantation— the *vina* would be. Giordan's vines, the weathervines, were the most stubborn, the most delicate . . . but even they were tinted with the red of Sin Washer's sacrifice. Even they were bound to what they could do, what they could be.

There were no unblooded vines left. The First Growth was gone, its tart, pale green spellwine as much a legend as Sin Washer himself. Therefore, the vines Jerzy had touched could not be unblooded. It was impossible.

But they were the closest thing Jerzy had ever felt. Even now, the magic in them was thrilling his bones like a deep vibration, an almost painful hunger and an ache and a longing all in one.

He had touched the vines, and they had touched him, and his mind was flayed open, his senses raw and ragged, and he could not allow the magic to rule him, could not allow it control.

A Vineart controlled himself.

And so Jerzy scrubbed the trace off his skin, and changed his clothing, and slicked back his hair—too long now for neatness, and too thick for a thong, he left it wet and tucked behind his ears—and rejoined the patient slave, who led him to the main hall, where the others had been keeping Vineart Esoba distracted, as Jerzy had requested.

There was another man with them, solidly built, with skin color closer to Ao's bronze than ebony, but dressed in the same brightly colored fabric, tied securely at shoulder and hip. A younger, darker-skinned man with a flat-nosed face like the slave boy's stood behind him, dressed similarly.

"Ah, there you are. I hope that your walk was satisfying." There was veiled curiosity there, but no suspicion that Jerzy could discern.

"My apologies," he said to their host, in response to the combined greeting and accusation. "It has been a long journey, and I felt the need to refresh myself, by touching soil more thoroughly than has been possible until now."

He did not care if the others thought he had rolled in a mud puddle—if Esoba was any kind of Vineart at all, he would understand.

"Yes, your friends tell me you traveled by water. You are a most enterprising young man, indeed; I have never even seen a boat, much less stepped on one." Esoba cocked his head, watching Jerzy with an unnerving intensity.

"May I introduce you to Merchant Benit, who handles the sale of all my wines for me?"

"Vineart," the merchant said, inclining his head in a polite, if neutral greeting, not bothering to offer his companion's name.

Normally a trader clan would handle such dealings. Jerzy looked at Ao curiously, but his companion looked down at his plate and said nothing.

"Merchant Benit," Jerzy replied, taking the cue to ignore the man standing behind Benit, and slid into the seat offered, to the right of the Vineart, next to Ao. Kaïnam sat on the other side, with the merchants, while Mahault was a little farther down the table, as though there were an invisible wall between the males and her. Jerzy looked at her, uncertain, and her chin dipped slightly, her attention never leaving Esoba. A female servant sat behind her, on a stool—a meek demure mouse of a woman, nothing at all like the scowling guard her father had set on her, in Aleppan.

Jerzy tasted the air, carefully, trying to determine if the scent of the taint hung over the two merchants. It did, but no more than what he had felt elsewhere, and with the hum of the vines still in his skin, Jerzy was not quite sure he trusted his judgment in anything just then.

"We are an . . . interesting group," he said only, carefully, in response to Esoba's comment, not sure what else his companions might have said previously. When he had asked them to cover for his absence, he had not warned them off any topics—but they were smart, and they knew what not to say. He hoped.

"Sadly, as interesting as you are indeed, I must excuse myself," the merchant said, rising with another, deeper bow of his head to Esoba, as his companion moved with him, a voiceless, nameless shadow. "My apologies, Vineart. But there are things that cannot wait for my attention."

"Of course," their host said carelessly, waving off the man's apologies. "You shall rejoin us when you are done."

"Of course."

There was a moment of silence as the two men left, during which a slave came forward to place a platter in front of Jerzy, and fill it with some sort of meat that smelled better than anything Lil had ever prepared—although some of that might have been due to living on ship rations for so long.

Ao, as ever, leaped to fill the gap. "When Jer's master asked us to find new places where he might try transplanting his vines, we never expected to find a Vineart here," he said smoothly. "Outside the Vin Lands . . . and doing so well. Your work is quite extraordinary." He lifted the glass he was holding, as though offering it to Jerzy. "This spellwine, it aids in the digestion," he explained. "A glass before meals, and no matter how inedible the food, no rushed trips to the privy, after!"

"A healwine?" Jerzy asked, picking up his own glass and sniffing at it carefully, looking for the telltale nose that would identify the legacy. He was not surprised when he could not recognize it at all. A spell like that could come from healvines or aethervines, according to Master Malech's lessons.

"Ah, not exactly healwine," Esoba hedged, looking both shy and sly, tilting his head and looking at Jerzy. "My vines are rather unique—that is why I have so few; they require most careful handling."

Jerzy would not doubt that for a moment. The power he had felt in those vines could outproduce Master Malech's main yard, even in a poor year. If the Vineart were able to craft them properly . . . It seemed impossible to Jerzy that Esoba could do that. But they might also all still be enspelled into thinking him a jovial fool.

Jerzy did not know, and the not-knowing was the problem. Was Esoba their enemy, or another victim? He needed information, before they went any further.

"How old are your vines?" It was a fair question, one that would raise no eyebrows even among the most conservative of Vinearts. The age of a House was one of its strengths; even Vineart Giordan, who had been a complete rebel in that regard, had taken his master's vines with him when he planted his new yards—for all the good it had not done him.

And yet, for all the innocence of the question, Esoba hesitated. "I have worked them for nearly two decades," he said finally. "I do not know how old the vines themselves are."

The others could not know how odd that answer was, and Jerzy hid his reaction under the guise of taking a sip of the spellwine. His Senses open, looking for any hint that this *vina* was more than Esoba claimed, he let it linger briefly on his tongue, and then allowed it to slip down his throat. As expected, it tasted much as the previous *vina* had—smooth and ripe, but with more of a structure than that altered pour. Beyond that, there was no sense of magic to it at all. A true *vin ordinaire*.

Jerzy was at a loss. He was not a scholar, he did not know the ancient legacies, did not understand the intricacies of the Blooding. He knew only that something was off here, that magic was being used on them, and he could not rely on the others—if he, with his own spellwine in his veins, could not be certain what was real, then how could they?

"How much of this spellwine do you produce," Ao was asking, leaning forward with his elbows planted firmly on the table, his dark eyes opened wide in an attempt to look honest and trustworthy and, perhaps, a little innocent. "Because no matter how good your merchant friend might be, there are courts I have contacts in where this would go for a plentiful coin."

Kaïnam laughed, breaking into the conversation with an easy chuckle enough unlike him that Mahault raised her head to stare, curiously. "Forgive Ao, Vineart Esoba. His instincts are sound, but like all the trader folk, he cannot resist the urge to bargain—even in social settings."

"I am not offended," Esoba assured them. "Sadly, I produce only so much each year, and I already have an Agreement with Benit. A local lord has been pressing me for Agreement, but I . . . I do not like his words. Benit suits me."

"So you have no contact with the Vin Lands at all?" Jerzy asked, although he already knew the answer.

"The old world does not know we exist." He seemed almost proud of that fact. "My master left there, cultivating this yard and building the House. He took his slaves from the local population—I have never known anything else."

So it was possible Esoba had no idea what he tended, how amazing, how impossibly rare. Or he was playing a deeper game than any of them suspected.

Master Malech had suspected a Vineart. They had not conceived of a Vineart who did not know his own strengths. Or unblooded vines. These were vines that could—in capable hands—potentially create the spells that their enemy had used: to animate dead flesh, strike a blow from an impossible distance, hear words whispered on a far-away wind, and send a blow of magic to eliminate a threat.

But was this man—this seemingly simple, comfortable host—the master behind the plot? Or was someone else using him, manipulating him as others had been? And if so, where was the whispering voice, the spell-bearing aide?

Step carefully, Jerzy could almost hear Ao telling him, teaching him how to get information, back in Aleppan. Go one way when you are looking in another.

"Where did your master come from, do you know?" Jerzy asked, and then turned to the others. "The slavers collect us from everywhere, and we are dispersed like seeds on the wind, the magic claiming us when we come to the proper vineyard, when we find the correct master." They knew this; he hoped they would realize he was trying to set a trap.

Their host frowned. "He never—"

There was a loud crash, coming from the front of the House, and raised voices, shouting. Kaïnam was on his feet in an instant, the chair sliding back behind him as he rose, while Mahault followed an instant later, more clumsy, knocking her chair over.

"Stay here," Kaï ordered the others, his hand going to where his blade should have rested at his belt. He swore under his breath, then shook the lack off. "Mahl, with me, to the left."

Mahault moved into second position by his side, as though they had trained for that when sparring on the deck of the *Heart*, and disappeared out the door of the dining hall.

"What?" Esoba began to say, and was interrupted by a sharp, shrill scream, and the sound of something large and heavy breaking open.

"The front door," Ao said, tensing, but not rising from his seat. "Someone's coming in. With a bit of violence."

"Impossible!" Their host stood now, his frame practically shaking with indignation. "I will put a stop to this immediately!"

Jerzy let him go: it was his House; he should be front and center of any defense that was mounted. That was Esoba's responsibility. But the image of Malech's body, still and bloody, made him stop Ao when the trader would have followed out of foolish—and possibly deadly—curiosity. "Wait until the others return," Jerzy said, when Ao protested. Mahault and Kaïnam were fighters. He and Ao could defend themselves, if need be, but their skills were in other directions.

With that thought, he picked up the goblet in front of his plate and drained it. *Vin ordinaire* or not, if this came from unblooded grapes . . . he did not know what it might do, what it might add to the magic pooling within him. That thought, rather than frightening him, made him more eager to discover the result.

The *vina* filled his mouth and his senses, intensifying the now-fading effect of the heal-all, and tickled the awareness of quiet-magic into wakefulness. He did not know what he could do that might be useful in this case, but he would be as prepared as possible.

There was another scream, this one longer, and the sound of voices shouting—then their host, angry and demanding. Another voice answered him, and there was the sound of running steps, heading toward them, not away.

"Come on." Mahault stood in the doorway. Her hair had come down from the neat knot at the back of her head, her skin was flushed, and she was carrying a blade she hadn't possessed earlier in her left hand. The edge reflected the candlelight in a way that said it was wet.

"Come on," she said again, more urgently, when they didn't respond. "We have to get out of here, now. Whoever came to visit, they're not interested in conversation."

"I'm not going anywhere," Jerzy said, the image of Master Malech, of the shocked, sorrowing faces of Detta and Lil foremost in his mind. A Vineart protected the House. . . . If Esoba were as feckless, as badly trained as he seemed . . . "He's our host. We owe him—"

"We owe other people more," Mahl said, and they stared at each other until there was an explosion of some sort, and the walls rattled in response.

"That didn't sound like blackpowder," Ao said, cocking his head to evaluate the sound. "Magic?"

"Magic," Jerzy confirmed, feeling the waves of it carry through the building, the taint hot and sour. The intruder was the source. He grabbed the pitcher of wine from the table, looking for something to carry it in without spilling. Seeing nothing, he took a long deep swig of the liquid, ignoring both his own uncertainty and the reactions of his two companions. It was not done, to treat *vina* the way one might ale or water, but he could see no other way to carry it.

The liquid splashed down his throat, the sense of the magic within it almost overcoming him, in such a dose. There was a reason spellwines were taken in small sips; more did not increase the power of the spell, but rather overwhelmed the user until the decantation was impossible to perform.

A Vineart was not overwhelmed. A Vineart *controlled*.

Jerzy took a deep breath, not looking at his companions, and then slipped past Mahault and out into the hallway. The door she had indicated was to the left. The fighting was coming from the right.

He turned right.

"Jer!"

He heard the others calling his name but did not respond. They could go if it suited them. Esoba could not defend the House alone. Jerzy would not abandon these vines to anyone who came in with violence, stinking of that taint.

That, in his mind, would be the true apostasy.

The hallway was disturbingly empty, the sleepy-looking guards gone, although he did not know if they had fallen, or run. A year before, the slave called Fox-fur would have hidden, hoped the violence would pass him by. Now Jerzy pushed through, unhesitating, to find the source.

The only noise now came from the main hallway, where they had first been greeted. The massive door had been battered down, now lying flat on the floor, and half a dozen bodies were sprawled, bleeding or already dead. Most were slaves, dressed only in their colorful wraps, but two bodies belonged to strangers, fighters, wearing worn brown leather trou like the solitaires and leather bands across their bare chests, with some sort of metal plate the size of a spread hand fixed on them, front and back. A sigil of some sort, but—not surprisingly—not one Jerzy recognized. Ao might, or Kaïnam.

A man stood in the middle of the carnage, dressed like the fallen soldiers, only he still held a thick, deadly looking blade in his hand. In front of him knelt a handful of others, including Kaïnam, his proud head bent, but not—if Jerzy could read him at all—subdued. The stranger looked up and saw him, then shouted words in a language Jerzy did not understand. The man—thick-muscled, with skin so dark it seemed almost to absorb the light around him—shook his head and then said again, in passable Ettonian, "You! Put up your weapons!"

Since Jerzy had no weapon in his hands, he held them up, palm front, to indicate he was obeying. A hard push came from behind, between his shoulder blades, as the intruder's men found him, and he stumbled forward, falling to his knees with the others.

The scent of the taint came to Jerzy's senses, like spoiled meat, or the aftermath of a charnel fire. This man was coated in it, but Jerzy did not think that he was the source. There was power in him, but no magic.

"You all fought well," the man said, switching back and forth between the two languages, one a liquid roll of sounds Jerzy could not understand, the other an oddly accented Ettonian. Clearly, Jerzy's arrival had interrupted him. "You fought well and there is no disgrace in that. But it is over, now."

There was another disruption—shouting and the clash of bodies—and Jerzy turned his head just enough to see Esoba dragged out to join them, a guard at each elbow and his hands bound behind his back. The Vineart saw the man standing in front of them, and his face—previously so open and friendly—folded into a fierce scowl.

"You dare?" Esoba was outraged. More, he was offended. "Sin Washer's Command—"

"Has no bearing in these lands, I have been informed," the intruder replied calmly, speaking Ettonian, as Esoba had. "These are not his lands, and we are not bound by those rules. I made my offer in good faith and tried to reach Arrangement. You refused. Now, I take what I want."

Jerzy started to object, that arrogance moving him where the violence had not, but a sharp elbow in his ribs stopped him.

The elbow had been Kaïnam's. His gaze was focused on the man in front of them, his face grim set and stern, but a faint twitch in the side of his cheek nearest Jerzy indicated that he was not as resigned or as calm as he seemed. His blade had been taken, and there was a ragged cut on the prince's arm that needed tending, but he waited along with the other defenders, demanding nothing, saying nothing.

"This is an outrage!" Esoba said, but he also did nothing, merely stood there, blustering, rather than raising a spell against this intruder.

He had no quiet-magic, Jerzy realized. Or his master had not taught him about it, how to gather and use it. Esoba was helpless without a spellwine in hand, at the mercy of this man brushed with the taint enough to make Jerzy gag from the stink of it.

In the midst of the carnage, a thought came, cold and calm: Esoba was no Vineart. He did not deserve these vines.

Jerzy could still feel the magic he had taken—from the heal-all; the spellwine they had been drinking; the vines, running in the flesh of his cheeks, limning his throat—and knew that, if he tried, he could raise quiet-magic enough to . . .

To do what?

Sin Washer's Command was clear: power or no, Esoba was Vineart here. Kaïnam had the right of it. Stay still, be taken for some of the Vineart's men. Kaï could pass as an exotic hire-sword, while Jerzy could still play the slave, if needed. Ao could blend anywhere, it was his gift; and Mahl . . . she could be a solitaire, or could disappear into the women's quarters. . . .

"If you agree to my terms, your people will be let go, and you will not be harmed. I will, of course, leave my men here. Merely as a precaution. All other terms will remain as per my offered Agreement." He smiled, as though to show that he was, in fact, a reasonable and generous man, as though the terms had been written by Negotiators, and signed in good faith, not scrawled in the blood of slaves. "Ah, Sahr Benit. As you can see, we have all come to terms."

Benit came into the room carefully, with the cautious movements of a man not accustomed to being around violence and a look of distaste on his face. Kaïnam let out a low rumble that might have been a curse, but otherwise remained still and quiet, and Jerzy felt the inside of his chest constrict, as though a giant fist were squeezing from the inside.

Layers of betrayal: merchant and lord, turning on Vineart . . . the taste of the taint grew in the room until Jerzy thought that he might gag.

Then a greater worry intruded: the man had been introduced, he knew who—and what—they were. If he said anything . . .

"You!" Esoba strained forward, his mouth working furiously, as though unable to say more than that. If looks could have killed, the merchant leader would be on the floor with the other bodies, the hate was so intense. "You betrayed me?"

"I merely pointed out a few facts to our mutual acquaintance," Benit said, his manner as cool as it had been while sitting at the table of the man he had betrayed. "Surely you understand that I must look out for my own well-being—and he offered a much better Agreement than you. Still, we all win, here. He gets access to your vines; I make my profit . . . and you are not dead."

The merchant swept his gaze across the room, passing over Jerzy and Kaïnam, but just as Jerzy began to think that they might be able to escape unharmed, if the intruder kept to his word to release any who did not resist, the merchant's attention returned to them, and he frowned.

"Sin Washer, defend us," Jerzy muttered, even as the merchant, his gaze now firmly locked on Jerzy's face, reached out a hand as though to gather the land-lord's attention. If Benit identified Jerzy as a Vineart, there would be no escape for any of them.

Jerzy tried to shake off the surge of magic that was trying to claim him, drive him into action. This was not his House. And yet, a vineyard was at risk—if he did nothing, the vines would fall under the control of a man of power. Worse: a man of power who stank of the taint. For the first time in his life, Jerzy understood hatred.

He felt Kaïnam shift next to him, and knew that the other man was readying himself for action, despite his earlier actions willing and ready to follow in Jerzy's lead. The only problem was, Jerzy had no idea what to do.

You are Vineart.

Distant, stretched almost to breaking by the distance between them, the feel of the Guardian's words was less weight and more a scrape against his thoughts, the rasp of stone against flesh, a rough caress.

A Vineart crafted spellwines. A Vineart shaped the magic.

A Vineart *protected* the magic.

The Washers claimed that they protected the people from magic, from the abuse of magic, keeping their eye on Vinearts, through Sin Washer's Command. But here it was not Vinearts who hungered for more. . . .

All this went through Jerzy's thoughts faster than he could acknowledge, a whirl of emotions and memories, not all of them his own. Out of that whirlwind, a tendril crept and grew, winding itself around his awareness until he knew what to do.

If he let them, the vines would tell him what to do.

His mouth watered, and Jerzy felt the quiet-magic come alive under his touch, drawing it onto his tongue until his entire mouth tingled from the sensation. Healwine, filling his body, protecting it, intensifying it until Jerzy almost passed out from the sensation of knowing every inch of his body so intimately, inside and out. Master Malech's healwines, the fruit and soul of vines he had tended for most of his life, the soil that was pressed deep into his skin, the mustus that was deep in his bones, his blood. It came to his call now, and met the unblooded spell-wine in his stomach, blending and re-forming a new spell, under Jerzy's guidance and the Guardian's knowledge.

Blooded wine would not re-form, once incanted. Quiet-magic could only go so far.

But those two, with the weight of spell-carved stone behind it . . . It might be enough. It might be something even worse.

The land-lord heard Benit's urgent whisper, and his gaze swung to Jerzy as well, his expression going from annoyed to incredulous to a dawning realization that did not bode well for Jerzy or his companions. The land-lord's hand slid to his belt, touching on a shorter, still-sheathed blade, and the last of Jerzy's hesitations fled.

"Healspell, unheal," he told it, barely moving his lips, thinking the words more than he was saying them. Quiet-magic did not need decanting; the Vineart *was* the spell, and even as Jerzy formed the words, the magic flowed from him, almost visible in front of him as it rushed forward, his eyes and mind shaping it into a winged form, sinuous neck outstretched, pointed muzzle aiming directly at the land-lord's gut, one wing slamming into the merchant standing beside him.

Jerzy could feel the backwash in his own stomach, even as the magic changed its shape, even as the lord doubled over, his hand falling from his belt to grasp at his stomach, his face twisting in pain and anger. Then his head bent forward, he fell to his knees in an uncanny echo of the captives in front of him, and dropped with a heavy thud to the floor, and did not move.

Beside him, the merchant had also doubled over, but the bolt of Jerzy's anger had gone into the lord, diluting the impact, and he yet lived. His head lifted, and he glared at Esoba, only to realize from the Vineart's expression that he had not been the one to strike them.

Before the merchant could switch his attention to Jerzy, Kaïnam reacted, lurching forward with a high-pitched yell in a language Jerzy did not know. He grabbed the short blade from the lord's belt, unsheathing and twisting and shoving it upward into the merchant's stomach before the man could do more than twist away from the attack.

And then chaos broke loose around them, as the previously subdued captives realized what had happened and got to their feet, and the fighters who had come with the lord rushed to counterattack, seeming not to realize that their master was already dead. Jerzy was quickly lost in the flailing of bodies, apparently striking at random; his training—keep an attacker off guard, run when you can, strike hard when you must—was totally useless in such a melee. And magic—anything he tried could hit friend as well as foe, even if he could think of anything. Firespell—no. A sleep spell? Then he'd have to wait for Kaï to wake up. . . .

The scent of the taint, suddenly even thicker in the air, jerked Jerzy out of his confusion. He looked up, his gaze going directly to the source, in the room with him.

The merchant, staggering upright, his hands clutching at his gut, trying to staunch the bleeding, his mouth moving in words Jerzy didn't need to hear to understand.

He was calling for help.

Not letting himself think, aware that it needed to be now or it would be too late, Jerzy launched himself at the merchant. Even as he moved, his mind was forming what he needed, calling up the last ready reserves of quiet-magic, forming it into another . . . not a spear. A rope, this time. Firespell, to encircle and contain.

"Hold and bind," he said, even as the magic rose up and left him.

He had used too much, exhausted from the first strike. The flickering dragon-shape was weak, fragile, and would not hold; he realized that even as he flung himself into action. His hands found a grip on the merchant's arm, the tricks Cai had taught him rising instinctively the way the weapons master had promised they would. An elbow, here. A leg, there. A knee and shoulder, like that, and Vineart and merchant fell, entangled, to the ground, both grunting in pain.

The taint touched Jerzy then, settling on his skin and making him shudder. He resisted the urge to pull away, holding on tighter to the merchant's soft flesh, as though the man might somehow wiggle away if he only held his clothing.

"Who sent you?" he demanded, his face in the man's sweat-flushed face. The blood was seeping from the man's gut, dripping over Jerzy's hands and arms, but it was less disturbing than the layer of ooze the taint laid on everything, this close. "Who. Sent. You?"

Jerzy could feel the taint on this man, and he would not let him escape, not without an answer. Master Malech was dead. His yards were in danger. He tasted a bitterness in his mouth that was neither wine nor bile, the tang of blood, and licked his lips, feeling another shudder run through him, but this one was not as unpleasant. His hand raised, reaching for the man's face, intending to . . .

To do what? a voice whispered again. What will you do?

The question stilled him—not long, but enough for the merchant to start mouthing those words again. A decantation: Jerzy recognized the pattern if not the language, but there was no spellwine, and this man had no quiet-magic. . . .

The taint rose again, enough to make Jerzy gag. No quiet-magic, but a feel of it, borne in that stench, and it came from the man in his hold. Jerzy slammed his hand hard enough to feel the merchant's nose break under it, demanding again in a cold, sharp voice he didn't recognize as his own: "Who. Sent. You?"

There was a quiver in the air, as though it were shaken like a cloth, and then something putrid slammed down hard over Jerzy, shattering against his skin in a thousand places, and the world disappeared.

Chapter 16

er?"

Vineart.

The combination of the two voices, one in his ear, the other deep in his mind, was enough to wake Jerzy into full awareness.

"Am I late? What?" He tried to swing himself out of bed, and discovered that he was not in his bed in his chamber in his master's House, or even the hammock cot on the *Vine's Heart*, and that his head felt like someone had broken a wall over it. A hand gripped his arm hard enough to bruise, keeping him from swaying or falling over, and slowly he remembered.

"He's gone."

"He didn't feel anything." Mahl was the source of the voice, kind and worried, and Jerzy craned his neck—carefully, slowly, not wanting to throw up—to look at her in confusion. There was sunlight coming in from the window on the far wall: pale light. It was morning.

He shifted his attention away from the passage of time and back to Mahault's confusing words. "What?"

"Esoba. He didn't . . . oh." She looked down, away from his gaze, as though suddenly realizing that he had no idea what she was talking about. Her hair was back in a tight braid, and her face looked drawn and strained. "I'm sorry, Jer. I thought you . . . they killed him. Esoba. We got there too late, and he just . . ."

"The merchant," Jerzy said, not caring about the other Vineart's fate at that moment. "He's gone." The last thing he could recall, the taint enveloping them, the man's soft flesh becoming even softer under his grip, struggling to hold on and knowing that he could not.

"He's nowhere in the House," Ao said, from across the room. He was sitting in one of the few high-backed chairs, holding something wrapped in cloth to his head. There was a dark bruise against the other side of his face, and his right leg was propped out in front of him as though it hurt. "We have his servant, though. Kaïnam caught him before he could fall on his blade."

"They didn't take the servant," Jerzy said, thinking that through. His bones ached when he moved; the healvine had burned from his body—had it been what saved him, when the tainted magic stole the double-dealing merchant away? "Did they not know about him, or was he not important enough?"

"Take? Who took?" Ao leaned forward, then hissed in pain and leaned back again. "Jer, what happened in there? You ran off, then we had to deal with some bullyboys. By the time we found you, Kaïnam just muttered something about mad Vinearts and idiot soldiers, told us to bring you here, and then rounded up what was left of the House-servants to do a search for survivors, or any of the lord's men who might have been hiding."

Jerzy's thoughts were getting clearer, sharper. The mindspell, whatever it had been, had not been cast at them, but those already here, either Esoba, to make him docile, or the guards, to keep them from fighting back. Whoever had cast it, the effects were gone.

"The merchant. He sold out Esoba to the local lord, the one who was harassing him."

"What?" Mahault's jaw dropped open, and even Ao looked surprised.

Kaïnam knew, but Kaïnam was not there, and obviously had not stopped long enough to explain.

"The vines here . . ." Jerzy stopped, unable to explain. He wasn't even sure he understood, himself, how rare and impossible they were. He didn't think the merchant or lord had known, either; they had been manipulated, led by promises they could understand.

But the source of the taint . . . oh, it knew. It knew very well what was hidden here. The merchant might have thought to take two Vinearts for the betrayal of one. But this had long been in the planning, long before they had arrived.

"They were all tampered with: merchant, and lord, and Esoba, too. Our bad luck that we were here when it all came to a head."

Mahault was more suspicious than Ao. "Over a simple vineyard in the middle of nowhere? It doesn't have any advantages—too far from the harbor, and forgive me, Jerzy, but one small vineyard is hardly such a prize. You don't believe that it was because of us?"

Jerzy shook his head, trying to think how to explain why this vineyard was so valuable. "Oh. Ow." The world swam in front of him, and his stomach revolted, dry heaving.

"You got whacked over the head with something even harder than your head," Mahl said, her hands gentling on him. "You're making a habit of that. Sit back, if you won't lie down."

He obeyed, because it seemed the better choice than falling over. He looked up at Mahl as she settled him on the cushioned settee, suddenly noticing that there was a bandage on her arm, and she was moving as though she was favoring her left side.

"Yeah," Ao said, watching him watch Mahault. "Everyone's banged up. But we won."

"Won?" Jerzy closed his eyes, willing the room to stop spinning quite so much. "Esoba dead, the source still unknown—this is winning?"

"We're alive," Kaïnam said from the doorway. "That makes us the winners." The prince was unmarked, but his shirt was torn and stained with blood, and his blade remained in his left hand, as though he had forgotten that he could put it down. "Are you well, Vineart?"

The formality felt odd, until Jerzy saw movement behind the prince, shadowed bodies waiting in the hallway. Waiting for answers. Waiting for a master.

Then it hit him, truly. Vineart Esoba was dead. The vines were unprotected. The slaves were without guidance. This House had no Detta, no Guardian.

It only had him.

Exhaustion slammed into a sick despair and uncertainty, what he desired fighting what needed to be done. The temptation to reach for the vines threatened to overwhelm him, drown him in the need, but he forced himself to focus on the more immediate problem.

"I am well."

Kaïnam came fully into the room then, letting the heavy wooden door close behind him and leaving the shadow figures to spread the word, as they would—and interpret it, as they would.

Once the risk of being overheard had been removed, Jerzy spoke directly to the prince. "The merchant was sent by our enemy, to specifically take down Esoba."

Kaïnam nodded, clearly having put the pieces together the same way, even with his more limited understanding of what had happened. "The lord did not act alone, nor did the merchant."

"They were played," Ao said, leaning forward, then wincing and leaning back upright again. "But who is this man, playing them? More, *where* is he?"

"*What* is he?" Mahl asked. The sword she had taken from one of the fighters rested across her lap now, one hand wrapped around the hilt as though itching to use it again, against something she could see, something she could hit.

"I don't know. He does things that are impossible. . . ." Even as he said it, though, something stirred in Jerzy's memory. Not the Guardian this time. Something else, closer. He wished he felt better, wished there were a flask of heal-all within reach. He considered sending Ao to find more, but wasn't sure if more *vin magica* would be wise, right now, after what he had done. Just the thought of holding a sip in his mouth made him feel nauseated. He ignored his body and focused on the question.

Their enemy had plucked the merchant away. The Guardian had moved him, and Mahault, the same way. But the Guardian was bound to him, and Mahault had merely been caught in that, by touching him. . . .

"I sense only the taint, laid upon others . . . no, not laid. Rising."

"Rising?"

"It touched me, coated my skin, but from the lord, the merchant . . . even the aide in Aleppan, it rose from within them, as though it were part of them."

"Is that possible?" Ao asked, and for the first time Jerzy could remember, Ao looked frightened.

"I don't know, and I have no one to ask. One by one, Vinearts of skill or courage are dying. Are murdered." Their disappearances, undermining the structure. The Guardian's fear, come true. The thing he was supposed to, somehow, prevent.

"The House here, outside the Lands Vin, beyond the claim of Sin Washer's Command—or, at least, the reach of the Washers," Kaïnam said, thinking out loud. "Whoever crafts this taint wanted Esoba under his control, or at least that of his proxies. But why?"

"The vines here . . . they are rare," Jerzy admitted. "A Vineart with no scruples, no adherence to the Commands . . . could do terrible things with them, if he had access."

"You suspected that Esoba's master had not taught him well; the training interrupted or unfinished, maybe, and he was given the yards without knowing what he was doing." Kaïnam was making the logical, political connections. "If so, the poor fool was ripe for the picking."

Like himself, the thought came creeping into Jerzy's thoughts, dark and sad and dangerous. Like him. Doubt and failure slid along his skin, and when Kaïnam touched his arm, he jumped slightly, shuddering hard enough that he removed his hand just as quickly. He wanted to apologize, but didn't know how—or for what.

"But . . . how is a failure like that possible?" Mahault asked, and then answered herself. "How would anyone know? You don't keep tabs on each other; you don't talk. It would be easy for some apprentice to take off one day, trying to leave his failure behind, then land here and find vines where there should have been none. . . ."

"And decide it was fate, and set himself up as Vineart," Jerzy said. "Magic calls to magic. These vines are . . ." He hesitated, then said only, "powerful." He would not—he *could* not—tell them what those vines were. Of all the things he had said, that was the one secret he could not share. No one could know, not if he wanted to keep them safe.

"Powerful enough to draw this taint-maker to him, as well as Esoba's master?" Ao had been quiet, but that drew his attention.

Powerful vines, perhaps the most valuable things in all the lands, Vin or barren. But they had not protected their would-be Vineart, in the end. Jerzy tried to remember the chaos of the fight again, tried to remember when Esoba had fallen, but all he could recall was the look on the merchant's face, the taint rising like a thick black-green mist over them, the sticky feel, the taste of something stale and unpleasant in his mouth. It disturbed him, made his throat close and his tongue curl away from the taste, but he did not know why.

"We have one source of answers," Kaï said. His tone was not reluctant, exactly, but cautious.

Mahault nodded. Her eyes had the same caution within them, and Jerzy felt a stir of unease, looking back and forth between them, even as he understood what the prince was suggesting. Kaï might know the ways, but it would be the Vineart who was feared.

"The merchant's servant?"

"Locked in one of the storerooms. Do you think that you can get answers from him?"

Everything in Jerzy shied away from the idea. "I do."

*   *   *

BEFORE JERZY COULD let himself rethink this, or question his judgment, they were out in the vineyard, with a sturdy wooden chair set in the middle of the yard, in between clumps of golden-brown vines. Just him and Kaïnam, and the servant, seated in the chair with Kaï's hand hard on his shoulder, to keep him there.

Ao and Mahault were back at the House; Jerzy had refused to explain himself, but told them to stay there and deal with the servants and slaves.

Much to his surprise, they had obeyed.

Kaïnam had brought the merchant's servant out, the man's legs tied with a loose loop of rope that hobbled him to a shuffling walk, his wrists bound behind his back. He looked worn, scuffed, but no less defiant, as though he did not know that his master had abandoned him, had fled and left him behind.

The aches and confusion Jerzy had been feeling since the tainted blast faded the moment they crossed the gate into the yard proper. He wasn't sharp, but he could focus. The vineyard was murmuring to him, the ropey twisted vines sliding into post-Harvest dormancy but still aware of him, now that they had been touched. There were no slaves to distract, no Vineart to control them, and so they reached for him the way they reached for water, or sun. Sin Washer had only enforced what happened naturally, when he bound them by Command to serve their vines.

Jerzy looked at the still-nameless servant, their gazes meeting, and something in the man's face changed as he realized what stood before him: not a soldier; not a feckless, untrained vine-tender, already befuddled by spells . . . but a Vineart, in full control of his magic.

Something inside Jerzy relished that sudden uncertainty in the man's expression, the first flickering of fear. He barely had to think what he wanted, this close to the vines, and they rose to do his bidding, creeping an inch at a time to wrap themselves around the servant's ankles above the ropes, locking him into the chair. His eyes went wide as he felt the first slither across his bare legs, and when they reached up around his waist, he tried to bolt. Kaïnam had to be just as startled, but the prince's hand kept their prisoner seated until there were enough vines binding him to the chair that he could not move even if released.

"One more," Jerzy said, and this time he made a show of lifting his hand, directing the single vine that slid along the back of the chair, then snaked down around the servant's neck, wrapping tightly once, then twice. The fear shivered through the man, and Jerzy hesitated; then the memory of Master Malech, his dark blue eyes cold and distant, came back to him, firming Jerzy's resolve for what he must do.

A Vineart never showed weakness. To defend his House, to protect these vines around them; to do what must be done, he must do what needed to be done.

Jerzy leaned forward, crouching down, resting his palms flat against his thighs. This close, he could smell the dirt, the early-morning sun barely warming it, mixed with the stench of the man's sweat, stale after a night spent locked in a small, windowless room.

"Who approached your master?" he asked quietly, looking the man directly in the face. "Who sent him to the land-lord, to broker this betrayal?"

The man might be sweating, but he was not frightened. Not enough, anyway. "I do not know."

"I think you do."

The vine around the man's throat tightened, and his eyes widened, his mouth working as though to summon spit—not to cast a spell, but merely to moisten his mouth. Now, perhaps, he was frightened enough.

"Tell me, and you may live. Hold back anything, and I will know— and the vines will break your body down and plow you into the field."

Jerzy believed every word he spoke, and the vines shifted against the man's skin, as though reflecting the anger within the Vineart.

"A Negotiator," the servant said, finally breaking. "A month ago. My master had just established Agreement with Vineart Esoba, but the Negotiator said that a local lord wanted the vines, wanted Esoba to work for him, but the Vineart had refused. The Negotiator said that he could tell my master how to make it all work . . . without breaking Sin Washer's Command."

Because Sin Washer's word did not hold outside the Lands Vin. True or false mattered less than the claim being believed.

That explained why the merchant had no taint in him; he was merely a tool. "Tell me who the Negotiator represented," Jerzy said, his voice turning soft, a coaxing croon that made the servant shudder even more. "Tell me, and live."

KAï FOUND HIM in the vineyard; not within the yard, but standing beside it, watching it, as the sun cast long shadows across the mountains behind them.

"Mahault has everything well in hand; she may not wish a Household, but she knows how to run one." Kaïnam's admiration was real. "Ao is busy sorting through the House stores, replacing what we'll need. We should have everything cleaned up in a few hours, have a night's sleep, and be ready to go in the morning. I figured you would want to go through Esoba's cellar, before we leave?"

Jerzy nodded. "There should be a cellar book; it will tell me what his racking system is, so I can find anything that might be useful." He was not certain taking those wines would be a wise idea; he had no knowledge of the methods Esoba and his master had used to incant them, no idea what magic might be stored within. But he could not bear to leave them behind, either.

Thinking about that, the details of choosing and packing, the forward movement, was easier than contemplating what he had done.

Kaïnam squinted a little as a cloud passed and the sun shifted lower. "Jerzy . . . let it be. You did what needed to be done. What none of us could have done. There is no shame in being skillful. And now we have the name of our enemy."

The servant, his face now flushed with fear, stuttering with the desire to tell whatever they wanted to know. "Ximen. Praepositus Ximen. The

Negotiator looked like a man of our land, but he had a strange accent; he said he was a man of Iaja, an explorer, who had discovered a land of great wealth and magic, and we would have a share in all things, if we only did his bidding. I know no more, I swear."

Jerzy did not know if the man spoke the truth, but Kaïnam had believed him.

A Negotiator could be hired by anyone. Even a Vineart, who could not leave his vines, but wished to cause mischief.

A Vineart who could work his magic through others, using Agreement to push his will through their mouths, his actions through their hands. Who could reach anywhere, be everywhere, and never show his face.

Jerzy felt a rumble within him; his quiet-magic no longer quiet, waiting, wanting to be summoned. It made him uncomfortable, as though he had eaten rotted fruit. He had done things he did not know he could do, learned things he should never have known. It was too much: he desperately craved a slave's life, the certainty of the seasons, the surety of the overseer's lash, the secure acceptance of what was and was not. All gone, the moment Master Malech had taken him from the yard and, with that first sip of spellwine, shown him what he could reach for.

For a moment, for the first time in his life, he hated his master. Hated him for what he had done, and hated him for dying.

"These vines."

Jerzy didn't say anything, listening to the rage inside him.

"These vines," Kaïnam said again. "People were killed for them. You said they were powerful."

Jerzy waited. He knew what would come. Kaïnam had his own reasons for being with them, reasons more urgent than Ao's or Mahault's personal desires, and it would not serve to forget that.

"How powerful? Jerzy, if the magic they hold is so strong, if whoever started all this, who could do all this already, wanted them so badly, shouldn't we—"

The unease and sickness in his gut rose into Jerzy's throat, the rotting smell almost enough to make his eyes water. "Do what? Destroy them? Burn vines and salt the land, destroy knowledge, things of beauty and wonder, for fear?" He had thought it, had lifted a hand to the flask of firewine in his pack, not moments earlier, and considered it. "Or would you have me stay here and work the yard myself, steal another's vineyard? Would you have me become what they claim—would you have me become what *he* is? Would that bring your sister back, Kaï?"

Thaïs, the Wise Lady: murdered, Kaï believed, to drive his lord-father into acts that would set their island Principality against the other Vin Lands, turning them into scapegoats for whatever actions their unknown enemy made.

Kaïnam, unlike Ao, did not rise to the bait. "You want to. Stay here, I mean. Learn these vines. Ao and Mahault, they don't see it, but I do. Ao sees people to be manipulated to his best advantage or possible profit, and Mahl . . ." His expression turned rueful. "Mahl sees people as either obstacles or allies. She's single-minded that way. But I was trained to observe the currents of power, to learn what people want, what they won't speak of—what secrets they hold. You're holding a secret from us."

Jerzy didn't look at him, didn't move, but answered in a steady voice. "It's all right. These vines survived before anyone came to tend them. They'll be all right here for a while longer."

It hurt to say it, knowing it for the truth. He wanted to stay, but he could not. More, he should not.

Kaïnam heard only the spoken words. "And then you'll come back?"

"I don't know." He could still feel the roots and leaves whisper, but he knew now that they were not whispering to him. They had not saved Vineart Esoba, because they did not care. They did not recognize a Vineart's hand. Feral vines. Unblooded, untouched by Sin Washer's gift, left- or right-handed.

They were powerful . . . but they were not his. They were not anyone's.

And the body now buried under their roots, its neck wrapped thrice with vines, its face blue from strangulation, made Jerzy wonder if, in truth, he wanted them at all.

The vines had sensed his fear, his anger, and acted. Unlike the plague ship, he could not claim that act had been anything other than murder.

And yet, he could not bring himself to destroy them.

"There's still a long way to go, yet," he said out loud. "This Praepositus Ximen took the merchant back; if the man survived it, then he knows who we are, must assume that we know who he is, now. He will not hesitate to attack—directly, this time. I can't let him find me. Not until we have a way to strike back—and win."

Chapter 17

Off the coastline of the land the maps called Greater Irfan, just beyond the confines of the too-shallow bay, the Brotherhood's ship waited. They had been at harbor for nearly a quarter-turn of the month, waiting for any sign of their quarry returning, taunted by the empty shore and the quietly resting ship. A score of times, Neth had thought to set fire to the cursed Vineart's boat and leave, stranding the boy in this benighted land. A score and one, he had come to his senses before giving the order.

And now he had been rewarded.

"Shall we go after 'em?"

"No. Wait, and watch."

"Aye." The captain shifted the pipe in his mouth and nodded at the Washer, stalking away. That left Neth, but not alone, for the ship swarmed with sailors above and below, working silently, for the most part. The men had spent the past weeks glancing sideways at the ship still moored across the bay, spitting and making protective gestures whenever the unnerving masthead swung around to follow them.

Ship-rats were superstitious, unlettered creatures, but he could not blame them for their unease. The way those pale, carved hands moved, constantly stroking the leaves of its wreath, was disturbing, no matter what magics had caused them to move.

Neth was not watching the figurehead now, however, but the figures on the distant shore as they pulled a small craft from the brush and piled their belongings into it, unhitching the cart they had been using and handing over the beasts to another figure, who led them away, back up the cliff.

Patience. A Washer learned it, just as a Vineart did. He waited, his hands opening and closing on the rail, as they set onto the water, the craft pitching on the waves as it made for their ship.

"Alyn."

The Washer, a young boy no older than the Vineart they chased, stepped forward, making an almost involuntary bow. He was too young to be on such a mission, should still be in the Collegium at his studies, but every man they had was on the road, to quell the rising unrest, and that meant putting children into men's jobs.

The Vineart-student was no older, in truth, nor his companions. Neth felt every one of his forty years like armor across his back, weighing him down. Children, all of them.

"Alyn," he said again, because he must. "Fetch the men. Tell them to bring their arbalests." Traditionally, the Brotherhood was not supposed to go armed with more than a bludgeon or cudgel, any more than Vinearts, but that did not mean they did not know how to use them. And Brion had made sure they knew how to use them well.

The sailors would not aid them; frightened of the *Heart* as they were, it had been all the captain could do to keep them from mutinying. Asking them to go against the masters of that ship? No. They would have to do this on their own, seven armed Washers against . . .

Children? He looked at the figurehead again and shook his head. He did not know what they went against, and that was what worried him.

*   *   *

"Jerzy!"

The sound of his name being called out across the water didn't surprise Jerzy; Ao had spotted the longboat coming toward them a breath before, and it seemed unlikely that anyone would be so purposefully cutting them off from the *Heart* without being either pirates or Washers.

The dark red flag hoisted on the mainsail of the ship they rowed from put lie to the first possibility, leaving only the second.

The Brotherhood had found them.

"Jerzy, stow your oars and let us come aside."

"Rot if we will," Ao muttered, barely within hearing. Mahault, who had been sitting on one of the casks of spellwine, reached down to where her own blade rested, sheathed and wrapped against the risk of water.

Jerzy knew the voice; patient and calm and fully expecting obedience. Washer Neth.

"They have arbalests," Kaïnam said from his position at the bow. "They could take us from there, if they've any skill at all. Closer, and we're done for."

"Swords?" Jerzy didn't expect much, but he had to ask.

Kaïnam shook his head. "Swords are useless here, and I'd have to get in close to use a knife. By then . . ."

"Magic?" Ao asked.

"They'd be expecting that," Mahault said, her hand still touching the blade as though disbelieving Kaïnam's evaluation of its usefulness.

"So, what? We just give over?" Ao sounded more annoyed than worried.

The longboat was moving closer as they argued. The Washers were not trained sailors, but perfectly capable of rowing in unison, with purpose.

"I have no waterspells," Jerzy said. "Healvines and firevines . . . useless here unless I want to set their boat afire, and Washer Neth is too canny for that, assuming any captain would allow his boats to touch water without protection."

Firespells could burn, or light without burning, but they could turn fire aside, as well. It all depended on how the Vineart incanted the firevine *mustus.*

But Jerzy had more than Master Malech's vines to draw on. His gut turned at the thought of using more of the unblooded wines; it was too much, too dangerous, and he was not sure he could continue to control it. Still, he had the flask of Vineart Giordan's weatherwine. Barely half left, now, but enough, if he could use it properly . . .

"Neth will be expecting anything I do," he said to his companions. "So we will only have one chance. Be ready, and take the chance when it comes."

"What are you going to do?"

Jerzy stood cautiously, keeping the flask below the lip of the tiny boat, out of sight. "I haven't any idea," he said, and turned to face Washer Neth.

"Vineart-student Jerzy." Neth's voice was perfectly modulated, carrying over the water as though he were preaching the comfort in a village square.

Jerzy waited.

"I sorrowed to hear of Master Vineart Malech's death," the Washer said. "He was a strong and talented Vineart. We are diminished by his loss."

"Do you know who killed him?"

"I know that you didn't."

Jerzy waited again, the two boats rising and falling in the gentle rock of the waves, held steady by their oarsmen.

"Jerzy, if you decant a spell against me, my men will take you down before you can swallow. You know that, don't you?"

"I can capsize you before they loose a single bolt," Jerzy said in return, his voice as even and calm and confident as Neth's. He could . . . he was mostly sure that he could. Neth would be waiting for him to lift the flask, to go through the steps, but if Jerzy needed, he had enough quiet-magic in him now to touch the windspell, stir the waters, and set them on fire.

Create a firespout.

"I could kill you without flinching," Jerzy said.

"No. You couldn't. I know you, Jerzy. I know Vinearts. Whatever you have sunk yourself in, whatever is driving you . . . you are perhaps a fool, but not a killer."

The waves were slowly bringing the boats closer and closer together, until neither of them needed to shout in order to be heard. Kaïnam tensed; the weapons were within range.

"I would do it, if I had to," Jerzy said. His hands were not clean.

"And so would I," Neth said softly. "And all would likely die, in what followed. Is that what you desire, Vineart? Because it is not my wish. Not here, not today. Not if we can be civilized, and avoid it."

Neth did not know what Jerzy had discovered. Did not know the powerful, unmastered vines hidden in the hills behind them. If he did find out . . .

No. That vineyard was Jerzy's to protect, if not to use.

But he *could* use it, if he was careful.

"There is a vineyard three days' travel to the north," he said. They had traveled south. "A strong, well-planted vineyard. The Vineart there was murdered, the very day we arrived. Murdered, and his grounds claimed by the land-lord of this place. The land-lord claims they are beyond Sin Washer's Commands, as they are no part of the Lands Vin."

Neth was too smart, too experienced to splutter, the way another Washer might. But his eyes narrowed. And in that moment, the way Jerzy knew when a Harvest was good, he knew the Washer's secret.

The anger he had felt before rekindled, like sour wine heated in his stomach, making him feel ill.

"You knew," Jerzy said, "All along, you knew that land-lords were being tampered with. You knew about the maiar of Aleppan. You meant to use Sar Anton to test the maiar, him and Vineart Giordan, to see what they would do. You knew—"

"We knew very little." The waves shifted, and Neth almost lost his footing in the longboat, one of his men reaching up to steady him. "But we knew some, yes."

Jerzy thought of Giordan and his open-handed generosity; of foolish Esoba; of the unknown villagers killed by serpents, the slaves vanished when their master died. . . . Master Malech, his stern face no softer in death than in life. "And what did you do about it? This . . . and what Master Malech told you, the information we gathered. The Lands are under attack—and what have you done, Legacy of Zatim Sin Washer?"

It was too far to tell, the afternoon light too uncertain, but Jerzy thought that Neth's expression changed, looking pained.

"Go back," Neth said. "Make camp on the shore. I will send a bird to the chapterhouse, to ask for instructions from the Collegium, with this new information. My orders were merely to take you into custody, not deal with renegade lords. I do not feel qualified to deviate further, without their consent.

"Go back, and we will discuss this more on the morning."

"Jer . . ." Ao didn't quite whine, but it was close. The tension was a physical thing, a fifth body in their little boat.

"We have no choice," Jerzy said heavily. "No choice at all."

He sat down and picked up his oar, nodding at Ao to do the same, and they turned their craft around and rode the waves back in to shore.

THEY LEFT THE boat intact, taking out only what they needed to set up camp for that night, and Kai tethered the craft in the shallows, a branch and a rope anchoring it on the sand. Ao and Mahault built a fire against the night's chill, and they tried to settle down to a subdued meal. The smell of roasted vegetables and fresh meat taken from Esoba's kitchen made Jerzy feel queasy again, but they all ate their fill, facing ship rations and fish again on the morning.

After cleanup, Jerzy left the fire and, barefoot, wandered down to the waterline. The sand was cool under his feet, and for a moment Jerzy could almost pretend that it was the fine-grained soil of the northern vineyard.

Malech had said that the ground deep beneath them was the same rock of the hills to the west, a pale brown rock riddled with caves. Firevines liked that type of soil, and a good Vineart learned to recognize it.

Useful information . . . not useful here. But the sense that the sand under his toes was somehow related to the soil back home let Jerzy's thoughts settle, and his breathing even out, until he was utterly calm, staring at the rush and ebb of the water.

"What are we going to do?"

He had heard the others come up behind him, but hadn't wanted to acknowledge them. They were expecting him to come up with a plan, some way to evade the Washers, to reclaim the *Heart* and figure out their next step.

Part of Jerzy wanted to give in; Neth had authority, Neth would have orders from the Brotherhood. Who was he to challenge them, again and again? Master Malech had . . . he was not Master Vineart Malech. He was not even a Vineart, in truth.

You are Vineart.

It was not the Guardian's voice; Jerzy knew now that while vines might grow here, it was not part of the Vin Lands, did not share the common bond in the soil, and the dragon could not reach him. But the memory was sharp as the dragon's voice, and goaded him into speaking.

"Opinions?" he asked them, not turning around as they settled themselves on the sand around him.

There was silence, only the quiet rumble of the ocean, cut by an occasional night bird calling from up on the cliff, where the village was dark and still.

"This Washer Neth may be an honest man, but I do not trust the Brotherhood." Kaïnam, his voice as dry as the sand, but far more solid. "They are political, and will do as they see fit, and once we give them control, we will never get it back."

It was an opinion, no more and no less than what had been asked.

"Mahault?" Jerzy felt like there was grit in his throat, blocking speech.

"You are Vineart," she said. "I will follow where you lead."

Solitaires were known for two things: a fierce independence, and an even fiercer loyalty to their employer. Mahault might, temporarily, have abandoned that path, but she had taken both those things to heart, it appeared.

Jerzy waited, then, when there was no third voice, turned his upper body to look at Ao.

The trader was sitting cross-legged on the sand to Jerzy's left, all traces of the carefree boy Jerzy had met in Aleppan finally gone from his face, even in the moonlight. He gave a subtle shrug. "I'd rather risk myself than let someone make the decision. That way, I know the cargo's of my own choosing. But I've no skill with this sort of route."

None of them would tell him what to do. Neth would. But Neth was wrong.

The Guardian was silent. Master Malech was gone.

"Ao. You have a map?"

"I have many maps," he said, a little stung.

"With you?"

"I go nowhere without maps." He said it as though Jerzy should have known that, should not have doubted him, and despite himself, Jerzy smiled. "Get me one. As wide a range as you have."

While Ao went back to their campsite and rummaged through his pack, Mahault smoothed a portion of the dry sand in order to create a makeshift map table, and Kaïnam moved closer to Jerzy.

"You have a plan?"

"I have an idea," Jerzy said, unwilling to say more. Kaï nodded as though that was all he needed to hear.

Ao came back, unrolling the map and placing small, rounded lead weights at each corner to keep the edges from rolling up.

"Light," Jerzy said, and three small flames appeared over his open palm. He placed them in the air over the map, chasing away the dusk's shadows and making the legends written on the map legible.

"Where would the name Ximen and the title Praepositus be used," he asked Ao.

The trader knelt down and considered the markings. "Ximen's a popular name here, and here. Southern Iaja, and Riopa. I don't know about the title."

"It sounds Ettonian," Mahl said. "But I don't know what it means."

"Nor do I," Kaïnam said. "But if it's Ettonian, odds are good it's a military title."

"Iaja." A Vin Land. So was Riopa, island-nation, home of strong earthvines. Etton, home of . . .

Home of the ancient Emperor. Home of Sin Washer, who would have destroyed mankind, had his heart not been touched by the kindness of the common folk, the ones who became the first Washers, the heirs to his Legacy.

Jerzy's mouth was dry with worry and exhaustion, and he searched in vain for the slightest hint of moisture to draw the quiet-magic forward. The lights had come, but he had used too much, was too dry. There was too much grit in his throat, clogging him.

"Mahl, fetch me a wineskin."

She stood to obey, then paused midaction. "Which one?"

"It doesn't matter. The first you find."

Jerzy wanted to tell her to take one from Esoba's cellar, but he held back. That was desire, not need, speaking. He would not need that power, not for this. He hoped.

She returned, and he took a scant sip, feeling the leathery smoothness touch his mouth, making the flesh pucker. Whether by chance or fate, she had chosen a Riopan earthwine. Perfect.

Holding that puddle of magic on his tongue, letting it seep into flesh, calling the residual magic living within him, Jerzy reached down for a handful of sand. The thought came that this was perhaps how prince-mages had worked, not so much decanting as evoking, allowing the power to rise and express itself to fit the need.

The thought, at another time, would worry him. Not now.

His need touched the magic, flowing without conscious direction. Like unto the soil that nourished roots. Soil and root, vine and fruit. He knew the taint well enough now, winding his awareness of that into his Sense, letting them mingle the way the wave mingled with the shore, the wind wove through trees, touching but separate, one staying still, the other leading . . . where?

The hand holding the sand opened, slowly turning and tipping the sand onto the map.

"What—" Kaïnam started to ask, then stopped himself even before Ao and Mahl both held up hands to hush him.

"Shhh," Ao said. "Watch it."

The grains of sand blew as though a gentle wind picked them up, swirling around the mage-lights, then dropping to the surface of the map, still moving in a circular motion, first one way and then another.

Jerzy's eyes were closed, his hand steady over the map, his lips moving silently, barely visible as the night grew darker, the mage-lights not enough to illuminate him. Slowly, the sands blew away, whisking off the map and returning to the ground, leaving only a thin trail on the map itself, leading from the shoreline they rested on to . . .

Jerzy opened his eyes as he felt the magic fade, and looked down.

The sand led not to Iaja or Riopa, but a place off the map, to the western margins beyond Irfan. . . . To where a sigil for sea monsters and mer-witches was inked in the bright yellow colors of warning and danger.

The Forsaken Sea, where not even Iajan sea charts knew what lurked—or what lay beyond.

"Well," Ao said into the quiet uncertainty, "the Washers certainly won't think to look there."

"We need the ship, first." Kaïnam stood, stretching his body into a long lean line, and looked out over the now-dark waters to where the Washers' ship floated at harbor. Lights came from the deck, and the shadowy figures of sailors and guards could be seen moving against the brightness. "They'll see us if we use the boat, and it's too far to swim. Jerzy, can you move us, the way you were moved back to your House?"

"No. I . . . No. That magic . . . it is tied to the House. It will not work here."

"Then we'll do it the hard way," Kaïnam said, then checked his movement. "With your permission, Vineart."

There was no mockery in his voice, and Jerzy, feeling oddly light-headed, inclined his head with equal solemnity. "As you will, land-lord." Vineart and land-lord, in formal partnership. What was one more Command bent, after all this?

"Ao, Mahl, load our things, be ready to go. Quickly."

"What—" Ao rethought his protest, rolled up his map, careful to avoid the mage-lights, and followed Mahault back to their campsite.

"I would have you send them fire, Vineart. Fire that burns."

Jerzy swallowed, feeling the bitter finish of the spellwine in his throat. "I will not burn the ship out from under them," he said. "The sailors have done us no wrong, and the survivors would blacken our name—the same blackening you seek to erase on your own people's name."

"Not to burn them," Kaïnam said. "Burn us. Our camp. Let it go up in flames, and bring their attention here—while we go there. Can you do that?"

It was less a question than a demand. Jerzy turned to consider the shoreline. It would be easy to set the underbrush aflame, but it was dry, leaf and branch alike, and a spellfire set on it would roar out of control unless he was careful—and if they were paddling for safety, he would not be able to keep that control. And if it escaped, it would threaten the village.

A memory rose: one of the children he had healed, face glowing with vigor where before it had been ashen with illness. A child who lived in that village, where the people had been nothing but curious and kind. He would not endanger them, not even to save himself. Not if there was another option.

"The sand." Jerzy was speaking to himself now. "It will be slow to catch, but it will burn." He thought it would, anyway. Master Malech had claimed that a well-incanted firewine could burn anything, even stone.

"That will get their attention," Kaïnam said. "How long will it take you to be ready?"

Jerzy turned to face him, calculating what spellwine he had left. "Now."

They worked in silence, moving slowly so as not to raise suspicion in the eyes undoubtedly watching them from the Washers' vessel.

"This had better work," Mahl said, casting an uncertain glance back at where their bedrolls lay, spread out on the sand, clearly visible, stuffed as though bodies lay within.

"Shh." Ao hissed.

"There's no way they can hear us," Mahl said, her tone impatient, but she said it quietly, her left hand resting on her sheathed sword as she climbed over the wale of the boat and found her seat among their packs and supplies. Her muscles were tensed, and she kept glancing over her shoulder to where the ships waited, then whipping her head around to stare stonily at nothing.

"Ready, Vineart?" Kaï asked.

Jerzy nodded. "Push off. I'll catch up."

The moment they left the shore, Jerzy forgot about the others. There was only the faintly glimmering sands in front of him, the spellwine in his hand, and his determination to do this.

Despite his easy words to Kaïnam, this was no sure thing. Sand would melt before it took flame. Even a firespell would have difficulty—unless it was decanted just right.

No blending of spells. No borrowing from another Vineart's work. This was purely House of Malech.

"I am Jerzy, Vineart of House Malech." He spoken in a whisper, letting the night air catch his words and carry them forward. "I nurtured these vines. I gathered their fruit. I crushed their flesh, and bound them with their skins, until the magic bound by Zatim Sin Washer answered to my command."

He could feel, like a whisper of leaves against his skin, the spellwine in his hand, the small amount of his master's own work becoming aware of him. Recognizing his touch, the sense of his quiet-magic. So far from the first time he had felt the touch of mustus, from the first time he had understood what he was, what he could become . . . the sensation still humbled him.

Aware there was little time, he lifted the wineskin and poured a dose into the silver cup of his tasting spoon, letting the air touch the surface, and the magic grow. When he sensed that it was ready, he put the spoon to his mouth, taking a shallow sip and letting it rest on the bowl of his tongue.

"Flame to sand. Burn it clean and high. Go."

Quiet-magic met spellwine, the first pressing against the latter, compressing it into a dense, thick mass, then drove the magic hard against the packed sand at Jerzy's feet.

There was a hesitation, as though the wind held its breath, and for that breath Jerzy thought he had failed.

Then the sand hissed, water turning to steam, and a bright white sheet of flame threw itself up in front of him.

The sands were burning.

"Jer!" A tug on his arm, breaking him from his fascinated stare. "Jer, come on!"

Ao, fingers curled around his wrist, tugging on his arm, pulling him toward the water, even as the fire spread along the beach, and a low horn sounded across the water—the fire alarum, coming from the Washer's boat. They had seen the fire; they would be coming to investigate.

"In!"

Jerzy and Ao splashed out into the water and were hauled into the boat by the others, Mahl's strong arm grabbing Ao, while Kaïnam dragged Jerzy by the scruff of his collar and one leg, dropping him unceremoniously onto the crowded floor.

Ao recovered first, pushing Kaïnam out of the way and grabbing his oar. "I'll row. You mind your weapons. We're not out of this yet."

Mahault and Ao set to work with the paddles, carrying them against the tide. They were aiming not directly toward the *Heart* but sideways to it, hoping to avoid being seen by sailors on the other ship. Jerzy got up on his hands and knees, his gaze drawn not back to the beach where his fire still raged, but out across the water.

The Washers' ship was a flurry of sounds and movement, longboats being lowered into the water, sailors going down rope ladders and picking up oars. They would be on their way, too soon. If any of them spotted the smaller boat, crossing their path . . .

The *Heart* turned against the wave, going broadside, hiding them from view.

"Thank you," someone whispered. Jerzy thought it might have been Kaïnam, from where the sound came from, but it was such a low whisper, he couldn't be sure.

Shouts reached his ears now, amid the repeated sounding of the fire alarum. The fire on the beach was no threat to either ship; even if it broke the command he placed on it, the fire would not be able to pass over the expanse of ocean. . . .

Jerzy paused. He didn't think it could, anyway. The decantation was simple enough; creating fire was one of the most basic of incantations, the second one he had learned. It was the intensity that was potentially dangerous. Once it had burned the offered fuel, the flames should die. If not . . .

"Oars up, heads down," Kaïnam ordered, his voice pitched to not carry beyond the four of them, and they all bent over, crouching as much as they could to create the smallest silhouette, even as Ao and Mahl let their oars be still, lifting them just out of the water so their momentum was not slowed. It was full dark, but the moon was full directly overhead, shining on the water, and an alert scout might see them, or hear the sound of the oars.

Jerzy's breathing came too loud, harsh and ragged, and he tried to modulate it, calming himself the way he would before a major incantation. But his legs trembled under him, and his back ached, and his thoughts refused to settle. What if the fire broke loose and spread? What if one of the sailors saw them? What if, even if they did reach the ship safely, the other ship caught up to them, even with half their crew on shore? What if . . .

Then the bulk of the *Heart* loomed in front of them, and Kaïnam was reaching for a rope that dangled from the side, just as they had left it, pulling them tight against the hull.

"Ao, you're quickest. Up and throw down the ladder, but quietly," the prince ordered, and Ao scrambled to obey, going hand over hand up the rope, barely making a sound. There was a pause, too many heartbeats waiting for a shout of discovery, or the twang of a bolt being loosed, hitting wood or flesh. Jerzy felt the itch to turn around, to look back at the shore, to see if the other ship had noticed them yet, but he stilled the urge. He was not superstitious, he did not believe that doing so might tempt the silent gods, but he would not risk that it might, either.

The rope ladder came down, making a banging nose as it hit the side of the ship, and Jerzy flinched, knowing how easily sound traveled over water, at night.

"Go!" Kaïnam urged them. Mahault was first, grabbing a pack and slinging it over her shoulder, then going up the ladder at a steady clip. Jerzy looked at the half casks, then at the ladder. He could lift the casks easily, but not without both hands. How would he get up the ladder? He would have to use magic, but it would take so long. . . .

"Lift the entire fool boat," Kaïnam said, sensing his dilemma. "After you're safe onboard." Jerzy blinked at the obviousness of the solution, then grabbed his pack and a wineskin marked with Giordan's sigil, and scrambled up after Mahault.

Behind him, Kaïnam tied the smaller boat securely to the tug-rope, then followed up the ladder.

On deck, Jerzy saw that Mahault was already at the wheel, checking to make sure that nothing had been damaged or disturbed while they were away. The small spell-light was still burning over the wheelhouse, catching glints of gold in her hair as she worked, her movements swift but sure as she unlocked the wheel and rechecked the map she had carried from the shore.

Ao had already lifted the weigh-anchor and was standing by the railing looking back toward land. Jerzy finally gave in to the urge, and looked as well.

The sheet of fire still raged, shards of angry white flame reaching twice a man's height, building a wall nothing living could pass. It was holding the narrow line Jerzy had directed it into, and Jerzy felt some of the tension leave him. The two longboats had made it to shore, but their captains wisely kept them in the water, directing the sailors—and, Jerzy presumed, Washers—to slog through to the sand itself. The flames blocked them from where the campsite had been, however, preventing them from getting close enough to see they were gone.

Neth was no fool, and he knew what Vinearts were capable of. It would not take the Washers long to realize they had been tricked. The *Heart* had to be under way before then.

"Clear space," Jerzy said to the other two, gesturing with his right arm as he lifted the wineskin and pulled the wax stopper out with his teeth. The skin felt warm in his hands, and he worried briefly that the rough treatment had damaged the wine. Spellwines were hardly delicate, once incanted, but it was still possible for them to become ruined by mishandling.

One sip, barely wetting his tongue before the crisp, bright aroma filled his mouth and nose, allayed his fears. The familiar sense of a weatherwine hit Jerzy's awareness, and with it came the sound of Vineart Giordan's strangely appealing bark of laughter, the way his hands moved when he spoke, the look in his eyes that last day, when he realized he had been trapped, and called up one final storm to try and free himself. . . .

Jerzy shut those memories off, and let the *vin magica* ready itself.

"Wind under wood," he whispered, enunciating carefully to ensure the decantation was clear. "Lift like a babe, safely stored. Go."

The command took effect, and the smaller craft shuddered and began to move, as though lifted by an invisible hand.

"Kaï, they're going to see us soon, if they haven't already. Can you show them we have teeth as well?"

"There are bows stored belowdeck," Kaï said grimly. "Night shooting is tricky, but if need be, I can prick them a bit."

"Go, do that." Jerzy did not want to use magic against them. He had killed three times, using magic, and the memory still made him feel ill, even though twice had been mercy killings, the last a matter of survival.

The smaller boat was almost even with the railing now, and Jerzy and Ao reached up to grasp it, untying the rope and preparing to guide it down onto the deck, when something hit the bottom of the *Heart*, making it rock, and them stagger. Jerzy's attention distracted, the spell wavered, and the smaller craft crashed to the deck, parts of its hull splintering.

"What was that?" Ao asked, looking around, even as they heard shouts coming from the other ship, and Mahl swung hard on the wheel, moving the *Heart* away from whatever had hit them.

"Someone, the sails!" she called, her voice high with panic. "Get the sails!"

Jerzy looked back at her and saw what she had seen, rising out of the water too close for comfort, too close for safety. "Oh, root and rot," he swore, even as he was scuttling backward, away from the side of the boat. He grabbed at the wineskin, trying to remember the proper decantation, then lifted the skin to his mouth, but another blow hit them, against the side of the ship this time, and he choked on the liquid, sending it down the wrong way, the misdirected magic making his chest burn.

And then the cause of the bump rose over the railing, illuminated in the starlight.

Up close, the serpent's head was even more terrifying than the ones he had seen at a distance, the head and sinewy neck covered with muddy brown scales, the milky-white eyes scanning for movement that might indicate prey. The Guardian might have the same basic shape as this beast, but there was no more relation between them, especially as the beast opened its black-lipped maw, revealing a ragged double row of teeth, and the stench of things long-dead and rotted.

Had he called it? Had his magic drawn the beast to do its master's dire bidding, the way he had called the cat's-paw on the road, that afternoon?

"Down!" Kaïnam cried, breaking Jerzy's panicked thoughts. Even as Ao threw himself to the deck, dragging Jerzy with him, there was the sound of something flying past them, like a hawk stooping to the kill, and a thick bolt embedded itself into the beast's head just below one dead-looking eye, where the scales did not completely defend.

The sea serpent let out a high-pitched keening noise, and more of the great, scaled neck appeared, rising up into the sky as the beast looked for its attacker.

Shouting, no, screaming came from the sailors, and Jerzy had a passing thought that it would be a terrible but useful thing if the serpent decided those on the beach would make easier prey, but the beast seemed intent upon them.

There was the sound of something soft and heavy hitting wood, and then the welcome noise of ropes being hauled on, and the mainsail going up, cracking and bracing in the night air.

"Shoot it again!" Ao cried, but it was taking too long for Kaïnam to reload the bow, and the serpent had found them. The head swooped down, even as Jerzy pulled all the quiet-magic he had in his body and threw it at the beast, imagining the shape to the Guardian, created to protect all of House Malech: stone wrapped in fire, aimed like another, far more deadly crossbow bolt.

He let the magic fly just as the serpent's head dipped closer and its mouth opened over him. The heavy stink of rotted flesh and sour *vina* rolled up from its gullet, too many rows of sharp teeth visible, and Jerzy knew in that instant that, no matter what he did, he would die.

Even as he thought that, consigning himself to Sin Washer's solace, there was a mad howl, the sound of a wolf in full rage, and Ao threw himself at the creature's head, knocking into it, distracting it from Jerzy even as the spell hit the beast directly between the eyes.

Jerzy rolled, trying to get out of the way, hearing only the crack and flap of the sails over his pounding heartbeat, all else fallen away to a dull roar of background noise. He landed facedown on the deck, waiting for those terrible teeth to come down on him, to swallow him whole.

Instead, there was a heavy, wet thunk, and an even heavier splash of something falling back into the water. And then silence.

A heartbeat later, the silence was broken by the sound of Mahault's scream, followed by the sound of feet racing across the deck. Jerzy got to his knees, pushing up against the deck, and realized that his hands were wet and sticky. He looked down, saw that he had placed his palms into a puddle of something dark and wet. He frowned. The serpent he had helped kill near Darcen the year before had not bled.

"Get a tarp, something to wrap him in," Mahault was yelling over her shoulder, knelt down by something. Jerzy crawled forward, not trusting his legs to hold him, leaving a trail of red handprints on the weathered wooden planks.

"And healwine! Jerzy, get healwine, quickly!"

Cradled in Mahault's arms, Ao lay, slack-jawed and ashen, his eyelids fluttering as he tried to focus. The blood was coming from him, Jerzy realized, even as Kaïnam dropped a handful of flasks on the deck beside them.

"I didn't know which one," he said, his gaze fastened onto Ao and Mahault, flinching when Ao let out a low, pained moan. "I didn't . . . Sin Washer's mercy, Jer, do something!"

Crawling closer, Jerzy saw what the others had already known; Ao's upper body was intact, barely scarred by the serpent's teeth—but both of his legs now ended just above the knee. The blood on the deck came from him, not the serpent.

His gorge rose up into his throat, and Jerzy forced it back down, refusing to allow himself to pass out. Mahault was still cradling Ao, murmuring something to him in a soft voice, while Kaïnam dropped to his knees on the other side, trying awkwardly to wrap a tarp around his lower body.

"No." Jerzy's voice was harsh, cold, and Kaï stopped midmotion. "Put him down. Both of you. Put him down."

"But he's bleeding, he'll bleed to death if we don't—"

"He's dead already, no matter what you do." Ao had gone from ashen to sickly, his skin coated with sweat, the pulsemark in his neck throbbing with effort, and the blood was still streaming from the ragged stumps, all—

Jerzy averted his gaze, swallowing hard. He couldn't think about the fact that this was Ao, bitten off like a . . . no. There was no time, no chance. No chance but one.

A Vineart did not show weakness. A Vineart stood apart. There was no time to calm himself, no possibility that he could be calm, or careful. Jerzy grabbed the nearest wineskin, not caring which it was, and pulled the cork out with his teeth, splashing the liquid down his throat.

Bitter-ripe, rough as bark but potent as fire, the spellwine resented being treated that way, burning his throat and making him gag and cough. He pushed Kaïnam aside, ignoring the blood drenching his trou and staining his hands, and put his fingers directly onto the wounds, feeling the wet warmth of his skin and the sharp jagged jut of bone.

"Stay with us," he whispered, not a spell but an order, risking a brief look at Ao's face. "Stay with us."

Ao's head moved, and Jerzy decided it was a nod of assent.

He knew the decantation he needed; Master Malech had taught him, in the weeks after the cart accident, when two slaves had died. "For when the worst happens," Malech had said. Not if, but when.

"Blood to blood, flesh and bone. Bind and succor, make him whole." Jerzy paused, feeling panicked that it wasn't enough, not powerful, not determined enough. He thought of the figurehead, of the hands holding the wreath of leaves, protecting this ship, and directed the decantation as much at it as the magic within him. "Go."

Jerzy thought he had known what to expect. He was wrong. The surge of magic pulled out of him like he had been thrown into the press himself and crushed with the Harvest, all the magic flowing out of his body. All he had, his magic, his anger, his fear, the memory of Ao that first meeting in the maiar's House, the offer of friendship to a young Vineart who had no understanding of what that meant; everything went into the spell, spreading up into Ao's damaged body, finding and mending, cauterizing the wounds and keeping him aware, and alive.

When it was done, Jerzy fell back, not feeling—or caring—when the back of his head hit the deck.

"He's breathing," he heard Mahault say, her voice catching on a sob. "He's breathing."

Jerzy turned his head enough to see her catching up the tarp and wrapping it around Ao's body, hiding the now-cauterized stubs from sight.

"Get us out of here," he told Kaïnam. "Now."

The serpent would keep the others from following; even if it was dead, the sailors would fear another appearing from the night-dark waters, stranding those on shore.

The serpent had allowed them to escape.

Jerzy laughed, knowing it was horrible, hearing the exhaustion, the fear, in his voice, but unable to stop as he felt the ship shudder underneath them as they picked up wind and headed back out into the wide sea.

The thought struck him, a cold blade to his throat that stopped the laughter, and left only exhaustion.

Too much water. Too much emptiness where there should be soil. No touch of leaves, no whisper of magic . . . it was empty, barren, and it left him weak and adrift. He could not fight an enemy that strong, could not hope to win, like this.